ISLANDERS

ISLANDERS

by Helen R. Hull

Afterword by Patricia McClelland Miller

THE FEMINIST PRESS
at The City University of New York
New York

This edition © 1988 by The Feminist Press at The City
University of New York
Afterword © 1988 by Patricia McClelland Miller
All rights reserved.
Published 1988 by The Feminist Press at The City University
of New York, 311 East 94 Street, New York, N.Y. 10128.
Distributed by The Talman Company, Inc., 150 Fifth Avenue,
New York, N.Y. 10011.

Islanders was originally published in 1927.

91 90 89 88 6 5 4 3 2 1

Library of Congress Cataloging-in-Publication Data
Hull, Helen R. (Helen Rose), 1888–1971.
Islanders.

I. Miller, Patricia McClelland. II. Title.
PS3515.U363I7 1988   813'.52   88–11174
ISBN 0–935312–91–9 (pbk.)

This publication is made possible, in part, by public funds
from the New York State Council on the Arts.

Cover design: Lucinda Geist
Cover art: Ellen Day Hale, June, c. 1905. Oil on canvas. The
National Museum of Women in the Arts. Gift of Wallace and
Wilhelmina Holladay. Reproduced by permission.
Back cover photo: Helen R. Hull, c. 1930. Courtesy of
Frederick C. Hull.

Printed in the United States of America

ISLANDERS

BOOK I

ISLANDERS

PART I

I

Behind the girl who walked so swiftly along the stretch
of muddy road lay the village like a cross, the church
steeple and a dark nucleus of houses where the two roads
met. Ellen's backward glance saw it caught in a fever,
a passion of men talking in excited groups, hushing as
a woman came near them; she saw in the gray sky above
it a taloned hand reaching down to pluck out all the
strong men. They're crazy, all of them, she thought:
wanting to set out into the wilderness, in search of gold.
West, in the direction she walked. Fields lay each side
of the road, black and soft with spring waiting, patches
of snow in corners of the rough rail fences. Against the
horizon trees marked the limit of clearing. Days and
years of toil. She had watched the fields stretch into the
woods, growing as she grew, and to-night she felt as she
strode along, the mud sucking at her rough shoes, that
she and the land were one, deserted by the wanton desires
of men who sat and talked, heads together in a frenzy
of fortune getting. She came to a huge oak left at the
corner of a field, the projecting root making a seat.
Behind her the village was lost under the slight curve of
land. Beyond her, over the line of trees, the sunset

3

brushed one long stroke of color against the gray. Gold, even in the sky, if she looked westwards! She sat down, pulling her cape close, her head back upon the tree. All about her in the grass tiny new leaves uncurled, pushed up spring arrows. Soon the nights would be mild, with clouds of loveliness over the fruit trees, and stars softened from their winter brilliance. But Matthew would be gone. He could go, leaving her. Her face glistened with horror. I can't keep him, she thought. She laid her hands against her temples, her fingers thrust into the dark hair drawn smoothly into the braids at the nape of her neck. He's going because he wants to go! That awful hour this morning, in the kitchen, when even her mother had cried shame upon her, and her father had said, "Your mother had more courage than you, Ellen. You'd tie your man to your doorstep, when he can make a fortune like this? Your mother says not a word to hold back her oldest son. Are you a puling infant? When your mother set out with me for this land, she was younger than you, and heavy with child."

"But she came with you! Matthew won't have me. You came to make a home together. Matthew is going away from home."

"To make a fortune for you, Ellie!" Matthew began. Ellen had laughed at him until his wind-burned face grew scarlet with rage and he strode out of the house, her brother at his heels. At daybreak they would ride away to join the rest of the band some thirty miles south. She would never see him again. She twisted her body along the rough root, one arm bent under her head, fury shaking her, a cold fury touched with strange wisdom that had grown in her during the weeks of futile struggle.

If other women weren't so meek, so docile! Her mother, her brother's young wife, and all the rest, believing the loud talk of men . . . that they started forth into danger for the sake of their women. Oh, if she were a man! Suddenly rough fingers pushed between her arm and her hidden face, warm, insistent, softening her fury, obscuring her faint wisdom; an arm tugged at her shoulders, rolled her gently around, and she rested against Matthew's knees, his face near hers as he crouched beside her.

"Ellie, dear—" His eyes, blue under sandy lashes, peered at her. "You won't be cross, not to-night?" He lifted her, his heart pounding under her arm. Ellen's hand pushed back his fur cap, touched his fair hair flattened on high temples, crept under his collar where the cords of his neck grew rigid at her touch. But as he kissed her, his excitement rolled between them, driving them apart, as if he were already miles on his wild journey.

"You'll see!" His breath on her cheek, his arm strong about her soft body, but his heart flung out days ahead, toward the west where a thin amber line marked the gray. "I'll come riding back with bags of gold. The rivers wash gold down the mountains out there, Ellie. You pick gold out of the sand. The rocks shine with it. What a chance, Ellie! You'd never have me stay here and drudge!"

Ellen drew away from him and rose, her back to the oak tree, to the west, her eyes lifting from Matthew's flushed, excited face to the dark acres of land within the margin of woods.

"I'll say no more about it," she said. "You've mortgaged the land we were to live on, and you're going."

Under her cloak her fingers pressed into her breast, where dull torment pulled. In the paleness of the swift spring twilight her face, its firm chin lifted, had no color : shadow of hair, of brows, deep shadow on her soft throat.

"You might wish me luck." Matthew was sulky, as if her white quiet face threatened his high mood. "You love me, Ellie. You'll wait."

"Oh!" She rocked her arms against her body. "Wait? What else is there for me to do? You go riding off and you want me to wave you good-by—"

"It's not easy to go." He stood close to her, his fingers moving along the fur of his cap. "It's as much for you as me, and you know that. Just a year."

Ellen looked up at him. Above them the oak spread its dark branches, blurred with swelling buds, through which the leaden sky showed. In the dusk she could just see the flare of nostrils, the widened eyes. He was armored in the fever of his dream. Not one crack where any weapon she possessed might enter.

"Just a year," she said, and her words drifted away in a mocking wonder. "It's now I love you." She stepped across the root and went hurriedly along the road.

"You won't stop." He walked beside her, his broad shoulders swinging in the heavy balance of a body accustomed to rough ground. His hand found hers, enclosed it. Ellen's hand was rigid; all her will held his touch there at her fingers, held it from flooding through her blood. The Matthew that was hers was lost, walled off behind this lust for gold, for wild adventure. Then, just as her hand betrayed her, and in an ecstasy of pain his touch crept through her veins, he spoke.

"By this time to-morrow, we'll meet the others. More

than a hundred of us. Think of it, Ellie. Rivers and forests and mountains high as the sky!"

To-morrow night. Her hand was cold now, and sep- arate, in his.

They were at the gate, the yellow of the kitchen candles shining across the yard, the pungency of fir wood blown from the kitchen chimney.

"Tell Bob I'll meet him at the crossroad. Your father said he'd ride part way with us. No, I won't come in."

His arms held her, roughly, as he kissed her. "Ellie, Ellie!" For a fleeting moment—ah, he was her Matthew, his madness stripped away. Could she hold him? Her hands clung behind his head, her lips moved on his; all her pride, her love, her unused young passion she flung out in a tether. The kitchen door swung open and with a mutter Matthew broke away.

"Ellen?" Her mother, a weary silhouette in the rec- tangle of light. "Are you out there?"

"Good-by, Mrs. Dacey." Matthew waved to her. "Good-by, Ellen."

II

The night sky had paled into a tremulous hint of dawn when Robert Dacey pushed his chair back from the kitchen table. His mother glanced at the windows, where the glow from the candle met the growing dawn in a queer opacity. "You can't eat more?" she asked. "Your horses are ready. Your father's seen to them." Her glance at Robert's wife, weeping in a corner, rang with scorn. Ellen, tying a handkerchief about the bundle of food for the day, was white and hollow-eyed. These younger women were soft. If her son chose to go forth

like a man, he should go. But, oh God, guard him! Her
little son, tugging at her breast—"God bless you, Robert."
She kissed him. "Your father will ride part way." Her
fingers brushed at his shoulder. Homespun she had
woven from her own yarn. Wool, keep him warm! The
touch of her fingers was a rune to guard him. Her first-
born. She had lost him a little when he married, but she
had him again, in her courage to send him. Past the
window moved the dark shapes of the horses, and the
door opened. Thurston Dacey, reins over one arm, stood
on the threshold. "Ready?" His bearded face looked
haggard in the half light, and Martha felt a curious
movement of pity in her body. All night he had lain
restive at her side, and she knew his thoughts. "This
is for young men," she had said, and he had made no
answer. When the small square of window grew separate
from the blackness of the room Martha had risen, heavy
from the sleepless night. Thurston had not moved until
she spoke his name, surprised that he lay after she rose.
He sat up then, tossing aside the blankets, fumbling for
his rough clothes. "Twenty-five years, Martha," he said.
So he had gone back, too, through the years of their life.
She had been fiercely glad for an instant that the room
was dark, that his eyes searching could not find her, could
not see the weight of those years in her stooped shoulders,
in her shapeless body, her abdomen flabby, distorted by
child-bearing, her jaws sunken, toothless, from ague and
nostrums. She pulled on her shoes and hurried into the
kitchen; for shame, that she could have thoughts of vanity, as if she were a girl! But Thurston was still handsome; toil had not broken him. He hadn't known that
he too was growing old, until now, with Robert and Mat-

thew and the other young men starting on their search.
As he looked in at the door she pitied him, knowing he
had yet to learn to find his remnant of youth again in
children. "Where's my gun?" he was asking. "I'll fetch
a rabbit."

Then little Thurston, the youngest boy, ducking under
his father's arm, rushed in to circle about Robert, his
thin face tragic. "Take me, Bob! I'm plenty big
enough!" Robert cuffed at him, and turned to bid his
wife good-by. Martha saw that the girl had shaken off
her tears for an heroic moment. That was better. Ellen
followed Robert to the door, and when he had swung
himself onto his horse, stood on tiptoe, pressing something
into his hand. "Give it to Matthew, Rob." Ellen took
things hard, if they crossed her will. But she was young.
Robert gathered his reins, the pack-pony nosed behind the
black mare he rode, the hoofs crunched on the dirt.
Thurston rode behind, as straight as his son, heavier,
perhaps. Young Thurston darted after them, crying,
"I'll run to town, at least." Martha pushed her shoulder
against the wooden frame of the door, hard. "Don't look
for me before to-morrow," Thurston called back. Mist
in the meadow, a floating veil of white, with the dark
figures of men and horses riding past; above the trees
the sky was cold and white. Thurston turned to wave,
and a sudden fear, white as the morning sky, fell through
Martha. Oh, she was a foolish old woman. That sobbing of Robert's wife bothered her. Ellen stood beside
her, looking after the diminishing figures. No tears in
her dark eyes: a kind of wild bitterness. "Your father
will come back to-morrow," said Martha. "And in a
year"—her courage flooded back as she heard her own

words—"in a year, the others." She would not watch
them out of sight.

In the kitchen Sarah, Robert's wife, her head down on
the table, sobbed dully. Across the table crawled a stream
of dark molasses, overturned by the girl's outstretched
hand. "Ellen!" Martha spoke sharply. "Come clean up
this mess. Sarah—" her hand on the quivering shoulder
was firm. "There's work to do. If you'll be about it,
I'll be obliged. Tears plow no fields."

III

All the next day a cold spring rain beat against the
land. By night Thurston had not come. Martha said
only, "He would not ride far such a day." Two days
later young Thurston came slowly up the lane, his face
puckered in sulky bewilderment. Martha, knitting by the
fireplace, saw him and rose, holding the wool and the long
wooden needles like a cross on her heart.

"They might a let me go, too," said the boy. "If old
men can go, I could."

"What have you heard?" Martha knew that Ellen
had come to the doorway, but she could only look at
her young son and wait.

"Pa's gone. He's gone with the boys. He sent word
by ole Saxby that he had to go. They might a let me,
too."

"Yes, it's a shame you didn't go! Why don't you get
you a horse and chase after them!" Ellen swept upon
him, shaking his shoulder. "You're a man, almost. Go
riding away, and leave the women behind, to work!"

"Ellen, hush." Martha sat down, her hands moving

automatically with the strands of wool. "Is that all your father said?"

"When he saw the wagons and all, ole Saxby said, he just had to go. It was a chance of a lifetime." The boy hesitated on the phrase. "Why, he"—his young, unformed mouth twisted grotesquely—"he ain't coming back!"

Martha's hands hung rigid a moment. Her lips sucked in over the sunken jaws, and her eyelids shut; a kind of numbness crawled up her legs, through her bowels, to her heart. The injury struck below her love, deep into the centre of her life, into the very spring that nourished her, her reason for living, her proud secret self. She had made her life into Thurston's, and he—she saw him moving darkly against the white morning mist. Her eyelids lifted. Ellen watched, and the boy, too.

"He knew we could fend for ourselves," she said. "Can you take your father's place, do you think, Thurston?"

"Not a word of blame for him?" Ellen gasped, would have rushed hotly on. But Martha, quiet in her chair, her eyes invincible over the gray sunken mouth, hushed her.

"He's your father and he has seen fit to go." She saw the boy let go reluctantly of the gay dream of riding after the men, saw him turn seriously toward her.

"He knew I'd be here," he said loudly.

IV

Three women and a boy. Acres of land to be plowed, planted; other acres cleared of trees but still to be

stumped. Thurston found the chain and iron bar where
his father had left them the day before he rode away.
Martha's eyelids twitched when she saw them.

"There's gold here, too," she said grimly. "In the
land. But you can't pull stumps, Thurston. Another
year, maybe." That thin, gangling body of his—she
wouldn't have it strained. "It takes two men," she added
slyly, as he lifted the bar to prove how easily he could
move a gaunt stump.

She planned the work with the boy. Ellen was strong.
Sarah could help in the house. Martha made a treadmill
of long, labor-full days, on which their feet could grind
out spring, summer, fall, winter, until the year would be
worn through. Not until the spindles of the corn were
shriveled and the long blades rattled in the breeze did
any word come. A letter for Martha Dacey, folded,
sealed, brought by a stranger who had it from another.
She shut herself into her bedroom to hide the trembling
of her body. She had never had a letter from her husband before. She broke the seal and spread out the single
sheet.

> Dear Wife, a party camped with us tonight is
> headed east and will carry word to you. We are well
> and trust you are the same. The trip is slow oweing
> to rivers in flood and roads to be cut through and
> Rob sends his love as does Matthew and also Yrs.
> Truely Thurston D.

From him, but remote, unhealing. Against her eyelids she saw the men like ants, crawling across rivers,
through great forests, with never a backward thought.
Her hand touched the paper curiously. What had her

husband thought as he made those letters? Within her
the wound of his going began to throb; she heard his
voice in the dark, "Twenty-five years, Martha."

Her door crashed open and Ellen, the sunburn strange
on her white-lipped face, rushed at her. "Is there a message? They said—". She was on her knees beside her
mother, her head bent over the creased sheet. "Is that
all?" Her eyes brightened with pain, and Martha laid
her hand, its long fingers work-swollen, on Ellen's rigid
shoulder.

"They are well," she said. "It is good to know that."

"It's not much," Ellen cried out, "after all these
months."

"We must tell Sarah." Martha Dacey rose, her dignity covering her fear that Ellen's rebellion might be a
spark to her own secret thoughts. So Ellen, too, had
empty spaces in her dreams, spaces made worse than
empty by reason of the strangeness into which the men
had gone. But Ellen hadn't years of life suddenly broken
across.

Sarah was sitting on a bench outside the door, her
hands idle. She sat there often, letting the sun warm
her heavy body. For she was waiting not for Robert
now, but for her child. When Martha showed her
the letter she said, "Poor Robert. He doesn't even
know."

Martha watched the younger woman shrewdly. Not
only her flesh, but all her thoughts, her emotion, seemed
drawn in toward the making of her child, and she had
nothing to waste on Robert. Secretly Martha was pleased.
For Robert had then the more need of his mother's love
and prayers. At night Martha stretched her weary body

in her bed, while her love went running, running, on
winged feet, down dark aisles of forests, to weave a
charmed circle about two men, her son, her husband. But
by day she watched Sarah with some tenderness. The
girl's own people were dead. Ellen was scornful of
Martha's protectiveness. "It doesn't hurt a woman to do
some work, does it?" Martha said only, "I lost two
myself, one from haying, one from doing a wash. Lifting a tub with ice in it. Sarah's no need to do our work."
There were things she could say to Sarah, too; bits of
old wives' lore, speculations. The sight of the girl with
the rhythm of change, of growth, was a finger touching
now this day, now that, in Martha's own young womanhood, enriching her dry, withered present with the sharp
invoking of earlier days.

"When Rob comes back, next spring, my baby will
be—" Sarah counted off the months on her knee.
"December, January— If they come in April, my baby
will be more than four months old."

V

Winter shut in early that year. Ellen, crashing the
dipper into the frozen water bucket in the kitchen, bleak
darkness still over the earth, wondered whether Matthew
was warm. It might be summer in the land of gold.
She knelt beside the hearth, brushing ashes from the
precious pink embers, laying the fire for the day. As the
flame leaped through the shavings and caught at the
wood, she held her hands toward it. Poor raw knuckles.
She should rub mutton tallow into them. She heard her
mother groan faintly, heard her moving in the next room.

The stitch in her side must be worse. Sarah still slept.
Ellen pushed the kettle forward and rose. It was wicked
to hate Sarah. "I am wicked, then!" Ellen lifted her
hands to twist her dark braid into a coil. Sarah was too
happy. Suppose—Ellen's hands stopped an instant. If
Matthew and I— Her mother stepped into the kitchen,
and Ellen moved hastily, bending over the jar of buck-
wheat batter, as if her shameful thought might be visible.
Matthew was so far away she could scarcely remember
how he looked.

Thurston was gone all day, at a logging camp in the
woods. Ellen had the stock to care for. Then there was
spinning, weaving. Martha's hands on the loom were
the most dexterous of the village, and she had promised
a length of cloth to Mr. Saxby, in return for shoes.
Ellen disliked the confinement of the house. It felt too
crowded, three women, each waiting: candlelight and firelight, a few hours of daylight, candlelight and firelight
again, and night. She made excuses to escape the walls.
She loaded a bag of grain on her sled and walked to the
mill to have it ground. The miller eyed her through
whitened lashes, and Ellen tossed her dark head. His
wife had died, and he needed a new woman. "Ain't
heard from Matthew, have you?" His grin, on his clown-
white face, mocked her.

"He's too busy digging gold."

"Any time you're sick of waiting for him . . ." He
meant it, enough to spice encounter with him.

She went to a spelling match in the schoolhouse.
Thurston was sluggish after his long day in the woods.
Ellen's cheeks were flushed above her dark wool dress;
she was as gay as if she weren't looking, hungrily, for

Matthew's square head over the others, in the corner
where the men shuffled and joked.

Then in late December part of the waiting reached a
peak. Sarah's time came, prematurely. More women
crowded into the house, a neighbor woman who was the
best hand in the village at a child-birth, other women.
Ellen hid her curious young fears under determined activity. She was glad when in the early twilight she had
the animals to feed. Familiar barn odors, quiet crunch-
ings and stampings: but even there she thought she heard
those inhuman sounds from Sarah. Sarah was a weak
little thing. Ellen stood close to White Star, the old
Indian pony, a kind of comfort in the warm, horsey
smell, in the snuffling among the feed.

When she pushed the wood-shed door ajar, and stepped
into the kitchen, she stopped, a flicker of terror in her
veins. The women were crouched near the fire, three of
them, dangling something, slapping at it, something pur-
plish and wrinkled. Ellen crept nearer, just as Martha,
with a low cry, seized it, covered it with the bit of blanket
spread on her knees and huddled over it. "You'd best
go in to Sarah, Marthy." One of the women touched
her arm. "She'll take on, when she knows."

Martha rose, holding the tiny stiff bundle. "It's as
if"—her face had a gray luster—"as if I lost another,
myself."

Again it was a house of women, waiting. Sarah
recovered slowly. Ellen thought that if Martha hadn't
insisted, hadn't run her own will through the younger
woman like an iron wire that would not break, Sarah
would have died easily. But Martha coaxed and bullied
and dragged her out of bed, out of the slow lethargy in

which she moved, into what was at first mere acquiescence in living. When the March thaws began, Sarah had regained her soft, fair prettiness, although her blue eyes kept an empty, puzzled look.

Spring again, with the frost working out of the ground, with plans for the spring work discussed seriously. Still no further word from Thurston Dacey, from Robert, or Matthew. Ellen went through the mud to stand under the old oak, her face toward the west. Perhaps they were coming back. Any day they might ride along that road. But all her desire, flooding back with the spring, couldn't give her a picture of Matthew riding toward her. If he had turned his horse toward the east, bags of gold piled behind him, would she feel him coming? He might be in the village now, and she not know it. Love was a feeble thing; it couldn't stretch through a single mile of air as clear as this between her and the horizon. At least there would be less time now for thinking, and at night she would sleep, too tired even for dreaming.

VI

Through the summer Martha forgot the sharp pain in her side. She watched Thurston with pride in his growth—he was taller than she, now, and across his lip, rimming his square chin, unmistakable light down. He would be a man, soon. He plowed, planted, harvested, with Ellen steadily beside him, in a kind of dogged faithfulness. But Martha knew he was no farmer. He looked like her father, as he grew. She recalled with amazement her own youth, in the small Vermont town where her father was minister. She had taught her own chil-

dren to read and write, and all she knew of books. If
Thurston, that older Thurston, did come back with gold,
the boy might have a chance. She sighed, knowing she
had no dream of wealth. Some core of disbelief stayed
impervious to hope. She knew too deeply that whatever
she had to-day she had made with her hands, with toil of
her body, with thought that turned into the shaping of
material.

In the later summer Thurston harnessed the oxen to the
heavy cart, loaded it with logs from the winter's work, to
drive to a neighboring settlement. As he started, Sarah
ran from the house, the full skirt of a sprigged calico
dress she had just made floating about her, a pink bonnet
shading her face. "Take me, Thurs, take me!" and she
scrambled beside him. Poor Sarah. Martha had borne
with her through the summer, in the unhappy pettishness
which had followed the slow climbing back to life. If
the baby had lived, the girl would have steadied into
womanhood.

All day Martha and Ellen worked cutting the dry bean
vines, wheeling them into the barn, stripping the pods.
Ellen was dexterous and silent; Martha turned her
thought toward her, since her son was gone. Russet
lights from the days of sun in the smooth coil of her
dark hair; dusky gold on face and forearms, soft cream
of throat where she had pushed apart her dark calico
for coolness in the sultry barn. She was thin, but strong,
well. When had the sharp line grown there at the corner
of her mouth? Had she hardened into resentment, as
if this second summer were a kiln, firing pliable clay into
rigid mold? Suddenly the girl lifted her face from the

pile of stripped vines she carried, and looked at her mother, her eyes defiant.

"Will they ever come?" she said. "Last summer we said 'next spring.' And now? They might be dead—"

"Hush, Ellen! God will keep them." Martha was stern against her own leap of fear. "It is a long journey."

"Thurston wants to go."

"What do you mean?" Martha stumbled across the piled dead vines, seizing Ellen's wrist. "What has he said?"

"I heard him talking with Saxby. It would be only a man's way. He's growing up."

Martha felt blackness before her eyes, as if the dust from the brown pods made a whirling cloud. Thurston, too, into that empty, voiceless distance? Oh, God, no! she prayed. Leave me one son.

"He's worked hard," Ellen said. "But he doesn't care about the land."

"He can find other work, then." Martha's stooped, gaunt body grew erect, and she stood in the wide barn doors, staring out at the west where the sun rode high, until black disks went sliding down a sheet of steel before her eyes. "You finish the beans. I am going to the village."

Not till after dark did the oxen come ponderously up the road, the lantern swimming in the zigzag of their slow step. Sarah jumped down from the seat and poised at the door of the kitchen, her fair skin flushed, her eyes animated. "Oh, you should have come, too." She let Ellen slip past her to help Thurston unyoke the oxen. "There were people to talk to, and a wagon train for the west. I sent a letter. The men might see Rob. I said if he didn't hurry back, I'd find me a new husband. One of the men there"—she smiled impishly at Martha— "promised to come if Rob didn't."

"You sound foolish," said Martha. "Sit down and eat, Sarah." She waited at the door for Thurston. "Did the boy talk with them?" she asked.

"They offered to take him." Sarah sat beside the table, smoothing the folds of her skirt, crumpled in the evening mist. "He wouldn't say a word all the way home."

Martha's hand pressed against her side, where that pain gnawed . . . or was this some new pain? Thurston clumped to the door, sent a quick glance at Sarah, stopped as Martha touched his shoulder in a curious, inquiring hesitancy.

"The logs got a fair price," he said. "I'm hungry, too."

"I told her about the wagon train." Sarah's head had a mocking tilt.

"Ugh." Thurston dipped water from the bucket and washed, silently. Martha laid the supper before them and sat down, her hands clutched under the shelter of the table. Ellen came presently to stand at the doorway, looking out at the dark night.

When Thurston had finished, Martha leaned forward, the candlelight shining up in the deep sockets of her eyes, in the hollows of her cheeks.

"Thurston," she began, "to-day I made a change. It's time we thought of your future." She saw the boy shrink away from her gaze, uncertainly. "If you think you must follow your father west, I couldn't hold you. But I had another plan." Slowly she explained; Ellen turned to listen, and Sarah stared, while Thurston moved restlessly under her intense and careful speech. When she had gone to John Abbott, in the spring, for an advance of a little money until the crops came in, he had asked about her son. John Abbott was the big man of the village; storekeeper, justice of the peace, banker. It was he who held the mortgage on Matthew's land." "He says—" Martha spoke with a desperate earnestness; she must weave a spell to bind him against the mad lure of the western gold. "He says there is a great future here, in this country. There is talk of a steam railroad through this county. New settlers are coming. He will let you come into his store, when the corn is harvested. You can help there while he teaches you what he knows of law, of all his business. He has no son, and he must have a young man. In the spring I said we needed you here, on your father's land. But he can find a man, another year, to work with us on shares. It is for you a greater opportunity than digging gold out of rocks." Martha pushed on, against a feeling of almost treachery to the older Thurston. "When the railroads come, and many families, this will be the great state of the union. And you may be one of its great men." Martha leaned toward her son, the sweep of her prophecy rushing through the candle-lit kitchen, catching in its wings the restless eager imaginings of her youngest boy, lifting him—ah, she saw it!—into a new dream. "We can manage, we three women, to hold the land."

Sarah pushed away from the table, her sparkle gone. This was too vague a dream for her; she wanted something warm and near. But Ellen stepped forward, and the candlelight showed her thin face stripped of its sullen-

ness, touched into wondering admiration as she listened
to her mother.

VII

Thurston was to have a room in the store building,
that he might have time in the winter evenings to read
in the volumes of law Mr. Abbott would give him. Ellen
stitched on his new suit, gray and black wool mixed, with
pride under which, deep beneath, ran a cold stream of
envy. Oh, to be a man! There had been a letter and a
package from that remote west. Thurston wrote, laconi-
cally, that it seemed better to wait until they had more
gold, that Matthew had left them to join prospectors in
a mountain farther north, that he would like to hear from
them. Dead Horse Gulch. Ellen hated the name. The
package, wound in strips of a blue handkerchief which
Ellen remembered, had a few lumps of dull metal. Gold
nuggets. They kept them in a cup on the kitchen shelf,
to show to their rare guests. Sarah had wept for a day
at the sudden cutting of her hope that Rob might even
then be travelling back to her. She dallied over her tasks,
snarling the wool she spun, spilling the candle molds. She
liked to walk to the village, to see Thurston in the store
until they quarrelled one day. Ellen did not know what
Thurston said: something about Sarah's manner with the
village men.

In November, when the first snow lay like a garment
stretched too thin and tight over the black earth, a neighbor brought a bit of news. An itinerant preacher, with
his family of sons and wife, was coming to the village,
to hold meetings. "He's been through Ohio and Illinois,"
the woman said, hugging her shawl about her shoulders.

"They say he has the gift of tongues, that he makes hell live under your eyes, and he never talks without the spirit of God taking possession of all who listen."

Sarah came in on Saturday evening, pleasantly excited. "They've come," she said, "in a covered wagon, with a big eye of God painted on it. The preacher is a great black-bearded man, and he has a son like himself. They'll preach all day to-morrow in the meeting house."

Martha listened, one hand over her sunken mouth, her eyes bright. "When I was a girl, a travelling preacher came to our town. He stayed in my father's house, and I remember before he left the spirit of the Lord entered into everyone. Some fell in a trance, some screamed. It will be wonderful if this man has the power."

Ellen felt her mother's excitement. This was a strange Martha who moved about the house, making preparations for an early start in the morning, her eyelids heavy with secret anticipation. Her usual rigid quiet had relaxed into an unfamiliar savouring of pleasure which Ellen could not understand. Early in the morning she called Ellen, and while the girl harnessed White Star, she laid the breakfast. They ate hurriedly, and then Martha knelt beside her chair, her face gaunt under the black bonnet, her lips moving. "Oh, Lord, make Thy handmaid worthy, let Thy awful joy descend!"

The three crowded on the one seat of the wagon, Ellen in the middle, driving. The gray sky hung low over the bare trees; the horse's feet broke the frozen surface of the muddy road. A cruel sound, thought Ellen, that brittle crack and the dullness that followed. The air had a bitter damp which numbed her fingers; she hated the smell of November, dead leaves, dead empty fields. Perhaps her mother's strangeness had drawn her nerves too taut. Sarah's small face, her nose reddened in the cold dawn, had expectancy, too, but not like Martha's.

Ellen blanketed the horse and followed the others into the small building. Already the benches were filling, but Martha walked toward the front row without a glance at anyone. Little whispers of excitement ran like insects through the room. Ellen looked about for Thurston. He would sit with the Abbotts, perhaps. It was indecorous to turn from the front bench her mother had chosen. She could only listen to the rustles and clumpings and scraping of benches. Suddenly the church grew still, and through the stillness marched heavy feet, feet pompous, assured. Ellen turned slightly. The man of God. He was tall, with long arms that hung loosely from great shoulders, with a black beard curled under a hooked nose, eyes as black under long black hair. Behind him, like him except that he walked more lightly and that no wrinkles cut through his bearded cheeks, another, his son. Behind him a row of children and a woman, small, shrinking into a seat under the platform with the children.

The two men towered above the little church. Ellen felt the hooked nose sniff her out at once. Martha was leaning forward, hands clasped, face lifted, the cords of her throat tight. The younger man sat down behind the rough Bible stand; his father stood, arms lax, eyes darting about the room. Suddenly he flung back his head, flung up his arms.

"Oh, Lord, pour into me Thy wrath! Fill Thy vessel!" His voice, husky, resonant, was a stone hurled at the throne of God. He shivered, crouched above the wait-

ing congregation, and began, softly at first, and then as if
he gained strength from the sound of his words, more
loudly, more violently. The familiar meeting house disappeared. The earth itself vanished. They were lost
souls, black with sin, fleeing without hope from the
vengeance of a pursuing, maddened Lord. Great beasts
of the Judgment Day, hounds of the Lord, tracked them
down. Hell, with ice and fire and cold, dreadful fear,
lay about them. Ellen heard sobs—or were those cries
of souls lost for eternity, whirling between the stars?
Martha had slipped forward to her knees, swaying in
the awful rhythm of that dark roaring voice. The voice
mounted into a high whisper, and the younger man leaped
forward, while his father knelt, hands clasped over his
contorted face. This voice was shallow, shriller, as it
shrieked a new picture, the bliss of the saved. For hours
it seemed the two men cried their antiphony. They
stopped, rigid, faces lifted, and the air moved heavily,
laden with sighs, with gasps, with groans, with the dull
sound of swaying bodies. Suddenly a woman rushed
down the aisle, crying, "It's come! I feel the Spirit!"
She flung herself down on the platform, clutching at the
feet of the older man, rolling over to lie rigid. Others
followed her. Martha crept forward, on her knees, her
face white, ecstatic. Ellen clung to the edge of the bench,
while the flood beat about her. These were people she
knew, feeling what kind of madness? She herself felt
no inrush of God, only fear of that black hooked face
that sought her out. Sarah had risen, swaying, the bonnet
slipping from her bright hair, her eyes closed. The
younger man caught her outstretched hand. "Are you
saved, sister? Glory to God." He half lifted her to the

platform, among the prostrate saved. "His Bride comes!"
His eyes ran back to Ellen, who huddled on her bench,
stubbornness mounting within her, a hate of those dark
bearded faces. She turned away from them. There were
others behind her, praying, or grinning in foolish embarrassment. "I think it's coming!" Old Mrs. Saxby, just
behind her, stared, wild-eyed, hands clenched.

If she weren't saved, hell gaped for her. Through the
small window she saw the flat disk of a pale sun sliding
through clouds. A kind of dizziness rocked her head,
and she rose. But the ravenous hand of the younger
preacher, reaching for her, drove her in quick flight
through the aisles, past unheeding eyes, to the door. She
was outside, alone in a world brooded over by a threatening Lord. If I can't be saved, I can't, she thought. She
went slowly around the building to the post where White
Star was hitched. The blanket had slipped half off the
mare, and Ellen dragged it back, stood a moment with
her arm against the horse's neck. White Star nuzzled
gently at the girl's shoulder. Ellen laughed, a laugh in
which hysteria broke away; she climbed into the wagon,
folding a blanket about her shoulders. It had been early
when she woke, and her stubborn resistance to the whirl-
wind in the meeting house had left her tired. It was very
still outside the church, with white slabs peering through
the fence of the little cemetery. Ellen had known some
of the people who lay beyond the fence. Sarah's baby.
An old woman. Were they tormented through eternity
by an angry God? The baby had never been saved. How
did it feel? That strange glow on her mother's face, the
pleased, dazed look Sarah lifted? Where did the thought
of Matthew come from, as her eyelids drooped and her

head swayed forward. Matthew, warm, close, holding her in strong arms. The jerk of her head woke her. Matthew had gone farther into the mountains. He might have fallen—she saw his handsome body, limp, shapeless, at the bottom of a dark ravine. It was Matthew who tortured her, not the Lord. It was Matthew she wanted, not God. She sat erect, her face sharpened in fright at her own wickedness.

Later, when she was cold with waiting, people came forth from the church, walking awkwardly, as if they were weighted with the load of their redemption, as if they had no bridge between that and the picking up of life again. Martha climbed beside Ellen without a word, and Sarah after her. Silently Ellen drove them back to the house. The road was muddy now, with no sound of frozen surface. When Ellen came in from stabling the horse, she faced her mother in a kind of defiant humility. Martha said, "I will pray for you, Ellen. So will Sarah. The preachers, too. One of them will come here to pray with us."

The next day and the next Martha and Sarah drove to the village, to be witnesses for the Lord at further meetings. Ellen refused to go. "Someone must do the work here."

On Wednesday when they drove home, the younger preacher sat beside them, his beard half hidden under a long scarlet muffler. A spasm of fear contracted Ellen's body as she saw him, and her hands were cold when she set the supper on the table. He prayed in a low sing-song, while Martha and Sarah sat with tranced faces. Then they ate, he greedily, setting strong yellowish teeth into his food, his dark eyes on Ellen.

When supper was ended, Martha opened the door of the small parlor.

"Brother Laing will pray with you, Ellen," she said. She set a candle on the table and closed the door. The room was cold. There were points of leaping flame in the man's eyes.

"Kneel beside me, sister." His voice was sweet, shallow. "Here." He knelt close to her, holding her frozen hands between his clasped palms. Over her head his voice flowed, invoking the spirit of the Lord. "Wait, sister. It will come. That delight, pouring through you. Joy, curling in your veins." His voice was close to her ear. "The Lord must have you as His Bride!" His beard brushed her cheek, his arm shut about her shoulders. "You tremble—it comes!"

Ellen dropped into darkness; something leaped within her, stirring in her pulses—was this the Spirit? She swayed toward him, felt a heartbeat. Was it his? His bearded lips were on hers, moving as if he still prayed, there was a kind of madness in the rhythmic pressure of his arm. Languor, heavy and sweet, flowed over Ellen. For long moments they knelt there, in that strange embrace. Then the man struggled to his feet, lifting Ellen, startling her with his sudden awkward violence. His hand closed harshly on her breast, and the girl's languor parted in sharp clarity. "Oh!" she shuddered, thrusting her hands against him, pushing at him. They stared at each other, the man's breath whistling between his teeth; there was an instant of naked meeting of their eyes. Hatred in his, and a threat of power trying to ride her down into submission; hatred in Ellen's, and a confusion of shame and fear. She slid backwards toward the door and the candle threw his shadow across her.

"Oh, God!" The man dropped to his knees, his hands clasped over his face. "Forgive this woman for her evil thoughts! She has tempted me! I have invoked Thy grace and spirit, but she is full of sin."

Ellen's fingers touched the latch of the door. Was it true, that she was full of evil thoughts? Then she saw his dark eyes peering between the strong, clutching fingers, she felt the startling violation of those fingers, and scorn sharpened her face. "Pray for other women," she said; "not me!"

She left him kneeling and walked proudly through the kitchen, where Sarah started from her chair. "Has he saved you?" Martha lifted her face from the Bible open on her knees. Ellen felt the tensity with which the two had waited while that door stood shut. She half lifted her hands, palms out, in a bewildered gesture. What could she say? They felt something, the grace of God, and she— She heard behind her the voice of Brother Laing, lifted in a sing song invocation, and she ran across the floor, clambered the rude steps to her own loft room, and shut herself in. Lying in the dark, she wept, for the first time in the long months since Matthew had gone riding away. She wept for her wickedness, for bewilderment at the ways of God, for pain at the treachery of her soft, yielding body, in which those dark caresses had stirred blind hunger. She should pray for forgiveness; she could pray only that Matthew might come back. She cried herself into a restless sleep. God, with a great black beard, pursued her down a steep road, to the edge of a cliff, where the soil crumbled under her stumbling feet, so that she fell, clutching at bushes, down, down, in white agony of fear, in which she tried to scream and woke to hear her own muffled groan, to feel her heart beating madly. The house was still, with all the remote hint of voices gone. Through the small window glinted one star. Matthew is dead, she thought. She lay, afraid and small, in an empty cold world, until the star dropped below the window sill.

The next day the caravan with the eye of God was to start again on its journey. Martha and Sarah prepared food for the preachers, a ham, bread, a sack of potatoes. When they drove away at noon with the provisions Ellen refused to go. Martha said as she lifted the reins, "Remember that my own joy in Heaven will be darkened at the thought of my daughter in eternal flames." Ellen turned desperately to the hardest tasks she could find.

After dark Martha drove back, alone. She had stopped to talk with Thurston. Hadn't Sarah come earlier? Unconvinced, Martha went into the small room next hers which Sarah had used. She called sharply to Ellen, who ran at the sound of her voice. Martha was holding back the curtain which hung before the row of hooks. Nothing dangled there, except a faded calico wrapper. Ellen lifted the cover of the wooden chest. In the bottom a pile of white things, the few garments Sarah had prepared for her baby. Nothing else.

"She's gone with them!" Ellen let the heavy lid clatter down. She had a sharp moment of insight: not a visual image, but pressure in her nerves—that dark, hooked face, its male dominance swooping upon Sarah's restless, empty fairness. "With Brother Laing!" Then she caught her

mother's arm, as the older woman rocked unsteadily.
"Mother!" She pushed her toward a chair. "I'll go after
her!"

"No." Martha let her head droop, her chin on her
shrunken breast. "Never. Let her go." She was silent
a long time, while Ellen waited. "They will not take her,
Ellen." Martha raised her head, her eyes full of doubt.
"Men of God." Ellen felt her face flood scarlet, saw
her mother's doubt harden into her old clear shrewdness. "Ah, you mean—the younger?" and then, "She
was too soft to bear the burden of waiting until Robert
should come. I have done all I could. My son—what
will I tell him?"

She rose, and Ellen saw that for all her rigid courage,
she was troubled. What did she think, now, of the
preachers? Then she spoke. "Ellen, you are still young
and stubborn. You don't know that the Lord is greater
than his servants, even than those through whom he
works. Brother Laing is an instrument of God. He is
only a man, too."

VIII

The years moved for Martha with a kind of circling
sameness, one spring to another, like the flowing loops
of a penmanship exercise. As she counted them, fifteen
since Thurston her husband had ridden away, she wondered a little. Time hurried as you aged, almost as if
life grew eager to be done with you, to reach the end
of the line where the last loop broke off—into death. She
held herself against its rush. She would wait until her
husband came back. One spring thrust itself up, jagged,
above the smooth drift of the other years. Robert had

sent for Sarah, how long ago? Five—no, eight years.
He had made provision for her to join one of the wagon
trains.   Martha remembered Ellen's pitiful outburst.
"Sarah! They send for Sarah! You and I who have
waited—nothing for us. But Sarah!" It had been worm-
wood for Martha to send Robert her news; he had left
his wife with her, his mother, and she had failed to keep
the girl safe for him.   Then Ellen, watching her seal the
letter, had cried out, as if the letter pried down the stones
of her endurance, "Let me go in Sarah's place.   They
have need of women now.   Place for them in their
camps.   Oh, let me go!"
    "Matthew has not sent for you."   Martha had been
deliberately cruel, but not cruel enough to speak her whole
thought: he may no longer want you.   Ellen guessed it
and brushed it aside.
    "He thinks it would be too hard for me, too rough.
Oh, let me go!"
    Then she stayed, to nurse Martha.   Perhaps the neces-
sity for the letter brought on her sickness, or her fear
lest her daughter shame herself by pursuit of a tardy
letter.   Rheumatic fever which left her knees stiff, so
that she still limped.
    That summer Judge Abbott had foreclosed on Mat-
thew's land.   Ellen had begged Thurston to buy it, but
he had refused, cocksure in his young wisdom.   "I've
got a better thing, in stock of the new railroad.   I can't
afford it."
    Ellen's youth had disappeared that year.   Martha hadn't
noticed it until later.   There was something bleak in her
face, as if she had walled up her heart alive, and the
soft contours of her body were worn down by toil.

There had come no answer from Robert. Thurston, her husband, had written, sending a little gold, saying that another year he hoped to make a big strike and come home.

But Thurston, her youngest son. Ah, she had saved him. When, five years ago, he had married Judge Abbott's daughter, soft, clinging Grace, Martha had relaxed. He was safe now, woven into the fabric of the growing town. A wife, two little children, a new square white house in the village, an air of importance about his serious, handsome face. Thurston had done well. Martha felt at times, as she saw the slow creep of change in the community, that she had helped to make the town when she had dreamed it. Then she prayed to be forgiven for her vainglory. She and Ellen still lived in the old house Thurston had built, but the town had come out to the edge of the east pasture. Martha had oil lamps instead of candles, and in front of the bricked-up fireplace in the kitchen, a solemn black stove. There was a new schoolhouse where Thurston's children would go, presently; a family from Ohio had bought out the general store, and Thurston Dacey was a partner of Judge Abbott in the banking and legal business of the county. Thurston talked of moving his mother and Ellen into part of his new house. Each fall Martha resisted with impenetrable solidity his suggestion that before winter they close the old house. When Thurston Dacey, Senior, came back, he should find her waiting.

There seemed little to do except to wait. Ellen in heavy boots tramped about the fields, supervising the hired man, helping at planting time, at harvest. But Martha's hands, with swollen joints, could no longer fly across her loom. Ellen told her it did not matter, that there was cloth for sale now in the village. Poor stuff, that would not wear three winters! Some days Martha could hold her knitting needles, but let the wind come east, and they were too heavy. After Ellen had found her crouched in a stupor of pain over the steaming wash-boiler she had tried to lift to the bench outside the door, the girl would not let her help with the washing.

"I'm not an old woman, not yet," thought Martha, stubbornly. Fifty-eight wasn't old.

"Maybe a person's got just so much work to him," said Ellen. "You did yours up early. It's as well. There's scarcely work enough for one of us, now."

So Martha came to sit for long hours with her Bible on her knees, and her thoughts moved with a pleasant confusion from the dazzle of pages of Revelations to the days of her own youth. Thurston, tall and fiery, leading her through the wilderness to the promised land. No milk and honey there: cold toil, childbirth and child-death, the fierce struggle with the wild land. Yes, she would wait until he came again. She had a reckoning with him. Without thought, in shifting planes of feeling, she brooded over his coming. He had in his going torn across the profound meaning of her existence; he had defied her part in his life. He pretended that he sought gold for her sake, for his family. Ah, she felt him, running wild, escaping her; escaping the network life wove about you as you grew older. Some day he would come. Never humbly; a Dacey man could not be humble. But his coming would be tacit submission and Martha's life would heal itself around him.

She liked to watch Thurston's children, Alice and

Robby, in the rhythm of growth which seemed so swift to her. She gave them an austere tenderness; they were her own people moving down the years. But they were more real as shadows in her past, and she often spoke of the little girl as Ellen. Their mother came at times to sit with Martha, her small hands busy with fine sewing, but there was no intimacy. Martha felt the younger woman as almost a creature of another race. She had a woman to work for her; she complained a little in her light voice of how much trouble children were, and how easily they tired her. Thurston was proud of her; he bought her a brooch and a silk dress. When Ellen and Martha drove in to church on Sunday, Martha had a secret delight in watching her son come down the aisle, Grace clinging to his arm, her dress rustling, her fingers on her husband's sleeve, white beyond the edge of her black mit.

Sixteen years, seventeen years. The surveyors for the railroad moved through the town, a further projection of Martha's dream. Thurston bought a silk dress for her, black, stiff. Martha's gnarled hands trembled above it. "Not for me. I never had the likes of that." But Ellen slashed into it with long shears, sewed the lengths with the tiny stitches Martha had taught her a quarter of a century before. Martha thought: I'll wear it when Thurston comes. She could see him stop in the doorway, dumb with amazement at her elegance, could hear the little cluck he made when anything surprised him.

Eighteen years, and spring, early, warm. Martha sat on the small piazza in the sun; the light on the page of the Bible hurt her eyes, and she lifted her head to look along the road, past the tilled fields. Tiny pale leaves

glistened on the maples; they cast scarcely a shadow, just
a deepening of the fresh green on the grass beneath them.
Under the three tall firs the shadow was deep and blue.
Someone walked under the trees. A man. Martha lifted
one hand to shade her eyes. She did not know him.
There were strangers in town these days, now the railroad
was almost built. An old man, walking slowly, with no
zest. He stopped at the gate. Martha creaked her chair
around to see him better. Gray beard like a tuft of moss
against his dark clothes, his body bent and brown like
a bit of potato peeling. He hadn't noticed her. He took
off his hat, turning to look at the fields; the wind lifted
his thin, long hair, which he seemed, outlandishly, to
have parted clear to the nape of his neck. Martha's hands
clutched at the arms of her chair. He had made a little
sound, a clucking. He came slowly toward the house,
blinking under bushy white eyebrows. It was an old man.
It was Thurston. Oh, not Thurston, not that old, old
man!

"Eh, Martha?" He peered at her, up the slight distance of one step. "Is it you, Martha?"

Martha's hand trembled up to her sunken mouth, over
her cry of halting, incredulous recognition. Then, terribly, she saw in his eyes that she was old. For a timeless
space they hung there, the years climbing over the recollection each had held. Then Martha rose and took a
step toward him; she stood erect, and for an instant she
was almost young again, her old courage urging her
blood. For she saw in Thurston's eyes that he was
uncertain, that he waited now for her to speak.

"Come in," she said. "I've been expecting you."

His hands touched hers, hard, calloused, bony hands,

and she drew him into the house. "You must be hungry,"
she said. "You've come quite a way."

"Yes, yes." He stared about the room, biting at his
stained, drooping moustache. "You've changed things
some, I see."

"Come out to the kitchen and I'll get you something
to eat. Ellen's out."

He sat down at the table, and Martha moved from
the cupboard to his side, trying proudly not to let her
stiff knees hobble, laying before him meat, bread, butter.
This is My Body. The words hummed in her ears. *Take,
eat.* He still felt strange; she saw his eyes wandering, a
little bloodshot, unhappy. He was tired, too.

"We didn't have a stove there, did we?" He fumbled
in a pocket. "I brought you something." He poured
from a red cloth a stream of nuggets. "I—I almost
struck it, Martha."

"We've got plenty." She sat opposite him, her knees
trembling. "Thurston's done well. And this farm."
She must heal him, quickly, before Ellen laid her hard
eyes on him.

"I thought I might as well come back home." Martha
nodded encouragement. "I thought I might as well."

He ate, pulling the meat apart with his fingers, gulping
the milk noisily. Martha watched. Thurston had been
a decent mannered man. These were rough men's ways,
eloquent of years of crude living. He pushed aside his
plate, rubbing the ridged, hard back of one hand against
his mouth.

"I meant to wait till I made a good strike, but I got
to thinking I'd better come home. You've got it soft
here, compared to what I been used to." He leaned

across the table, one fist clenched, the knuckles huge, pro-
truding. "Martha, I never planned to go. It came over
me all of a heap, that morning, seeing them all ready to
start, that I had to go along."

Martha's hands pressed against her knees, and her heart
quickened in triumph. He knew! He too was seeing
that morning when he rode away, and the wantonness
of his desertion. She had waited for this moment.

"I never thought it'd be so long." He stumbled, hunting for justification. "I tell you I worked, Martha. It
wears a man out, work like I did. When you get older,
you can't stand it. Luck wasn't with me."

Martha's eyes were quiet under their drooping lids.
He couldn't say more, being a man and Thurston Dacey.
She had to take those few words and turn them to her
own great need. A sound of wheels on the road. Ellen
was driving into the yard, the yellow paint of the cart
gay in the sun, little Alice beside her on the high seat.
Thurston cupped a hand over his burned-out eyes.
"Who's that?" He scrambled up and stood at the window, the unfamiliar arc of his body making him again a
stranger.

"That's Ellen, and Thurston's girl," said Martha.
"Where's Matthew? That's all she'll want to know. And
Robert?" She was a wicked old woman, rolling triumph
under her tongue, forgetting to ask for her son. "Where's
Robert?"

"Rob went to the coast, to settle. I heard he was
married."

"Married? But Sarah—"

"She was gone, wasn't she? He needed a woman."
Thurston turned, pulling at his yellowish moustache.

"Why didn't Ellen get her a husband?" His voice crackled with petulance, and Martha thought he was afraid Ellen would hold him to blame. "That Matthew—he went off prospecting with a party. He'd been drinking, too. We helped stake him, Rob and I, and we never heard a word from him again. Struck it rich and hogged it. I know." He shook his head toward the door, his thin hair agitated. "She needn't think she'll ever see him."

Martha pushed herself to her feet. "Don't you tell her all that, Thurston." She felt a curious, tender pity lifting her into a clear sight of him. There was hatred in that rude life of men alone, hatred as well as rough, hard ways. And her son, Robert, with a strange woman . . . a wife, if she was a wife. "Come out and see Ellen, and Thurston's child. We must send word to Thurston."

IX

Ellen had driven back from town in excellent humor. She had made a good bargain for two of the calves; the spring air was pleasant; she enjoyed the skittish feel of the black colt, his vitality rippling through the reins into her arms as she drove; she liked to have Alice on the seat beside her, the two neat braids of fair hair shining on her bright pink dress; projects for the farm moved in her mind and muscles. Then, as she slipped the shafts from the lugs, she saw her mother and an old man crossing the patch of fresh green toward the barn door. Like flame, like the spring restlessness in the colt, hope that she had done with years ago burst through the stones she had laid heavy over it, swept in a storm through her hard, strong body, so that she twisted her hands into the

mane of the colt and clung there, the warm clean smell
of the horse in her nostrils, watching across the arch of
his neck those two figures coming toward the wide door.

"Why, Pa!" Her voice was hot metal in her throat.
"Watch out. Flash doesn't know you." The colt took
a dancing step, and Ellen moved with him, strong, fiery.
With a sweep of her arm she tossed the bridle off, with
a firm slap she drove Flash into his stall.

The years had worn him down, this old stranger who
brushed her cheek with his gray beard. "This is Alice,
your granddaughter. Another grandpa for you, Alice!"
Ellen pushed the child forward. "She's like her mother,
not dark like the Daceys." She felt dry fibres in her
body expand, grow living again, under flooding, sweet
rain. When could she ask? Then she saw her mother's
face, stern, warning pity in the sunken eyes. "Did you
come alone?" she cried out, but she knew before she asked.

"Rob has settled somewhere on the coast," Martha said.
Ellen turned to hang the harness on hooks along the wall.
"He doesn't know where Matthew is now."

Oh, fool, fool, to let hope trick her! Her knuckles
scraped the rough wood, and the smart gave her angry
relief. The spring sun had done it, and the suddenness.
What was Matthew, or any man, to her? She was old
and done with dreams. She turned steadily enough. This
was her mother's day. "We must let Thurston know,"
Ellen said. "We'll have them come to supper. To cele-
brate." One prodigal, at least, had returned.

The excitement which had started as a flood of hope
stayed with Ellen all that day, in a frenzy of work.
Martha brought out a suit that Thurston had left, which
she had cherished against moths, and if he looked rather

piteously shrunken, at least he was less shabby in it. When twilight came, Martha in her black silk sat at the head of the table, Thurston in his salt and pepper at the foot, Thurston, Junior, and his wife on one side, the children across with Ellen between them, and the feast of welcome spread. Ellen's excitement had risen into a mood of hypersensitivity, as if she were part of each person that the hanging lamp shone down upon. She felt her brother's mixture of resentment and self-approval. His boyhood stood like a ghost at his father's shoulder; this bent, oldish man, with no bags of gold, had been the hero Thurston had longed to follow. It was the younger Thurston now who could, faintly, patronize the older man. Ellen felt Grace's thin sympathy and disapproval. She was glad that Thurston's father had come back, but what an uncouth old man! Then, deeper, a tinge of satisfaction that he compared so poorly with her own father. Next Ellen felt the children; their thoughts were little nibbles of wonder and indifference, with attentive eyes on the generous feast. But Martha—the meaning of the day lay in her heart, touching her old cheeks into unwonted color, steadying the motions of her crooked fingers, marking with pride her glance about the table.

Supper finished, Ellen refused the offer of help from Grace and from her mother. "This is my business. Go talk," she insisted. As she stood at the wooden sink, she heard Thurston with his father in the yard, explaining how the value of the farm had increased. "I'd like to talk with you about selling part of it." Ellen stood motionless, her hands idle in the dishpan. Sell it, the land? Why, it was hers! Her life spread over the smooth acres. Then her hands rattled the cups. Thurston was just showing off. To-night she could not think, she had to keep going.

Later Thurston and his family climbed into the surrey and drove away. Ellen waited at the door until the sound of the wheels was gone. From the swampy hollow across the fields came the shrill sweet repetition of hylas celebrating spring. Strange to hear in the house behind her, not only her mother's shuffle, but the heavier thump of boots. Strange, too, to think that the house which had been a house of women for so long now sheltered a man. Would he have notions about the farming, want to run things? Ellen stretched her tired shoulders. He was her father, but he had been eighteen years away from this place. Maybe she could manage him, too. She turned reluctantly to enter the house. Loneliness wrapped her about, keyed to the shrilling of the hylas, cold with the soft damp of the spring. Not for Matthew; that had been a rush of madness, which the steady habit of the day's work had pushed out of immediate pain. For her mother, for the routine of their life together. All that was gone, now. Martha would want her husband dignified, important, as head of the family. She'd side with him, against me. Ellen's thought was vague; she had a premonition that this homecoming threatened all she had found satisfying. I ought to be glad for her, and instead —she sighed, as she entered the empty kitchen.

As is she had been waiting, Martha came to the door. She had taken off her black silk, and her dark wrapper was buttoned close to her wrinkled neck; under the frilled edge of her cambric nightcap her forehead was powdery white and calm. "I want to say good-night, Ellie." She waited for Ellen to come. "My cup runneth over." The bent fingers reached Ellen's shoulders. "Surely goodness and mercy shall follow me." Ellen felt the old arms tremble, and bent, her eyes closed to hide her quick, unaccustomed tears. The soft lips brushed her forehead; she was a little girl again. "And you, too, Ellie. Goodness and mercy for you. You are a good daughter." Then she went with her hesitating step to her own room and Ellen heard her door close.

Ellen lay in her narrow bed, arms crossed over her breast, waiting for sleep. Bits of recollection beat against her, as if she drifted down a swift stream with whirling flotsam. Sarah, weeping the morning Rob went. Sarah and her dead baby. Brother Laing's black beard. Thurston, listening to his mother's prophecy. A nest that Matthew had found in an elder bush, one afternoon as they walked along the little river. Matthew would be a stranger, now. Her hands clenched into fists. Matthew was dead. Dead, he stayed always young and straight and ruddy. She was old. Too old for such wild, foolish thoughts. She twisted her spare, unused body against the hard bed and hid her face.

She was wakened by a strange voice, shouting her name. She sat up, and the tone of that "Ellen!" jerked her out of the daze of sleep. It was light; over the terror in the call she heard the morning twittering of birds. At the foot of the narrow stairs her father stood, a shrunken, frightened figure in the old yellowed nightshirt Martha had found for him.

"Ellen!" She hurried down to him. "Your mother— I can't wake her."

X

The day of the funeral, when Grace repeated the one remark she had made too often, "Suppose she had died a day earlier, or he had come a day later!" Ellen broke her silence with a fierce, "Don't be a fool! She wouldn't have died till he came, no matter when." She didn't care if Grace was indignant. She herself had washed the body, her mind busy with strange thoughts as her hands worked, and dressed her mother in the black silk. She knew when she kissed me good-night, Ellen thought. She listened to the minister, solemn in his funeral garb, praising "Our Sister." He doesn't know half, thought Ellen. Courage, pride, fidelity: Martha Dacey's spirit was woven of rare fibres. Thurston, her husband, in new black his son had furnished, had a dazed, grieved air. "Why, I'd just come home," his eyes said. "What call was there for her to die right off?"

Ellen, driving home, her father silent and bent beside her, thought: here I was, worrying about her siding with him. Wicked thoughts. Now it's him and me together, with her gone. Thurston Dacey's homecoming had carried out that premonition, however wicked her thoughts that night had been!

The next week Ellen drove herself and the hired man with fury, hurrying up the spring work on the land. Her father followed her about, offering suggestions which Ellen scarcely heard. If he made a forlorn figure, in a field corner, she was too busy to notice. His notions about farming were a score of years behind time, and Ellen, struggling against resentment that it was he and not her mother who waited for her to come to the house, brushed aside carelessly his suggestions. He objected to her young orchards, the centre of her pride; he thought she'd starve them with no more acres in wheat and corn. The morning that the purchaser of five calves arrived to drive them away, Ellen found her father at the pasture gate, brandishing his arms, while the man hesitated in amazement.

"I haven't sold any calves! I ain't planning on selling any."

"I have, Pa." Ellen had hurried from the kitchen, the flush from the stove over which she had been working deepening into anger. "I sold five. It's all right, Mr. Tracy." Then she added, grudgingly, "It was before you came, I made the deal."

Later, as she drew from the oven the bread she was baking, and turned the brown loaves onto a fresh cloth, she felt a hostile inspection of her movements Her father stood at the door, mumbling into his beard.

"Have I any say on my own land, or haven't I?" He stamped into the kitchen.

Ellen's hand slipped, the rim of the iron pan leaving a red welt on her wrist. "I didn't think to speak about the calves," she said.

"You've had your own will here so long you think you can make a laughingstock of your father. I'd have you know this is my land. I settled it. I cleared it and made a home."

"You left it, didn't you?" Ellen held one hand against her smarting wrist. "You left it, and for twenty years I've worked day in day out. You didn't care then what I sowed or reaped."

"If I'd come back rich, you'd find respect in your heart

for your father. If your mother—" His rage throbbed in a vein along one temple, and he stamped out of the door.

Ellen followed him, after a moment, and saw him walking toward the village, head down, arms swinging, long uneven steps. He was going to see Thurston. Well, Thurston hadn't bothered much about the farm, not since the winter he had moved to the room above Abbott's store. Then shame smarted through her, as if the burn on her wrist spread, that they had had words. He was her father. Oh, give me more patience, she sighed. Maybe, if she could pretend to take his advice, he'd be content.

He didn't come home at noon. When Ellen came in late in the afternoon, she found the dinner she had set out for him still untouched. The sun, the hours in the garden, had relaxed the morning tension. She busied herself with the milk the hired man had brought to the door, straining it, pouring it into pails, into flat pans. Some of the children from neighbors would come presently for the pails. Her mind was busy with little phrases for her father, placating words, words that Martha would have liked.

Thurston and her father drove into the yard, the older man climbing stiffly down from the seat. Ellen went down the neat path, and her father brushed past her, with a triumphant snort and swagger.

"Ellen." Her brother looked down, his fingers rubbing the leather rein. "We've got great news." His eyes, under his prominent forehead, were uneasy, and he brushed one hand against his crisp side whiskers. "We did a good piece of business to-day."

Ellen stood close to the cart, her fingers closing over the wheel, so that the strip of bright steel at the rim ran under them, round and round in a dizzy circle of fear.

"The railroad wants the brook and west pasture, and Father agrees to sell it. His hand's out of farming and he thinks it's too hard for you. Swanson, the Swede, will take the house. There's room in my house for you. I've said so often enough. You'd be a real help to Grace."

"Sell it, this?" Ellen's head swung in a slow arc, toward the fertile, growing fields. "Thurston Dacey, you couldn't!" Her hands lifted from the wheel, desperate, empty hands. "Land I've worked—it's mine! What are you doing?"

"Now, Ellen." Thurston crossed one leg over the other knee, and flicked the end of the rein. "It's not yours. It's his. And he sees eye to eye with me. This is the time to sell it. I can invest the money to take care of both of you. You can't work like a man all your life."

Ellen thrust her hair back from her gray face and pulled herself close to the cart. "I could work like a man to give you your chance," she cried. "To clothe you, to feed you, while you learned to be a big man. Why, we hadn't enough to eat those winters, and now you do this!"

"I didn't ask you to starve." His face was harsh. "You wouldn't let mother come to my house, you wouldn't come. I tell you I don't want you crashing around in men's boots, while I make the Dacey name mean something. Grace doesn't like it, either. If Father wants to sell his own property, he can, and you ought to be thankful there's a good home waiting for you." He gathered the reins in an angry hand. "Let go that wheel. You'll get hurt."

"Thurston, it's just because I made him angry this morning. About the calves. I'll let him have his way. Only he's been gone so long."

"It's as he said. You've had your way too long. It wasn't calves, except that he made up his mind quicker, maybe. There's no use arguing, Ellen. It's done." He clucked at the horse, and the gritty edge of the wheel scraped through Ellen's hands. "You'll have a good home with me as long as you live." He whisked the reins, the wheels grated in a turn, and he was gone.

Inside the house that old man waited, with his air of triumph. He had shown her, hadn't he, who owned the land? She couldn't go in. She hurried around the house, across the field, out to the road toward the west, as far as the great oak which still stood in the fence corner. The late twilight of summer lay in translucent green over the quiet slopes. Anyone passing might see her, think her crazy. Well, wasn't she? She pressed her hands against the rough bark of the tree; through her passed a notion that the tree had grown strong, that its acorns had grown bitter with pain that had run these twenty years from her fingers, from the pressure of her arms, through its fibres, into its mounting sap.

She sat down on the gnarled root, crouching forward, her forehead damp in her cold hands. Nausea more bitter than any physical rejection twisted through her. Presently she sat erect, looking into the deepening twilight at the familiar shapes. A good home until she died. They would give her that. Without these acres she was nothing. Profoundly she knew that she had been less barren, living there, making the land yield. What could she do? Until she died. Soon she would be forty, then fifty . . . sixty. Listening to the light voice of Grace making complaints, watching her button together her thin lips. Her brother and father: they could do this. They were strong against her impotence, in wanton, male arrogance. She closed her eyes against the shadow of beloved trees on a small hill. Thurston wanted money. She had suspected that, before her mother's death. He had been unable to touch Martha's will, her determination to wait for her husband's coming.

Ellen lay back along the root, lethargy creeping over her tired nerves. A night wind moved in the oak above her, and a few stars pushed through the darkening sky. No use to struggle. They would have their way, being men. If she had been more careful of her father's pride —but that would only have postponed the moment.

Later she rose, stiffly, and started toward the house. "I'll not say a word to him," she thought, and her smile was bitter. "That'll bother him a little." And then, "The only thing I could do would be to get me a husband, and I don't know of any I could stand." She could see the glow of the kitchen lamp now, and she stopped, caught back into another evening when a candle shone through that window and Matthew walked beside her. Well, she thought, I lived through that. Her mother had called her, from the doorway there. Ellen's hand pressed against her trembling lips. If Martha were sitting in the kitchen. The old hands seemed to rest on her shoulders, the steady voice said, "Goodness and mercy for you, too, Ellie. You have been a good daughter."

She had loved her sons more, Ellen knew. And her

husband. But she had lived with Ellen, and it was to Ellen she had given her farewell. She knew how to endure, thought Ellen; her mother, the oak tree, the summer night enclosed her.

PART II

I

It was well that Thurston had built a house to fit his ambition, Ellen thought. Even so, it seemed too small for the people whom it sheltered. First Thurston and his wife, then the two small children, then Judge Abbott, now Ellen and her father. One old man on each side of the central hall downstairs; Thurston upstairs with Grace, and Robby in the small room next Ellen's. It was a household of men, with Thurston as its Lord, and each of the older men lord by proxy in Thurston's absence, accomplices, abettors in his presence. To Ellen, after almost twenty years of self-sustained existence with her mother, the first year in Thurston's house was a kind of imprisonment in a torture chamber, where one by one her habits of living were plucked out. From the time she woke in the morning—breakfast for men, for children, instead of soft, moist eyes of animals in a dusky barn—until she could climb the stairs to hide herself in her room—where the ceiling, high and white. lacked the brown friendliness of sloping rafters, and there was no space beyond her window for trees and stars—and all the intervening hours, when whatever she worked at seemed tiny bits fitted into the life of many other people, never her own proper work, belonging to her own schemes for a day or a year—all this time the wrenching at the ways

of her life went on. Work, whatever it was, became the
only sedative she knew for the pain of adjustment, and
Grace found her more of a help than Thurston had fore-
seen. She complained a little that Ellen wasn't good company, she went around so sullenly.

"It takes a while to get used to being here," Ellen tried
to explain.

"You old maids have such set ways!" Grace watched
Ellen ironing the fine pleated bosom of one of Judge
Abbott's shirts. "You haven't made that too stiff," she
added, sharply. "He doesn't like it stiff."

"Any other ways are stiff, I notice," said Ellen tartly,
holding the iron near her cheek, testing its warmth. "I
don't know anyone more set than Thurston about what
he has to have. If things aren't just so, you'd think the
earth was falling down."

"Thurston is particular." Grace had satisfaction in
her tone. "But he's a man."

Ellen set her lips and thumped the iron against the
board. When Grace had gone, she stood for a moment
easing her tired shoulders, staring out of the window at
nothing. Queer she got so tired, she who had worked
all day in the fields, with only a pleasant need for sleep
when night came. With competent, firm strokes she
returned to the ironing. At least no one could say she
didn't earn her keep.

She thought with a tinge of amusement that Robby
was the only one of the men who liked her. When she
heard him shrilling through the house, 'An' Telly!
An' Telly!' she felt less cold and shrivelled. Judge Abbott
gave her small heed; Ellen remembered how great he had
seemed to her in her girlhood, with his sharp nose and

clipped beard. Still shrewd and hard, he had retreated further into his pompousness. Between him and Thurston Dacey the older there went on a secret warfare, as if the two men kept in the air between them with skilful strokes the need of each to be superior to the other. Ellen heard their whacks at the uncertain ball; Thurston boasted of his adventures, John Abbott made himself the core of the growth of the town; then Thurston alluded to his wisdom in settling on land that had grown so valuable, and Abbott referred to his training of young Thurston.

Abbott, however, had his office and his partnership with Thurston, while old Thurston had only his leisure and hints at great plans. Ellen might have found malicious pleasure in the breaking in of Thurston to this new life, except that her Dacey pride added her father's discomfort to her own. His son took him in hand, at Grace's disapproval. He wasn't in a mining camp now, and there were some things—cuss words; if he had to chew, he couldn't spit in the house. Ellen heard the first of that filial protest, saw the rage of humiliation that flooded old Thurston, and hurried away from the door of his room, out of hearing. He'd brought it on himself, yielding to his son's schemes, but it was hard for him. They dwelt in the tents of strangers; for Thurston, her brother, had become a stranger.

Ellen's life narrowed so into days of dull endurance that she was slow to hear the first rumbles of change. Talk of a new President, a man from Illinois, a railsplitter. Talk of states' rights. Her father and John Abbott had new fuel for their struggle. Thurston was irritable. Something was wrong with his schemes for money. A neighbor woman brought in a story about a strange sight one night, a band of negroes tramping east toward Detroit, bound for the shores of Canada. None of all this touched Ellen with much significance until the day when the town suddenly changed from its existence as houses where separate human beings dwelt, into a feeling, an emotion, that went leaping from one body to another, making faces similar, sounding alike in the voices that spoke, penetrating closed doors, running down the roads: as if the town were submerged in a strange fluid and for the brief time of the impact of the news, nothing existed separately or unsubmerged. War. War of the Union against seceding states.

Old Thurston stood in front of the house, waving his hickery walking stick. "By God!" he shouted. "I'm going! I can shoot!" John Abbott, older by five years, danced in front of him, brandishing a fist under his nose. "They won't take you! You're an old jackass!"

Thurston the son came down the street, the tumult in his jerking stride shouting aloud his share in the common flood. Grace pushed Ellen aside and rushed out, to fling herself at Thurston, her arms beating at his shoulders.

That night, as Ellen heard Grace weeping, she remembered another woman weeping by night. Sarah, before Robert went away. When Thurston in his new uniform said good-by, Ellen wondered if he remembered. No, he wouldn't. It was his turn now to ride away. For all the riding was different, it was the same. Another Dacey riding away, while women waited. Old Thurston's desire rode with his son, although he stayed behind. Thurston had come to Ellen, the night before his departure. For the first time since his boyhood, he paid her tribute. "You'll take care of them, Ellen. I know they can depend on you. The Judge will look after the business, what there is. The children and Grace—well, they've got you."

"Yes, they've got me." Ellen had a glimpse of the young, eager Thurston peering through the hard mask of twenty added years. "You're glad to go, aren't you?"

"Glad? It's my duty, any man's duty." Thurston hesitated, and added softly, "I'm not sorry. You can't say I haven't worked hard, been faithful." Ellen knew then that the desire of the boy, which Martha had opposed so skillfully, had never been fully diverted into his years of money making. It had only waited a chance to break through.

II

During the first months after Thurston's departure, Ellen found herself hoping that the Lord would forgive her for her wicked delight that her brother had gone to war. "I'd pray to Him about it," she thought, "only, since He's a man—" Was that why she never felt that devoutness, that intimacy of religion which her mother had possessed? Almost shocked, she retreated from the dangerous edge of such irreverence. She had little time for thinking. For with Thurston gone, the household had unwittingly focussed about her, as if she alone had the necessary force to carry it through the troubled days. Grace dragged herself about the house, her face swollen, tear-blanched, unaware of her children except for moments when she flung her arms about one or the other of them and wept afresh because they were fatherless babes. Ellen had a scornful pity for her; it's as if she guessed she couldn't hold him back, she thought. To her questions about household affairs Grace said, "I don't care! Can't you see I don't care!" Ellen, with caution at first, and then boldly, as she saw that Grace persisted in indifference, took charge of matters. Grace complained of pains in her head, in her stomach, and then one morning in weeping that grew hysterical, she confirmed what Ellen had suspected, that she was with child again. "Oh, I can't bear it!" She clung to Ellen, who bent over the bed, smoothing the blankets. "I can't go through it alone. It's bad enough with Thurston here. But he's gone, leaving me like this!"

"It'll give you something to think about." Ellen pushed down her secret delight that Grace would need her the more, would leave her free. "You'll begin to feel better soon. You just lie still and don't worry yourself."

Alice was in school all day, but Robby trudged after Ellen as she went from one task to another. "An' Telly, what you doing that for? An' Telly, what's that?" Ellen liked the way he planted himself before her, feet wide, face serious, and made stubborn insistence on an answer. Her own life mounted in swift crescendo; she looked younger, with the harassed wrinkles about eyes and lips gone, with her gaze serene, as if the sight of five people depending on her gave her energy for life. She liked to swing Robby up in her strong arms, liked the feeling of his small bones under her hands, liked to touch the dark wisp of hair that curled in the little hollow at the nape of his neck. She was always gentle with Alice, but the child had a way of fretting too like her mother. Ellen never laughed with her as she did with Robby.

Thurston and the Judge were fighting the war, day by day; if they couldn't go, they could escape by means of it. The Judge dressed with care in the clothes Ellen laid out for him, and went down to the office. But he wagged his head at Thurston, saying that if the war lasted two years the country would go to wrack and ruin. The bottom was out of business. No one wanted money, except for mortgages and more mortgages. He caught cold, and Ellen plastered him with mustard and red flannel. After that he lost his pompousness with her, and even looked for her when he came into the house at the end of a day in an uneventful office. Ellen had started a garden in the stretch of ground behind the house; her father watched the plowing, Ellen with the family horse and a borrowed plow. Then he clumped down himself to take the handles of the harrow.

"I been thinking we ought to raise potatoes," he said. "And beans. With a war, we ought to raise things."

Ellen nodded; she had planned to wheedle him from his restlessness, marooned in a village with women, children, and other old men.

Letters from Thurston came, rarely, like an alien wind, blowing Grace into fresh tears, touching Ellen with a chill. Of course he would come, some day. She wanted him to come. But—

The child was born, another son, a baby protesting and peevish, whose mother's forlorn months seemed to have embittered his life, even before he tried it for himself. Thurston came home for a week's leave, before marching south; brown, upright, with captain's strips on his blue shoulder. His father and his father-in-law hung about him, thirsty and feverish for a draught of his adventure. Grace showed him his new son, John Thurston, subtly making a reproach of the child's ailments, almost of its existence. Ellen watched the silent devotion Robby offered to his father, and tried to tear out the jealousy that leaped in her.

The morning that Thurston left, he came into the kitchen, his spurs rattling, pushing shut the door, speaking hastily. "Ellen, do you think you can manage? The Judge says nothing's coming in. I'll send my pay. It's not much."

"I'll manage."

"I don't know how long it'll be." He stared a moment, one hand pulling at his moustache. "Why, you look like Ma, Ellie."

"She would be proud of you, Captain Dacey!" Ellen made a little run toward him, seeing his face in a mist of tears. "She'd say, 'God bless you, Thurston!'" She kissed him firmly. "There. I hear Grace calling."

Later that day she found old Thurston behind the woodshed, showing Robby how to hold a piece of wood against his shoulder. "Here, fingers on the trigger. Aim! When you see the whites of their eyes, fire!" His bang! and the child's boomed together. Ellen turned away, shivering. She was a fool, upset by Thurston's going. Of course Robby would grow up, like any man, and if he didn't go to war, he'd ride off somewhere, like any Dacey. "I can love him now," she said to herself, "before he grows up."

Late that fall Ellen heard that the draft had taken Swanson, the Swede who had bought the Dacey farm. She walked out one afternoon, talked with the stolid, full-bosomed woman, looked about the kitchen, full of tow-headed children, all of a size, and came back driving a black and white cow. There was room in the small barn, and the children needed milk. Mrs. Swanson lacked grain for the winter. As she tethered the animal in the stall she stood a moment, the end of rope dangling. She had gone there, to the old home, without a single ache of longing, without a stir of the bitterness which had distorted her last days there. I must be getting old and sensible, she decided. Or was it only that her days were so crowded now with other thoughts?

The winter was long, shutting down in snow and sleet, and short, dark days. The Judge waited for Ellen to wrap his gray muffler about his ears before he started cautiously along the street. "Why not stay home to-day?" she would ask, knowing that he would shake his head, that he needed the pretense for all its emptiness.

Another spring, another winter. Thurston was ill, was in a hospital, was better, and no news for months, except the tales of battles, of marches, of men wounded, of a neighbor boy who had died. Robby started in school, in a suit Ellen fashioned for him from one of the Judge's coats. She missed him. John Thurston was beginning to follow her about the house, in a scrambling mixture of crawling and unsteady steps, but his shrieks and tearful rages never reached Ellen's heart. She nursed him through croup, when Grace was sure he would die. She kept him quiet when his mother, whose youth had been rubbed down into consistent melancholy by the friction of the years of waiting, said she couldn't stand that child another minute, and why should she have a child that cried and fretted all the time? When Robby came home from school, his shout, "An' Telly!" satisfied the unconscious, slight strain which the hours of his absence accumulated in Ellen. The same shout roused John Thurston, always. He would drop his attempts to walk, descending to creeping as a surer method, and like a speedy turtle, track them to the kitchen. No use to close the door. He had to come in, had to share the bread or cookies Ellen gave to Robby. Ellen liked to sit in the rocker, listening to some small epic of the day which Robby brought to her. But John Thurston pulled himself up to her knee, lifting his gnome face—his head was large, domed above the blue eyes—and insisting, "Me too, me too!" If Ellen tried to hush him or to send him away, he would stiffen into the preliminary stage of temper. Sometimes Ellen would lift him into her lap, in a kind of repentant pity for him. Absurd to fancy that a child of three could feel jealous; but that queer look in his face! Then Robby; "Aw, he's always hanging 'round."

"Tell me about it to-night, Robby, when he's asleep."

"Won't go to sleep." John Thurston squirmed on her knee, and when Robby went off, defeated, looked up at Ellen with solemn, old eyes, before she set him down and returned to some one of her many tasks.

Old Thurston was sick that winter, with grippe and a stubborn cough. He was sure he was going to die, at first, and clung to Ellen in obedient fear. When his fever dropped, he grew querulous, complaining that Ellen neglected him. The Judge asked after him with solicitude. He missed their scraps, thought Ellen. One evening as she came down the stairs, after tucking each child in with a heated soapstone, she heard the old voices peppering at each other.

"So you aren't dead yet?" That was the Judge. "I never thought to see you up and about again."

"You'd best get yourself out of my room. If you should ketch it, you'd never see the light of day again, a man of your years!" Thurston sounded as if he were bouncing in his bed.

"It's constitution that counts, not years."

"Ketch it and see! I won't have my girl nursing you if you ketch it!" Thurston's voice roared into the hoarse cough which had followed the fever, and Ellen hurried into the room.

"What are you up to, hollering yourself hoarse?" She would have laughed if she had been less weary, at the pair of old roosters, feathers all askew—Thurston's scant hair brushed out past his ears, the Judge pulling at his whiskers. "Get out of here, Judge, where it's warm. And you, Pa, you lie down."

"Well, if you'd come and see to my blankets, instead of flying about making milksops of boys."

Ellen's hand was harsh enough as she thrust him under the covers to break off his reproaches. She felt his old eyes prying at her as she tidied up the room for the night. "There. Now I'll be right here on the sofa, and your door's open so some heat can come in."

"Kin I get up to-morrow, Ellie?"

"Not if it's as cold as to-day. You go to sleep."

The Judge poked his head out of his doorway. "It's your nursing does it, Ellen," he said, shaking his whiskers. "He'd never pulled through. I never expected him to get out of bed again."

"You better get into bed yourself, Judge." Ellen poked chunks into the round iron stove, adjusted the checks for the night.

"If I took sick, ever, some time, I mean, wouldn't you tend me?"

"My land, yes, if I had to."

Ellen buttoned her flannel wrapper, wound a shawl about her feet, and lay down on the hard sofa she had pulled into the hall. As she dozed she thought of the quiet house, with cold winter creeping along the floors, pushing icy fingers under the doorsills. A house full of children. They were all children, even the Judge, and she could tend them all.

Then it wasn't the Judge who "took sick," but the children. Alice complained one morning that her head ached. Ellen told her impatiently that she could go to school or to bed. Later that morning Ellen was hanging out the washed clothes, in cold that turned them into brittle icy ghosts before she could pin them to the line. She stopped to hold her aching fingers together under the edge of her shawl, when she saw Robby crossing the yard, slow-footed.

"I feel funny." He looked up at her, his face crimson.

Ellen hurried him into the house, propped him in a rocker while she unwound his muffler, drew off his leggings, afraid of his drowsy, unnatural eyes. He shivered away from the touch of her chilled hands. She made him herb tea, sent Grace up to look at Alice. They had something, both of them.

Scarlet fever, the old doctor said. Some of the other village children had it. Ellen drove Thurston upstairs and turned his room again into a hospital. Grace would have to keep John Thurston quiet, and out of that room. The Judge and old Thurston tiptoed about, fetching wood, bringing hot water for Ellen, offering comforting words about all children having such fevers. But the day Ellen heard that one of the Swanson children had died, she knelt beside the bed where Robby lay, offering queer phrases. His very bones were hot under her fingers. "Oh, God!" She tried to find a prayer, placating, potent, to offer that remote, terrifying God of her people. "Oh, God! He's so little. Don't let him die. I never asked for much. Don't let him die. I never asked for much."

If it strikes in, it's dangerous, the old doctor told her. If it comes out, it's all right. "It" came out swiftly with Alice, in blotches and blisters. Ellen bathed her, consoled her, tied mittens over her hands. "You mustn't scratch!" And all the time her heart lay under the feet of God, imploring, while her hands and feet ministered.

Then Robby's fever dropped; he was fretful, restless, irritable, and Ellen's heart, strong, singing, was hers again. Her patience flowed out in a sea with no horizon, and when at last they could burn sulphur candles, and John Thurston pounded his fists on her knees, screaming, "I wan'a be sick too!" she swung him up to her shoulder, laughing at him, until he was quiet, with one fist curled in her throat.

III

Spring again. Ellen planned with old Thurston for a larger garden and the Judge spoke of land on which he held a mortgage. "You could put it into grain, wheat," he suggested. Ellen dosed herself with sulphur and molasses against the strange lassitude she felt. She'd been cooped up too much all winter. She dosed her family, too, even to the Judge. "Purify your blood," she asserted, a tyrant with spoon and bottle. News trickled through the town, of fresh stirring of the fighting, frozen through the long winter into rigidity. The railsplitter was President again; some time, surely, the war would

end. Or would it go on forever, while old men talked
and children grew taller? Ellen wondered if it had reality. Was it like that gold the men had gone in quest
of, something women never saw?

She walked along the edge of the garden one afternoon, thrusting a pitchfork into the ground, sniffing at
the cold wet soil. Still early for plowing. Frost too
deep. She heard a shout, a quavering call, and saw the
Judge running, waving his stick, his white whiskers bristling around his scarlet face.

"It's come!" His voice squeaked in his windpipe.
"Ellen, girl, it's come! Lee has surrendered. The
Union's safe!"

Ellen held the gate ajar for him, thrust her arms
through his. "You ought not to run that way." She
felt the old man shaken by the frantic pumping of
his heart. "Here." She pushed him down on the
steps.

"Where's your father? I told him Lee would crash.
It's come." He thumped his cane, his hands knotted over
it, tears, rolling into his whiskers. "A messenger, on a
horse, riding through."

"What's come?" Grace ran out, her hands gathering
up the folds of a dress she was ripping apart. "Thurston?
Has Thurston come?"

"He will come, Grace. Lee's surrendered. The
Union's saved! Listen!" He pointed with his stick.
Over them came the sudden jangle of church bells, as if
hands as tremulous, as mad with excitement as the Judge's
had seized the ropes. The spring air was full of bells.
Under their sound the village was a second time submerged, drenched in one single emotion. Old Thurston

came down the street, one hand against his back, holding together his old bones while he hastened.

"What'd I tell you?" he shouted at the Judge.

"What'd I tell you?" the Judge yelled back.

Ellen felt a tug at her skirt. Robby, taller, thinner since his illness, frowned at her. "Will my father come home now?" he asked.

Grace, wiping tears away with the width of skirt she carried, pulled Robby toward her, held him while he squirmed. "Yes, he will come home now!" John Thurston pummelled at her. "My favver?" he demanded. Ellen stepped backward from the group there on the edge of the piazza, lifting her face toward the sound of the bells. They rang the end of war for all the people, and what else, for her? They were bells of great rejoicing. Why did their tone echo mockingly? I'm a fool, she thought, sternly. A selfish fool.

IV

Thurston Dacey came home, one shoulder stiffened from a bullet wound of which he had not told them, a new bruskness of manner. Four years older and more than four years harder. Grace blossomed amazingly, curling her hair again, hurrying to finish the new dresses Thurston wanted her to have, clinging to his arm as they walked down the street to church. She was like a bean vine with no prop, thought Ellen; now she's got a pole again. Alice, too, fluttered about him, coaxing for his attention. Robby tried to copy his stride, even his peremptory speech. Only John Thurston, who had never known his father, resented this intrusion into his familiar household, roared back at him, sulked at his "Did you hear me, John? At once!", defied even punishment. Ellen learned to keep the child out of his father's path. That, after the first few weeks, was easy, for Thurston was seldom at home. After the incredible shock of Lincoln's assassination, business was getting on its feet again, he said. Ellen had a picture of Thurston astride the shoulders of business as it heaved up, cow-like, while the old Judge panted apologetically behind, humble because Thurston found things in such bad shape on his return.

The change in Ellen's existence was subtle. At first there seemed no change, except that there was more money for food, for clothing, for fresh paint on the dingy house, for a new carpet in the parlor. When Thurston first returned he said to Ellen: "You've had a hard time, but things will be easy now. The Judge says he couldn't have got on without you." That was during his first week, and he never amplified his statement. Grace had no desire to take back any charge of the house, except to say, "You know Thurston doesn't like oatmeal. You might make another pie for him." Outwardly Ellen's life ran the same course. Something had gone from it. Old Thurston missed something, too; he was like an old crow with clipped wing feathers, flopping about in circles. Ellen thought: now that he's won the war and saved the country, he hasn't anything to do. For herself the trouble was not that her hands were empty. She had plenty to do. But each day had a separate round of tasks, and the days together made a dull repetition of one note, without meaning. She did not think in clear words that her energy lacked purpose, but her self, straining beyond the work of her hands, could only drop back, thwarted.

Work on the railroad started again; men cleared the ties of grass and weeds, and the rust red rails stretched in long lines. Thurston planned a new business block, the Abbott-Dacey block. All day the whine of saws in the lumber mill made a faint, scarcely noticeable accompaniment to the familiar village noises. There were church socials, and women found time to call on each other, after dinner. Grace grew plump, her satisfaction with her position as wife of one of the biggest men in town finding physical expression. Ellen was shy with outsiders; her life for more than forty years had expanded only to the limit of the family, and external, superficial contacts made her shrink into awkward dumbness. Since someone had to stay with John Thurston, even if the older children no longer needed her, Ellen's withdrawal from the new social life of the town was convenient.

The second winter, the Judge slipped on the ice, and after a few days of suffering from a badly fractured hip, died. Shock, the new doctor said. Only Ellen thought that the old man might have been relieved to die, to escape his bewilderment at the rapidly changing world. Old Thurston wagged his head, blustering, "He was a good bit older than me, eh, Ellen? And he'd had a soft life. That makes a man tender." The younger Thurston said, "He'd been a big man in his day. He didn't know enough to let go when he got too old." Ellen heard the relief he thought he hid. Now he was alone, with no interference. Grace wept a little, she wept again, proudly, at the eulogy the preacher delivered the day of the funeral. Two weeks later Thurston sent carpenters to the house, to build bookcases and cabinets against the walls in the room the Judge had used. It was to be a library. A whole room for books! Ellen had never heard of such a thing. "There are his lawbooks, to start with," said Thurston. "Anyway I want a room to myself in my own house."

There were other extravagances. New dishes for the table, white with a red band. Water pumped in to the kitchen sink. A suit of store clothes for Robby, who would outgrow them long before they wore out, so fast his legs and arms were stretching. A new carriage, two seated, with blue cloth cushions.

Ellen climbed through the years, day after day, as if she took step after step along a flight of stairs that slipped under her feet, with nothing at the top. Grace had a kind of habitual indifference toward her which rose into brief moments of petulance. "If you'd only get you a good dress and comb your hair decently, Ellen! But then, you never go out anywhere, so—" Alice copied her mother. Robby had outgrown his daily need of her; he defied anyone to show him affection as he clattered through the house, all feet and hands and mouth. He still shouted "An' Telly!" when he wanted something to eat, and he had moments when he sprawled across a kitchen chair, yarning about the fellows at school, taking great bites of the ginger bread she had baked because he liked it. John Thurston still tagged him about. "Gee, An' Telly, that kid's something fierce! Can't stir without him. He oughta know he's too little to go with us boys." For John Thurston a queer feeling had grown in Ellen, a defense of him against the rest of his world. He was still a solemn-faced child with a large forehead and eyes that strained at what they saw; his fits of rage were rare, but he kept a certain sullenness, except for hours when he and Ellen were alone in house or garden. Then he followed her, talking, long rambling stories to which Ellen paid little attention. If she listened, she would interrupt; "Why, John Thurston, you didn't really have a fight yesterday!"

"Yes, I did, and I licked every one of 'em, and they said I was the best one. An'—" he would stop, under her quiet gaze, and finish, "Well, maybe I would lick every one."

There was talk of sending Thurston to the legislature. Grace brought it home one day to supper, from a call on the doctor's wife. Thurston sucked in one side of his lower lip, frowning. "Don't go talking about such foolishness," he said. "I've got my hands full enough as it is." A few days later a committee "waited on him." Ellen had answered the knock, and led the men, one a son of old Saxby the shoemaker, two newcomers, into the library. She forestalled John Thurston, who had curiosity like a hound dog and whisked him off to the kitchen.

"What do they want?" he insisted.

"They don't want you, John T.," she said.

"I expect they'll take him to jail," the boy said. "It's too bad to have a favver in jail."

Ellen stared; was there a malicious glow under the solemnity of his face? "Jail? What ails you? It's the legislature they want him to go to." Then she had to explain that, as well as she could, before he would go to bed. As she descended from his room, the library door opened, and she heard Thurston: "Yes, gentlemen, I appreciate the honor. I wish to serve my country, as I did during the war. But it's been a hard pull, putting my business on its feet again. Let me serve you as banker, as justice of the peace. For the present, at least. Another time—"

Ellen waited till the door closed after them, before she finished her descent. Thurston, twisting at his moustache, started as Ellen appeared, and half turned toward the library. Then he swung back. "I can't do everything." His eyes were harassed. "I'd stand to lose all I've got if I went off right now. Grace wants the glory of a senator's wife. She wants cash too, doesn't she?" He stared at Ellen, and then with a shrug, went into his room.

For a day or so Ellen wondered about the expression on his face. He looked anxious, not exactly frightened. Whatever was in his life outside the house was far outside her knowledge, except for vague talk of railroad stock and building.

V

Spring again. Ellen had started a new garden, in spite of Grace's protest. "I don't want you working out there, like a hired man."

"Pa needs it. Robby can help him, if you don't want me to." Ellen had gone ahead. Thurston her father, for all his grumbling about his back, was happier for the season if he had growth to watch. She stood at the edge of the rows while Thurston and a reluctant Robby stuck in brush for the peas.

"When your pa was no older than you," old Thurston was saying, "he could run a farm. He didn't have no time for school and such."

Ellen couldn't hear Robby's answer, for his averted head. It was true. Her thoughts moved slowly backward. When her father and Robert rode away, Thurston was only a year older than Robby. Well, these children had an easier time. Take Alice—against all Ellen's attempts to teach the girl something useful, like making bread, Grace intervened. "Her father's got money enough. She won't need to work." Alice was sixteen. And I, thought Ellen, am nearing fifty. She looked down at her hands, large, black-streaked at the finger tips. Soon she would be old. Thirty years and more, and still in the spring rebellion lifted stubborn head, as if life weren't over for her.

Her brother Thurston came around the house, the tails of his long black coat flapping, hungry excitement in his nostrils, in the quick bite of his eyes.

"Ellen, I've got news for you," he began. "You're going to be surprised."

Old Thurston had lifted his head; his son seldom appeared at this time of day. Half a row of black scraggly brush, and beyond, the thin tender green of new peas. Ellen looked back at her brother.

"A letter has come, from Robert. After these years. He enclosed one for you, from Matthew Eldon."

He might as well have said, "Mother sends you a letter, from heaven." The words would have had as much reality, for the moment, to Ellen. There was a barrier between her and the words, as if they were in some foreign tongue. "You remember Matthew Eldon," insisted Thurston, as he reached for the pocket under his, coat tail.

"Yes," said Ellen. "I remember him." Suddenly the barrier was down, the words crashed through her, stirring the forgotten, young Ellen, waking her to struggle through a prison of old flesh, of tired quiet heart, of walled-up hope. Still the prison answered Thurston. "What is in the letter?" Then as his hand moved toward her, and he

said, "I haven't read it. I know what Robert says. . . ."
the young Ellen moved violently through her muscles,
seizing the letter, turning for flight through the house
to shelter.

She locked her door and stood with shoulders against
it, lest someone find her out. Then she read the letter,
the only letter Matthew had ever sent.

Dear Ellen: I heard the other day your still living with
your folks. I thought youd got married before this. I didnt
get back as soon as I expected and I aint got anybody else Id
like to leave my pile to so if you can use it your welcome to it.
Im giving up my claim kinda sudden but the horspital folks
will see you get this. I wisht it was more but maybe you can
use it. Yrs,   Matthew.

Ellen's knees were water and she melted to the floor in
an awkward heap, her head back on the door, her eyes
closed. "I'll come riding back with bags of gold for us,
Ellie." Where had his voice lain, all these years, that
it should ring so clearly now? Presently she leaned forward, to look at the other letter. Robert's. A little
formal. The hospital had informed him of Matthew's
death, bloodpoisoning from a gun wound got in a quarrel.
The bankbook he enclosed—made over legally to Ellen
. . . several thousand.

A knock on the door, a cautious trying of the latch,
Thurston's voice. "Ellen, let me in."

Ellen pushed herself up to her feet and stepped away
from the door before she answered. "Ellen!" Thurston
knocked more loudly. "Aren't you coming out?"

"No!" said Ellen. "I'm not." She waited. Silence
outside the door for several minutes, then Thurston again,
peremptorily, "Get away from your aunt's door, John

Thurston! Get away, I say!" A scuffle, as if Thurston reached for his son, missed, started in pursuit.

Ellen sat down in the little rocker. It had been her mother's sewing chair, and the broken arm gave a familiar wabble. Under the window stood the chest Ellen had brought from the farmhouse, and in it, as if they gleamed through the pine wood, Ellen saw the few linen sheets she had woven for her home with Matthew. Matthew was dead. That old vision of him flashed for an instant— his strong body crumpled at the foot of a cliff, bits of twig, of moss, in his bright hair. Vaguely, a shadow, the agony of that vision drifted past her memory. Now the fact that he was dead stayed in her mind; it was true, but it had no power to make her suffer. She stretched. her hands along her knees, her body sagging, relaxed and heavy. I should think I'd feel bad, now I know. She touched her cheek with slow fingers. Tears rolling down, tears of pity for herself, for Matthew, that even by dying he could no longer stir her into tumult of grief or despair or joy. For a moment only, in the first shock of his name, that young self had stirred. But in the real Ellen that youth had no more part than the sound of Matthew's voice across the many springs. I've lived through all that, she thought, and I'm different, and Matthew wasn't with me. Yes, that was it. The Matthew she knew was young. What had he to do with her, to-day, a woman nearing fifty, a body too old for the uses of love? If he had come back, and they had lived together through those years—rage thumped in her for a moment, and remembered bitterness for the emptiness of the years.

She read the letter again, each word separately, as if she could pry beneath it, find him out. At least he had remembered her, for the space of the letter, perhaps. What had he been, those long years? A wastrel, drinking, shooting, whoring—ah, she had heard her father's stories! She would never know exactly. The young Matthew had not been meant for wasted years. Her heart ached now, softly, as if she watched him growing older. Suddenly, like a hand thrusting up a flaring torch, the realization of the money flashed upon her. For her, Ellen Dacey, thousands for her. She sat erect, her secret self, so long subdued, tramping with loud feet through her warming blood. She stared at the grimy pages of the bankbook, the figures of entry and withdrawals racing under her eyes. She rose, thrusting the book into her dress, under her breast, where the corner prodded when she laid her hand against it. Now—she said the words aloud, listenning to them, believing them—now I can do what I want, myself. I am delivered out of bondage. She had, as yet, no single image of what she wished to do. She stood in her bare room, her head, the smooth hair just touched with gray heavy at her neck, thrown back, a flush on her high cheekbones, a brilliancy in her dark eyes. Through her head, unaccountably, ran lines of one of the war songs.

"My ears have heard the marching of a hundred thousand
        feet,
They are trampling out the grapes of wrath about the judg-
        ment seat."

When she reached the last line, she sang it aloud.

"My soul goes marching on!"

"Ellen!" Thurston still at the door, startled by her outburst. He had been waiting, had he? Ellen sang the verse through again, loudly. "Ellen Dacey!" He rattled the latch. "Are you crazy?"

Ellen opened the door. "Wouldn't you be crazy for a minute if somebody set you free?" Then she stopped. No use to talk like that, no matter how she felt.

She swung past him, down the stairs. Time to put dinner on. She better get to work, before she did some really crazy thing. Singing like that—the tune was in her heels down the stairs.

"Ellen, how much is it? You haven't told me. Where's Matthew's letter?"

Ellen looked back at her brother, one hand curved over her breast. "Matthew's letter is to me," she said.

"Robert says several thousands." Thurston pushed past the barrier of her proud reserve. "Is it?" He chewed at his lip.

"All of that." Ellen went on into the kitchen.

VI

Curiosity, excitement, admiration washed about Ellen. The news spread through the village, with varying rumors about the size of her fortune. What was she going to do with it? Thurston could invest it for her; she was lucky to have him for a brother. Women spoke enviously to her; a lover faithful through so many years glittered more than a husband at one's elbow. Ellen was less an old maid than a bereaved widow. A woman who never married because her lover deserted her was one thing; a woman who could inspire devotion which produced a fortune out of mysterious distance was quite another.

"Of course—" Grace, undaunted by Ellen's unresponsiveness, kept scratching about her. "Of course your home is with us, just as it always has been. I've said to Thurston for a year or more that we ought to get a hired girl. I suppose you'd rather pay board now that you're rich."

"I didn't know you had a fellow, An' Telly." Robby inspected her with frank curiosity. "You're kinda old. Some of the girls in school have fellows. Say, did you send him off to make a fortune?"

Ellen answered that. "He went because he wanted to. I didn't send him. He went with Grandpa and your Uncle Rob."

"Well, why didn't he come back sooner?"

"Robby, don't bother Aunt Ellen with foolish questions!" Grace had a new habit of hurrying into the kitchen, to see if she couldn't help. She told Alice, too, to wash the dishes, to brush up the dining-room floor. Ellen didn't want them around. She needed the routine of the day at present, as a solid ground from which her thoughts could take their daring flights.

John Thurston alone had no questions. He listened to the others, his eyes blinking solemnly. One night he called to Ellen as she passed through the dark hall. She stood by his bed, in which his small body made scarcely a bulge, looking down at him—his head cocked up from the pillow, his breath puffing as if he had been running. "When I'm a man, Ellen," he whispered, "when I'm a man, I'll give you twict as much as that fellow. Five times so much." He stared defiantly at her.

"Why, John Thurston!" Ellen laid her hand on the pillow, and for the briefest instant the child turned his cheek against it. "You would?" Perhaps her own intensity of

living made her sensitive; she felt him straining a puny
self against a hostile universe. In a rare gesture of tenderness she bent and kissed his forehead. As she closed
the door, she heard his sigh, faintly content.

The effect of the news on old Thurston had been at first
a renaissance of all his recollections of mining days. He
rambled, pulling out ragged bits of what had been whole
memories once. Slowly his tales circled, in small and
smaller circles, until they focussed on one fact. He had
financed Matthew, and never had any return. "We set
up his stake, fitted him with grub and tools, and he said
we'd have a share. What did we ever get? Did I ever
get a cent back?" He shook a fist at Ellen's silence. "Did
I? No!" One day he added, slyly, "Matthew would like
to have his honest debts paid off."

Ellen turned on him: she was mixing bread, and the
dough clinging to her fingers made a grotesque of her
angry gestures. "That was between Matthew and you. I
have nothing to do with it."

"You got the money he made."

"What I've got, I mean to keep." The flour sprayed
over the floor. "Ten years ago you sold the farm, the
house. Some would have thought I had a share in that,
if works counts. You've got all Thurston made for you
then, and I have had nothing."

Her father glanced cautiously toward the door, and
thrust his leathery old face toward Ellen, his arms jerking. "Now, Ellie, you had as much as anybody. As much
as me. Thurston never gave me a cent. He's got it all
invested." His voice cackled in exasperation "All tied
up. You'll get it when I'm gone, your share."

Ellen turned back to the table. "See what you've

done! Made me mess the floor all up!" Her hands slapped at the dough.

"I tell you, Ellie, Matthew would want—"

"I don't care what anybody wants, but me. You might as well save your breath, Pa."

He clucked and coughed and presently shuffled away. Ellen saw him pass the window, his hands still gesticulating, his old legs rocking. He was aging, drying inside his wrinkled skin. So Thurston had kept the money from the farm. She had thought as much.

Only her brother, Thurston, said nothing to her. Sometimes she found him looking at her, his lip caught in between his teeth, his eyes speculative. He had not even asked again how much Matthew had left. Grace said one day, "I should think you'd give Thurston that bankbook and have him put the money to use in his bank."

"Did Thurston suggest that?" asked Ellen, and Grace's denial lacked the bone of truth. "Tell him I like my own bank."

Ellen, meantime, walked in dreams. Never before, except for the brief time when she had begged Martha to let her go west in Sarah's place, had she imagined herself outside the town where all her life had passed. Now, that corner prodding at her breast, why, she could go anywhere! The thousands seemed limitless. At first she ventured only as far as Detroit, the town growing on the river between two lakes. Then farther east, to Martha's old home. To the Atlantic. Farther. The world was small for the strengthening wings of her dreams. Haphazard bits of knowledge made her pictures: Greenland's icy mountains and India's coral strands; the Blue Danube; a mixture of geography and the rare missionary stories

she knew . . . camels, elephants, and cannibals. She
would return with strange gifts and stranger stories.
Slowly, a kind of fear sprang up, that she might find herself in some remote part of the earth, alone, among people she did not know; that her very dreams might trans-
port her thither. What would she, Ellen Dacey, *do* on a
coral strand? Then, under her dreams, her glittering
but with human warmth, as if she knelt, parting waving,
fringed grasses, and found close to the earth a small
thing to cherish between her hands, her decision shaped
itself. She couldn't separate herself from Robby, even
from John Thurston. With miles between them, what
would she have to love? She needed the familiar town;
herself apart from it would be lessened, diminished by the
absence of its roads and houses and horizons.

Eagerness mounted as the decision became tangible; she
had need for haste. Why had she been so slow to see
where her real desire pointed? Here it was already late
summer. The moment that the decision reached past
thought and pressed into action, Ellen was ironing ruffles and ruffles on a white dress of Alice's. She stopped,
one hand wiping the moisture from her forehead, the
odor of hot muslin stifling in the warm kitchen. Outside
in the grass an insect shrilled. Why—now's as good as
any other time! Ellen set the iron on the stove, left the
dress dangling over the board, and climbed to her room.
She heard the creak of a board on the piazza as Grace
rocked; during the weeks since that letter from Matthew,
as Ellen gave no outward sign of any change, Grace had
slipped out of her solicitude, especially as the warm
weather settled over the land. Ellen bathed her moist
face and neck, dressed in a clean black and white print,

and went down the stairs. She pressed one hand to her side; that dragged, heavy feeling bothered her, from ironing, perhaps, standing so long.

"Why, Ellen!" Grace stopped rocking, let her fan drop to her knees. "Where you going in this sun?"

"I didn't finish that dress Alice wants," said Ellen, and walked up the street, holding for a moment some amusements at the blank way Grace's mouth had dropped open.

It was supper time when she came back. She heard Grace as she entered the hall, her voice lifted irritably. "Well, if Ellen's going traipsing off like that, you've got to get somebody to help me, that's all."

"Where did she go?" Thurston's voice was sharp.

Ellen left her hat on the hall rack, and stood at the dining-room door. Everyone turned toward her, Robby with bread halfway to his mouth, old Thurston wagging his head suspiciously, and her brother sending a furtive sidewise peering toward her. John Thurston ducked his head with a breath of relief. She sat down at her place beside her father, letting them stare at her. When she said nothing, their silence splintered into bits of irritation.

"My dress is one sight, Aunt Ellen," Alice began. "It dried up, and here I want it, to-night."

"Going to have a beau?" Robby grinned. "Boo-hoo, my dress is awful."

"Leave Alice alone," said Grace. "If you'd tell me, Ellen, when you mean to rush off—"

"I'll tell you," said Ellen, calmly. Their curiosity was like the summer heat, persistent, hard to breathe. "I just made up my mind all at once. Now it's settled." She looked at her brother. "I've bought back the farm," she said. "Swanson wants to go to Dakota, to try a bigger farm, and he's glad to sell. I'm going to fix up the house and live there."

"Alone?" That was Grace.

"Unless Pa wants to board with me. I feel at home in that house."

"When you've got a good home here?" Thurston shoved his chair away from the table, a vein bulging along his temple. "Why should you waste money on that farm? What'd he want for it? You don't mean you've bought it, without a word to me?"

"He asked a little more than he paid you, Thurston. Says it's worth more. I'm going to have a home of my own."

"Board with you? With my own daughter? On my own land?" Old Thurston came up spluttering from his amazement.

"Mine." Ellen rose, her face undisturbed. "I'll be glad to see any of you there, any time." She climbed to her own room, her knees quivering. If she stayed, she'd say things she'd be sorry for. She felt drunk with assurance. They could talk it out without her; she was safe, invulnerable.

Swanson wanted a month or so, to finish the harvest. He would sell much of his stock, of his farm implements. Ellen spread her bankbook on her knee. Money for repairs on the house; the raft of towheads had worn it down. She was still strong enough to manage a small farm, with a hired man, perhaps. That weight inside her body would disappear, once she got outdoors, on her own land. Her own!

VII

Thurston Dacey watched his sister walk serenely from the dining room, his muscles taut; not his mind, but his muscles, his stretched nerves ached to seize her, to throttle her, to search out that bankbook she hid so complacently. The old wound in his shoulder ached, as if Ellen's thwarting had been physical. From a black distance he heard his wife's trickling complaints; "Thurston, you must make her listen to reason! Such a foolish waste of money. Make her consider others a little. After all we've done for her!" He stared at her; how would that round, smooth face of hers look if he shouted out, "I'm ruined!" Eyes swollen shut with weeping. What a wife for a man with ambition! Old Thurston was doddering something. "You oughtn't to have sold that farm, Thurston. That set her against us. She's always held it up against you and me, too. I never got anything out of it, and now she says I can pay board!"

Then John Thurston. "If Ellen goes away, who's going to do the work? I'm going to live with her."

Thurston sprang to his feet, a hot knife driving through his shoulder. "You young fool!" Ah, that was better. His shout fused the others, all of them, into attention, submission. "Do you think your aunt does everything in this house? Don't be insolent!" He towered a moment, the silence brushing his torment, and then flung himself out of the room, into his study. There he began a steady pacing, across the room and back, hands under the long tails of his black coat, nervous fingers flicking at the cloth. Gold watch chain on his vest, dignified, impressive; the

Judge's gold watch in his pocket. His eyes clung to the
glitter. Damn that shoulder! He sat at his desk, lifting
one elbow carefully, trying to ease the pain. Back and
forth paced his thoughts. It was the war, putting madness
in the country. That railroad in northern Illinois going
bankrupt last week, a bank in Ohio failing. A few thousands would swing him safely, and Ellen had it. Women
had no sense. Selfish, scheming creatures. A man's life
had to reach out, shaping the affairs of the world. No
woman knew anything about a man's concerns. Wave
after wave of weariness broke over Thurston, washing
his head down on his arms, drowning him; and as to a
drowning man, bits of his life rushed past. His father,
his older brother, strong men, ordering him about, indifferent to his straining eagerness, leaving him to the
women. Where would his father be now, without him?
His mother— "And you may be one of its great men,
Thurston." She had placed his hands on his own boot-
straps and commanded him to lift himself. Well, hadn't
he? Year after steady year—what boyhood had he
known, except in awkwardness and ignorance? Grace, a
young girl, remote and fair. He had climbed up to her.
All the excitement had been in reaching up to her; none
since. A good wife, savorless. Only Ellen had guessed
how he leaped into war. "You want to go, don't you?"
Moments in those years, sharp and clear. In spite of
all the cold and dirt and suffering—his nostrils quivered
at a whiff of acrid smoke and rotting flesh—you were
bound somewhere. Men heard your voice and followed,
a purpose drove you. The dull, curious emptiness of the
days after his return, as if his self were a snake, coiled,

with head swaying this way and that, uncertain where to
strike. The old Judge, warning him. You want too
much, Thurston. These are bad days. A man had to
want something. Money. That was it. Men listening
to your voice again, giving you that meek lift of eyelid.
Send him to the legislature, would they, so that other
fingers might poke among his affairs . . . that state
inspector, sniffing at the bank securities. . . . He pushed
himself erect, his hands clutched over the edge of the desk.
He was back in the present, his thoughts darting like
minnows. The money he'd lent on that new town, Boom
City. He'd heard families were leaving it, going back
to their original homes. The railroad running north—he
needed more stock there. That question yesterday: "If
we had to draw out our money, you'd have it, of course?"
Was fear running under the surface of the country, sucking down the men who worked for it, who made it?
He'd have that money of Ellen's. He had to! A year
from now he'd give it back doubled. She'd listen.
Quietly, his head catching the querulous ripple of Grace
and Alice, somewhere back in the house, he ascended the
stairs to Ellen's room, whispered her name, lifted the
latch.

VIII

Ellen, sitting at her window, tensed into wariness as
she saw her brother. He closed the door, drew a chair
near her, and sat down.

"I want to talk a little." He squared his shoulders,
professional sternness in his tone. "You're buying land
just when the price is up. Another year, and I can get
you anything for half the price. What's more, I can

double for you what you've got. I can make you rich, Ellen."

"I've got enough." Ellen turned toward the window; the sultry evening was crowded with village sounds— rockers on porches, children calling in some game. "I don't want to wait a year."

"Can't you have some sense?" He touched her knee, and she shrank away. "You don't know anything about money, and it's my business. If I tell you you are foolish—"

"It's real nice to be able to be foolish." Ellen brushed his coercing hand from her knee. "It won't do you any good to talk to me."

"Have you given Swanson the money?" as she hesitated—"Have you?"

"That makes no difference."

"You haven't! Thank God! Listen, Ellen. You've got to let me have it. I swear I'll more than double it for you. But I've got to have it! Now! I can't explain. You don't understand business. That cash, to-morrow or the next day, will stand between me and penniless ruin. Is that clear?"

Ellen looked at him. In the pale, thick air, his face moved toward her like an awful threat, his eyes prominent, his mouth unsteady. The folds of skin about his eyes, his mouth, seemed stricken with illness.

"What about Pa's money? You have that. And the Judge's."

"I said you wouldn't understand." His voice sank into a husky whisper. "It's tied up. I can't get it."

"And you want mine, too, to lose?" Ellen was stiff with cold. Was this a trick, a last attempt?

"If I go down, there are the children, disgraced, shamed. If you've no decent feeling for me— You are a Dacey, aren't you?"

Blind resistance, as if death threatened her, swung Ellen to her feet, one hand on her side where all her fear throbbed in that dull pain. "You can't have it!" She thought she shouted, but her voice came back to her ears in a thin, high note. "It's all I've ever had. If I didn't have it, if you hadn't known it, hadn't grudged it every second since it came, you'd find some other way out of ruin. Well, find it! I won't—I won't!" The room swelled into enormous blackness, her voice roared in her ears, she was falling, falling, in empty spaces between the stars.

IX

Thurston caught her as she swayed, but her heavy body slipped through his arms to the floor. He knelt beside her, breathing heavily. Just a faint. Her face, half-closed eyelids, blue lips, offered him a mask of resistance. "Grace!" he shouted. "Grace!" Then, as he heard her feet hurrying on the stairs, he plunged his hand against Ellen's heart, and as Grace pushed the door ajar, drove it deep into his pocket, clutching at the bankbook.

X

Ellen floated, very small, head to her knees, in a flood of nothingness. A hand, enormous, cruel, plucked her out, dragging her up, up where consciousness pulsated like flame about her, touching her, entering into her, beating in her own heart. Her eyelids were sealed. She longed to slip down into that sweet nothingness, but the hand prodded her. Voices loud and meaningless rocked over her. If she could lift her eyelids—she could not stir a finger. Like the stroke of a bell a thought hung in the air: I have conceived and in my womb, not a child, but a monster fanged, clawed, tears at my flesh, grows to devour me. She must hide where none should know her shame. With slow effort she escaped that hand, to drift out of the pulsating light into darkness again.

But it was herself that was the hand, dragging her back, hating that narrow rim between life and death. This time it dragged her across the threshold, and she heard the voices. "She's coming to. Drink this." Liquid burning her throat, her lips. The room brimmed with faces, retreating as her eyes opened.

Later she heard Thurston. "Can you hear me, Ellen? Do you know what I say? The doctor says he must cut out something, a growth. The young doctor from the east. We had both of them. You can't live unless he does."

Ellen heard. They had discovered her shame. Thurston's face grew clearer in the shadows around her, and with it a memory—he wanted something. Her heavy hand moved, as if from a great distance, to her breast.

"You'd want to leave a will, in case anything did happen."

Knives, cutting into her, violating her. Thurston's face, insisting.

"Who do you want to have it, Ellen, in case—"

Robby. Thurston laid something under her hand. She couldn't see it for the glitter of knives.

"Write your name here, Ellen, for Robby."

XI

Spring again, with warmth in the sunshine. Ellen sat on the porch, her thin hands stretched idly on her knees. At her feet was a basket piled with balls of grayish black, stockings for John Thurston and Robby. The thought of holding a china egg in the gap in a heel and working a needle back and forth ached protestingly in her arms. Queer that a thought could ache. She watched the man who plowed the garden behind the house, and her feet grew heavy with his plodding. Another month, perhaps—

John Thurston came down the street, running a stick along the pickets of the fences, rat-tat-too. "Hullo, Ellen!" He stood in front of her, hands behind his back, gray mud smeared to his knees. "I got you something." Mud even on one ear; his cap, an old one of Robby's with broken visor, drooped over his forehead as he blinked at her. "Mieow! mieow!"

"Pussy willows!" He laid a few twigs in her lap, and Ellen drew her fingers over the gray fur ears laid so neatly to each branch. "In the swamp?" Only last night she had told him how she used to gather them when she was a little girl. "You better brush off your legs before your mother sees you."

John Thurston grinned, gap-toothed, and pelted away to the garden. Ellen bent slowly for a pair of stockings, and as slowly ran her hand inquiringly through them. That young doctor said her strength would come back, now she could get outdoors. Being sick was queer. For weeks she had been a log, with desire only for comfort, for the end of pain—warmth, sleep, relief. Where did

your soul go when you were sick? Or your brain? She
hadn't even known when Thurston's buildings burned, the
whole row of stores, and his bank. She hadn't cared
what happened to anyone. Enough to feel her own heart
beating, to feel the pain grow less, to sleep. She had not
wanted to stir out of bed, even when the doctor said she
might. That meant the beginning of life again, the weary-
ing impact of people. They would say, "How do you
feel to-day?" They would force her into thinking, about
them, about herself. Then she had found that it was
pleasant to sit, hands idle, and wait for thoughts to come.
All her life she had turned her thoughts into the demands
of the day. Now that she could scarcely lift a finger,
indifference to things settled in her. Perhaps she never
again would have time to think.

At first her thoughts went back through her life; under
her quiet, attentive waiting, hidden memories stirred.
Slowly she came to feel that she was hunting for something, that she would never quite return to days that followed one after another like a row of pebbles, with no
thread of meaning. She had no curiosity outside this
quickening search, whether for Thurston's affairs, or for
her own. Was it God she wanted? She could see her
mother, the Bible on her knees. No. She might be
wicked, but God wasn't her answer. Something deep
in her own heart. Had she been so near the edge of
death that her eyes failed to focus when she looked again
about her? What *was* she, Ellen Dacey? Was there
any meaning in her? She began, secretly, to look at the
others in the house, not at the futile things they made
their days out of, but at them. Her father, her brother,
Grace, the children. Perhaps you weren't meant to have

time for thought; it turned the whole world queer. If she had married—Matthew—some other man—and borne children, instead of this scarred, empty womb—why would that seem to give some answer to her life? It's natural to have children. Her search ran deeper than that answer. Was it being a woman that shut in the reason in life? Hemmed in, your self tied up.

She laid aside the darning and with the branch of pussy willow in her fingers, walked to the edge of the freshly plowed land. The odor of the soil, damp, sun-warmed, floated many springs through her veins. In a blurred rush she thought of growth; seeds, tender shoots, blossoms, fruit, and brown, wrinkled death again. A tingling at her nerve ends, as if some meaning pressed close.

The horse and plow approached her; the broad, square breast of the horse moved upon her with steady flow of muscles under shining brown skin, the horse's head nodded with the alternate motion, and the dark eyes, rimmed in white, gazed unblinking at her. Ellen waited. The man following the plow, engrossed in his struggles with the blade polished to silver by the earth, had not seen her. Down moved that great beast, and Ellen could not stir. Like a child making a game she thought: if he crushes me down, and the plowshare drives me into the earth, I may find some answer. But the horse tossed his head, warm breath brushing her face. It was only Ned, the farm horse. Ellen laid her hand between the wide nostrils and turned away, not heeding the ejaculation of the man at sight of her.

There was her father, coming home, shrunken, brown, with wide uncertain steps, as if his mind pulled strings for his old bones. He was at the end of the cycle. Winter. Ellen watched him into the house, and made her slow way back to her chair. Why—she thought—maybe he had to go away as he did. When he went west, he had been a little younger than she was now. Perhaps he had a search for more than gold, and being a man, he thought to find it, this obscure, vague *it*, by riding away on a horse. Though I take the wings of the morning and fly to the uttermost parts of the earth. Was it wicked to search past the edges of the preacher's wisdom? Love God, love thy neighbor, do good to them that spitefully use thee, honor thy father and thy mother. Ellen's mind, still tracing through the progress of the seasons, flashed a queer picture; piles of hay raked for a sudden storm, with square canvas covers tied at each corner, inadequate, hay bulging out. That was the preacher's wisdom, that old bit of canvas.

She had stood too long, waiting for the horse. The fatigue of her body defeated further thought. She climbed the stairs, drawing herself up each step with a hand on the railing, and stretched herself on her bed, where fatigue eased softly into sleep.

XII

Ellen watched the garden in a leisurely dream. The first tiny points of green filled her with incoherent excitement; the tender bent heads the peas pushed up were soft notes of a song, and their straightening, their unfolding of leaves moved in her blood. Walking back to her chair, she heard Grace inside the door.

"She's queer, Doctor. You don't think her head is

touched? She pays no attention to anybody, and she doesn't care what happens in the house. If she'd do a little something—"

"Give her time, Mrs. Dacey." Why, it was young Doctor Willis. Ellen strained forward. "She's been a sick woman, and she's worked hard all her life. Wonderful constitution."

"Doctor Willis!" Ellen lifted her voice. "I'm out here." He had come to see her, hadn't he? His first visit for days. She liked his hard, young hand on her pulse, his serious clear eyes attending to her. She knew, for all her indifference, that Grace envied her that inspection, and Alice—hadn't she seen the way the girl hurried into a fresh dress and hung about?

"Well, good day, good day." That slight pompousness was part of his smart youth. "How's my best patient?" He looked at Ellen with a tinge of possessive pride. All the village knew he'd saved her life. His first important case. "Fine. That strong heart's what pulled you through." He sat beside her, frowning earnestly. "Time you began to take some interest in things. A little work about the house. Some of the things you women like to do. Nothing heavy."

Ellen sighed. Grace had put that notion in his head. Still, if she was getting well— "I never sat still before," she apologized.

"You mustn't work hard for a year or more." He sat back in his chair, assured, brisk. "Just try your hand at easy things. Make an effort. You have to get back to normal life, you know."

Ellen sighed again. She had been sitting about, listening to her thoughts, longer than she had a right to do.

Well— "You won't need to call any more," she said.
She would miss him. She liked the flavor of difference,
in his queer accent, in his neat clothes, in his manner. A
finish over his youth. If Rob could be turned into that
kind of young man—Ellen forgot her own guilty regret.
"Dr. Willis, tell me some more about your school, where
you studied." He had, as she lay dull and lethargic, sat
by her bed, talking about himself, his ambitions, his past
life. She listened now, reaching for a toehold on which
she could climb out of herself, into the days ahead of
her. Robby was a firm rung. If he could go east to
school—a daring, absurd idea. "Can you learn to be
other things besides a doctor?" For Robby had no use
for anything ailing. It was John Thurston who had hung
about her door. Robby was too robust, too occupied
with all his boy's affairs.

"Yes, anything." The doctor boasted about his college. Finally he rose. "I'll have to come to see you,"
he said, "just to talk." He shook hands, as if they were
friends. "Not many here are interested." As he started
toward the gate, Alice came out of the house, her ruffled
skirt swaying about her slim figure, her fair crimped
bangs shining under the brim of her small hat.

"Are you walking toward town, Doctor?" She moved
down the path beside him. Ellen thought disdainfully
that the very back of her waist quivered. If the girl
thought she'd capture that young man! He had hinted,
ever so remotely, at a girl in Boston. She'd tell Grace.

The doctor had torn through the comfortable indifference in which Ellen had lived. When she went in to
supper that evening, she went as one just back from a
journey, who looks about with senses sharpened for things

once too familiar. Thurston, her brother, sagged in his
chair, lifting his hand to stop the twitching of an eyelid.
He looked older, wrapped in a dour unawareness, except
when he shouted out at Robby, "Keep still, sir, if you can't
be civil!"

Rob pretended to sulk, but Ellen saw him wink at
Alice, who flushed with indignation from his sly queries
about the doctor. "Did you have a tummy ache, and have
to tell him all about it?" He snickered, and looked innocent as his father's head thrust at him again. Rob was
as tall as his father, now; he seemed taller at the table,
and handsome, for all the uncertainty of his young mouth.
John Thurston ate quickly, darting glances at the others,
as if queer ideas hurried under his domed forehead.
Grace, plump, unaltered, said, "Now, children! Don't
bother your papa!" and her eyes slid away from Thurston's silence. Old Thurston broke bread into his cup of
tea and mumbled it, separated from the others in the
obliviousness of age. Ellen's quickened senses marked
Thurston her brother; his dark coat was buttoned over
some gnawing thought.

For the first time there pushed into her memory that
evening on which her illness broke past her control.
Something in Thurston's face pulled down the barrier.
She had forgotten his coming to her, had forgotten that
he had her bankbook. The thought of her money had
been as remote as all her contact with life, something she
would turn to, later. The farm—she looked at her wrists,
all bones. She couldn't work a farm, yet. But she must
speak to Thurston.

After supper, instead of climbing at once to her room,
she hesitated outside Thurston's study door. She had no

strength yet for encounter, but surely, to ask for her bankbook was simple enough.   Thurston lifted his head.

"I'd like my bankbook, Thurston."   Why should her voice quaver?

"Um. Yes. Your bankbook."

What crawled over his face, graying it?   "You don't need it to-night, do you? Later—"

"No. I want it now."

"My dear Ellen—" He rose, leaning heavily on his hands, spread over the papers on his desk. "You've been sick so long. You don't understand. Many things have happened."

"What?"

"I'd rather wait till you are stronger, more yourself."

"What have you done with my money?"

"I?" He lifted a deprecating hand. "I did all I could. Banks have failed everywhere, among them Matthew's. Since you insist on knowing. Utter failure. Now I, even with the blow of the fire, you remember there was a fire? I paid a little on each dollar. This western bank, though—" His gesture was final. "I'm sorry. After all"—he slid his tongue over his lips—"you are right where you were. You have a home with us. As long as I can keep a roof over our heads. Your loss is nothing to mine. I can't be bothered with your paltry loss!" His voice lagged with reproach. "My God, I face utter ruin, and you stand there talking of a few thousands!"

"How do you know it's all gone?"   Ellen retreated a step from the sinister, dark passion of his face.

"Letters, papers. They were destroyed with all of mine, when the block burned. You've been well out of it, lying sick. I've paid your bills, you've nothing to complain of."

Ellen backed toward the door. A moment she stood there, summoning all her courage to look into his eyes. Then she turned, and climbed the stairs, pulling her body which quivered with weakness, up each step.

As she lay in bed, with healing darkness about her, she felt the push of some memory trying to reach her mind. Pain, whirling blackness, Thurston's voice plucking her out. As, she had it! She had written her name, for Robby! Suddenly, white conviction chilled her. Thurston had lied. I'll find out, she whispered, and relaxed, as her weary flesh dragged her into sleep.

XIII

Ellen settled by slight stages into the domestic harness. Thurston had said one noon: "I should think three women could do the little work of this house without hiring a fourth. Money's close just now." Grace, dolefully, dismissed the hired girl. Cooking was easy, and dish washing, for Ellen could sit down occasionally. One week she attempted the washing. Robby and John Thurston filled the tubs on the bench outside the kitchen. She began with childish bravado: wasn't she as well and strong as ever? But the sheets, water-soaked, were leaden in her hands, her wrists had no strength to lift the weight, and pain ground through her back. She leaned against the tub, her hands clutching at the long coil of cotton, when Dr. Willis driving past, hauled his horse up sharply, jumped over the low picket fence, and strode to her side.

"See here!" He pushed the wet sheet out of her hands,

shoved her back to the step. "What you think you're doing? I said light work. Look at your color!"

Ellen grimaced. "I thought I could do it." Hurrying about the corner of the house, her full skirts oscillating, came Alice, drawn by the Doctor's shout.

"See here, Miss Alice, you shouldn't let your aunt do this. You don't want to kill her, do you? I can't have it. See that she lies down." He was off, as quickly as he had come.

Alice watched him drive away; her hands twisted at her small waist, her face quivered into tears. "You needn't have done it right outdoors," she sobbed. "Just to be seen!" She fled past Ellen into the house.

Ellen saw John Thurston's head rise over the washtub, and the two grinned at each other. Poor Alice, just as she thought she had his cool heart touched a little. "I never knew I showed from the road," said Ellen.

"Well," said Grace, "if you hadn't been so stubborn about that money, you might be able to pay something. Thurston could have invested it."

Ellen, sitting by the table scraping thin skin from new potatoes, thought: so Grace knows nothing about it. Outside the window the clothes flapped white in the sunshine. A woman down the street had finished the washing. If you didn't do a thing, someone else did. That was a new idea for Ellen. Still—there was her keep to pay for, if it was true about her money.

Then, at the end of the summer, she dressed, with pride in the fact that her dress no longer could wrap twice around her, and walked along the main street of the town. She had not seen the ruined Dacey block, and the blackened débris, charred beams crisscross in what had been cellars, one wall standing with sky through its ruined windows, gave her an ominous feeling of disaster beyond the ruin, a feeling that tightened her breathing and prickled over her skin. Months since the fire, and Thurston had done nothing. In the older wooden buildings across the street, where patches of blistered paint spoke of the reach of the fire, several of the merchants had reopened their stores. Thurston's sign hung over the old office of Judge Abbott, next the general store where Thurston the boy had gone to live, more than thirty years ago. Ellen crossed the dusty road and looked through the window. On the wall hung a large map of the state, the mitten threaded with red lines of paper railroads. She saw Thurston bent over a table, and a stranger following his pointing finger. Quickly she stepped beyond the window. She had not meant to go in to-day. Not yet. She could bide her time.

The bank had reopened, but Thurston Dacey was no longer banker. No money there, he explained, when Grace brushed him with questions. They want me back, but with the new regulations and all— No, I've got a better thing than that. Stocks, all these railroads. If there's any money in the country, it's there. I can't help it if it was your father's bank. Times have changed."

Then fall, with Rob and John Thurston again in school. Rob's last year. "You're about old enough to help me feed this family," his father said. Ellen waited. "When I was your age, I wasn't stewing over books."

"I'll go to work to-morrow." Rob's clear skin showed red.

"Nothing you could do." Thurston dismissed the matter, as if his satisfaction lay in rousing the boy's defense.

"Times are different. You might as well stick this year."

Ellen waylaid Rob, later that evening. She had a small gray catalog, a gift from Dr. Willis, with a cut of the college on its cover.

"Have you thought, Robby, what you want to do next year?" She had the book open. The boy pushed out his lower lip, scornfully.

"What's there to do, here? Clerk in a store, be a hired man——"

"Engineers and lawyers and doctors and——" She was breathless, pointing out the words.

"He says I'm old enough to go to work now."

"If you make up your mind you want to go, I'll see to it." She hovered near him, so calmly confident, that the boy sobered into attention. Although he shrugged, he carried the book away to his room.

Alice, as the fall darkened into winter, grew thin, with a nervous brightness which shivered into tears at slight causes. During the summer she had gone to drive at times in the doctor's buggy, but now she stayed in the house, working feverishly to remake a dress, flinging up her head at a sound outside. "Why doesn't Dr. Willis come any more?" Grace asked, too frequently.

"Who? Oh, him. I'm sure I don't know and don't care." Alice tossed her crimped bangs.

Ellen, in the room next the girl's, was wakened at night by a muffled sound. She sat up. A piteous sound of lonely, hidden crying. She lay down, folding her hands over her breast, frowning. Alice wouldn't thank her for going in, for overhearing. Several nights later, when she couldn't sleep, waiting for that sound, she shuffled into slippers and wrapper and went silently into Alice's room. The sound of weeping stopped. Ellen sat down on the bed, her hand found the girl's thin shoulder. "Alice, it's just me, Ellen," she said. A convulsed sigh against the pillow. "You'll just make yourself sick, taking on so."

"I wish I could die." Ellen's hand moved in a slow caress down the girl's arm.

"Folks die hard," she said. "I've found that out."

Alice twisted over in the bed, her hand closing on Ellen's. "I thought he cared—a little." She caught her breath on a sob. "He acted—as if he did." Her long quiver woke an echo in Ellen's past. So . . . he'd made a little love to her. Poor child, she'd invited it. "All the time he had a girl, back home."

"You knew it, Alice." Ellen was gentle. "I told your mother."

"I didn't care! He pretended he liked me. Oh, I wish I was dead!"

"I expect he was kind of lonesome, and you made it easy for him. You'll have to stand it, Alice."

"It's Pa's fault. Losing money . . . so we can't have clothes. If he thought I was rich . . . he can't send for her because he hasn't money enough. If——"

"A poor sort of husband he'd be, if you bought him." Ellen's brisk voice tried to whip the girl into decent courage.

"I wouldn't care how I got him. I can't bear it."

"Yes, you can." Ellen held the cold hands close in her own. "You listen to me, Alice Dacey. You make up your mind to bear it, and you can. You never had to bear much, and you got a chance to find out how. You have to stop feeling sorry for yourself. You tried to get a man away from the woman he was promised to, and you didn't. You're shamed, as much as anything. You got to hold your head up and put your mind on something else. I'll help you all I can, if you let me. First you stop lying awake and taking on about how bad you feel." She pulled the covers up around the girl's shoulders. "Nobody but me knows, and if you go on this way the whole town'll know you threw yourself at a man and he wouldn't have you. Have some spunk! Now you go to sleep. To-morrow we'll think up something for you."

Ellen got back into her own bed, shivering at the cold blankets. She lay for a time, thinking, looking back as if she read an old book at the page when Matthew had ridden away. Alice didn't feel like that. She was unhappy, but it was conceit that ached in her, as much as love. "I said I'd think up something, but I don't know what."

Then a taunt from Thurston, irritated by Grace's request for money, prodded Alice. "Money? I haven't got it. Look at this household, all hanging on me. Look at Alice. If she can't get a husband, why don't she get something to do? She's old enough."

"What can I do?" Alice was white.

"Well—" Thurston looked at her, and Ellen knew he had some plan in his taunt. "You can't do much. I heard this morning the teacher's sick in District Three."

XIV

That winter, whenever people met on a street corner, at church, at a school entertainment, they talked of hard times. At first they sounded to Ellen like an echo of her

brother. No money for anything . . . building, buying;
no credit; the dollar wasn't worth a quarter; failures,
bankruptcies. The South was to blame, the freed slaves
were to blame, the President was to blame, foreign countries were to blame. Since hard times was in the mouth
of every neighbor, Grace recovered from her reluctance
to admit that the Dacey family, too, was pinched. Ellen,
listening to the talk, reflecting on mysterious phrases like
wild-catting, and no value to money, listening to the minister's long prayer, "Lord, help Thy people in these days
of tribulation and panic," watched Thurston with changed
eyes. She had supposed, if a man worked hard, kept
honest, and had sense, that what he did would have its
reward. Perhaps what he did was mixed up with what
other people did. Not alone in their small town, but in
towns scattered like dots all over the country. She felt
her mind stretch, trying to follow her new idea. Take
the young doctor: he wasn't making money, because people
had too little to pay him; so he couldn't send for his girl;
so Alice had been bruised. Still— Ellen's thoughts hurried back to the clear precepts of her childhood; if Alice
hadn't tried to entice the doctor away, she wouldn't have
suffered. It seemed dangerous to blame the country for
the girl's pinched face. (She was working hard, rising
earlier than ever in her life to walk the three miles to
her school.) If you got to blaming hard times and distant places for what happened to people, where would you
be? If you weren't responsible for your affairs, what
was there to keep you going?

Old Thurston, cupping his vein-ridged hand behind one
ear, listened to anyone who would talk to him, wagging
his wispy old head. He remembered a panic when he

was a boy, before he started west. People ate anything they could get hold of. He hinted at worse days than any these young people could know.

Ellen watched Robby. He had almost over night changed from a healthy indifferent male animal into a young man who stood before a blurred looking glass, sleeking his hair back, who slid out of the house evenings, wearing his good suit. He had a girl, a plump, pink-cheeked farmer's daughter. Ellen saw them in the gallery of the church, at prayer meeting. She knew Robby took her on the sleigh ride after the first snow. Silly, empty face, thought Ellen, in angry fear. Suppose she caught Robby, what would he be, then? Ellen's jealousy reached into the boy's future, and grew cunning with the years it fed on. She stopped one day to talk with Dr. Willis. Later Robby confronted her in the kitchen.

"Now, see here, An' Telly!" Ellen brought a plate of cookies from the cupboard. "What you going round telling I'm going to college for?"

"Aren't you?"

"How can I?" The dignity of his roaring protest was muffled in a mouthful of ginger cooky. "You make me look foolish, people speaking to me about it an' all."

"Who spoke about it?" Ellen sat down in the rocker.

"Well, that doctor. He says, 'Glad to hear you're going to my old school. Anything I can do for you?' How'm I going anywheres, I'd like to know, when all Pa says when he opens his mouth is about hard times?"

"The doctor might help." Ellen rocked slowly.

"But . . ." Rob glowered over her, exasperated.

"I told you, if you made up your mind, I'd see to it. What's more, I will. Only we ought to plan pretty soon.

You have to ask 'em to let you in. You'd have to study up some things, the doctor says, instead of running around so much."

"How can you see to it?" The boy's mouth twisted with the effort of his thought to follow hers. "It takes money. . . . Oh . . . that fellow?"

She saw him stop, caught in a recollection of the mystery about Matthew. That night she helped him plan a letter. "Don't tell your father just yet," she said. "When it's time, I will."

"If I go there, I could get rich, couldn't I? Do . . . anything?"

Now if that little plump snip could catch her boy! She'd drop a hint to the doctor to tell Robby some stories about the place, concrete pictures for the boy's desire to work on.

One noon at dinner, Thurston stared at his son. "What's all this?" he asked, holding out an envelope. *Mr. Robert Dacey,* with Harvard College in one corner.

Rob's hand shot out. "It's mine," he said, and leaped up as his father tore it open. Ellen tugged at his arm.

"Yours, is it?" Thurston pulled out the sheet. "You're my son yet, aren't you?" Ellen patted Rob's hand. Thurston had to puff himself into authority, the boy had to hurl himself against it. Her own nostrils widened; her moment was coming, coming!

"What's this mean . . . send letters of recommendation, credentials?" Thurston flipped the letter across the table. "College? You plan to go to college, do you?" He laughed.

Grace fastened her round eyes on her son. "Robby, what have you been up to now, vexing your papa?"

Rob turned a crimson, frustrated face toward Ellen, seized the letter and started to rise.

"Sit still!" Thurston roared. "Eat your dinner, and explain what your fine idea is!"

"It's my idea." Ellen leaned forward, her blood pounding in her ears. "Mine. You'd better wait till after dinner, Thurston, and I'll tell you about it. You better not press me now."

He stared at her, one hand pulling at his clipped whiskers. With a shrug he bent over his plate, while Grace murmured, "Well, I never!"

John Thurston slunk away from the table first, leaving his food scarcely touched. Ellen could not bother with him. Presently Thurston rose. He pretended not to look at Ellen, but she caught the swift corner glance as he left the room. She folded her red checked napkin and pushed it into the wooden ring before she followed him.

"Well!" Thurston turned from the window, hands clasped under his coat tails. "What are you trying to do, coming between father and son and making a threat before my family? Are you crazy?"

Ellen closed the door softly. "I'm not crazy. You were scared enough to keep quiet, weren't you? What you afraid of, Thurston Dacey?"

"You haven't been right since you were sick. I didn't want you making a fool of yourself."

"I couldn't remember everything at first," said Ellen, slowly. "It took me quite a while to remember the name of the bank. Matthew's bank." Why, she was almost sorry for Thurston; she'd thought she'd like to see him down in the dust, while she waved banners above him—but that tormented twitching in his cheek, his eyes staring until the dilated pupils were rimmed in white—"I did, finally. I wrote and asked them about my money."

"I told you they failed."

"But they paid you first, every cent. 'We have closed your account, as per your instructions giving your brother power of attorney.' I don't know what that means." She watched Thurston jerk back a chair and seat himself at his table. "Forgery and stealing, too."

"It's a lie. They failed. You signed the paper yourself."

"You must of thought I was going to die, didn't you?" Ellen stood at the edge of the table, her clasped hands resting on it. "So nobody would know. You stole twice, from me and from Robby."

"If you knew anything about business . . ." Thurston hunched his shoulders, tightening his muscles. "I used my best judgment. Everything's going to wrack and ruin. You'd have lost it all later."

"No Dacey's ever been a scoundrel, before." Ellen's eyes were heavy with reflection. "I guess you thought you were too smart. That's why Robby's going to have something different. He's going to school some more, and you're going to help him. There's no use my asking for my money back. You haven't got it. You can get enough to start Robby. Maybe he can learn how to stay honorable."

"I won't be told how to run my family!" On Thurston's grayish forehead a vein bulged. "He can go to work! I've got your signature. The money belonged to your father, anyway. He'd staked Matthew. You needn't think——"

"I think your mind's crooked, Thurston. I never

signed a paper giving you my money. Oh—" She lifted
her hands against the sickening twist under her heart.
"When I wanted Robby to have it . . . you could do
that?"

"I'd begged you to help me. You wouldn't, even when
I crawled at your feet." His breath whistled.

"You've got some shame left, then." Ellen was
upright, firm again. "You'll send Robby east to school,
or everybody will know what you did. I'll tell them,
if it kills me. You've had everything of Pa's, and of
mine. You think you're safe, because I have a feeling
for our name. I did have. Now I don't care. There's
other lawyers besides you in this county. I'll—I'll bring
a public law suit!"

Thurston's belligerence relaxed; he slumped in his
chair, chin down on his chest, and stared under his eyebrows at Ellen.

"You can't get blood out of a turnip," he said. "A law
suit'd get you nothing."

"It wouldn't do you any good."

"I haven't a dollar."

"You can get it. Easier than you'd ever get much,
once people knew."

"What good'll it do him?"

"Why—" Ellen's grim face softened. "If there are
things to learn, to help a man along, so he doesn't get
mixed up. . . . Robby's smart."

"He's too damned smart now, thinking he's a match
for me."

"What would he think if he knew about you?"

Thurston flung out his hands. "Oh, Lord, let me
alone! How much would it take? I've done the best

I could. Oh, God!" His head went down on his arms, his fingers digging into his hair.

Gray hair. He was getting old, too. Ellen lifted one hand to her dry throat. "Not much. A few hundred to start with. There's lots a boy can do to help himself. You tell him you'll do it. Tell him yourself. He'd like that."

She closed the door upon Thurston. She had to sit down on the lowest step of the stairs, until her heart stopped its frantic beating. An ashy, pinched look hung about her eyes and nostrils, as if she had run too far. Robby, on cautious, ungainly tiptoe, came through the hall, peered at her.

"He won't do it. I knew he wouldn't."

Ellen lifted her face, the mist clearing from her eyes. Thank God Thurston hadn't forced her into her threat . . . public shame, disgrace. . . .

"Yes, he will, Robby." She could smile at the eager toss of the boy's head, the smack of his hand on her shoulder. Like a young horse, Robby was, with life rippling close to the surface. "He'll talk it over with you. Not just now."

XV

The household seemed shrunken when Rob finally had gone. Another Dacey riding away, thought Ellen. This was no wild-goose chase. Alice had another school, fifteen miles away, so that she came home only on Sunday. She no longer crimped her bangs, and she complained that her eyes bothered her. The reddened lids dominated

her face, warring against the shallow prettiness she had
possessed. Until Rob's departure Thurston had avoided
Ellen, never letting his eyes meet hers. But during the
winter she heard him boasting of his son, and gradually
habit crusted over the uncomfortable edges of that scene.

Times were picking up a little. The railroad changed
its route, men came to pry up the miles of rusted rails,
and laid them some fifty miles to the north; the village
lost its dream of youth. Thurston talked of raising capital to rebuild, but snow capped the gray débris. His arm
stiffened; the doctor said the old wound had injured
important nerves.

The following summer Rob did not come home. He
had a job in the east, and the distance stood like a wall
between him and the village. The doctor had gone on a
lake steamer as far as Buffalo, returning with his bride;
Ellen's interest in the quiet, slight stranger centered in
one thing. She had seen Robby. Dr. Willis had asked
him to call on her. For a long time, whenever Ellen saw
them driving past, she hurried out, catching up her apron
in one hand, to ask again: "Rob looked well, when you
saw him?" Not even when she saw Alice behind the
parlor curtain, peering out with red, hungry eyes, could
she give up that moment of inquiry. "Why, she might
remember something else he said," Ellen defended herself
when Grace asked, "What are you talking to the doctor's
wife about?" and then, "You've asked her a hundred times
about Rob."

John Thurston had a job that summer, too, as chore
boy on a farm near town. He stayed there nights, in
order to be on hand mornings, but Sundays he came

home, his soiled clothing slung in a bundle at the end of
a stick. His legs and arms were stretching out like splin-
ters, and his neck was too thin and long for his large
head. He asked always about his brother. Was there a
letter? What kind of job did Rob have? Did he make
more than John Thurston?

"I think he's working too hard for his strength," said
Ellen one Sunday evening, when the boy's figure disappeared at the end of the street. "That farmer's a rough
hand, too."

"Never hurt me, when I was his age." Thurston
scraped his chair over the porch floor. "He's just
scrawny, that's all."

"I don't see who he takes after." Grace rocked, slapping at mosquitoes. "He's not like my people."

Ellen went into the house. She had the washing to
put to soak. The boy's clothes, stiff with dirt. Something in a pocket of the patched canvas pants . . . a
sheet of one of Rob's letters, worn cottony on the folds.
She smoothed it. John Thurston still tagged his brother,
funny little chap. Sense, though, in those solemn eyes.
Then the letter drew her thoughts away from John
Thurston.

The next winter was one with wind and snow and sudden spells of bitter cold. Thurston went to his office on
good days. More often he sat in his study, wrapped in
a shawl of Grace's. He spoke of important plans. There
was talk of a new pension bill, with an increase for
wounded officers. Thurston declared, "I'll take no pension for serving my country!" Grace coaxed him.
"You've never been the same since you came back. For
all you work so hard. It's that shoulder. . . ." Gradually Thurston's rejoinder changed from its loud refusal

into a grudging admission. "If I can't work. We've
got to live. If other men are taking it."

Old Thurston, bent like a shaving, spent days beside
the kitchen stove. One morning he refused to get out·
of bed. His breath rattled between his ribs, and he waved
his arms at the covers Ellen piled over him. The next
day a film spread over his faded eyes. He thought Ellen
was Martha, and cried, tears catching in the wrinkles of
his cheeks, if she left the room.

"Marthy!" Ellen bent close to the rattling breath.
"Marthy, I never meant to stay away so long. You
might of waited, running off the minute I got home.
Where you been?" He fell asleep and Ellen sat beside
him. She had not slept all night, and her eyelids were
heavy. In the soft vision between waking and sleep she
saw three men, riding through white morning mist, three
tall, strong men on horses, dark shapes on a vague and
shifting background: young Matthew, young Robert, and
her father. "Marthy!" She started, full awake, the
vision still clear before her eyes, the figure of her father
turning, waving. This brown shell on the pillow. She
drew the sheet gently over the empty face. He had
ridden away, again.

Ellen sat for a little while beside the dead man, thinking how the years moved together as you grew older.
Perhaps that helped you to bear life. When you were
very old, a year was less than an hour of youth, and at
the end, the whole span shrunk into nothing, as if time
were hot water—she smiled at her homely fancy—and
you dipped into it the woolen garment of your life. It
was unseemly to sit there, thinking. She rose. Her
father lay there, dead, and with him, part of her own life
closed. The part that reached into the past.

BOOK II

I

Alice **Dacey** pressed her finger tips into her eyeballs; she'd only make her eyes red again, but that dry ache. . . . At a step in the hall her hands pretended to smooth her hair.

"Now, Alice, if your eyes are bad again, you ought to see about glasses." Her mother came in, with the pattering steps of feet too small for a heavy body. She sank into a chair, fluttering a cardboard fan. "Mercy, it's warm for September. You wouldn't need to wear them all the time."

"I don't need glasses." Alice let her hands fall. "It's just that chalk dust makes them smart. From the blackboards." Glasses, hideous admission of weakness! She'd be an old maid schoolma'am then. She winked her lids. "I won't wear them!" Why, she was scarcely thirty. . . .

"I don't know as I blame you." Grace set her chair rocking. "They don't improve anybody's looks. Land, isn't it warm? You don't feel it so much as I do."

"I feel uncomfortable." Alice looked toward the street; was someone passing, or was it only that shadow under her eyelids? She sighed, catching at her hand as it twitched to lift to her eyes.

"What you got that dress on for?"

"I thought maybe I'd go to church. That missionary is going to talk. It isn't time yet." The women sat in silence, and through Alice's mind wisps of thought drifted. The missionary had looked at her that morning; twice, she'd seen him look. He had a long throat above his black tie and great white ears. He was a brave, good man. If she sat on the front row . . . or the second, maybe, and listened . . . would his look pick her out? She might drop a hymn book. A man like that would be above a pretty face . . . he could see a soul . . . like his . . . full of longing to serve the Lord . . . heathen crowding to touch the hem of her garment . . . black natives with nose-rings . . . see, Lord, I bring you these souls. . . .

"I hear his wife died last year," said Grace, rocking. "In the Ganges, or somewhere."

Alice knew that look in her mother's face, that speculative scheming. Here's another man, her eyes would say. Why can't you get one?

"He's going to be in town a week." Her voice carried tags of that look. "We could ask him. . . ."

Alice got to her feet in a quick movement of escape. "Oh, for goodness' sakes!" She hurried into the house. Her mother always spoiled things, putting her plump fingers on them, hauling them out of shadowy possibility into daylight, where they vanished. Good thing the day was so hot; at least no one would want to go to church. Up the stairs she hurried. She should have something for the missionary box. Under the pile of handkerchiefs in a drawer lay her knit purse. Two quarters and one large silver dollar. She was saving for a new winter cloak. She could see the man look up at the sound of a dollar falling into the box. She wrapped it in a handkerchief; it pressed assurance into the palm of her hand.

Then she peered at her reflection. The soft evening light was kind; she saw herself slim, refined, with quiet charm. Little rosettes of blue ribbon holding the ruffles of her dress. She'd have no such dress without her teaching . . . that awful school room, rows of stubborn young wills fighting against her, until she wanted to scream out at them and whirl in a mad circle, the way the inside of her head whirled. Not to-night, though. No school till to-morrow. Why spoil this hour? She walked to the door, with a mincing step that swung her skirts. Hand on the latch, she listened. Her Aunt Ellen moved in the next room, with a purposeful, even step. Would she ask to go to church? Well . . . it might look better. Yes, there stood Ellen, in plain gray, silver gleam of braids under her black hat.

"Your mother says you're going to meeting. I'll walk along."

Alice felt still more slim and ladylike, walking beside her aunt. Younger, too, although Ellen's spare, colorless face changed so little with the years. No wonder she'd never married. She was too—Alice peered at her clear profile, hunting for a word to measure the difference between her aunt and other women. Men liked women to be soft, depending on them.

"Why don't you ask the doctor about your eyes?" said Ellen. "They look worse since you started school this fall."

"They don't look a bit worse!" Alice trembled with anger.

"If your father gets that increase in pension, I was telling him you ought to give up teaching. It seems too hard for you."

"I guess if you tried it, you'd see how hard it is."
Alice wriggled her narrow shoulders. "I have some other
plans, anyway."

"Well—" Ellen's glance was tolerant, and Alice
clutched hard at her dollar. Sometimes she hated her
aunt, looking as if she spied the fringes of the dreams
Alice cherished.

Then, sitting beside Ellen in the front row, she forgot
her aunt, her solicitous mother, her school. Something
noble about that gaunt, tall figure, shaking dark hair
from his forehead, towering above the elderly village
pastor. Stories of heroism, of souls saved. Let us pray.
. . . Alice leaned forward, hands over her face, surreptitious fingers on her eyes, her hunger spinning a fabric
of gossamer. He had looked at her, bidding her rise
and follow, a stern, tender look. Ellen nudged her. "Are
you asleep?" The prayer had ended, the missionary himself was stepping from the platform with the collection
plate. Alice laid her dollar among the small coins. He
saw it! At the end of service he pressed her hand, calling
her Sister. He turned to speak to someone else. Still,
that pressure. . . . Alice dreamed homeward through the
warm night.

"He thinks he's pretty fine." Ellen broke through her
visions. "I expect it turns a man's head, feeling he's the
special messenger of God."

"Of course he's better than other men."

"I always think," went on Ellen, "that being a missionary or a revivalist is a grand job for a man, he can
feel so stuck up without having to hide it. It's funny
the way their wives die. This one's had three. I got
to wondering about Sarah. You know, your Uncle Rob-

ert's first wife. She ran away with a revivalist. This missionary looks some like him." Ellen was silent a moment. "I expect she had a hard time."

Alice floundered in unspoken retorts. She walked more quickly, bent on reaching her own room, where nothing could drag her away from the obscure, delightful pictures that awaited her. If she didn't get away from Ellen, they would fade out of her reach, and she would know . . . she trembled at the margin of that realization . . . that to-morrow the missionary would be gone, like all the preceding figures in her dreams. She ran up the steps without heeding some sleepy query from Grace, and on to the shelter of her own room. By the time her light was out and she had drawn the sheet to her chin, she had safely forgotten that threat of reality. She relaxed, waiting, and slowly the ritual of her phantasy began. She clung to the missionary's arm, people waved her good-bys, a long feather drooped from her hat over one shoulder, the doctor pressed through the crowd. "All my life I have realized my mistake, but honor forced me. . . ." More darkly, someone kissed her. If she lay very still, her body recaptured the distant thrill of kisses on summer evenings. Shameful and sweet. That school principal lingering in her room, his red round face swimming close like a moon. The clerk in the grocery store, curly hair, white apron, thrusting an apple into her hand, his eyes saying, "I am so far beneath you, how could I hope?" They were older figures in her fancies, dim now. It will be hard, my darling, to share the Lord's work in heathen countries. Nothing is hard for a woman who loves. She stirred faintly, one hand over her eyes, as sleep dragged her under the rim of pictures, down into dreams.

II

Ellen heard the new sharpness in Alice's voice, expected the sick headache with which the week ended. The missionary had come to supper on Wednesday. He had produced a tin-type of three children, a boy standing with one hand on the shoulder of a solemn girl, a younger girl on a hassock in front of them. "Their mother's sister, a God-fearing woman, has consented to take their mother's place as my wife," he explained.

"Your fourth?" Ellen spoke hastily, before he looked at Alice. "She must be God-fearing."

"Yes." He replaced the tin-type. "I have had many losses."

Ellen, carrying gruel to Alice on Saturday, thought: she'll get somebody else on her mind soon enough, poor little fool. It was hard on a woman when she couldn't get her mind off herself. She sniffed at the acrid odor of the closed room. "Don't you want some air in here?"

"The light hurts my eyes."

Ellen reflected as she descended the stairs. Suppose she went away, would Alice take hold and run things? Teaching was bad for her, made her too edgy. But where could I go? Ellen stared at the familiar shabby chairs and carpet, the doors behind which so many recollections hid. She had a repetition of a feeling that had come often during the past years, that her own life had stopped its onward flow, that it spread into a motionless pool with no outlet. Since Rob had gone east. Ten years of nothing. Rob was so far away, his life ran so remotely for hers, that for all her pride in him she had no pull from the dull circle of the pool. Once he had

been home, when he went for the summer with a railroad
gang into the west. Just a few days, scarcely enough to
believe it was Rob. Now he was in business in the east,
vague term that left her unsatisfied. And he had a girl.
If I could see him, thought Ellen, I'd feel better. As for
going somewhere, to see if Alice would take hold. . . .
The only thing I'm good for is work. I could work for
other people, but they wouldn't any of them hear to that.
She shrugged herself out of her idle moment, and looked
onto the porch. There sat Grace, rocking, brushing cake
crumbs from her dress, in spite of the doctor's warning
about being so fleshy.

Grace was lots easier to get on with than she ever had
been in her slimmer days. Perhaps her weight was an
outward symbol of the laziness she had longed for, and
at the same time a valid reason for no exertion. Since
she found it difficult to walk far, she had lost her resentment at Thurston's financial straits. Rocking on the
porch in summer and in the living room in winter, she
could forget that her husband was no longer the prominent man of the town. She sucked in her breath commiseratingly when Thurston burst into a tirade against
changing times, against the perfidy of some concern in
which he had invested, and then apparently forgot his
trouble. Ellen glanced again at the porch. Grace had
picked up the pink-covered weekly journal, and was reading again the continued novel, reading with slow mouth-
ings of the words. Ellen went to the kitchen, conscious
for the moment of the hard, alert movement of her body.
Probably, if you were as fat as that, your thoughts and
feelings had the life squeezed out of them. She smiled
drolly; Grace took her increased weight as occupation.

Supper to think about. Alice wouldn't come down. Grace would waddle in, animated at sight of the table. Thurston would come. Perhaps John Thurston, although you never could count on him. Ellen with a basket went out to the vegetable garden, brown and almost dismantled at the summer's end. Tomatoes. She bent, closing her hand firmly about the sleek red globes. Love apples, her mother had called them. She walked down the row, her feet pressing into the dry soil. Most of them would ripen before danger of frost, unless this spell of heat rushed suddenly into sharp weather. Sometimes it did. Her fingers yellowed, grew aromatic with the breaking of the stems. She sniffed at them, standing at the end of the row. Another winter, season without growth, before she could plan another garden. Spring, summer, were better; there was a feeling of accomplishment, for all you knew it ended in dead vines and crackling leaves.

Why, John Thurston was home already, pushing open the kitchen door with that hang-dog, listless air of his. Ellen walked briskly the length of the garden. He'd want supper, and then go off again, where she didn't know, in spite of looking tired enough to drop. She didn't know what ailed him lately; she wouldn't ask him again, just to have her head snapped off. Hard on a boy in his early twenties to have to help the family as much as he did. His boots outside the door, dirty, odorous of the livery stable where he worked, looked sulky, toeing toward each other. In the kitchen she heard him overhead, stumping about in stocking feet.

As Ellen sliced the tomatoes, she frowned. Whatever had reminded her of the first time she'd asked John Thurston for money? He was just a boy . . . eight years ago.

She had to buy flour, and Thurston had dragged the gray cotton linings of his pockets out when she told him. That was their worst year, before the pension began. At the end of the summer, John Thurston had not gone back to school. "I couldn't do anything for him. I'd done it all for Robby." Ellen pushed the memory out of mind.

Thurston came in, the tails of his black coat flapping with his jerky, busy gait; greenish along the seams, that black coat. John Thurston was in a good humor; sometimes, when his thin cheeks flushed under the high cheekbones, and he was freshly shaven, he was almost good looking. He talked, amusing his mother with livery stable gossip. A funeral the next day, and he was to drive the hearse. "I might borrow Pa's coat."

As he jumped up from the table, Thurston shouted after him, "Where you going?"

"Out."

"Why can't you stay home a single night?"

"Here?" He thrust his head forward, truculently. "I've some things to attend to."

"I don't want you hanging around that woman, you hear? Yes, I know all about her. If you can't respect yourself, think of your father and mother!"

"You—you let me alone!" His voice rasped, as he flung himself out of the room.

"What woman, Thurston?" Grace's full cheeks quivered. "Is he after a woman?"

"I know all about it." Thurston thumped the table. "I'll put a stop to it. As long as he's under my roof! He's my son. . ."

Ellen rose abruptly. "It's some thanks to him there is a roof," she said, "and if he's found somebody he likes—"

She wanted to bang the door, but she closed it discreetly. At the outer kitchen door was John Thurston.

"Ellen! Pst!" he whispered. "I forgot my cap."

She tipped down the hall and returned with it. As she slid the door open, the boy grinned impishly, and bolted.

III

He swung carelessly down the village street, his anger blurring under the flood of excitement. Old fool, what did he matter? What mattered was the night, patched with yellow glow of lamps behind windows, full of that queer smell, as if the dark laid a cool hand suddenly on sun-parched leaves and withered late roses; that early fall odor that thrummed in his blood like the very essence of all longing. He sniffed at his sleeve; did that awful livery stable hang about him? He felt sometimes that his skin soaked it up. No matter. On, across the dark stretch of the mill race, where the fragrance of still water floated, out to the edge of town.

The small, low house that was almost the last on the road looked dark. John Thurston walked to the latticed porch, disappointment swelling in his throat, breaking in a sigh of relief as he caught the thin line of light along a drawn curtain. She was at home. After his knock he heard the startled scrape of a chair, and then a voice. "Who is it?" A frightened voice.

"It's me, John Dacey." His hand was eager on the latch, but as the door opened, he pulled off his cap and stood still, thrilled with embarrassment at the sight of the small woman who lifted a worried face to him.

"Oh, come in." She pushed the door hastily shut, and

retreated to her chair, reaching for the mound of dark wool stuff, beginning again her busy stitching. A little girl slid from a chair beyond the table and pushed against her mother's shoulder, looking at John Thurston. "I didn't know you were coming to-night. I'm glad to see you."

John sat down, thrusting his cap under the chair. "I didn't know I could get away in time." His heart was beating fast, sending a strong, sweet contentment through him, as he looked at the two, the woman with untidy fine hair dulled from the fair, shining texture of the child's head so close to her arm, the small pointed faces so much alike, except that the child's smile was puckish, and the mother's blue eyes kept the startled look from his knock.

"Did you get some sewing?" He pointed to the goods on her knee.

"The woman two houses down. To make over a winter dress. If I suit her, she might have a new one."

"It must be warm to sew on that to-night." To himself he said: her face is like a white lilac leaf, her eyes are the color of a full blown lilac blossom; suppose I called her *Lilac*. Just a month since he had heard of her. Sim, who drove the hack from the station, had said, "There's a new widow in town, come from the east. Going to live in the old Carter place." The next day John himself had driven out with a trunk, a shabby black trunk with a high curved lid. He couldn't get out of his head her small white face and the narrow hand that trembled as it handed him the money. He had watched for her on the street. A few days later, as he sweated over washing down a carriage, he had seen her coming, scurrying along like a partridge in her brown dress. He jumped up, dripping sponge in one hand, and when he saw the frightened stare change into a smile of recognition, he felt as if his heart turned over and ran down out of his muddy boots, to blow like thistledown after her along the street. He had looked for her in church on Sunday, and not seeing her, had waited until evening. Then, irresistibly, he had walked as far as the Carter place, past it to the woods, back to the house, and with a desperate impulse, straight to the door. She had been frightened at the knock, and he had said, "I thought, as you were a stranger, maybe there'd be something I could do." She had asked him to come in. Florence, her name was. Mrs. Florence Brown.

"It's hard to get started." She held her needle out, stabbing the thread at it, her eyelids puckering. "Go sit down, Flora." She pushed the child gently away from her arm. "I might go out by the day, only I hate to send her to school yet."

"She has to go some time." John Thurston sat quietly in his chair, but his longing to help ran through the dark streets of the village. "She'd have a nice time. My sister teaches. I could speak to her."

"Would you?" Her eyelids lifted for a grateful instant.

"If you'd come to church, the way I said, and get to knowing folks——"

"Yes, I know." Her needle hurried. "I mean to come. But people aren't very friendly . . . to a stranger."

"That's because it's such a little town. Not like the cities you know. Why . . . they'd have to be friendly to you." He was breathless at his daring, but the woman smiled faintly over her sewing, and he dared still more. "They couldn't help theirselves!"

"They haven't been." Her small mouth trembled. "Except you."

"Well, in a town like this"—John Thurston stumbled among his confused thoughts— "they have to know about you. They want to know why you came here, and everything." He stopped as Mrs. Brown gathered folds of the stuff to her breast, her eyes aghast.

"I . . . I'd heard about it, that's all. I had to come somewhere. I thought it was a good place for her."

"I'd rather go back to the city." The child had been standing quite still, just where her mother had pushed her.

"I just mean they wonder about it, first. Then they get used to the idea, and by and by they forget you weren't always here." A wave of bitterness that he had no power against the stubborn town, old bitterness rooted darkly in all his past years, rolled over John Thurston, threatening this new amazing contentment. As if the woman saw the threat, she dropped her sewing.

"Let's not talk about it. I made a cake to-day. We'll have a party, Flora, help mamma clear the table." Her voice had altered, and her face. To John Thurston she seemed to open dull wings, showing inner radiance. The child, too, had changed, as if her mother's voice plucked at a wire of excited delight. They swept spools and cloth away, John held the lamp while Mrs. Brown threw over the table a white cloth, fragile and darned. Cake, cider, and apples for the child. "Now are we lords and ladies?" The child's color deepened into rose, "or are we sailing away on a boat? Tell us, Mamma."

"Which would you rather be?" Mrs. Brown lifted her

hands in a gay gesture.   John Thurston saw the pricked
forefinger, saw, above the pleated muslin frill at the neck
of her dress, a pulse beating close to the thin white skin.
A foolish game to fill him with such delight, a strong,
mounting pleasure, full of calmness, with none of the
thwarted, baffling turning in upon himself.   "I'll tell you
both . . ." as if he were a child, too! . . . "about a party
once, in a great city, miles and miles away."

All too soon there were crumbs of cake, and golden
dregs in the glass cider pitcher.

"Now you must go."   Mrs. Brown stood, one arm
around the little girl.   "It's late, and the party is over."

John Thurston twisted his cap between his hands.

"You . . . you don't mind if I come again, soon?" he
said.

"Not too soon."   Was that fear, again, in the movement
of her eyelids?   "Some time.   Good-night."

"I want him to come."   The child beat at her mother's
hand in a flurry of spent delight.   "Then it's nice, when
he comes."

John Thurston walked home, his face up to the stars,
past dark, still houses.   Lilac, Lilac . . . the small pale
face shone nearer than the stars, but more remote than
thought.

IV

The next week the heat broke, in heavy rain.   The line
storm, the villagers called it.   Summer was washed away
in flooded gutters, along with dirt gullied from hillsides
and brown leaves.   Alice picked her way home from school
around puddles, her draggled skirts slapping at her ankles,
the wind buffeting her umbrella.   An awful day for a

woman to have to be out. No other women were out,
except that one who had come to school in the morning.
Alice made a buttonhole of her mouth. As she passed
the church and the adjoining frame house of the minister,
she hesitated. No, she'd tell her mother first.

Grace had retired from the porch rocker to a corner of
the dining room, where some warmth from the kitchen
stove entered, if Ellen would leave the door ajar. She
clucked commiseratingly at Alice and her wet skirts.
"Hurry and change, or you'll catch a cold." Alice hurried, returning presently, the end of her nose pink with
excitement.

"You know that woman Mrs. Cole was talking about,
Ma?" She drew a chair close to her mother, whose face
puffed at the whiff of gossip. "That one that calls herself a widow, and lives in the Carter place? She came
to school this morning, in all the rain. With her little
girl. Could she start her in school, please, she'd never
been, and her name was Flora, and she wouldn't have
come such a bad day, but she had a chance to help with
some plain sewing. I said it was late to start, but if she
was past six, and she said she was going on seven and
knew her letters. So she went away without a thank you,
and I had another young one on my hands. She acted
scared to death all the time." Alice lowered her voice.
"Is Ellen out there?" Grace shook her head. "At recess
I asked Flora when her father died, and what do you think
she said? 'I don't know.' I asked her what her mother
came here for, and she said the same thing. Her mother'd
told her to say that."

"Well—" Grace rocked busily. "I told Mrs. Cole I
didn't see why a widow should move away to a new place.

It looks funny.   Now I wouldn't think of moving . . .
not that your father's sick, or anything.   Mrs. Cole said
she was a nice appearing little thing."

"Nice?"   Alice ground her hands, and the pink tip of
her nose quivered.   "When they've seen men coming
away from her house late at night?   And John Thurston's
been there."   She leaned back in her chair, hearing again
that creak of hall boards as her brother passed her door, a
dreadful creak of a man returning . . . from who knew
what infamy?

"Your father did say something."   Little folds crept
into Grace's cheek.

"I think it's time something was done."   Alice felt her
anger stand up like a candle, lighted for righteousness.
"She puts her child in school with honest children. Folks
answer questions if they aren't hiding things."   As Ellen
came through the room, she was silent.   Ellen had a queer
way; you couldn't count on her.   With her in the kitchen,
further talk was impossible.

"I don't see what there is to do."   Grace reached for
the paper she had laid aside.

Alice flounced to her feet.   Do?   She'd find something
to do.   The minister wouldn't have such a woman in
town.   Satisfactory, resounding phrases from Bible texts
rolled under her tongue as she left her mother to the
pages of her serial.   Scarlet woman, painted Jezebel; she
looked innocent enough, with her shrinking, pale face. It
was her soul Alice battered with Biblical invectives.

Through supper Alice sent cautious glances at her
brother, jerking her eyes away when she met his.   She
seemed to meet his often, as if he knew her thoughts.
Only lately had he taken to cleaning up so fine before he

ate, dark hair sleeked straight back, eyes anxious. Why, she had a duty to him, too. Her brother. Not like Rob. If Rob were home, handsome Rob, he could take her around a little, as brothers should. John Thurston was queer, silent, sulky. His mouth looked different, firmer. Alice felt a spiral of fire in her head, as if the nearness of John Thurston, who had come at night from that woman's house, brought sin so close that she could almost faint for her own virtue.

She expected him to follow her into the living room, so sure had she been of his investigating glance. And he did, moistening his lips, his flush springing into scarlet.

"I just wanted to say . . ." he looked at her entreatingly. . . . "You had a new child in school, to-day. You . . . sort of help her along, while she's new, Alice. She's timid. You could be nice to her, till she gets used to it."

Alice trembled with eagerness; why, he had put himself within reach of her burning hands. "What child?"

"Flora. I met her mother, and she told me. You see, the little girl's never been away from her mother before, and."

Alice watched the Adam's apple above his clean collar. Slowly she lifted her eyes to his confused face.

"I heard you knew her mother, the Widow Brown," she said. "I never supposed you'd dare ask me . . . *me* . . . to show her favors. A woman nobody knows a thing about, even the child says she doesn't know anything about her father, and you ask your sister to show special favors. Who is she, and what have you to do with such a woman?"

Alice was dramatic, she was outraged virtue, all her secret fancies fuel to her blaze. John Thurston stared, incredulous horror crinkling his skin. He raised his fists, and Alice stepped hastily backwards.

"My God!" he cried, "she's better than you are! You nasty-minded old maid! You—" But Alice screamed aloud at the stable epithet that followed.

"You'd strike your sister?" She burst into sobs, and saw the door and Ellen, amazed, at the threshold.

"I didn't touch her. I should of," said John Thurston.

"What are you two quarrelling about?"

"She'll tell you, and it will be all lies." The boy's face was white, except for disks of color on his cheeks. "Lies! Anybody who'd think such things——"

Alice, sobbing, peering between her fingers, saw Ellen tug at his arm, saw his wild backward look as he went with his aunt. After a moment she shivered over a final sob, and tiptoed along the hall. Her mother rocked, oblivious. Alice couldn't cross the dining room. She slipped through the outer door, and stumbling in sodden grass, the rain cold on her head, she ran to the woodshed outside the kitchen. Through the window she could see Ellen standing, and her brother crouched in a chair. They moved, and Alice squatted behind the piled wood. The door opened.

"You go see her, yourself, Ellen." The boy's voice was steady. "I'll tell her you're coming. If they're all against her. . . . Oh, damn good women, anyway!"

Ellen laughed. "There, John Thurston, you're just riled up. Yes, I'll pay her a call some day. Button up your coat."

John Thurston's step shook the woodshed. Alice closed one hand over a stick of wood, rough, splintered. When Ellen left the kitchen, she'd creep in. Wonder, so

remote that she scarcely felt it, crept over the rim of her
anger. Why had she said so much? Ellen's calm voice.
. . . There, Ellen was gone.

But as Alice closed the door on her stealthy entrance,
Ellen was there again, her eyes on Alice's drenched head,
on her muddy shoes.

"Are you crazy?" she said, sharply, "or what?" She
made no motion to stop her, though, as Alice stalked past
her.

V

John Thurston splashed through puddles; he shook his
head as the wind drove rain on his face. What a fool
he'd been to say a word to Alice, what a purblind, stag-
gered fool! When had she ever lifted a finger for him,
except to wag it contemptuously? Just as well Ellen had
opened the door. Good old Ellen! If Alice had gone
on, he might have knocked her flat. She deserved worse
than that. What ailed her? What did she have against
Florence Brown? He wanted to run, but the very thought
of his feet pounding down the deserted street seemed to
fill the windows with staring eyes. When he came to the
little house near the end of the road, he saw no crack of
light along a drawn curtain, and to his knock there was
no answer. He knocked again and heard the wind roll
the sound down the street. As he turned slowly away
he thought he saw a shadow move in the dark porch next
door. Some other she-cat, like his sister. No wonder
Florence wouldn't answer his knock. What had Alice
said, or done, to that child? Frightened her, badgered
her with questions. John groaned. There he'd promised
to speak . . . and his own sister . . . what must she think

of him? If Ellen would go to see her, she might forgive
him. Ellen would be a good friend. She could persuade
Florence to go out more, so people could know what she
was like. Once they knew her . . . the consciousness of her
grew in John Thurston like a glowing light, a light with
fragrance: her flying, fine hair, her small face, her serious, sweet timidity. Why, they'd like her. All of them.

He had come to the block of stores. The street lantern on the corner, smoky under its pointed roof, dropped
shimmering reflections into the puddles. Two new buildings stood up like teeth on the empty side where the Dacey
block had burned. Across the way the buildings were
dark, except for First and Last Chance. John was cold
and wet. He'd stop for a glass of beer, and see who was
out this kind of night.

Sim was there, lounging over a table. Well, he lived
above the livery stable. Two country fellows. They'd
stayed in pretty late. John leaned on the counter, watching the beer foam into the huge mug, when Sim began.

"Johnny's got a girl. She ain't sent you out this chilly
night so early as this, has she, Johnny? Only she ain't a
girl, she's a widow."

Snickers from the big, red-faced fellow. "Widows
are better'n girls, any day."

"You shut up, you Sim." John Thurston's fist shut
over the mug handle. "You're drunk."

"I didn't have no nice warm widow—" Straight into
his loose, grinning face John's hand let the beer fly. He
stared, amazed, at Sim, spluttering, drops of beer rolling
from his eyebrows.

"Hey!" The proprietor jerked about from his barrel.
"Hey, you!"

Sim was at the good-natured stage. He thrust out a thick tongue, licking at the froth. John Thurston, without a word, strode away from the counter, out of the door. As he hurtled down the street, he began to blubber, softly. "Damned dirty-mouthed . . . son of a——" He shook his fists at the dark houses. What a town! What a world! For a woman like that, alone, helpless. At the gate of the Dacey house he stopped, shivering. The night was full of sound, of hostile shadows. What could he do, poor stick, flying into rages that had not even honest blows for a finish? He lifted his face and the cold rain beat against his eyelids. Maybe he'd taught Sim to keep his drunk jokes off her. The rain was harsh, bitter with the odor of dead leaves, of cold earth. Strength in it and in the wind. The boy's hands gripped the pointed palings of the gate, and he stood quite still. Something in the wind, in the rain. He saw her, scurrying along the road, like a partridge, all brown, frightened. He opened his coat, and straight against his heart, soft feathers. . . . Why, he loved her! My God! (it was a prayer. . . .) He hadn't known it!

VI

Ellen heard John Thurston climb to his room above the kitchen. She had been afraid his father might intercept him. Echoes of that scene with Alice had lasted, although Alice had disappeared.

"What are those two fussing about?" Grace insisted. When Ellen denied knowledge, Grace nodded into her rows of chins. "That woman. Alice was worked up."

"What woman?" That had jerked Thurston's head up from his paper. At Grace's explanation, he bristled, crackling his sheets of news. "I told him to stay away from her."

"Do you know any harm of her, Thurston?" Ellen stood between them.

"I know she's no better than she should be."

"I don't know as any of us are." Ellen smoothed the red checked table cover. "But we don't talk of it."

"There's talk of her. A strange female with a child and no reason for coming to town, ensnaring my son."

"Um. I thought as much." Grace pushed her rocker into motion. "Alice said she couldn't get a word out of the child."

"This is a nice Christian village," said Ellen. "Full of brotherly love. I'm going to see this woman to-morrow. You let John Thurston alone. I would, if I was you. He was riled up. The first time he ever showed so much spunk."

She had stalked off with that, leaving them. Fortunately their own dullness had driven them both to bed before the boy came, early as he was. She'd go the next day, just for a call on Mrs. Brown.

In the morning, as she gave John Thurston his breakfast, she found a moment to tell him. The flash of white gratitude on his face gave her a foolish ache in her throat. It meant that much, did it?

By afternoon the rain had stopped, although the wind still drove ragged clouds low over the trees. It would be colder, now. An early winter, perhaps. Ellen got out her second best merino. It was pleasant to walk through the village. She ought to go out more. Young faces in

the town she didn't know.   Farmers' wagons tied along
the hitching rail in front of the stores.   Carter's house
was quite a way, for so small a town.

She rapped, and thought she heard light feet behind the
door.   At her second knock, the door crept back and a
child with yellow hair looked up at her.

"My mother isn't home," she said.   "I wasn't to open
the door, but I peeked and saw you."

"When's she coming home?"

"Soon, maybe.   She's sewing and the dress was most
done."

"Could I wait for her?" Ellen stepped in, doubtfully,
and sat down in the bare, neat room, her hands prim in
her lap.   It was intruding, perhaps, but she didn't know
when she could manage to come again.   The little girl
stood in front of her, with sober blue gaze.   She looked
like someone . . . just a faint stirring of recollection down
a dim corridor.   "You didn't go to school to-day?"

"No, ma'am."   The child frowned.   "I went one day.
I didn't want to go any more.   I'll tell you——" she moved
a step nearer.   "The teacher isn't nice like her brother.
Do you know him?"

"I'm his Aunt Ellen."   How delicate the child's face
was, with the quick flush under the skin.   Ellen sighed,
pressing her lips together.   If she didn't watch out, she'd
be leading the child on to talk.   As bad as Alice.   A hurried step crossed the porch, a voice, anxious.   "Flora, are
you all right?" and on the threshold, Mrs. Brown, to
answer for herself.

"It's his Aunt Ellen," exclaimed the child, and Ellen saw
how color fainter than the child's touched the older face.

"I hope you didn't mind me coming in. I'm Ellen Dacey, and John Thurston said. . . . Well, I thought I'd call."

"It's good of you." Mrs. Brown took off her hat and sat opposite Ellen, the little girl decorous on her small chair. Ellen frowned. Again that stir of recollection, so distant that she couldn't capture it. "I ran . . ." she was breathless, and some agitation worked in her eyelids, her mouth. "Leaving Flora . . . alone. . . ." Ellen saw in the taut knuckles she flung up to her lips, her struggle to push down whatever emotion had run with her to the door. "I took her to school yesterday."

"Yes," said Ellen.

The woman's eyes clung to Ellen's an instant, fear showing in them. She rose. "Flora—" she had the child's hand. "You go sit in the other room a little while. Please." She shut the door, standing against it with her hands out at her sides, palms extended. "You look like a good, kind woman," she said, her voice drooping, exhausted. "I haven't meant any harm, coming here. Why can't I stay? And work? Do you know . . . the woman where I was sewing . . . she said I needn't come again. At school, they scared Flora so. What can I do?"

"You better sit down," said Ellen. "You're tired." She waited until Mrs. Brown moved to a chair. "You see, folks aren't used to strangers, and they don't understand why you came here. They don't mean to be cruel. You act scared, and that makes them think worse. If you could explain a little and act different."

"I thought it would be a nice place for Flora. I'd heard about it."

"Where'd you hear about it?" Ellen's voice coaxed

gently. Back in her mind that likeness to someone eluded
her, flitted like a bird through thick branches.

"If I tell you"—the words were a gasp—"will you help
me? My mother told me. She lived here, once."

"Did she?" Who had lived here, and gone away? "Did
I know her?"

Mrs. Brown nodded. "She lived with you."

Ellen's head flew back. That likeness was clear, now,
a bird beating in her hands. Sarah! That fair, sweet
helplessness. A head like that, down on a kitchen table,
with sticky molasses crawling from an overturned jug.

"She always talked about how pleasant it was here. I
didn't know any other place."

"Oh, my good land!" Ellen drew cold fingers across her
forehead. "Sarah. You are Sarah's daughter." That
baby that died in Martha's arms. Another child . . . that
preacher. . . . "Was she happy, with that preacher? What
was his name? Your father's name?"

"My father wasn't a preacher." Florence Brown huddled in her chair, her face gray. "He had a canal barge."

"The preacher, the revivalist? Laing." His image
leaped, black beard and all, out of the past.

"She couldn't stay with him." Her small hands, twisting, spoke of pain and entreaty. "He was cruel."

"And then . . . she married your father, on a canal
barge?"

"Not right off. She had . . . oh, a dreadful time! You
don't know . . . you've always stayed right here . . . you
don't know what happens to women. My father, she said
he was kind. He died. Then it was worse, because she
had me. Finally there was the saloon keeper, Markey."

Ellen stared and stared. Forty years ago Sarah had

run off. This woman was scarcely thirty. Her daughter.
Years of . . . dreadful times.

"She used to tell me about this village. About you.
And your mother. How your brother left her and her
baby died. But he's not here, is he? I thought—" a gesture of her weary head toward the door which had shut
out Flora. "I thought he might help her. Not that she's
any claim, except that he went away and left my mother."

Poor Sarah, looking back from her years of dreadful
times at the village she had hated, at the farm, clothing
them with enough of longing so that they drew her daughter back. "You better tell me the rest," said Ellen.
"Where's your husband? If you knew the Dacey men,
you wouldn't of thought of asking Rob for help, when his
wife didn't wait for him. I'll help, if I can. Only you
might as well go on. Where's Sarah now?"

"She's dead. When I was sixteen. Markey was good
to me, as good as if they'd been married. He'd let me
go to school before she died, and have things. It was in
a big town. I kept house for him until he got another
woman. She didn't like me. She shamed me before the
men who came, calling me names. The names were
true!" Florence Brown stopped, peering helplessly at
Ellen. "Why was I bad? What had I done? And my
mother . . . oh, she wasn't a bad woman! She had to
live. But the men who heard her . . . Markey's woman
. . . thought I ought not to mind, since I was nothing.
So I went away. Only I couldn't get far enough so I
wasn't afraid someone would know who I was."

Ellen sat quiet, while broken pictures shifted with the
words of Sarah's daughter, pictures incomplete because
her own experience could not finish them. I ought to be

shocked, she thought. There was that woman north of town, with a crippled child. She never left the house, althought some spoke of seeing her at night. You were good or you were bad, weren't you? A life of sin, a child born out of wedlock. Sarah had to live. And this woman staring with piteous, frightened eyes, with beads of moisture glistening on her upper lip. Dew of agony. She had to live, too. Why . . . Ellen brushed through cobwebs of colloquial phrases that blinded and prickled, out into a clear space. If I'd been like Sarah, I'd of gone. Almost . . . that prayer of Brother Laing. . . .

"And then?" Ellen cupped her hands over her knees and leaned forward, amazed at the anger that quickened her heart beat. "Your own child?"

"I said I'd marry the first man who'd give me a name. Any name. So I'd be something. I did. Only he found out, later. I ought to'v gone farther away. He couldn't forget. He watched to see . . . if I had men. He was a railroad man, so he wasn't home enough. I couldn't complain. He'd been told things. I had to stand it. Then he got killed. When he had a jealous fit, he'd drink. We had a little money, and I went away, because the neighbors knew. I want my little girl to have a chance. I thought—" Her voice was a thin thread spun of misery. "If she could stay here, if I could leave her, I would go away."

Ellen lifted her head, at a faint noise beyond the door, as if a child brushed a longing hand against it.

"I don't see what you've done to punish yourself for," she said, bruskly. "Giving up your own child that you're fond of. Even if Robert was here, he'd never think he owed Sarah anything, for all he went away knowing she didn't want him to go. If you could stop acting as if you had something you were ashamed of——"

"How can I?" The woman's bruised, tormented self stood in her eyes for Ellen to see. "I try."

"You poor thing." Ellen rose and laid her hands on the thin shoulders, as if she could pour rage like a stimulant through her. "You poor little thing. Giving up your child . . . oh, my goodness! There——" She's like a drenched white feather, hurried Ellen's thoughts. And I feel as if she was a kind of relation of ours, when she isn't, rightly. "You haven't said anything to John Thurston, have you?" she asked.

"I shouldn't have let him come. Only he was kind." Florence pushed herself up to her feet, facing Ellen with a sudden gathering of dignity. "I won't let him any more. If you tell him, he——"

"He's only a boy. I want to talk to Thurston, his father. He knew Sarah. I want to think about it." She frowned. How did you take action against a feeling intangible as mist? Ugly currents beneath the surface of the town? "You hold your head up as if you felt proud. If you stand up, folks'll believe they were mistaken." She held the small, cold hands of the younger woman for a moment, and suddenly bent to kiss her. "There, we'll see."

VII

She walked home through whirling, jostling memories. Her father, Rob, Martha, young Thurston, Matthew . . . faces, voices, feelings pushing into her sober thoughts. Men, twisting the lives of women and putting the blame on the women. Women were as bad, letting men do it.

As she hung away her hat and her merino dress, her mind made little speeches, to Alice, to Thurston, to John Thurston. They wouldn't need to know the whole story . . . bargeman, saloon keeper. Just that Mrs. Brown was Sarah's daughter, and her husband was killed on the railroad, and they ought to have a decent friendly feeling for her, a stranger, alone. She'd had a hard time. A hard time! Ellen's anger rushed back, at the memory of that shrunken white face. Why, she thought, it's as if her soul didn't have any skin left on it, and what's she ever done?

John Thurston wasn't home for supper. That made a better start. Ellen waited until the end of the meal. Then, as Thurston pushed his chair back, she said, "I went to see Florence Brown this afternoon." Alice blinked her red eyelids. "I was surprised. She told me about her folks."

"Ts . . . ts . . ." Grace speared a second piece of cake. "I asked you where you were going and you . . ."

"She's Sarah's daughter." Ellen watched her brother, saw the name cut through the years for him, as it had for her. "Sarah, Rob's wife that he left."

"Her that disgraced us by running off with the preacher? That woman?"

"I knew there was something wrong." Alice expanded in triumph. "For all you said I was crazy."

"There's nothing wrong with her, except she's had a hard time."

"Nothing wrong? When her mother was a sinful woman, and she . . . why, she's a bastard! Her child, too, I don't doubt." Thurston whacked the table with the flat of his hand. "Coming back to stir up old shame . . . she thought to find Robert, and when he wasn't here, she enticed my son, as her mother before her tried to tempt me."

Grace purred in shocked pleasure; Alice hung, avid, on every word of Thurston. Ellen stared at her brother in pitying anger. "You were just a boy when Sarah went. You never liked her, more likely because she didn't notice you." They had quarrelled about something; Ellen saw memory twist at Thurston's scowling face. "It's not Sarah who's here. It's an innocent woman whose husband is dead and who wants to make a living for her child."

"Innocent, with a harlot for a mother? Unto the third and the fourth generations. And my son may be there at this moment!"

Ellen began grimly to pile plates together, rattling steel knives, jostling the heavy cups. The familiar motions drained enough of her anger so that she could speak again. "If you're quoting from the Bible," she said, "there are some other passages . . . about strangers within the gates and casting the first stone, and . . ."

"You can't warp the Bible into countenancing evil!" shrilled Alice.

Ellen carried an unsteady pile of dishes into the kitchen and let them down recklessly on the table. She had drawn the door shut with her toe, but the voices came through, just a vibration of righteousness and anger without words. It would be the voice of the town, too. That tone, beating through doors and walls poisoned the air for such as Sarah's daughter, until there was no place she could draw a breath of fearless self respect. No wonder she'd been foolish enough to think she might find help for her child. Ellen stirred into the habitual acts of setting the kitchen

in order, and as she worked, fragments of thoughts moved
in her mind. Sin ought to be punished, of course. People had a queer eagerness to see some kinds of sin punished. Sarah's kind. Thurston never got worked up
about . . . well, stealing money. The difference between
men's sins and women's sins. Men were strict about
women. Why . . . Ellen's hand drove a towel round and
round a dry plate. They're scared not to be. If women
got off as easy as men, there'd be no stopping the down-
ward course of the world. Alice, too, was all worked up.
Ellen felt the image of Alice's worn face, with greed pressing under her air of moral triumph. Almost . . . almost
as if she was jealous. Jealous of those who tasted for-
bidden fruit. No, not jealous, exactly. More as if . . .
and other people, now, not just Alice . . . as if they made
a scapegoat where they piled their own secret thoughts
of sin.

The door opened.

"If John Thurston comes in," said his father, "I want
to see him. I'll tell him just who this woman is, and
maybe he'll have pride enough to stay away. If he won't,
I'll have her driven out of town. That's all there is to
that. She can't come shaming the name of Dacey."

"It's a great name," said Ellen, her eyes travelling over
her brother, his thinning hair, leathered skin, shabby coat.

"There's Rob to think of, if you've no pride for us."
He slammed the door.

Rob, and she hadn't thought once of him. He was
far enough away. What would he say? That young
cocksureness of his ran on another level, where things
were sharply black and white. The thought of him lighted
candles in her heart; he was climbing, surely, to the top

of the world, her strong, handsome Robby. Almost reluctantly she thought of John Thurston. Pride. Would he have that kind of pride, that masculine resentment? As she swept the floor and carried the broom to the wood-shed, she heard him on the path outside. The wind blew past her, making the lamp flicker and smoke; Ellen waited until he came into the shed. She would see him before his father began to roar.

"Ellen!" The furtiveness of his bent head vanished. "You went out there, to-day? She wouldn't let me come in. She said you'd explain. She's not mad at me, is she?"

"No." Ellen draw the door almost shut, to stop the crazy leaping of the flame in the lamp behind her; the thin line of light struck across the boy's face, danced on a metal button of his canvas work coat. "She wanted me to tell you . . ." and hurriedly, lest someone in the house hear them, she told him, watching the pencil of light on his thin face. She saw the frown deepen in his forehead, saw anger flare under his cheekbones.

"Is that all?" he said, as Ellen finished. "Why wouldn't she see me?"

"She didn't know just how you'd take it. She's had a hard time, with folks looking down on her."

"Down on *her!*"

"Sh! Your father's real mad."

"If he says things against her——"

"You make it worse for her if you make him any madder."

"Oh, if I was only somebody, Ellen!" He ground his fists together.

"It's too bad she came here. Some other place, where no one knew about Sarah." Ellen stepped back into the

kitchen. "Have you had your supper?" If she could
keep him quiet, till his father went to bed. . . . But the
boy walked toward the dining room.

"If he says too much——'"

As he laid his hand on the latch, a muffled cry sounded
through the house. Ellen heard it with stupid awareness,
it seemed a knot tied in the conflicting feelings of the
day. It sounded again. Alice, shrieking, "Ellen! Where
are you?"

Ellen ran. In the hall, at the foot of the stairs, lay
an inert mound. Grace, her face with its chins a waxy
purple, and Alice tugging at her shoulders. "She'd
started to bed. I heard her fall."

Ellen knelt beside her. The doctor had warned her.
Like a tiny cricket deep in soft flesh . . . yes, her heart
was beating. "Run for the doctor, John Thurston!"

VIII

John Thurston sat in the kitchen, waiting for Ellen to
emerge from the sickroom. His mother was better;
unless she had a second stroke, the doctor said, she'd
recover. She couldn't speak yet, nor move her ponderous
body, but that would come in time. For three days John
Thurston had come home from his work to sit all night
in the kitchen, keeping the fire going, heating water for
Ellen, making coffee for her in the thin white hours before
dawn. His father was no good; he acted, Ellen said, as
if the stroke had slapped him, too. He chewed his lip
and muttered things about what a good wife Grace had
always been. He had wanted to send for Rob, but the
doctor prevented that.

"Ellen!" John Thurston jumped to his feet as his aunt came in. "I'm going out, if you don't need me." He ran his fingers guiltily over his fresh shaven chin. "It's all right if I go, isn't it?"

"You ought to get to bed early." Ellen's shoulders stooped, and under her eyes the skin sagged. "After these nights."

"Aw, yes. I slept more'n you have." He oscillated on eager feet, hand at the latch. "If you don't need me—" He had to go. For three days he had held himself there, as if he were iron like the old stove, while within him, like the stove, strange fires leaped. He had said; it's my mother lying there, sick, almost dead. I belong here. And he had almost thought he would find himself at a house on a dark road, so often he felt the very pebbles under his feet.

"Run along." Ellen made a friendly, weary gesture with her hand. "You've been a good boy."

He had no thoughts as he went through the town, only the blessed ease of release, of doing at last what his desire had driven so many hours against the necessity of sitting there in the kitchen. When he reached the house, fear prickled in his palms. Was it empty? Oh, she couldn't have gone! His fear made his knock peremptory. A light showed, moving from another room. Then, through the opened door, as Florence Brown blocked his eager way, her face shadowed, he saw her trunk, its high curved top strapped down.

"What do you want?" she asked.

"You aren't going?" John's hand reached toward her, and at her retreat he stepped forward. "Where are you going?"

"I was going to-day." The woman sat down in a straight chair; over her face a stiff quiet, like a film of ice, was drawn. "But Flora wasn't well. She caught cold."

"Where are you going?" He stood in awkward despair; she had shut herself away, hostile, unapproachable.

"I was wrong to come here. I see now. It was all I could think of, for my little girl." She lifted her eyelids, and the boy saw her fine lashes catch the light from the lamp. "But I'm going. I won't bother you any more." The curve of her lip hardened.

"I couldn't come any sooner," John Thurston entreated her. "My mother had a stroke. I had to stay, to help. Ellen told me. I wanted to come."

"You—you haven't just stayed away?" One hand doubled over her heart, the other covered the first, fingers fluttering.

Suddenly John Thurston understood; the self doubt, the suspicions nourished on humiliation of spirit, like bruised flesh shrinking from further blows. Dimly he felt her struggle in a dark, tormenting universe, like his, but far more bitter through her greater helplessness. He knelt beside her, not touching her. She was so small, so white, so piteous. His blood sang in his ears. As if her need offered an answer to his unhappy, thwarted search, his heart grew strong, indomitable. Under his steady gaze color mounted, tingeing her slender throat, her face.

"I'm going with you," he said.

"You mustn't! You can't!"

He caught her hand, beating him valiantly away, and held it between his hands. "I'm going!" he repeated. He had no words for the tumult that grew within him until he was mightier than the world, but his hands cherished the cold hand they held.

"I'd only spoil your life. I'm older. I've had too much shame."

For a moment the glory darkened. "You don't want me. I've nothing to give you, nothing."

"Oh!" He saw her quick breath lift her breast. "I have nothing, nothing but need of you!"

He drew her hand within his coat, against his heart. "Listen!" he said. "That's you." Then silence, weaving for him the delicate fabric of illusion, in which he was no longer alone, solitary, undesired. "Why"—her eyes were dark, with dilated pupils—"if you wouldn't take me, I'd follow you. I'd stand outside your house until you'd take me for pity."

"Not for pity!" Her free hand brushed his cheek. "Never pity! I thought you were angry. I meant to go away, far. I ought to send you away, and I can't." She drooped toward him, and suddenly John Thurston was on his feet, lifting her into his arms. She lay there, quiet, and his first kiss was gentle with awkwardness. A bird, blown by the wind; a small, wild bird. "Oh, I'll take care of you, I will," he whispered.

As he strode homeward beneath a sky where stars shone high and clear, he thought, "I've never breathed before. Now, if I draw a deep breath, the stars will tumble out of the sky!" He laughed aloud. "Stars, be careful! Stars in my blood, now!" With the softness of touch, a word brushed through his lifted head, through his swinging body. *Cherish.* Not a word, but a feeling. Cherish. A feeling drawing him to a high altar, where he lifted his spirit in an urn with two handles and poured it out in a

great flood. That was love. All his life he had struggled
for love as something to be given him, a prize, a possession, which always was dragged out of his jealous, hating
fingers and given to someone else. Ellen, or Rob. Instead of that, love was this flood of self, poured out at the
feet of another.

He came to the Dacey house, its square bulk dark except
for two windows at the side, his father's room and the
room where his mother lay. They gleamed at him like
eyes in a sardonically averted face. John Thurston stood
outside the gate, his feet wide. "Soon! Let's go away
very soon!" Florence had begged. "Before anything can
happen to us. I am afraid to be so happy." He had promised. The light in his father's window went out, as if
the eye winked. Think you'll get away, the house said.
Deserting your folks? Your mother sick, no money.
Where were the stars now? Blotted out by the high roof
of the house. He thrust open the gate and walked up the
path. Get on without me, his thought assailed the house.
Not one of you wants me. She does. Easier to cut and
run, but he wouldn't. He'd face them.

In the front hall the familiar odor of ingrain carpet
underlay the whiff of drugs from his mother's room. Old
fetters ready to clamp about his ankles again. They
needed his money, didn't they? Years he had worked. . . .
Ellen came through the door and behind her he had a
glimpse of his mother, massive, waxy eyelids closed.

"She's asleep," said Ellen. "She's lots better to-night."

John turned from the door, pity flickering in him. His
mother, bearing him reluctantly, estranging him in her
very womb. She had been young once, she had loved; the
years had hidden away that youth. As he followed Ellen to

the dark dining room and waited for her to light the lamp, the match making a yellow star in the palm of her steady hand, he smiled a little. This new emotion, to-night, was like a lamp, shining into queer dark corners of the years. How he had badgered Ellen for her love—ugly, sullen little boy, clamoring for more than the dispassionate justice she had given him. She looked across the lamp at him, the planes of her austere face touched with light. He felt at peace with her, now, as if love lifted him to a level road where men walked, out of the ditches he had struggled in.

"Ellen," he said, "I'm going away. With Florence. I'm going to marry her and take care of her."

"Are you?" Her eyes were compassionate. "Well——"

"They won't like it." He jerked his head toward the hidden household. "But you saw her. You know what she's like."

"No, they won't like it. But if you're sure it's what you want——"

"Sure?" At a quick gesture of Ellen's, he turned. His father, in flopping carpet slippers, bore across the room toward him.

"I won't have it, you hear? A son of mine, disgracing us, with that—" Wrinkled eyelids, twisted lips, vein in his temple bulging—why, he was like the face of the house! Ellen caught his brandishing arm.

"John Thurston's made his mind up."

Suddenly John was sorry for him, too, this elderly man in slippers.

"There's no reason why he shouldn't choose his wife, that I know of." Ellen's hand, her voice, were firm.

Thurston dropped into a chair, his eyes moving from his son to Ellen.

"Your mother . . . helpless. You're needed here. Your sister . . . she ought not to have to work. I'm getting on. I can't do what I have done."

"You think I ought to stay and work for you." That was the voice of the house, years of dull service. "That's all I've ever done. Since I was a boy. What chance have you given me, ever? Get Rob to help you." His loud words shouted down his stirring doubt. "He's the one you've helped, all of you." Yes, even Ellen. He wouldn't spare her, for all her fairness. "Tell him what you need. It ought to be his turn now. I'm going. To-morrow, or the next day." He started for the door, and turned. "If I get a good job"—his thin face had a beseeching earnestness, as if he threw a bribe toward some dark god of fortune—"if I do, I'll send you money, all I can. But I got to go." Of course. He could hear that soft voice, "Soon! I am afraid to be so happy!" It was she who had need of him, her need that made him indomitable at last. He stumbled in his haste to reach his room, to plan, to find the stars again.

IX

Ellen helped pack the old carpet bag. Not much to put in it. She folded two handkerchiefs she had hemstitched for Rob; she had picked out the carefully embroidered R in the corners, but there was no time to make another initial. Alice shut herself in her room, refusing to speak to her brother. Ellen wanted to go to the parsonage the

morning of the marriage, but the doctor was coming to see
Grace, and she couldn't get away. She called John Thurston back from the gate to put her arms about his shoulders
and kiss him again. "I hope you'll be happy," she said.
"You write to me."

She had tried just one protest, the evening before. "If
you'd wait a few weeks, till your mother is better, folks
mightn't talk so much."

"I won't hear 'em," said John Thurston. "I can't
wait."

And then: "Why don't you stay right here, where
you've got work and people you know?"

"Here, where even my own folks blame her for what
her mother did? No, we're going away, to a new place."
He had been silent, clenching his hands, the long stubborn
thumbs curving outside the fists, grime-etched. In the
gesture, and in the brooding frown on his high forehead,
Ellen caught a flickering sense of what that new place
meant to him. It was John Thurston's riding away! He
thought he would leave his old self in the familiar village; the unknown new place was a symbol for the future,
limitless in possibilities. Hope and courage in the mystery of some other spot on the earth. Florence, too,
would have that hope. Ellen remembered her pitiful, "I
ought to'v gone farther away."

So Ellen watched him, carpet bag in hand, walk down
the street. Perhaps, if the doctor came in time, she could
get to the railroad station for the westbound train, just to
wish them good luck. She looked in at Grace's door.
John had wanted to say good-by to her, but Ellen thought
it might only excite her. "I don't know how much she
knows of what we say, yet." Why . . . had Grace

moved? Ellen ran toward the bed. Her head was off
the pillow, at a queer angle, and one arm, the long sleeve
of the cotton nightgown pushed up from the deep wrinkle
at the wrist, hung over the edge of the bed. As Ellen
touched the dangling arm, her fingers recoiled. She saw
the line of eyeball under the lids. With an effort she
tugged the figure back on the pillow, and searched for her
heart. No, the tiny cricket was silent. "It may stop at
any moment," the doctor had said. No use to try the
futile stimulants he had left. Ellen straightened the covers, and stared out of the window, at sunlight on gray
branches of a tree. If Grace had waited another hour,
John Thurston would have been gone. Now . . . she
ought to send for him. Getting married, with his mother
just dead. That white, nervous expectancy on his face,
that stubborn fear: "I can't wait. Something might
happen."

"I've got to send word to him." Ellen dragged her feet
across the room. Then she glanced back. How calm
Grace looked, all her little hungers and frettings done with.
It wouldn't matter to her now, who came or went. The
indifference of death marked her with strange dignity.
Slowly Ellen recrossed the room, to stand beside the table
with its bottles, a glass covered with a plate. The quilt
at the foot of the bed, a log cabin pattern in blue, was one
Martha had made. If I just stay here, thought Ellen, and
no one comes . . . for a little while . . . maybe . . . it
isn't decent. . . . If I were dead, I'd want him to go on, if
he wanted to. As if he had imbued her with the fear of
his premonition, as if she sided with him against a slip
of fate, Ellen stood, waited. The house waited, too.
Thurston was down town. Alice still protested her

brother's conduct by a closed door. Time itself seemed sluggish, as if death laid a finger on a swinging pendulum, retarding it. I'm doing a dreadful thing, thought Ellen. I've never done much for John Thurston. And you didn't . . . she glanced at Grace. I ought to feel bad, living with you all these years, and I guess I will miss you. She heard her own heart beat slowly through heavy seconds.

The bell at the front door jangled, startling Ellen. The doctor had come. As she hurried to let him in, she heard, at the crossing below the town, the shrill, distant shriek of the whistle on the westbound train. Now we can't send for him, she thought, with horrified triumph; he didn't even say where they were going!

X

Alice did not go back to her school. For several weeks after her mother's funeral she lay in a darkened room, bandages on her eyes. Dr. Willis shook his head. He didn't know what the trouble was. "You mustn't cry any more about your mother," he said.

"I try not to." Alice reached for a damp handkerchief. "But how can I teach any more?"

"Not this year, I guess."

When he had gone, Alice thought over each word he had said. He didn't sound happy. His voice had sympathy under its bruskness, as if he said, "I realize how sensitive you are, how you suffer." Surely he stayed longer than he had to, lingering beside her.

Ellen came in, with a letter from Rob. He had been full of regret that he couldn't get home in time for his mother's funeral. He'd come some day soon to see them. He was getting on fine, learning the business in the plow factory. Finally, he hoped to be able to marry in another year. Let him know if they needed anything. What did Alice mean about John Thurston? What had he done?

"What did you say to him?" Ellen asked.

"I told him the shock killed mother."

"But she didn't know a thing about it!"

"You don't know what she knew. She felt it happening, such a disgrace. And that morning. . . ."

"If you'd get up, instead of lying here, you wouldn't have such notions." Alice heard the angry plump of Ellen's feet on the stairs. She wept a little. Ellen was hard as iron, and now there was no one . . . she could hear the "ts . . . ts . . ." of sympathy her mother had always given. Still . . . Dr. Willis. "Yes, I shall always be your friend." The bandage hid the hard world, and behind it strange pictures drifted.

The next day Alice waited for the sound of the doctor's wheels in the gravel at the front gate. At night when Ellen brought her supper she asked, "Did the doctor come to-day . . . I forget . . . the hours are all alike."

"Of course he didn't. Here, that's soup. Don't spill it."

"My head is worse to-night."

"He said he'd be in to-morrow."

The next morning Alice waited again. If she laid her fingers on her eyeballs, green rings swung against blackness, with orange spots slipping through the rings. She'd tell him that. Someone was talking in the hall below. She crept out of bed, feeling her way across the room, pushing the bandage up from one eye enough to peer at dim shapes.

"Is there anything really wrong with her?" Ellen, in an undertone.

"Miss Dacey, you know as well as I do. She's the kind that gets a good time out of being miserable."

Alice clutched at the door, her head rocking in a whirl of fury.

"What about her eyes?"

"If she'd let them alone, they'd be all right, too, so far as I can see. There's no use my coming any more. I don't like to charge you for nothing."

Something further, so low that Alice could not catch it. She fled back to bed, and lay rigid, her hands in tight balls. To the inquiry of the doctor . . . oh, Ellen had poisoned him against her! . . . she said, coldly, "I'm going to the city to consult a real oculist. I can't waste more time." He pried off the bandage; she shivered at his cruel fingers. "They're not so inflamed. Go on bathing them." He turned away. Had he seen the loathing in them, for his treachery?

When he had gone, Alice wept again. Only for a short time, as her tears were unobserved. She would get up, ill as she was, rather than lie helpless while Ellen maligned her. Rising, dressing, was a series of tasks full of indecisions. Something had snapped the string of habits that bound her to ordinary life, and each step in the process . . . washing, brushing her hair, putting on garments . . . was like a loose bead rolling away from her fingers. In the days that followed, the beads rolled farther, and her mind had to pick them out of dusty cracks. Should she brush her teeth to-day, or was it

enough that she had done it yesterday? She buttoned
one shoe, and there was the other, with its long row of
gaping button holes. Tasks all so complicated and weari-
some, once you began to think of them. She sat in her
mother's chair in the dining room, as Ellen had not yet
set up the stove in the living room, resenting Ellen's
methodical bustle through the house.

"Why don't you find something to do?" Ellen would
ask.

Alice shrugged her narrow shoulders under the black
wool dress. "It hurts my eyes to read or sew."

"Get outdoors, then. It's a fine day. Walk over
town."

Alice considered such a walk. That meant getting her
coat from the closet, brushing it, putting on a hat, going
out through the door, setting her feet down, one before
the other. She felt herself reaching the main street.
To-morrow she might go. Not to-day. Ellen only wanted
to be rid of her.

One afternoon she did start out. Little flurries of
November snow pricked her cheeks, blew like sand in ripples along the walks. In the window of the small hotel
sat a strange man, his chair tipped back. He stared at
her. Alice ducked her head to peer back. Bold eyes, following her. Her heart quickened. He wanted to speak
to her, yes, he had left his chair. He needn't think she
would pick up a stranger that way. She hurried on, pleas-
urably thrilled. Another day the grocer brushed her
hand as he dropped a package into her bag. She jerked
her hand back, her eyelids fluttering. She walked home
with an exaggerated mince that swung her skirts about
her overshoes. The grocer was married. Even if he did

admire her, he shouldn't make advances. She longed to
tell someone about her adventures. She did say to Ellen:
"I just hate to walk past that hotel, with all the men
ogling me through the window," but there was too little
sympathy in the way Ellen crinkled her nose for Alice to
say more. Of course Ellen was so old. She couldn't
understand. But if Alice weren't a good woman . . . if,
for example, she was like that creature John Thurston
had run off with. . . .

She began to go to church. As she prayed long, devout
prayers, she felt admiring eyes on the back of her head.
Just whose they were, her sidewise glances sometimes
failed to determine. Then she prayed again, to be forgiven for such thoughts in church. Sometimes at night
she woke with her heart beating so that she felt it in her
back, against the mattress. But by morning she never
could recall what her dream had been.

XI

Ellen found that winter the longest she had known for
years, since her youth had counted time in dragging days.
She missed Grace; after all, she had been easy to get on
with, and somehow . . . Ellen's thought was vague . . .
she had made a reasonable household. Or was it John
Thurston that Ellen missed? There had, at least, been
some kind of orderly life, with him going and coming,
with a wife for Thurston and a mother for Alice. Now
things felt at sixes and sevens. Thurston was by turn
moody and excited. He had some new project for growing rich; it was all Ellen could do to get money out of him
for the house bills. Yet she was sure he had more money;

there had been that talk of increased pension, and accumulated back pay. And Alice . . . Ellen sniffed. She got queerer every day. She'd never been exactly neat, but now her room was always in a mess, and her clothes! Ellen had carried off the black wool dress to sponge the grease spots from the front breadth, but in a few days it looked as bad as ever. Alice didn't seem to have any interest in anything.

One letter came from John Thurston, marked Chicago. He thought they might stay there a while; he had a job driving a horse car. Florence was well and sent her love to Ellen. Chicago was a big town, very different from Coldspring, but he thought he would like it there.

Ellen wrote to him, care of general delivery. She spoke of his mother's death, "soon after you went." She sent him news of Rob. Of Alice and Thurston she said nothing. She hoped he'd write soon again.

There were new neighbors at the left, with children. Ellen watched the little boy playing in the snow. Dark, like Robby, but not so strong and handsome. An' Telly . . . Why, she'd never thought he'd be gone so long. She might not have driven Thurston into sending him. More than ten years. They made a wall of strangeness through which she could not see him. Ten years of a different life. Ellen tried to think how Rob must feel, now. If you stay so far and so long away from your own people, you forget you belong to them. And yet, he was building his own life well. I'm just lonely, thought Ellen. I need somebody to think about. She wrote, saying they hoped he'd bring his wife to visit in the spring. Then she looked about the shabby rooms. He might not wish to bring a new wife there. He might even be ashamed of them, an

old aunt, a sister . . . she didn't finish her thought of
Alice . . . a father whose only moments of grandeur
and dignity were when he wore his uniform to a meeting
of the new lodge he'd joined.

She watched for the coming of spring with a wistful-
ness which caught at every sign of thaws, of rains, of
changing skies. The first crocus, before the snow had
really gone, might have flowered out of her own heart.
She caught cold, running bareheaded out to beat the carpets in a frenzy of spring cleaning, and for several days
went about with aching body and heavy head, in a muffled panic. Suppose she were really sick! She felt the
household fly to bits, like spokes of a rimless wheel. By
the time the man had plowed the garden she felt better.
She helped with the planting, kneeling to pat the moist
earth over seeds with firm hands.

Rob was married on Easter Sunday. He wrote that
he couldn't come so far as Coldspring, that his father-in-
law was giving them a honeymoon at Niagara Falls, but
he had to get back to work in a week. Ellen looked at
the shiny cardboard picture he enclosed . . . a new kind
of picture, much more stylish than a tintype . . . of his
wife. Perhaps she was pretty, her eyes stared under a
pale halo of frizzed bangs. Niagara Falls. Oh, if he
came as far as that!

Alice said, "I don't see what he sees in her."

"Her folks are well fixed," said Thurston. "He wants
to look out, though. He's flying pretty high. Neglecting
his own folks. Who sent him away to college, I'd like
to know, and gave him his start? What thanks have I
ever got for that?"

Ellen looked at her brother, grimly. After a moment

she said, "He can't very well come so far, with his work.
He'll come later, he says."

"It would make a lot of work, entertaining a stranger.
She looks stuck up, too." Alice sighed.

Ellen carried letter and photograph upstairs, to lay
them in a box with Rob's other letters, with a little tin-
type of Rob at twelve, a soft curl of brown hair tied with
a bit of red yarn. I'd like to see her, she thought. I
can't tell from this.

XII

Summer wheeled past with heat and dust and thunder
showers and maturing gardens. Ellen found drama in her
conflict with potato bugs and pea lice. As the evenings
began to shorten she sighed, regretting the swift season.
The little boy next door grew friendly. "Now, Miss
Dacey," his mother called across the fence, "if he bothers
you, you send him right home. He can be such a
nuisance!" Ellen tempted him with ginger bread men,
raisin-eyed, such as she had made for Robby years ago. It
would have been nice, she thought, if Robby could have
settled next door. One night she watched the evening
star, steady and golden in the opaque pallor of the sky
near the horizon, recalling suddenly nights in her youth
when she had stood under a great oak tree, watching western stars, with all her longing reaching past that distant
western horizon into the mysterious country where
Matthew had disappeared. Now her heart stretched east-
ward. All her life she'd lived here, in Coldspring, while
her love was dragged across a continent. She could
almost see it, a fine silver thread of longing. Suppose
Matthew had stayed. The star was sinking, larger, red-

gold as it dropped. Her own children would be gone,
now. She folded her strong, work-hardened hands; if
she gazed steadily at the darkening sky, she could see
another star. Queer, how you made your life out of other
people. From the minute you were born, you seemed
entangled with them, nothing apart from them. They
died, one after the other, or rode away, or grew up, and
here you were, yourself. Whatever that might be. Ellen
looked at her hands, a blur in the twilight. You don't like
to have to know how lonesome life is, her thought moved
slowly on. If you can keep enough folks to love. . . . The
evening star had gone and in the deepened blue of the sky
others showed, small and brilliant. Well . . . Ellen rose;
it was too cool to sit there longer. Somehow, from her
drifting thoughts, had come serenity, as if, cutting through
longing into an admission of solitude, she gave firm
ground to her feet.

She had need of firm ground somewhere during the
winter that followed. Thurston grumbled that times were
hard again, that expenses must be cut down.

"You've got a good pension, Thurston. I can't run
the house on nothing."

"My money's my affair, not a woman's. I'll see to the
bills." He scowled. "I won't be bothered. I've got
something big brewing." He shut himself into his study
until the weather grew bitter. When he appeared, he
always rushed, hurrying up the street with muffler and
arms waving.

A new doctor had come to town, young, sympathetic,
and for some weeks Alice was interested in a new malady,
something wrong with her heart. His bill arrived, and
Thurston, chewing his lip, said he couldn't spare a cent

just then; the man could wait. He came less willingly,
and Ellen noticed that Alice forgot to lose her breath half
way up the stairs, to sink down, one hand on her heart.

Another letter from John Thurston, from Arkansas.
Florence wasn't so well, and they were moving away from
cold weather. She had a bad cough. He hoped they were
well. In February, a letter from Rob; his wife's father
had died, her mother had gone to live with an older sister
near Albany. There was valuable property not far from
New York, on the Sound, and they talked of moving to
the old house there, if he could transfer the business from
Bridgeport. He was afraid his wife might be lonely
there. Perhaps some day Ellen could visit them. They
expected a child in the early summer. Ellen answered that
she was afraid that was too long a trip for her. For days
the letter glowed in her thoughts. Robby had, however
slightly, given her a sign; for the first time, as he strode
up through his distant, unimaginable life, he had turned
to call back to her.

She boasted a little, at a church supper. Her nephew
in the east wanted her to pay him a visit. Well, she
wasn't sure whether she would go or not. She wasn't
much of a traveller. Alice wasn't strong; she didn't know
as she ought to leave her niece and her brother. But
Rob's letter made a part of the slow on-coming of another
spring.

At the end of March Ellen's vague anxiety about Thurston's affairs struck substance. She had stopped at the
grocery store to order a barrel of flour, and old Mr. Case,
pushing his glasses up his forehead and growing red,
had said, "I hate to mention it, Miss Ellen, but there's
that bill. If you could pay something on it. Dacey

credit's good, but what with the winter and all. You know how it is, I need some cash."

"I thought my brother—" Ellen stopped, as someone entered the store.

"He's overlooked it." Mr. Case rubbed his hands, relieved he had spoken out. "Just a word to him. . . ."

Ellen hurried home, indignation in her step. All her life she'd lived here, and never before had anyone had to ask for a bill. Oh, Thurston shouldn't humiliate her. Her helplessness screwed her anger into a higher pitch. The money was his, but hadn't she worked?

She found him in the dining room, hands under his coat tails, stopping his pacing as she entered. As she looked at him, her anger dropped into a clutch of fear. He sat down, hands trembling between his knees, his mouth sagging under his long gray moustache. "You've heard, then? Over town? Everybody knows, eh?"

"No." Ellen waited.

"I wrote to John and to Rob. I've done enough for them. They can take a hand now." He dragged one hand across his forehead. "It was a sure thing, Ellen. I meant to be a rich man again. And now—" he flung his hands out as if he let the whole world slide from them. "The bottom's out."

The bottom was out, all right. Ellen picked up details slowly. Even the house they lived in was gone. Oil wells, a silver mine in Peru. She didn't quite know how those distant ventures sucked up a house in Coldspring. Notes Thurston had signed. "I meant to be rich," he repeated.

"You haven't anything, is that it? You even owe . . . how much do you owe?"

"I'll talk that over with Rob or John. You wouldn't understand," he blustered, climbing into a battered piece of male armor.

Three of them, penniless, impotent. Ellen climbed the stairs to her own room, refusing for once the brief anodyne of household tasks. If they wanted supper, they could get it. She stood in the middle of her bare, spotless room, and thought: I'm sixty-three years old. I haven't a roof nor a penny. I'm too old to go out to work; folks wouldn't have me, strong as I am. Shame, more bitter than anything she had ever tasted, curled the tips of her nerves, choked in her throat. A beggar, waiting for charity. The county poor farm, where old women huddled in the sun, while shame dried up in their faded eyes, waiting to die. She fumbled to a chair, her whole body sick with rejection.

This has happened because I am a woman, she thought, finally. First the farm, her father's place, which she herself had helped to hew out of wild timber land. Her father had had his own way about that. She saw it, like a tiny colored picture, very distant. One of Swanson's boys had a dairy farm there. Thurston had lost that. Then her brief hour of independence, when Matthew's bankbook—her hand moved toward her breast; for years she had not thought of that comforting prod of the corner of the little book. Thurston had destroyed that independence, wantonly, because she was a woman. "If I should tell Robby"—her thought crawled—"how it was I made his father send him—" Oh, shame, shame, that she should try to find a chain to bind herself, an undesired burden, to the boy. Thurston's sons would help him; that was their duty, being sons. Alice was their sister.

"And me?" Her mouth was parched. "Doling me out something for bread. Oh, God! If I could die, I'd have a grave to call my own then." That was a wicked thought, and she wasn't likely to die, not for quite a while, she thought grimly. "In my Father's House are many mansions" . . . was that her mother's voice, dropping the words? Small comfort right now. She lifted her face; under the smooth bands of gray hair, her eyes were bright and dry with pain.

Later that night Thurston came to her door, a paper in his hand.

"From Rob. A telegram message. He's coming."

Ellen stumbled to her feet, stiff, and laid a hand on the yellow paper. Not Rob's writing. No, it couldn't be, sent over thin wires so far. It said, "Letter received. Will come at once. Robert."

The house must be set in order. Ellen even drove Alice into a kind of slovenly activity. She almost forgot, for moments, why Rob was coming. At least she would see him, touch him. An hour, perhaps, of greeting and talk, before he realized what she was. He might call her An' Telly, might remember the little boy who had loved her. Just for a little time. Then he'd know her for an old woman, a burden.

XIII

The morning that Rob was due, Thurston came downstairs in his blue uniform. Ellen stared at him.

"There's a meeting this afternoon." He brushed lint from the braided cuff. "It looks better than my suit." He went off, his stiff shoulder high, his arms swinging.

"The poor old fool," thought Ellen. "He's Captain Dacey in that, and that's all he's got left."

She waited at the front door, watching the fine silver of April rain shine between her and dark tree trunks, between her and wet gray roofs. He's coming. Her heart made an irregular tattoo under the white net she had folded about the neck of her dark wool dress. Coming. The whistle of the train at the siding swayed her against the door, half faint, as if her heavy body stood there while all her longing swept down the street to meet him.

He came. Her first glance saw a stranger, tall, in unfamiliar clothes, spectacles, with serious firm mouth. He took the steps in a bound and hugged her. It was Robby, strong and solid. "Well, An' Telly!" When he smiled, square teeth showing, he lost that important seriousness.

As they went through the house, she saw his quick, hard glance at everything. He had forgotten, all these years. Did he find pieces of himself in the old shabbiness? One instant she had him, her Robby, and then he disappeared behind the stranger who frowned about.

"Say, something smells good!" He had his arm through hers. "I bet you planned a good dinner for me. Now I tell you—" he hesitated. "I have to go back to-night. I want to find out what Father's been up to I'll go talk to him."

Ellen heard the study door close upon them. Exhaustion crept through her limbs; she had consumed herself in anticipation, and now the brief moment of encounter was ended. She must see to dinner. She went slowly about the tasks: burnt offerings before an idol with blind eyes. She had remembered every dish that Robby used to like. Perhaps he had changed—new ways. If she knew what they were saying behind that door!

Dinner, with rushes of conversation and awkward lulls. Alice told about her eyes, her heart, and how she'd had to give up teaching. "We thought you must have forgotten your folks, you stayed away so long." Thurston blustered about the changes in the village, about old neighbors. Ellen felt his bluster as a struggle to drag his feet out of the quagmire of chagrin into which Rob had driven him. Rob talked a little of his business, his wife, New York. Ellen scarcely heard what he said. He was again a stranger, assured, with an air of other worlds about him, an alien in this house of shabby, ageing things and people. If he were sick, or poor; if he had any need of her. Why, she was almost wishing him ill luck, just a chink through his wall of prosperous maturity through which she could glimpse the child.

After dinner he followed her into the kitchen, lounging against a cupboard, hands in his pockets.

"Well, An' Telly." Ellen dared not turn, lest he see the foolish tears in her eyes. "Why didn't you tell me what was going on?"

She could only shake her head.

"We had a bad hour. He tried to bluff, but he realized finally that I'm not the young simpleton I was when I left this town. He's gone through everything, and he'd do the same thing to-morrow if he had a cent. He needs a guardian. You don't know where John Thurston is, he says."

"Not exactly." Ellen hesitated. "But he can't have much."

"Um." On Rob's face lay a bland superiority. "Too bad he married that way."

"He helped a lot, before he went away."

"Of course I wasn't in a position then to do much." Rob straightened his tall body, flicking with a finger at the gold loop of watch chain across his vest. "Now I am. Father doesn't want to come east, but I don't see what else to do. I can't run a house here and my own too. And there's no house here, anyway."

"You'll take him back with you? He's got enough, with his pension, if he'd let someone manage it for him. Enough for Alice, too." Ellen spoke with sternness. Rob must be fair; that tinge of complacency bothered her. "He is your father, and he gave you your start."

"Certainly." Rob was curt; no one need tell him his duty. "But I never knew. . . ." He looked at Ellen, his head lowered, his eyes magnified under his spectacles. "How you made him do it."

The kitchen was a black whirl about Ellen, in which she groped toward a chair. Tell him, now's your chance. She set her lips stiffly against her prodding, hungry self.

"I tried to get it out of him to-day. He rubbed it in about how he had to scrape to get the money, and that's all he'd say. What'd you do?"

"I . . . just persuaded him." Ellen sat down in the chair her hand had found. At Rob's laugh the blackness retreated slowly, and she could see his face again, strong square teeth gleaming at her. She gave a long sigh. At least she had kept herself decent.

"Good ole An' Telly!" Rob's glance wandered about the kitchen. "It was right here in this room you decided

I'd go, wasn't it? Only you've got a different color paint now. How soon can you get packed up?"

"Me?" Ellen pressed her elbows to her sides to keep her hands from shaking. "I can manage here. You don't need——"

"We've got a huge house. The old Vleet place, that was Mary's share when her father died. I've wondered if you'd like to come there. I wrote you once. It's lonely for Mary, and now, with the baby coming . . . I've told Mary a lot about you, and she thinks you're fine. I hadn't planned on taking them too"—he jerked his head toward the door—"but it's a big house, and they're my folks. We'd have to have you to manage things."

Ellen let her hands slide forward, work-calloused palms up. "You don't have to have me," she insisted.

"No?" Why, he was young Robby again, jeering at her, his hand on her shoulder. "An' Telly! You aren't crying!"

"Did you ever see me cry?" She sat erect, away from his touch. "Are you sure?" Oh, how could she be sure! If this was charity, or pity, or a kind of necessary gratitude, she couldn't have it. "Sure you thought of me coming before your father sent for you? There's plenty I can find to do——"

"Don't you want to come?" He frowned, flicking again at his chain. "I thought you'd like it, and I'd like my kids to have an An' Telly."

Ellen had to believe him. A clear wind was scattering the ashes of shame from her head. He was so young, and a man. How could he speak a word of perfect reassurance, when he had never tasted, even on the tip

of his tongue, the bitterness she had been drinking? "I
want to come." His children, and work for her to do.

"Well, then?" That familiar impatience of his . . .
the little boy, tugging at her skirts. . . . "It's settled?"

Suddenly in the old kitchen, the ten years of strangeness
seemed to matter not at all. It was Robby, saying that
he wanted her. Ellen let the ragged shreds of doubt
flutter away. "Yes, I'll be real glad to come," she said.

BOOK III

PART I

I

Ellen woke, her breath quickened in momentary panic at a strangeness in the dark. That sound, insistent, faint, unlike the familiar sound of wind. Water, lipping at yellow sand. Every night it woke her, creeping under her dreams. Lifting her head she saw through branches of trees the inverted red crescent of an old moon just rising, with glimmers among the leaves where the sea caught its dull light. She was foolish to mind that small noise, but it seemed to wake her deliberately, to remind her where she was, how far from still inland nights with no voice of water.

I'll get used to it. She lay down again, hands quiet over her breast, her eyelids held too firmly over her eyes. Five weeks now. She hadn't known she cared much about Coldspring until she came to pry herself out. Perhaps the place you grew up in always grew into you. There had been moments, when she cleaned out the attic, burning old things, when neighbors dropped in to say good-by, moments when she thought she couldn't finish that uprooting. Nothing else was possible, and Robby had said he wanted them, wanted her. The change had been good for Alice; moving her a thousand miles had fanned the ashes off some hidden embers. Thurston still floundered, subdued, uncertain of his step.

177

And Ellen. . . . Under her eyelids she could see the water, in long dark ripples on the sand, could see the house, large, brown, with its queer third story and roof. French, Robby said. She could almost see herself lying behind the concave wall at the corner. "If you don't mind the stairs," Mary, Rob's wife, had said, "that's much the best room."

Five weeks. Rob was busy, so busy that having met them at New York, from which Ellen, who had been train-sick, had no impression beyond that of mortification and bewilderment, and convoyed them by train and hack to his house, he then turned into an important, engrossed young man who scarcely saw them. His wife. . . . Ellen wondered whether the mixture of Danish and Dutch blood made Mary Vleet Dacey different. She wasn't a foreigner, of course. Her people had been around New York and the Sound for generations. I can't make her out, Ellen admitted to herself. I don't know her a bit better than the day I came. Lots of women would have been more offish than she was, with so many relatives of their husbands dumped suddenly on them. Mary wasn't offish, but she wasn't really friendly. Under her fair, youthful prettiness she had a streak of hardness. Well, it was natural for her to be absorbed, with her first baby coming soon. She was pretty, or would be, again, later, with her small neat bones under creamy skin, and her soft hair the color of ripe wheat. She admired Robby; Ellen had detected her pride. She had no mind to share him. These strangers whom her house must shelter could stay outside the charmed circle of her love for him. Perhaps Robby had glanced across that circle inquiringly the first day or so. Was An' Telly comfortable? Was she going to like her transplanting? Then he had settled into a sort of emotional invisibility.

For all Mary looked so young and almost helpless, she had her own ideas about how everything should be done, ideas alien to Ellen's life. Mary had been brought up differently. Money, a select boarding school, society. The house had elegance; slender legged mahogany furniture, her grandmother's from Denmark. She used her good linen and silver common. Had her meals served in courses, instead of put on the table so you could see what you were going to like best. No wonder the hired girls, two of them, maids she called them, didn't have time to clean decently. Ellen found whiskers in the corners of her room, and swept it herself, surreptitiously. Well, ways like that might be all right, provided Robby could make money enough. They left Ellen stranded on a rock of ineptness; she didn't even know how silver should be laid on the table. She sighed, and tried to drag the frayed edges of sleep about her thoughts. After she grew more used to things, perhaps she could find more to do. The sound of the water filled her room, as if the waves reached to the walls of the house.

A few weeks later, a mild hazy night of late August, even Ellen forgot the sound of water under the other sounds with which the house was filled. Childbirth, thought Ellen, submitted to no bewildering refinements. Doctors, the rustling step of a nurse, the clean sharp odor of disinfectants, the sweet smell of chloroform drifting down the hall. Ellen made coffee for Robby. He was a boy, nuzzling at her shoulder in the kitchen, his pompous-

ness stripped off, his charmed circle broken. "Lord, I'm
glad you're here. Why, she's only a girl, Mary is.
An' Telly, I never knew it was so damned awful!"

"There's things men don't know." Ellen smoothed his
hair with a gentle palm. "It'll be over. You stay here
and I'll see if I can do anything."

As she closed the door of the kitchen she found Alice,
bathrobe twisted in nervous hands, nostrils wide in fear
and curiosity. "Is she dying, Ellen?" Her scanty, fair
hair strained back from her forehead. "I couldn't sleep."

"Don't be foolish. Go back to bed."

"But she's not screaming any more."

"That's good." Ellen pushed Alice toward the stairs.
"This is no place for you." She saw the prim, shocked
look fold over the fearful curiosity in Alice's face as she
shuffled out of sight.

Hours later the child was born, with dawn a smoky
crimson over the sea and eastern sky. A girl, in spite
of Mary's determination to have a son, a girl with a comical tuft of black hair on her scarlet, wrinkled head.

"Can you take it?" The nurse gave it, squirming, to
Ellen. "She's all right, but her mother——"

So Ellen had Anne Dacey for her first difficult hour
of life. When she had bathed her and pinned various
bands into place, and folded soft white wool about her,
she sat with the bundle on her knees. Slowly she lifted
one finger and laid it delicately against the soft tiny head,
with its astonishing tuft of dark hair, against the soft,
rapid pulsation of the skull. With that beating at her
finger tip, a kind of ecstacy crept into Ellen, as if life
and growth entered her, as if her emptiness shrivelled at
the touch of this new thing.

Days, then, before they were sure that Mary would live. Fever, lacerations, delirium. The nurse was glad enough to leave the baby in Ellen's hands. Rob stared in sulky amazement at the small thing that could so upset his household, threaten his wife.

"There's no use your hiring a stranger to take care of the baby." Fear leaped under Ellen's cursory words. "I've nothing else to do." She had moved the cradle to her third-story room. If young Anne cried there, she would not disturb her mother. Rob was indifferent. Between his absorption in the new branch of the factory and his concern for his wife, he had not as yet recognized in the infant any emotional claimant. Mary couldn't nurse the baby. Ellen was ashamed of her delight, but the baby seemed more completely hers. When, in November, Mary at last could come downstairs, a fragile Mary with tracings of blue veins on her temples under the pale hair, her interest in her daughter was decorative rather than maternal. "She is a pretty baby, isn't she?" Dark eyes under long lashes, and dark fuzz all over the small head. "She likes you better than her mother, Ellen!"

"She's just used to me." Ellen rescued her as the eyelids puckered in the preliminary stages of a wail. "She's good as well as pretty."

"Lucky for her she's got an An' Telly." Mary relaxed in her cushions. "I haven't strength enough to lift her, even yet."

Ellen could not have explained her devotion. She had loved Robby, but she was younger then, with more sidetracking for her interests. Now, when she woke at night it was not to the sound of water, but to the quick, light breath of the baby in the cradle close to her own bed.

Pushing the wicker perambulator along the cinder path
through the November woods, with brown leaves rustling
underfoot, she lost her dislike of the coming winter,
thinking: with a warmer blanket, I could take her out
even when snow comes. Rob, driving home early one
frosty Saturday, met them near the gate and pulled up
his horse. "Say, she's getting human looking, isn't she?"

"Robby! She's the handsomest child I ever saw!"

"She's got a handsome aunt, anyway." Rob stared
down from his seat. "Getting younger every day, too.
How do you do it?" and then, "You like it here, don't
you?"

"Yes." Ellen's hands trembled on the handle of the
baby carriage. Like it? Why, it was her life.

"Wonderful for Mary, having you. The poor girl . . .
but she's getting on, too." He drove on toward the
house.

Ellen wheeled the baby after him, a serene content in
her step. Younger? She had forgotten how old and
dried up she had felt. Years ahead of her, while this
young thing grew up. Grew up to be a woman. . . .
Ellen felt a prickle along her spine, like fur standing on
end. She would forge some armor for Anne, from the
steel of her own hard years.

II

In the spring Mary gave a tea, a formal announcement
that she was again of the world. Sandwiches and cake
from a caterer's, an extravagance at which Alice pursed
her lips. A frilled cap and apron for the second maid.
Mary herself in blue silk with real lace in a frill from

the high, boned collar. Alice had a new dress. Ellen
had. watched for the long envelope with Thurston's pension check and waylaid him. "Mary is beginning to have
company, and Alice ought to go. You must give her
some money. You don't want your daughter threadbare,
and certainly Rob's doing enough." Thurston wriggled;
he had some obligations. But Ellen was firm. Alice
had been much better, until the long, dull winter had
slack'ened her response to the new situation; Ellen saw
her developing sensitive feelings again, leaving the table
in tears, shutting her door for a day. Since Mary's
strong sense of decorum included her sister-in-law's
presence, Ellen was determined to keep Alice out of 'her
burrow. Mary helped select the dress. If Ellen, seeing
them together, thought that Alice's faded blondness was
a parody of lean years on Mary's pale gold and blue fra-
gility, Alice seemed excitedly unaware.

Carriages grating on the cindery lane, rustle of silk,
quiver of maribou and ostrich, whiffs of scent from lace-
edged handkerchiefs in white-gloved hands, medley of
voices. Ellen must bring in the baby. She sat on her
mother's knee, her dark eyes wide and sober, while ohs
and ahs and isn't she too sweets fluttered about her. Ellen
was relieved when a gloved finger presuming against her
cheek brought a loud wail, so that Ellen was free to carry
her out. "Didn't like it, did you?" She tied the bonnet
under the small chin. "No more did I." She laughed
at the funny change of quiver into toothless smile.

Outside, along the path, the rows of daffodils were
already crisping into tarnished paper flowers. Ellen
watched the man from the town nursery setting out a
bed of tulips. Spring had a new savor this year, salty

like the wind from the Sound, strong on the tongue. No patting of soil around withered roots. Anne was bouncing against the strap, with little gasps to incite Ellen into entrancing motion. Ellen wheeled her around the house, past the bed of perennials taller since yesterday, to the rough path which edged the wood above the water. There no flattering guests would discover them. Ellen had a suspicion that Anne at six months might absorb their fulsome admiration, and she wouldn't have her baby spoiled if she could help it. A feather of smoke at the horizon from a steamer, a gull with wings flashing silver as it wheeled in the sunlight. Ellen suddenly liked the ocean. It stretched spring to a further horizon, in the soft tones of blue on its windless surface.

III

The new rector and his wife had been conspicuous guests at Mary's tea, and the following Sunday Alice rustled into the hall in her blue silk, her face small and flushed between the huge puffs of sleeves. Ellen saw Rob's glance make inquiry of Mary.

"I can walk." Alice drew on one black lace glove. "If you haven't room."

"Of course there's room. I didn't know you cared to go." Mary was punctilious.

As they drove away, Ellen, left to a sunlit morning with Anne, wondered whether some new notion had sprouted in Alice's head.

As the weeks warmed into summer Ellen, absorbed in the cycle of changes in her baby, thought of Alice only that it was fine the way she was taking an interest in things. Church every Sunday, devout attention to her new prayer book. The Welfare Workers Guild on Wednesdays . . . she walked the distance to town and back even when the heat of July glassed the Sound. In August, when the rector had his vacation, Alice went the first Sunday to hear his substitute.

"He's much less spiritual than our own rector," she complained at dinner.

"Barton's spiritual, all right." Rob grinned over his dexterous serving of thin slices of rare roast beef. "He looks to me as if his liver and other unmentionable organs got left out when he got created. That too rare for you?"

"Rob!" warned Mary, with a discreet glance at the maid.

Alice flung a hand up to her cheek; it left white streaks along her sudden scarlet as she shook it at her brother, while she stumbled up from her chair. "You are given over to carnal things," she cried. "Like all men. What do you know of spiritual things?" She vanished on a wave of rage.

"She's probably right." Rob was intent on his serving, but Ellen shared his discomfort at the expression of Mary's fine brows.

The later Sundays in that month Alice had headaches which kept her at home.

Rob's vacation came in September. He begged Mary to go away with him. They could take a boat up the river to Albany, see her mother, and spend a week in the mountains. Mary demurred properly at leaving her baby and household.

"But Ellen is here!" Ellen was afraid he might make her seem so competent that Mary's pride would keep her at home.

"I ought not to leave the baby, but Rob doesn't want

to take her." Ellen said nothing, and presently Mary was
planning her wardrobe for the trip. She decided to give
the second girl a holiday, too. With so small a household,
one woman in the kitchen would be enough.

Ellen expanded in guilty pleasure when Rob and Mary
had driven off in the station hack. A fortnight of blue
September days, with wind in the drying leaves and
feather-tipped waves on the Sound.

"It's like old times, eh?" Thurston took Rob's seat
at the table, diminished by two leaves. "We might be
in Coldspring, except for the baby." Was he homesick?
Ellen realized how little heed she had paid him this year.
In Coldspring his shadow, however vacillating, had dominated the household, and here. . . . She scarcely knew
what he did with his days.

On Sunday Alice dressed for church. By nine o'clock
the water of the Sound held an uneasy coppery reflection
of the sky, and gusts of wind snapped at the tree tops.
"You better wait." Ellen came to the window, Anne's
fist shut about her finger, while her feet plumped along in
the unsteady arcs of her new game, walking. "That looks
like a real storm."

Alice thought not. Just a fall wind. Even as she
spoke a wall of shining steel between water and sky moved
swiftly toward them and hurled itself at the house. "I'm
glad you hadn't started." Ellen lifted Anne shoulder high
to watch the dark flood of rain.

"This place is no better than a prison, so far from
town." Alice raised her voice in a wail of frustration.
"I'm not going to stand it much longer. If you weren't
such a slave to that child, you'd know how unendur-
able. . . ." With a flounce of her long skirts she hurried
out of the room.

"I suppose she can't help being that way," said Ellen.
"You'd have an easier row ahead of you if you'd chosen
to be a boy, young lady. Whoa, there. Want to get
down?" She set the bundle of squirms firmly on its feet
and followed the tug of small fingers on a fascinating
exploration of the house. "She was always sort of
la-di-la, even at your age," she continued, and then laughed
at Anne's chant of "wa-di-wa-di. . ."

Later in the week Ellen pushed the wicker baby carriage
along the lane, looking at sunlight through yellowed, thinning leaves, when she saw coming toward her, like a moving tree trunk, a man; the rector, his black solemn in the
golden light. He stopped, sweeping off his broad hat, his
gray hair stiff above a high, narrow forehead.

"Ah, this is Miss Dacey." Ellen disliked his careful, deep voice, and his finger under Anne's chin.
"And you"—he straightened—"you must be the good
aunt."

"I'm Ellen Dacey."

"Ah, yes. I haven't seen you at service, have I?"

"I'm not an Episcopalian." Ellen's air said, "Take
that!" but the rector's next "Ah!" was commiserating.

"A lovely place." He glanced toward the house. "A
lovely day. What a charming baby!" Ellen saw no
chance there to satisfy her desire to contradict him. He
was edging past her. "I shall find the rest of the household?"

Ellen reluctantly turned the cart. "Mrs. Dacey is
away," she said. "If you care to sit down, after your
walk——"

"But Miss Dacey. Let's see, she is your, ah——"

"Niece. She's in."

He walked beside her, lifting his narrow, long face

ostentatiously, Ellen thought, murmuring things about
the glories of the fleeting year. Then, cautiously, "Miss
Dacey, your niece, has had a tragic life. She is a brave
little woman."

"Alice?" Ellen pushed the cart ahead, in order to see
around the line of gray hair and flat white ear. "She's
had no worse than most in this world."

"Ah, I'm afraid you're a pessimist." He wagged a
reproachful finger. "The death of her fiancé, the loss
of her fortune. Such trials make noble women, I tell
her."

Ellen felt a crimson shock spread to her forehead.

"Was it just before you came east to join your good
brother?"

"I don't know when it was."

"She needs human sympathy."

Ellen shoved the carriage rapidly ahead. The rector
lengthened his stride. I better get in the house, thought
Ellen, or I'll let her down flat. The poor simpleton!

"You'll tell her I'm here?" He settled into a porch
chair, unfolding a large square of white linen. "No. I
am comfortable here." His whole air rebuked Ellen for
her hardness. She backed the perambulator into the hall
and lifted out Anne, who struggled to escape to the porch
for more of this ingratiating stranger. Ellen hesitated a
moment, one arm about the child, her eyes on the stairway. Then she went through the house in search of
Katie. Katie left her afternoon chore of polishing silver
to tell Miss Alice Dacey that the rector waited for her
on the porch. She came back after quarter of an hour,
grinning.

"She was real excited, and wanted I should help her into

her good dress." Ellen went on spooning bread and milk into Anne's round mouth. "Now she wants some tea made. There ain't much for tea."

"Bread and butter will do." Ellen kept to herself her thought: he looks dyspeptic.

When Katie disappeared with the tray, Anne decided to follow. "See man!" she insisted, in spite of Ellen's divertissements. Finally Ellen carried her, shrieking, up the rear stairs to their corner room. When, presently, she had yielded to the blandishments of a woolly dog, Ellen sat down at the window. "I suppose he'd think you had a tragic life, too," she said. Suddenly she gave a loud snort, which brought Anne to her knees, thumping the battered dog. "She's borrowed Matthew! What next?"

When Anne had gone to sleep, the dog tucked beside her, its shoe-button eye shinily alert, Ellen looked down at her, hazy thoughts brushing her mind. The child's face was changing, betraying hints of . . . was it character, so early? That soft, full under lip, with the sweet, almost pouting curve of the upper; dark feathers of hair curling from the wide brow. Was life marked for you before birth in secret ways, so that all your days you worked out a plan hidden in your flesh from the beginning? Ellen shivered. Thurston, and Robby, and John Thurston, and Alice. What had they done but live out themselves? Your struggle to have what you wished grew out of your very bones. A preposterous, wicked thought, dropping you beyond the need of effort. It couldn't be true. And yet, Alice. From her beginning hadn't she grown from herself? You couldn't make an oak from a poppy seed. Ellen couldn't remember just

how Alice had looked as a baby. Still . . . Ellen's farm
lore rose to rescue her. Even oaks differed. Soil or care
or rain. Grace, waiting for Alice to marry, spoiling her.
Thurston's failure. Maybe you did start as a radish or
a rose or an oak. You still had a chance at the kind you'd
turn out to be. If other folks made some difference . . .
Ellen's faint sigh over the sleeping child was more devout
than a prayer. Her own strong, beating heart would go
into the soil at Anne's feet.

She went down to supper, meeting Alice with pitying embarrassment. But Alice was talkative, cheerful,
unaware that Ellen guessed she had been warmed at an
illicit fire of appreciation. She had been asked to take
charge of some of the parish visiting, worthy cases.
Thurston's inquiry as to how she planned to get around
so much and so far, when she complained all the time
about her health, did not dim her glow. Perhaps Rob
would drive her in to town mornings. If not, she'd find
a way. Ellen thought grimly that Alice was finding more
satisfaction from her borrowed romance than it had ever
given its owner. No use to accuse her of purloining. If
the rector was a sentimental fool, all right.

IV

Mary and Rob came back from their holiday with a
new doll for Anne and tales of fish Rob had caught.
Mary felt better. She spent several delightful days dis-
covering things neglected during her absence. She had a
seamstress in for winter clothes. Even Ellen was to have
a new dress, a gift from Rob. Mary suggested black
silk, as being both rich and serviceable, but Ellen chose

from the samples a green, dark as pine needles. Mary admitted she looked well in the dress. With Rob's home-coming, Thurston had shrunk again into inconspicuous-ness. Rob tried to find something at the factory for him to do, but Thurston wasn't going to work for his son. Didn't he have an income? He never spoke of it as a pension.

Mary spoke of seeing more of the baby; the child ought to know she had a mother! Somehow it was always more convenient for Ellen to take Anne for her airings, and there was no point in moving the crib downstairs since Anne was used to sleeping in Ellen's room, and Rob didn't want a baby in their room. Mary joined a club of young married women, a literary circle, from which Rob drove her home, charming in brown velvet, in the deepening dusk of successive Friday evenings. She planned a series of dinners, just a few guests.

One morning in December she came down to breakfast with blue smudges under her eyes, smudges like shadows of the fear which looked out. She felt wretched, and Rob must ask the doctor to drive out during the day. Ellen saw how tensely she listened for the sound of wheels. Ellen had taken Anne upstairs for her morning nap when the doctor came. She heard their voices from the living room; she thought she heard Mary crying. When Katie appeared, saying the doctor wanted to see her, she hurried down. She had a glimpse of Mary, small and white in a corner of the sofa, and watched the doctor stroke his long moustache with one finger while he explained. Another baby. Mrs. Dacey felt unduly alarmed. Then, in a confidential murmur; it would have been better, of

course, if a year or two had elapsed. Still, no cause for
anxiety. Lots of women were better after the second.
Natural processes. If she'd keep Mrs. Dacey cheerful
. . . see that she took care of herself.

When he had driven away, Ellen sat beside Mary,
touching her knee in a tentative caress. Poor, frightened
child!

"He says you'll feel better for having a second."

"So soon!" Mary twisted her handkerchief. "I can't
go through it!"

"Maybe it will be a boy. Robby would like that."

"He ought to!" Mary's small face looked like a
drenched, angry kitten. "If men had to have babies, they
wouldn't want them so easy!"

"Well, they can't, and that's all there is to that," said
Ellen, practically. A little fanged memory struck at her,
Grace, hating her pregnancy, poor John Thurston. "It
isn't good for your baby," she spoke shyly, "not wanting
it. Some day I'll tell you about Rob's brother. I think
a baby feels it, the way his mother feels about him."

Mary patted away fresh tears.

"Dr. Kirk said be cheerful! And all the nice things
I'd planned to do this winter." Her small mouth looked
spiteful under her terrified eyes. "I wish Rob was home."
She moved her knee, and Ellen withdrew her hand. "I'll
go lie down. The doctor said I should." She rose, her
head drooping. "I've got to get used to the idea," she
added, defensively.

If she was fond of me, thought Ellen, I'd be able to help
her more. Something like a thin sheet of glass between
them, invisible, preventing warm contact. Like the cool
satin cheek Mary presented for her kiss.

V

Rob was delighted. In the following months Ellen had to admire with secret amusement the rôle Mary played so well. The child she carried was a special favor to Rob, since he desired a son, a favor granted in spite of peril and hardship. You'd almost believe the world had been peopled some other way, thought Ellen, and Mary had consented to try a new scheme. During the winter Rob was rushed at the factory; the spring orders were heavy. He never forgot Mary's whims, her slight errands. He had a telephone installed, an amazing instrument. Flowers, a pearl brooch. One day with sheepish triumph a long yellow box which disclosed a set of carpenter's tools. "For the boy!" Rob declared, and hid them away when Mary, unaccountably, burst into tears. Nervousness, explained Ellen.

In the spring he urged Mary to drive with him. She needed more air. She demurred; she didn't want to show herself. Rob came back from New York with a cape, an elegant garment of blue broadcloth, wrapped it about his wife and carried her out to the buggy. After that she rode with him often as the evenings grew mild and long.

By the end of May she refused to do more than to lie on the couch under the long windows at the end of the living room, where she watched the candles of the horse chestnut tree scorch and drop, while she waited for Rob to come home and sit beside her. Anne's vigor tired her, so that Ellen kept the child on the cautious leash of her attention during the moments when she went in to see her mother, and spent hours with her on the shore. At low tide there was a long crescent of sand, tipped at each end with rocks; even at the higest tides the arc of the diminished crescent was left. Anne could run and shriek and fall, while her skin warmed into gold. Ellen, sniffing sea odors, watching sea birds and occasional distant ships, feeling the yield of sand under her feet, included in her affection for the earth this water, the voice of which had at first been so alien.

Sometimes in the long June afternoons, Thurston wandered down to the beach, his stiffened shoulder hunched high. He had been made an officer in the G. A. R. chapter in town, he had joined a lodge, but those diversions stretched thin over all the days in a week. Caught in sand and beach grass lay a huge tree trunk, blanched silver, where Thurston would sit, chewing on his pipe stem, silent for a long time, and then breaking out:

"That boy's bit off more than he can chew. He won't listen to me. Extravagance everywhere. He oughtn't to try to run this place, putting on style. You'd think he'd listen to me. I've had more experience than he'll ever have."

Ellen let him talk, on and on, thinking: it's good for him to get it off his chest, so he won't say it to Robby. She found herself regarding him as an old man, a garrulous, crochety old man. And he was her younger brother! Perhaps his having gone to war . . . perhaps the crooked, devious paths his mind took, justifying and explaining his failures . . . for some reason age had come to meet him. Perhaps . . . a kind of panic furred Ellen's thoughts . . . perhaps to other people she seemed old. As old as Thurston. She looked at Anne, humped over a red pail she filled with sand. She couldn't grow old, not while the child needed her. Ten years, twenty years. She wouldn't count them!

One day Thurston plumped down on the log, a defiant excitement twitching in his wrinkled cheeks. He complained of the heat, rubbing at his forehead. Then, in a whisper, with a glance at the bank down which he had come, "Ellen, I've got news." His fingers spilled tobacco grains on his knee. "You heard talk of an increase in pension? Another, I mean? It's going through. I'll get a lot. I'm going back to Coldspring. Going to open my office again. Going to have my own roof over my head and eat my own bread."

"Why, Thurston, you can't. You're too——"

"I ain't old. What's sixty odd?"

"You can't live alone."

"I thought you'd enjoy Coldspring again. Your own house, no more charity."

Before Ellen's eyes the blue of the smooth water changed to a queer sulphur yellow, against which danced innumerable small dark heads. "Charity?" She closed her eyes dizzily, and a demon mounted within her. "What else have I ever had, thanks to you?" *Anne, Anne.* A scheme to tear her away. "If the bread of your own son is bitter to you, what have you done for me?"

Thurston got up hastily. "Just like a woman," he muttered. "Harking back. I don't want you to go." He scrambled up the bank, and turned to shout, "You needn't say anything. This ain't settled. I don't want you!"

Ellen dropped on to the log he had abandoned. I didn't know I could feel that mad. Settled? I should think not. Rob wouldn't let him. But she waited uneasily.

Thurston glowered at her at dinner. He didn't appear again on the beach. During the last week in June he was suddenly occupied with plans for a July Fourth parade, in which the G. A. R.'s from several towns were to march.

"Be too warm, won't it?" Rob inquired.

"Too warm for men who marched through Georgia? Humph. Have to show this milksop generation what men were."

The night before the Fourth Thurston knocked at Ellen's door. She opened it, finger at her lips. Anne, grumpy at the end of the sultry day, had just yielded unwillingly to sleep.

"You got any peppermint?" He had started to bed, apparently, and yellow folds of neck sagged over his collarless shirt. "My supper didn't set real good."

"I'll get you some." Ellen, returning with hot water and a bottle found him huddled on a chair, hands clasping his stomach. "You've been out in the sun too much," she said. "You ought to stay in to-morrow."

"Guess I can have a little stomach ache." He gulped obediently the dose Ellen proferred. "All that fancy food does it." Was that an echo of their last conversation? Ellen departed before his testiness tempted her into retort. He didn't look well; those pouches under his eyes. . . .

Anne woke early the next morning to such an outburst of energy that Ellen, lest she wake her mother, hurried to dress and to escape with the child to the safe shore. A quiet, cloudless morning, with a glaze over the Sound from the climbing sun, a sense of waiting in motionless leaves. They couldn't stay long on the beach, until the afternoon shadows came. Just till Mary was awake. The kind of day they called a weather breeder back in Michigan.

"Now we'll go to breakfast." Ellen laid aside the rounded pebbles Anne had piled in her lap. "You need more'n that glass of milk." At the porch door, Rob met her.

"Have you seen Father?" He looked chagrined. "He must have gone off without breakfast. I said I couldn't drive him down till later, and he didn't like it."

"Well . . . it's not so hot yet."

"No reason why he shouldn't have waited. I don't want to rush off without seeing Mary the only day I have a chance to stay home, do I?" For an instant he was the boy appealing to Ellen against his father. Then he stooped to pick up Anne, battering at his knee.

The sun was a red-hot penny spinning on the opaque, grayed blue sky, the noon shadows huddled under trees where leaves hung in air thickened with the heat. Mary said limply, "Why must you go to town? Surely they won't march in this heat." And Rob, "I'm afraid they will. Father'd never forgive it, if I didn't show up." Alice decided she must go, too. It was her father as well as Rob's, wasn't it? Rob waited, the horse twitching her flanks under the yellow fringe of the fly net, until Alice hurried out, her face moist, her large hat with its wreath of forget-me-nots askew, the ends of her blue sash fluttering. Rob's eyebrows were ludicrous, but he gathered the reins without comment, except for, "Don't eat all the ice cream before we get home. We'll need it."

Through the long afternoon Mary slept; outside in the

grass insects shrilled, like insistent plucking at a thin wire.
Ellen felt the heat throb in her temples. When the afternoon shadows lay over the beach, she took Anne to the
water's edge, where a faint whiff of salt rose from the
inrolling tide, like a promise of coolness. The tide was
almost high when Katie shouted to her from the bank.
The telephone. Mr. Dacey wanted to talk to her. Then
Rob's voice humming at her ear.

"An' Telly? Is that you? Can you hear me? It's
father. He's dead. He fell, making his speech. I can't
get home yet. Is Mary all right? I'm sending Alice . . .
she had hysterics, taking on. . . ."

"What is it, Aunt Ellen?" Mary cried out from the
darkened living room. "Was that Rob?"

Ellen fitted the receiver carefully on its hook. She
mustn't shock Mary.

"Is something wrong with Rob?"

"Nothing." Ellen crossed the dim room. "He says it's
Thurston. His father."

"Rob warned him not to go out in this heat. What's
happened?"

"He says . . ." Mary hadn't been fond of Thurston,
but any death was a sort of shock. "He was making his
speech when he fell."

"Is he dead?" demanded Mary. "Oh, poor Rob! This
awful day." She whimpered softly. "Ellen, are they
bringing him here? I don't want to see him . . . dead. . . ."

"Rob didn't say. But he hasn't any other home." Poor
Thurston, and his bitter bread!

"Of course. He's Rob's father. It's only that I don't
feel well, and a dead . . ." she quivered . . . "just now."

"I guess Rob will see to things."

VI

The funeral was at the church. Rob thought that best, since Mary was so nervous. A cortège of Thurston's lodge members and the G. A. R. chapter followed the hearse to the station. Robert was going west with the body. Thurston should lie in the Dacey plot, beside his wife, near his father and mother. Ellen stood beside Rob, waiting for the train. "I'd like to go with you," she said. "But one of us ought to stay here." Nostalgia ached in her, as if Thurston's return wiped a film of dust from old recollections.

"I feel easier, knowing you are here," said Rob.

Sarah's baby. Would Thurston like to lie so near that little grave? "We ought to let John Thurston know," she said, with contrition that she thought of him so seldom.

"Outrageous, his not writing." Rob was crisp. "Not decent, sending us no address."

Ellen climbed into the hired carriage, as the train jerked out of sight. Rob had a right to feel superior to his brother, perhaps. He'd cause to have pride in his conduct. Yet Ellen wished he would let other people feel the pride and superiority for him. Self-righteousness, and he was still young. Oh, well. . . . Wasn't she a critical old fusser? Who was it. . . . I thank Thee, oh Lord, that I am not such as they? Robby wasn't that bad. Just a touch. She must be tired, finding fault with him, and all he'd had to think about. Three days at least before he would be home again. Thurston had gone back to Coldspring, and there had been no question as to where Ellen belonged. Mary should be all right; several weeks before her time.

And Alice . . . queer she'd taken her father's death so
hard. The shock, the doctor said. Ellen had never suspected her of much feeling toward Thurston.

The nurse had come. Rob had seen to that, too, before
his departure. She was Scotch, red haired, with a set
of little jokes as starched as her blue and white uniform.
Anne disliked her, scrambling for Ellen whenever the
brisk rustle approached. But she prescribed for Alice,
whisking her out of retirement by the second day, and
Mary enjoyed her professional deference. The household
became hers, swung about the event of which she was
high priestess. Ellen and Anne were interlopers, evad-
ing notice, slipping away for long hours.

One noon Rob was home again. Ellen had left Anne
asleep when she heard him, talking with Mary, thumping
about the bathroom as he hurried into fresh clothes. She
waited on the porch.

"Hello, An' Telly. Whew, this sea air feels good, after
the middle west and that oven of a train." His neat
moustache tickled her cheek. "Who do you think showed
up? John Thurston!"

Ellen caught his sleeve before he could rush away.

"Tell me about him."

"To-night. He'd seen a notice in the papers. He's
somewhere in the west. Kansas, I think. On a newspaper, he says."

"Is he well?"

"All right. Kinda shabby." Rob frowned. "He's
pretty cynical, I'd say. He promised to write to you. I
got to hustle now."

Cynical, shabby, on a newspaper. Ellen couldn't build
much of a picture from those bits. She'd make Rob tell
her more when he came home in the evening.

But she didn't that evening, nor for many evenings. Mary was dangerously ill, with what the nurse called, appallingly, complications. The doctor, a surgeon from the city, another nurse. Ellen dwelt on the periphery of terrifying conflict. Nothing she could do but keep Anne out of the way. The third morning Rob followed her to the beach, to sprawl on the sand, his eyes haggard, his face shadowed with neglected dark stubble. Anne, enraptured, brought shells, coaxing his attention.

"This business . . ." he pushed the child away . . .

"The child isn't to blame." Ellen tried to divert Anne to a house in the sand. "Papa doesn't feel good. You play there."

"If anything happens, I'm to blame!" He dropped his head between his hands.

"Nonsense, Robby! You got born once, didn't you? You're just worn out, with no sleep, and your father's death, and the trip. Why don't you just lie down there in the sun?" She patted Anne's red cushion against the log. "There." Rob consented to stretch out, his face hidden in a bent arm, while Anne gravely trudged back and forth collecting treasures which she laid in a row beside him.

He made a convulsive leap to his feet, crunching Anne's shells, at the sound of the doctor's voice above him.

"There you are, eh?" The doctor nodded. He looks real pleased: Ellen's thought lifted a shield against her fear. "Well, well. May I come down?" He slid plumply down the grass. "Well, my boy, prepare for news. You have quite a family."

Rob stared, rigid.

"Your wife is pretty cute. She must have known she couldn't try motherhood again."

"For Christ's sake, man, what!"

"Twins. Twin boys. H'm." The doctor rubbed his hands and grinned at Anne. "Your nose is more than out of joint, young lady."

"Twins? Oh, my God!" Rob began to laugh, broke off to stare at the doctor as if he suspected this ludicrous ending, and then bolted for the house.

"A fine brace of boys," the doctor assured Ellen. "And their mother will pull through." He shot his cuffs down under his coat sleeves. "I was worried a while, though."

As he followed Rob, Ellen let herself down on the log. Twins. They did seem humorous, for Mary. She had a comical idea that Mary might be chagrined, as if twins weren't exactly. . . . What foolishness! She should be feeling thanks that Mary was coming through. Rob's shriek of nervous laughter had upset her, that was all.

Whatever Mary's first emotion was, by the time the nurse thought she ought to see her sons and carried them in on a pillow, two tiny scarlet heads with wisps of almost invisible fair hair above a white embroidered cover, Mary was ready to take the doctor's attitude. She had been pretty smart to produce two sons. Her glance at them, before she drifted into sleep, was calmly proud.

The room Thurston had used became their nursery. Two new Daceys in place of one outworn. Ellen felt some gratitude when Rob said, "Too bad father couldn't have seen 'em. He'd have enjoyed two grandsons." When she took Anne in to see her brothers, the child scowled at the nurse and tugged at Ellen's hand.

"Uh huh!" The nurse bent over the two red dots. "She knows she's not the baby any more. Don't you even want to see your darling brothers?" As Anne scuffed her feet, trying to draw Ellen away, she added, "She's a jealous little piece, isn't she? You ought to watch out for that disposition."

"She's only a baby herself!" Ellen was indignant. "Come, Anne."

One morning later, as they passed the nursery door, a sudden "Wahwahing" drew Ellen within. One twin beat the air with pink fists, while his brother sucked contemplatively on a bottle propped in a fold of blanket. "Poor baby! He's lost his breakfast." Ellen rescued the bottle, laughed at the sudden glug with which the wahs stopped, and patted the blanket into a prop. At a shriek behind her she turned; Anne plumped herself down with a clatter of sand pail, her face screwed into rage.

"Why, Anne Dacey! Hush!" Ellen picked her up, toys and stiff little body, as the nurse appeared at the door.

"What a noise! Your poor mother!" The nurse was severe.

"She fell," prevaricated Ellen, as she carried Anne down stairs and out of the house. For a time the child sulked. Then a sandpiper teetered at the edge of the water, and Anne, chasing the bird, forgot her ill humor.

Ellen remembered John Thurston, with his gnomelike face, trailing determinedly after her and Robby. She must ask Rob about him. Cynical and shabby. An instinct of protection delayed her inquiry. Alice was always at the table for breakfast and supper, and Rob seemed always to be in Mary's room when he wasn't rushing off to the factory. Ellen didn't want John Thurston's shabbiness and cynicism, whatever they amounted to, paraded in front of his sister or his sister-in-law. One

morning Alice wished to ride into town with Rob; she'd
be ready immediately. Ellen followed Rob to the front
steps. He snapped his watch cover, muttering that he
couldn't wait all day while Alice prinked.

"You haven't heard any more from John Thurston,
have you?" Ellen dropped her question rashly into his
early morning mood. "You didn't ever tell me what he
said."

"Just last night I was thinking about that. Mary wants
to name the twins after their grandfathers, and I . . .
well, Thurston doesn't seem a very lucky name."

"You didn't tell Mary that?"

Rob laughed at Ellen's flare. "No. I guess my son
could make it lucky."

"It's a good name." Rob settled himself on the high
seat of the road cart. He looked lucky enough, erect and
impatient, shining yellow wheels and sleek sorrel mare
details in the picture he made of prosperous young business man. "Has John Thurston had bad luck?"

"He said he'd write you. We didn't talk much. He
. . . well, frankly, An' Telly, we didn't hitch. He acted
as if he resented my getting ahead. All I said to him was
he hadn't worried much about his folks. That woman he
went off with died, he says. He's moved around a lot,
which may be why he hasn't done any better. He's in
newspaper work . . . . but I told you that."

The screen door clattered for Alice's emergence, gloves,
handkerchief, purse, feather tibbet floating symbols of
her taste. "There, I didn't keep you waiting, did I?"
She scrambled up beside Rob, clutching at her para-
phernalia.

"Less than an hour." Rob tightened his reins. "Hang

on! I'll have to drive like fury!" He winked back at Ellen, over the sudden lurch of Alice's wide hat, as the horse's hoofs scattered cinders and gravel.

Ellen turned heavily toward the house. She'd never thought of death, in her speculations about John Thurston and Florence. She had imagined them moving through the world into new, strange places, wayfarers who thought to leave the shadows of their old selves under a stone at an old crossroad. What was it Florence had said: "I ought to'v gone further."

A shrill pipe, "Telly! Come right here, Telly!" Anne, her small nose flattened against the square mesh of the screen door. The little girl, Flora. Did John Thurston have her?

VII

Mary's reappearance in the world came with the christening of her sons. A mild Sunday late in October she descended the front steps slowly, leaning on Robert's arm, and sank into the corner of the closed carriage from the livery stable. "You're sure the ride isn't going to tire you too much?" Robert spread a shawl over her knees, thrust smelling salts into her white-gloved fingers.

"Even if it does—" Mary let her sentence hang as the nurse came out, followed by Katie, each with a trailing bundle of embroidered white flannel. "Help her, Rob. Aren't they adorable?" Alice rustled down the steps. "You sure there's room for me?"

"Yes, and for Ellen too. Come along, An' Telly."

Ellen shook her head. "Anne's too young for church, and I guess I'm too old." She watched the stowing of the pink and white cargo, one in the nurse's arms, one in

Rob's. "You know which one is Charles Vleet and which is Thurston?"

"Charles has the pink bow. Katie, remember the rector will be here for dinner." Mary fluttered a handkerchief triumphantly as they rolled away.

"Well, young lady." Ellen turned to Anne, who was deciding ruefully that she wanted to go, too. "If they both cry as loud as you did, they'll make quite a chorus."

"Did Anne cry in church?" Katie clucked, and Anne twisted her face into an indignant, "No! Bad babies cries."

Anne had her dinner and had gone to sleep, and Ellen, in her green silk, sat on the porch when the carriage returned. Rob beside the driver to make room for the rector. The children had been angels; the rector regretted that Miss Dacey had not seen them. No, Mary was not too tired to sit up for dinner. Alice, lagging as the nurse disappeared upstairs and the others went on to the living room, confided in a flurried whisper to Ellen: "I was so mortified. Just before the ceremony . . . when the rector was praying so beautifully, the nurse had to take them out . . . into the entry . . . to change their. . . ." Ellen laughed. "Too bad you can't remember being a baby, Alice, if that mortifies you." Alice flounced into the house with an injured glare.

Dinner began with a rehearsal of admiring comments the twins had elicited. The rector had stories of other christenings. Ellen noticed the skilful way he managed to eat steadily while he ran the conversation. Praise of Alice's assistance in the welfare work, at which Alice winked and tried to blush. Several references to the need of money, for church repairs, for a new chapel. A cryptic remark: "Some of those who long to give their money, are inhibited, whether wrongly or not I cannot say." The rector was looking at Alice, and Ellen was puzzled by the dull color which rose from Alice's throat to her ears. As if the high boned collar of her net yoke was too tight.

After dinner Mary admitted fatigue, with the ebbing of the stimulus of her exhibition. The rector thought he'd enjoy a walk back to town. Perhaps Mr. Dacey would like a walk this fine fall day? Ellen, climbing the stairs in answer to the distant call of "Telly!" that announced Anne's wakening, found Alice at the hall window, her hands clenched on the sill, her face a curious sallow mask.

"What's the matter?" Through the window Ellen saw the two men standing a moment while Rob lighted a cigar.

Alice without answering darted into her room.

Ellen tied a scarlet hood over Anne's dark head, and fastened the scarlet coat. "Now, little Red Riding Hood," she said, "let's go meet Daddy in the woods." Those babies look nice, they're so pink and yellow, she thought, but you're handsomer.

Anne scuffed through the leaves, intent on a secret game. Ellen, strolling behind her, let thoughts drift through her, aimless as the leaves. Why should Anne gather the leaves and toss them with such absorption? How deeply blue the sky hung through the branches of the maples, and beyond, where the oaks held their dark canopy intact, not a scrap of blue showed. Did her oak still stand? She almost felt its ridged bark under her fingers. Rob wouldn't have noticed, of course. Alice's face, as she turned from the window. Was she building foolish ideas around the rector? Something pitiful, wasted about Alice. Anne must have a different life. It would be different, and yet . . . a thought drifting, leaf-like, just out of reach. . . . When Ellen was young, there was a kind of whole into which she had fitted, making life at the margin of the wilderness, men and women together; no chance for anything pitiful there. Thurston, her father, had defied that wholeness when he rode away, but he had come back, too late, in search of it. In Alice's time, her father was separate, running his man's affairs secretly. Ellen tried to catch her elusive, drifting thought. It meant something for that bright figure of Anne. Rob's life, like his father's, had that separateness, that secrecy, from which he returned at evening to his household. It made an emptiness for women. Mary didn't mind; she'd been brought up to fill that emptiness with pretty things, teas and clothes and admiration for her husband. She had a husband and Alice didn't. And twins. Still, Rob had the twins, too, and at the same time he had his important separate life. If Anne could, some way, have both. Ellen shrugged. You'd think I was one of these bloomer women, and here all my life one man or another has decided what would become of me. Nor of *me*. The strong fibre of her heart tightened in protest. Matthew, her father, her brother Rob. They had decided things that happened about her. Before she could clear away the tangle of her thoughts, she saw Rob striding toward her, violence in the thrust of his chin, in the hunch of his broad shoulders. That preacher's riled him, thought Ellen. She slacked his stride. Anne ran to meet him with precarious swiftness which landed her in a scarlet heap at his feet. Rob picked her up and she clung about his neck, her fists full of crumbled leaves.

"Hello." He scowled over her head at Ellen. "What you doing way out here?"

"We came to meet you." That rector was irritating.

Rob bent to set Anne firmly on her feet. "You run along, Anne. I want to talk to An' Telly. Here, you can have my walking stick." He curled her fingers around the smooth branch, and grinned as she thumped along the path. His grin contracted as he looked at Ellen. "Is Alice crazy? She never had any man so much as look at her, did she? I never heard of one, for all her efforts. You ought to hear the cock and bull story she's poured into that damn fool rector. He swallowed it, hook, line, sinker. He's been taking me to task, me, An' Telly! After all I've done for her. For stealing her money! What's she thinking of?"

"What did he say?" Ellen caught the stick which Anne was trying against her ankle. Guilt warmed her eyelids suddenly: that tragic life of Alice's he'd hinted at . . . and she'd never said a warning word to Alice or anyone else.

"Alice never had a lover who went off and made money and died, now did she? Why—" he stopped, amazed. "That's like you, An' Telly! You and what was his name? Luke . . . no. . . ."

"What did he say about money?"

"Alice told him she'd like to build the chapel he wants, but she couldn't get her money. Father'd had it, and then I used it, to go to college, to start business, she told him. Now she couldn't get it. He felt he ought to protest, even if she never gave it to the church. Unbrotherly conduct toward a woman whose life had been tragic.

Bah! He said Alice hadn't actually told him all this, she'd let things drop, and he'd come to understand and felt it was his duty to speak."

"What did you say, Robby?" Had Robby labelled his sister as liar? Poor Alice. . . .

"I put him off, said there was some misunderstanding. Alice didn't know anything about money, and I didn't know of any she'd had left her. I gave him to understand it was my father sent me to college, though." He stared at Ellen, the flickering sunlight on his face like reflections of his quick thoughts. "Why, An' Telly, it was you. Did Father. . . . You went into his room and made him. I never knew how you did it. You had some money left you. Folks thought it was a fortune. Is that what Alice is blabbing about? Did Father . . . he threw that to the wind with everything else, did he?"

"He's dead, now." Ellen spoke with dignity. "It was a long time ago."

"Matthew! That was his name. He went off west when Grandfather skipped off. You were going to buy the old farm. . . ." He scowled with his effort to bring up bits from the limbo of his youth. "Then did you let father have your money?"

"Thurston wasn't lucky with money." Ellen looked resolutely away from Rob. Something indecent in exhuming old bones. "It's Alice we're talking about," she added. "She's mixed things up. Though I don't see how she knew."

"What does she know? How you made father send me east? You needn't button your lips up that way. I won't try to pry it out of you. But he must have done something pretty crooked to let you bully him. I never suspected. Instead of getting after him yourself, you did for me, eh?"

"I thought you might do fairly well if you had a chance." Ellen was prim with rising irritation. Rob needn't press her. . . .

"Well, I have, haven't I?" His glance embraced the signs of his accomplishment, his daughter, the curve of road, the glimpse of brown house.

"In some ways," admitted Ellen.

"That's partly why this business about Alice makes me so raw, her spreading a story like that."

"Sh!" said Ellen. As if she had been waiting for them, straining through that hall window, perhaps, Alice came down the path, with a jerky run. Ellen bent to brush leaves from Anne's coat. Alice's rush blew guilt over her and Rob. A kind of wildness in her face, the pale hair straggling around a distracted brow, white dents in her nostrils, hands clenched.

"You've been talking about me," she said. "I know. I can tell."

"What'd you expect, after the yarns you've been concocting?" Rob's truculence was interrupted by Ellen's hand on his arm.

"The rector asked Rob"—Ellen pitied the fear that dilated Alice's eyes—"about the money you spoke of. Maybe he misunderstood you."

"And you said there wasn't any, I suppose!" Alice breathed quickly. She was a mouse in a wire trap, her sharp face turning this way and that. "You denied you'd had everything, and nobody else anything. Ellen would stand up for you. She always did. The rest of us stayed home and starved."

"Now, see here!" Rob pulled away from Ellen's restraining hand. "What's the use of such talk? You've filled the rector up with a story about you and a rich lover and money you'd build a chapel with if you could only get it, and I want to know what the idea is. Here I've treated you white, and you start a yarn like that!"

"You don't know anything about my life!" Alice swayed in the wind. "What did you say to him?"

"Rob, take Anne home." Ellen laid her arm about Alice's shoulders. "Go ahead," she ordered, and Rob, with a sulky shrug, started toward the house. "Now, Alice." Her arm was firm against the tense, spasmodic quivering. "Rob just said there was some misunderstanding. That's all. He had cause to feel upset."

"When I saw them going away together, I felt a warning. I knew he'd belittle me before Dr. Barton. I saw his smile when the rector praised my work. He's never liked me. They don't want me here." Her words tossed out on rapid, shallow breathing. "You don't like people you've wronged."

"Nobody's wronged you, Alice. Stop shaking that way! Your brother's given you a good home, and what possessed you to tell the rector he'd kept money of yours? Why, you never had any and you know it."

"I've never had anything, have I?" Alice was quiet as a stone, except for the furtive slipping of eyelids over her thoughts. "Nothing. I didn't say it was my lover sent the money. You didn't get it back, did you? I wanted to build a chapel. My father had plenty. He should have left me some. Rob's got it. Rob, who's had everything."

"Way last year," said Ellen slowly, "the rector asked me about your fiancé who died. I thought if you got any satisfaction out of making up such stories, you could have it. But you haven't any right to mix my affairs in it, nor to say things against Rob. You ought to explain to the rector."

"It's not enough for Rob to worm my confidences out of the only friend I've had. . . . You think I'll humiliate myself. . . ." Her voice choked, and she ran toward the house, head forward, elbows gyrating. Ellen hurried after her, to hear the scrape of the key in Alice's door. Well, let her cry it out. Bitter bread, but her own foolish mixing.

"An' Telly!" Rob's cautious voice summoned her back to the living room. "Katie's giving Anne her supper. What'd Alice have to say?"

Ellen looked at him. Handsome, young, firm-fleshed; she had a notion that his very thoughts were hard-muscled, direct. How could he comprehend the inept, erratic weavings of Alice's mind?

"I wouldn't be too angry with her." Ellen brooded across a gulf of inadequacy. "She didn't mean to make trouble. She's never had much in her life, Robby. She sort of made things up for herself, always. I guess she felt more interesting that way. The rector must have egged her on, hoping he'd get something. She wanted him to admire her."

"What did she lie for?"

"She just borrowed Matthew." Ellen smiled. "She says she never said it was her money, but she let him think so. You couldn't understand, could you, how hard it is for a woman when she hasn't anything of her own, and wants to do things? She wanted to give that chapel."

Rob thrust his fingers through his hair. "You sound

sorry for her, An' Telly! You ought to be sorry for me, with a yarn like that. . . ."

"You don't need anybody being sorry for you. I guess I can make her clear it up with the rector."

"You might tell him yourself." Rob grinned. "Then he'd think you were an interesting woman. Well, you are!" He hugged her. "You can tell me one thing. Was it your money sent me east?"

"I got to put Anne to bed." Ellen moved hastily toward the door. "Not exactly," she added. "Don't say anything to Mary, Rob."

"Lord, no. She thinks Alice is queer enough. An' Telly, is she a little off?"

Ellen pretended not to hear that last question. Off or on . . . she didn't know.

VIII

Alice sat in a small chair backed against her locked door, her shoulders hunched, her fingers creasing and smoothing tiny folds of her silk skirt. Darkness flowed into the room, lapping about her feet, sucking at bright fragments of the garment she had woven about herself. Explain to the rector? That attentive sympathy in his face, like a caress. Why, she had lost a lover! He must have been hers. Ellen was an old woman. Absurd that she had had a lover. They were all against her, tearing away bit by bit that lovely Alice, disappointed in love, but brave. If they destroyed her, what was left but a skulking shadow? Money? Something Rob was angry about. That wheel in her head, striking sparks into the rising darkness. The Alice Dacey memorial chapel. She'd never said it was her money. The rector urging her, gleams in the caverns of his eyes. "Someone should see that justice is done you." He'd promised to say nothing, and then he had betrayed her. Judas. For pieces of silver. Wasn't it hers? Someone had gone away, leaving her. Explain to the rector, Ellen said. Show herself naked for their ridicule, the tired, empty shadow with the wheel spinning. Why, that wasn't the real Alice. Not the Alice who had gone so brightly about the rector's work, visiting the sick, comforting the needy. Come unto Me. The darkness rose above her knees, above her heart. Stars through the window . . . or were they sparks from that flying wheel? The last shred of her fair garment washed away. They had denied her story to the rector. And yet . . . it had been her lover! Far more real than this huddled, empty shadow.

Still, the shadow moved, as if the busy wheel had at last jerked some spring of action. Stealthily Alice slid the chair from the door, turned the key, listened, fitted the key outside the door, and locked the deserted room. Life in the house; Rob's voice, and his wife's, behind curtains. The distant clink of dishes on a silver tray, a baby's sleepy cry. Alice's shadow on the stairs, on the dark porch, across the turf to a path, to the beach. Under the soft noise of the windless tide, the sound of sand cut by quick heels. Along the rocky tip of the crescent, the plop of seaweed bladders under pressing feet, the crunch of tiny snails. A shadow kneeling where the water lifted a dark mass of seaweed in a lazy undulation. Cool night saltiness drifting over the water. Alice lifted her face; low in the east a great star dropped a taper of dim flame into the sea. What was she doing there? The wheel in

her head froze into fear.   She sprang to her feet to run,
away from this terror.   But seaweed on water and on
rock is black at night.   The darkness lapped at last above
her head.

IX

Anne wanted to play on the beach, but Ellen refused.
It was too cold.   Anne could trundle her cart along the
wood path.   Perhaps by spring the rocks would no longer
be haunted.   That sprawling figure, hands clutched on
broken seaweed, foot caught.   "Miss Alice Dacey, sister
of Robert Dacey, prominent manufacturer, met her death
by accidental drowning."   Ellen wished she could be sure
of the accidental.   Had Alice slipped, walking there in
the dark?   Had she, fleeing from the wreckage of her
foolish stories, wanted to die?   Ellen had knocked at her
door that Sunday evening; if only she had seen the key,
outside the door.   "Thank Heaven the coroner calls it
accidental!"   Mary had said.   "Think of the disgrace . . .
suicide?"   Rob said nothing.   Ellen, afraid of strengthening her own fear at this, did not ask him.   But the beach
was no place for a child to play, not this fall.

Alice, dead, seemed to stay in Ellen's thoughts more
than Alice, alive, had ever done.   Her life, being ended,
shrank into a small thing Ellen could hold in one hand,
could turn and examine.   A living person kept himself
shut up, secret; he went about his affairs, giving you
signs from time to time of what he was, or wished.   Dead,
he couldn't prevent you from picking up what he left scattered about; he couldn't brush it from your fingers with
some sudden action.   Ellen had pity for the empty husk
that was all she could make of Alice.   Alice, a little girl,

ISLANDERS 217

with her mother so proud of her yellow curls. Whatever
happened to Anne, it mustn't be emptiness.

One day a letter came from John Thurston. Ellen
had almost forgotten that angular, hasty script, but she
knew it when Rob handed her the envelope. Her glance
at Rob was stern. This was her letter; he needn't expect
her to read it there, to him. In her own room she cut the
end, carefully. Letters were rare in Ellen's life, and
webbed in troubling emotions.

Dear Ellen: I've thought of writing to you a thousand
times, but haven't. Rob explained how ashamed I ought to
be for shirking my responsibilities, but I told him if I'd been
around he'd never had a chance to show how noble he was.
He didn't like that much. But he probably told you about our
meeting.

Florence died a year ago. She had consumption and the
doctors said she didn't have will enough to get well. She
was happy, I think, the little while before she died. But the
good people in the world killed her before she came to Coldspring. Flora is growing fast and is a nice girl.

I'm on a paper here. Florence persuaded me to try it.
Rob says you're well and happy, with his kid to take care of.
I suppose he has another by this time. I'd like to see you.
Drop me a line sometime.

Yours,

J. T. DACEY.

Ellen found a bottle of ink and a pen. She fastened a
paper to the light, so that Anne's crib was in shadow.
Then she began a letter to John Thurston. Her thoughts
moved laboriously, stiffening at the point of the pen. If
only she could see him, could talk, could try to exercise that
awful bitterness that clouded his grief for his wife. "I
am well and busy, since there are twin boys and I take
care of little Anne. I don't think Rob feels noble. He
has been real good." Alice. John Thurston didn't know

about her. "I'm sure Florence was happy, for she had you. The little girl must be quite big by this time." Oh, cold, limp paper, and stiff black marks, and in her heart, beating at the hard edge of the table where she labored, love, tenderness. "I would enjoy seeing a copy of your paper if you would send it. Do you write pieces for it or what? I hope you are getting on well." Nothing more about Rob, nor Anne, for she was Rob's daughter. With them counted out, Ellen could think of nothing to write about herself. "I was real glad to hear from you and hope you will write again soon." She waited for the ink to dry. That yellow wooden sand-shaker her mother had kept on the kitchen shelf—what had become of that? She folded the sheet, sighing, and hurried through her simple preparations for the night. Sleep might ease the heaviness which fogged her thoughts.

She slept restlessly, waking at times to a sense of dreams that slipped between her fingers, dreams of Sarah, of men riding through morning light across a meadow, of spring soil dank and heavy as it curled away from the plow share . . . dreams that were forgotten doors at which John Thurston's letter tapped. Toward morning she woke, clinging to a dream which grew thin as the outlines of familiar objects pressed into sight. She had been running swiftly, her body winged with joy, along the road toward the oak tree, where Matthew waited. Behind her Alice called, and Ellen turned to laugh, in young exultation. The laugh had wakened her. She pushed herself up in bed, her fingers trembling over her lips. Unbelievable, grotesque, that in her sober, ageing body, dream fire like that could leap. Did that young Ellen hide in the marrow of her bones, creeping out at

night? Her mother, carefully sanding a sheet of paper,
sealing it. The letter to her son, when Ellen had begged
to go west in Sarah's place; sealing under the fire of the
girl.

My writing to John Thurston got me stirred up. Ellen
propped a pillow under her shoulders, and stared through
the window. A faint low band of smoky orange in the
east, above dark water. Almost dawn. Anne would
wake soon. Ellen folded her hands outside the counterpane. She wouldn't sleep again, not with such dreams.
The morning light crept coldly into the room, white on
the ceiling, and Ellen, not asleep, not awake, thought she
stood apart, looking at the years of her life. From one
end they stretched away, vague, interminable, undeter-
mined; from the other they shrank into a hand's breadth,
settled, irrevocable. Yesterday and to-day were of a
piece. Life was too short! Ellen leaned away from her
pillows, awake. That was the difficulty; there was no
time to make over your first start. She bent toward Anne,
her dark head a shadow, one small fist doubled under her
chin. To-morrow, the next day, and Anne would have
her life made, set. And I can't do it right for her, for
all I know, now, the way it's done. The morning light
troubled her with its cold clarity. She longed for the
beginning of the day, when she could forget what she had
come, unwittingly, to know.

X

With the cold weather, Mary grew stronger, losing
the tracery of blue veins at wrists and temples. She kept
the nurse for the twins, although occasionally, on her

good days, she helped bathe and dress them. Ellen wondered uneasily how Rob made money enough to run his household. Just adding up the items she knew drove her into surreptitious economies such as checking the fires or turning off the gas. Rob didn't seem to share her anxiety. He wore new impressive gold-rimmed glasses and dropped mysterious phrases about expanding his business, buying out some small concerns, selling stock. To Ellen his phrases sounded reminiscent of the abra- cadabra Thurston had muttered over his disappearing for- tune, but Rob's manner was so padded with assurance that Ellen was ashamed of her thought. He drove Mary in to church on pleasant Sundays. The rector had paid a visit of condolence after Alice's death, and Ellen guessed from his polite, curbed inquisitiveness that Rob had in some discreet way explained poor Alice's romancing. Any- way, Alice was dead, while the Robert Daceys were impor- tant members of his flock.

"I couldn't entertain this winter, anyway," said Mary. "With two deaths. By next year I'll be stronger."

Real convenient, darted Ellen's mind. Having death and birth together.

Rob had to go to New York; something about capital for his expanding business. Why couldn't Mary come along? They'd see the town. Mary couldn't possibly go: no clothes, she couldn't leave the children, the household. But she went, to return a week later in a wonderful new hat, black velvet, from which an ostrich feather curled against her shining hair. They had stories of driving in Central Park in a red cutter behind silver belled horses, of the hotel quite far up Fifth Avenue where they had stayed, of opera.

"We might live there. Rob's going to open an office."

Ellen listened, cold with horror. She had heard about the city, houses like packing boxes piled together, noise, wickedness, scarcely a tree nor a blade of grass. People were potted plants, with no roots stretching into the earth. "The children"—she hurried into speech—"it would be no place for them."

"Don't look so scared, An' Telly." Rob laughed. "We won't drag you in just yet."

"You'd leave me here." Ellen could see beyond the living room windows the winter pattern of a maple, strong, black, lifting into delicacy at bough tips. Her body had a tree-feeling, feet rooted, immovable, in soil. Yes, she'd stay. But Rob and Mary seemed to forget their threat almost with its utterance. "When the twins are older," Mary said.

Anne grew by stretching, like a rubber band; she was long and thin of neck, wrists, legs. "What a contrast!" was the usual comment when she appeared with her twin brothers. Even Mary said it often. "She's a regular little gypsy, and they're such cherubs. I wish she had their disposition, at least." Anne no longer flew into queer tempers when people forgot to speak to her in their amused delight over the two boys. The winter she was four she developed a habit which persisted in spite of Ellen's attempts to divert her. As dusk came on, her attention pointed toward the hall down stairs, and sounds which would announce Rob's home-coming. When she heard him, she would plant herself on the top step, waiting. For Rob that Winter, liked to visit his sons in their nursery before their scampering round legs were tucked under blankets. "They're better than vaudeville, the pair

of monkeys!" Usually he passed Anne with a casual pat
on her dark head. Sometimes, rarely, she could hold him
for a moment. "See, Papa, I scratched my leg." Or,
"Papa, look at the stone I found." She came with curious trophies to her stand on the stairs, anything her hands
could close over when she heard Rob's entrance. When
he had hurried past her with a "Yes, yes!" Anne would
cling to Ellen's hand, her full upper lip firm with sulki-
ness. "She's not an appealing child, as they are," Mary
explained. Ellen dreaded the one afternoon a week when
the nurse left the twins in her charge. "You don't
mind?" Mary had asked. It was the afternoon the Ladies'
Guild met. "Anne's getting old enough to be a little
mother, isn't she?" Ellen couldn't, without betraying the
child, admit the pressure of those hours. A moment of
inattention was long enough for some mild catastrophe;
ink bottles, or buttons disappearing on pink tongues, or, if
they were out doors, one plump baby in a mud puddle.
Anne's demon transformed the two cherubs.

Then Anne was five, and in kindergarten. "She needs
to be with children her own age," said Mary. Ellen felt
the rest of the sentence . . . instead of with an old woman
all the time. True, but to Ellen it was a first gleam of
the knife of separation. Anne liked it. "When is to-morrow, An' Telly?" she demanded. "I want to go some
more. I was smarter than the little boys, too."

When is to-morrow? Ellen lay awake, her arms crossed
beneath her breasts, her fingers pressing into the firm
flesh of her arms. Her body did not change, much. Age
was deeper than flesh. Anne slept in the small bed
between the windows, restless after the day's excitement.
That appalling shrinking of time . . . that was age. She

was the child Anne, pushing a great wheel up and up a
hill; the shining spokes were days, yesterday, to-morrow,
and in the dark revolving rim hid the seasons. Up and
up, toward the mysterious summit of life. No, she was
Ellen, old woman. Suddenly, breathlessly, without a hint
that ⁄he crest lay behind you, the wheel began to whirl,
dragging you down, spokes, rim, blurred in a disk of
flight. Before Anne was plunged into that headlong
down ward slope she must know the summit. Stop there,
however briefly. Surely something existed between the
slow climb and the swift ending. Something Anne must
know.

Her thoughts slid away from the child, peering through
the silent house. Rob. His face hung clearly an instant
against her eyelids before it melted into darkness, hair
thinning at the temples, sleeked over the prominent forehead, that trick of twisting his lips, as if words meant
more when he felt their shape; assured, impatient. Time
hadn't started to drag him, not yet; but what did he find
on his summit? His face was a shell. Ellen saw it again,
briefly, the eyes hard, uncommunicative. I wanted something for him, she thought. I ought to be pleased. He's
good, he works hard, he's an important man. And Mary
. . . her thoughts moved through the dark house . . . a
queer fancy threaded her thought of Mary. She had
changed, a little, skin crinkled faintly from ill health.
Something had stopped inside Mary, as if she didn't
tick any longer. She wouldn't grow old. A little helpless, set in the frame of house and Robert and children,
like a picture of herself, with colors dimming. In the dis-
torting light at the edge of sleep their images moved away
from Ellen. Rob, intent on his affairs, a sleek figure from

which teeling slipped off; Mary, pursuing him with quick, short steps; Anne, a small defiant shape, scrambling after them. They were too young, too absorbed, to love the child . . . to love her enough. It leaves her for me. In her dream, her love floated out of her body in a warm cloud, kissing her on brow, breast, and feet before it wound itself about the child asleep between the windows.

XI

The next years slipped along with the blurred swiftness of Ellen's recurring picture of the wheel of time. She caught sometimes for a brief hour Anne's intense living in the present. "Christmas can't ever come, An' Telly! Here's this day, and another, and next week, and everything." Saturday afternoon, when the three children played on the beach, and Ellen watched them from her camp chair; sometimes time stood still then. "We'll play Injuns. I'm Big Chief One Eye, and An' Telly's the pale face mother and Charles is her baby and Thurston is my band of wild Injuns."

"You can't be the chief." Thurston squared himself in the sun, his blue eyes indignant. "You're a girl. I'm the chief and Charles is my men an' . . ."

"Whoop!" Anne was after him, whirling a piece of driftwood. "I'm Chief One Eye! I'm going to scalp you!"

His plump legs carried him hastily to Ellen's knees, and he shrieked at Anne's too realistic scalping. Her black hair flopped with her dance about them. "Whoop! Me big Injun. Me plenty scalp 'em." Usually her wild vitality bullied her brothers, for all there were two of

them, into submission. Ellen felt a humorous sympathy,
sometimes, for their pink stolidity, which yielded reluctantly to Anne's dark violence.

Mary had tried the experiment of a governess for the
three. It seemed much more convenient than transport-
ing Anne to the village each day. But after a few unhappy weeks, the governess spoke. "I think she needs
other children to keep her in her place, Mrs. Dacey. She
feels so much smarter than her little brothers. Of course,
she's older."

Robert had a serious interview with his daughter. "See
here, why do you annoy Miss Thorne this way? Why
can't you be a nice little girl?"

Anne's eyes were innocent. "I am, Papa. Really. I
am nice." Tears shone in the dark pupils. "It's only
. . . they're such babies, Charles and Thurston. I have
to listen to them . . . stupid . . . can't even read. You
wouldn't like it." She ducked her head, ingratiatingly.
"Miss Thorne isn't smart like you. She's all right for
babies."

"She says you pinched Charles."

"Did she say that?" Anne's soft lower lip pouted. "Isn't
he a cry baby?"

"You make a lot of trouble, it seems to me." Robert
look at his watch. "Don't you want folks to like you?
You can't expect me to love you if you aren't good." He
closed the front door sharply.

Ellen, descending the stairs, found Anne on the bottom step, her head on her knees, her dark hair falling
away from the white stem of neck. At Ellen's approach
the child darted up.

"I don't want to be nice!" she cried. "I won't be!"

Violently she hurled herself at Ellen, her defiant face down on Ellen's breast. Ellen held her a moment, until she pulled away, with a toss of her head like a pony.

When Miss Thorne, that afternoon, indicated just how bad it was for the little boys to have this example of unruly vanity with them, Mary telephoned the school in town and arranged for Anne's entrance.

Robert was spending several days a week in New York, where the firm had opened a new office. Mary complained gently: "My husband is so busy that I never see him. The penalty of success." She had a round of social affairs: a church bazaar, a series of musicales and readings, an occasional tea, a formal dinner. Ladies called, to chat of their children, of their clothes . . . styles were so extreme, with bustles discarded . . . of changes in the town—so many foreigners were coming in, to work in the factories, some of the old families were leaving. Conditions are changing, they said. Mary would add, "Yes, my husband refers to changes in business. Too much criticism and agitation, he says." Then they would nod, with knowing, blank eyes.

One evening there was a new word in the dinner conversation—(Mary had dinner at night, now)—an unpleasant word, thought Ellen. Muckraking. "These magazines are just being sensational," explained Robert. "Attacking the roots of society, without knowing the danger. How do they think we can run business, anyway? Do they think I run my factories to make a living for dago immigrants?" His chest swelled as he stared about the table. "I wouldn't touch one of those articles with a pitchfork." Ellen might have forgotten the talk and the word, if Robert hadn't appeared some weeks

later in a state of rage. "Look at this! I want you to
see it, too, An' Telly!" He let a magazine sprawl on the
table. "John Thurston, The Truth about Trusts! My
own brother a loose mouthed agitator! Porter at the
bank wanted to know if that Dacey was any kin of mine!"
Mary purred deprecatingly, but Ellen carried the magazine
to her room. Extraordinary that John Thurston had written those words printed on pages, whatever they said. She
read slowly; he sounded as if he knew a great deal, and
if what he said was true—Still, Robert was a business
man, wasn't he, and he wasn't sucking blood out of poor
people.

More articles, comments in papers, at dinners, even in
pulpits; red flags at which Robert lowered his head and
charged with wordy bellows. Talk of new laws to regu-
late big business, all as remote from Ellen as echoes from
another star, except that Robert lost his temper and called
John Thurston "one of those vile muckrakers!" She
kept secret her pride that John was smart enough to have
things printed. Mary wished that Rob wouldn't talk
business at home; it seemed to excite him so much. Ellen,
listening to the echoes, thought: we're on a little island,
Mary and the children and I, and Robby just lands there
a few minutes in the evening, after voyaging on seas we
don't know anything about. Presently the twins would
follow him. And Anne? Ellen could feel her tug to be
off. Would she, being a girl, remain on an island?

John Thurston wrote that he was coming east to do a
series of articles for a newspaper, and hoped to see the
family. Love to Ellen and his nephews and niece. Before
he came a bomb tore a hole in a ship, and suddenly there
was a different note in the echoes washed over strange

seas to the island of Robert's house. "Remember the Maine." Buttons on coat lapels and war against the oppressor, Spain. Ellen remembered that day, almost forty years ago, when feeling running through the veins of Coldspring had almost fused separate identities into one being. This emotion was less potent; it produced excitement with less fusion into action. Robert was silent until the telegram from John Thurston. "Coming Tuesday on my way south as special correspondent." Then Robert said, "If I were younger, with no responsibilities." Mary gasped, "Rob, dear! There are plenty of men who like to fight."

"I said if I had no responsibilities, didn't I?" Rob scowled at the tremor of Mary's lips.

On Tuesday afternoon Anne came home early, with mutinous red mouth and grimy tear stains under her eyes. Ellen saw her arrival; she was perched on the high seat of the grocer's delivery wagon, a red apple in her fist. She scrambled to the ground, dodging the man's attempt to help her, and ran into the house.

"I met her at the entrance to the wood, Miss Dacey." The man shouted as if he thought Ellen might be deaf. "She said she was running away, and I had to coax her to come along with me."

Mary's voice, high and sweet, floated into the hall. "Yes, this is Mrs. Dacey. What? No, she's not here. What? Just a minute . . ." Faint rush of feet on thick carpets, and Mary halted, seeing Ellen. "Anne's not here, is she? It's the school. She's run away."

"She just came," said Ellen. Mary's face stiffened in the indignation of arrested fear. "What's happened?"

Mary ran back to the telephone, and Ellen listened.

She couldn't make much of Mary's end of the talk. Just, "She is here. Yes? Oh . . ." with descending cadence, and another "Oh! Oh! I'm so sorry." She turned from the instrument, her eyes cold blue. "Ellen, she scratched a little boy. For no reason. Badly, Miss Wallace says. She shut her in the cloak room until she would apologize."

"What made her scratch him?" Ellen tingled humbly with shared guilt.

"No reason! Little Freddy Alger." Mary's voice rose. "Terrible! No, I'll see to her." She moved agilely past Ellen up the stairs. Ellen sat down to wait. If Mary insisted. . . . The picture of Freddy Alger, plump and white, hung before her. Even in her distress, Ellen chuckled. She scratched him for something, I know. Mary would come down, presently, defeated; Ellen knew that look on Anne's face.

Mary did return, soon, flushed, her skirts rustling irritation. "She won't say a word. I told her to go to bed at once. I don't see why I should have such a child! I ought to send her back to school, but she seems feverish."

"I'll go wash her face." Ellen rose briskly. "Maybe she'll tell me."

"This is serious, Ellen. You'll baby her."

"No. But we don't want her sick, and John Thurston coming to-night. They shouldn't have shut her up. She never would stand that."

"She's been a wicked child."

"Maybe I can find out." Ellen walked past Mary, adding, "Miss Wallace was careless, letting her start out alone. Anything might have happened, only the grocer's man saw her."

Anne sat on the floor, yanking at a knotted shoestring

She wouldn't lift her head. Ellen drew a low rocker close to her and sat down. "Put your foot on my knee," she said, and after an instant, Anne did. Ellen untied the knots. "Now get your wrapper," she said. The child's feet lagged, but she came back from the closet with the fuzzy yellow bathrobe and nightgown. Ellen helped with the buttons, slipped the nightgown over her averted head, down over her rigid, shivering, thin body. "Now I'll have to wash you a little." The heavy feet dragged after her to the bathroom. Stubborn small face, with closed eyelids lifted to the dabs of the washrag, a shiver that was almost a sigh. "Now get into your bed." Ellen's voice was dry, without a revealing cadence. She smoothed the sheet over the edge of pink blanket. As she reached the door she heard a scramble. Anne had rolled over, thrusting up her dark head, stiff-necked. "Are you going away?" Ellen waited a moment. "I might sit down a little while," she considered, crossing to the window. She sat down, hidden from Anne by the footboard of the bed. Presently a small voice travelled over the footboard. "Now I can't see my uncle, can I?"

Ellen rocked. "Not very well."

"I don't care." A jouncing of the bed, and a cautious head rising over the foot. Ellen did not turn. "I hate ever'body." She banged her forehead against the wooden rail and sank out of sight. "Will they put me in prison, An' Telly?"

"What for?"

"I made him all bludgy." Hushed surprise in her voice.

Ellen rose and looked across at the heap of blankets and child.

"You better lie down and cover up," she said.

"I was running away and the grocer man grabbed me and said he'd tell my pa. He was bigger than me and I couldn't help it when he brought me home."

"He saved me a lot of trouble. I'd had to look for you, of course."

Anne peered at her through long lashes. Suddenly she began to cry, accumulated sobs muffled in the blanket she wound over her head. Ellen sat on the edge of the bed and waited until Anne emerged again, desperate confusion on her damp face. "He kept saying 'Anne Dacey thinks she's smart! Anne Dacey thinks she's smart!' He wrote it in a paper and the other boys giggled. I skinned the cat better'n he could an I had two buttons for 'member the Maine an' he said I couldn't be a soldier, an' he grabbed my buttons because he said they were for boys."

"I'm sorry you scratched him. Aren't you?"

Anne shook her head violently, and in the shaking managed to move closer, until her cheek rested on Ellen's arm. "I couldn't stand it in that closet, An' Telly! Rubbers and ole clothes. I thought I heard 'em coming to take me to prison an' I climbed through the window."

"Scratching isn't nice, even if boys tease you."

Anne curled her fingers into her palms. "I didn't know I was scratching him," she admitted. "But he was all bludgy."

"Couldn't you feel sorry about that?"

"Maybe—to-morrow." A sob choked Anne's breath.

"Boys don't think you're smart when you scratch. They think you're like a cat." Ellen rose and dexterously straightened Anne under the blankets again. "That's no way to show them how much smarter you are. Now you go to sleep and get rested."

"I didn't hate you, An' Telly." Anne's arms clung about her neck. "I feel sick here." She pressed one hand to her stomach.

"That's because you got mad." Ellen brought her a glass of water, drew the shade until a semi-darkness filled the room. "Lie still and you'll go to sleep and the mad feeling will go away from your stomach. I'll come back by and by." A subdued voice stopped her again at the door.

"Can I see my uncle you told me about?"

"I don't know, Anne. Maybe, when you wake up, you'll be———" Elen hesitated; if she didn't go on, they'd say she spoiled the child, and yet—"you'll feel like being sorry for Freddy. Then we'll see." As she closed the door she sighed, amused at her own sense of shame.

Mary had a caller. Ellen could hear the voices of the women from the parlor, polite voices in a sort of game, making charming tissue paper packages of their phrases, winding them in pale ribbons, tying bows with the final cadence. For an instant Ellen thought she heard a familiar voice, with the puffy breathing of a fat woman. Grace! She had liked to talk, that way. John Thurston's coming mixed the past and the present in her thoughts. She sat with Grace, waiting, until the train whistled at the siding, and he was gone. Now, years later, she kept that twinge of apology toward Grace, while she walked in the sun around the house to watch the gardener remove the winter overcoats of burlap and straw from the shrubs. She sat down on the iron bench and wished that John Thurston would come. It wearied her, this weaving back and forth of her thoughts. The callers were going; she heard the arrival of their carriage. Across the lawn marched the twins, one on each side of Miss Thorne, as if they timed their approach. Ellen heard the flutter of words: "These are your little boys? How adorable! Haven't they grown!" and the twins, unabashed, "How'do! How'do!" Miss Thorne was training them well.

Mary wanted Ellen. She asked the gardener. . . . Ellen rose. That bench needed fresh paint, the rust crept through its green. "Here I am." Mary was in excellent humor. Ellen had a flash of the contents of her feeling; spring sun, nice little boys, gardener, house, all as it should be. "They want to meet Rob's brother," she said, a little breathless, "they think he's so clever, and now going to war. I thought maybe an informal dinner, if he is here long enough." She was so pleased that she thrust her arm through Ellen's, as they walked toward the house. "Would he——"

"He's probably in a hurry." Ellen couldn't fit John Thurston into one of Mary's dinners.

"I mean to tell Rob he mustn't argue. His brother may be famous, who knows? If he's here so short a time . . . he'll want to see the children. Oh!" Her mouth hardened, at a discordant stroke in the composite of herself. "What did Anne have to say? I can't understand. . . ."

"That boy's been picking on her," said Ellen. "She's told me about him more than once. Jealous. She's smarter than he is and he don't like it. She's sorry about the scratching."

"She ought to be punished. And just now, when

her uncle ought to see her. . . . No, she can't come down."

Rob telephoned. John Thurston was at the office; they would be out at once. He had to get the six something to the city, to catch the special train south. Mary thought it ridiculous to hurry off so, when she had planned such a nice dinner.

Ellen waited at the front door until the livery hack swung into sight. A thin, loose-jointed stranger stepped out on the stone block and came toward her, gray hair tumbling over a high forehead, deep lines cutting across hollow cheeks. Not a stranger, a baby with solemn face crawling busily after her, a boy with dark, excited eyes turning to wave good-by as he reached the street, shabby carpet bag banging at his knees. His hands were on her shoulders, and as he kissed her Ellen heard that old whisper of contrition: "I never loved him enough, and he needed it more than Robby." Behind them Rob's voice pushed, bland and managing. "Too bad John's in such a rush, after all these years. Twenty minutes. I've told the driver to wait. He's got all my family to meet." Mary, exhibit one. The twins, clattering downstairs. "This one is your namesake, Thurston." A wave of Rob's hand indicated the house. "We've made lots of changes. Sorry you couldn't have stayed, to go over the factory. Got a big plant."

John Thurston plunged his hands deep into his pockets and looked unmoved at all these evidences of Rob's expansion.

"Where's Anne?" Rob had discovered a missing detail. "She's An' Telly's pet."

Mary fluttered deprecatingly. "She was naughty, very. I'm afraid she can't come down."

"I'm going to take John Thurston up to see her," said Ellen, suddenly bold. Twenty minutes, and half of them already gone! "Come along." Hand under his elbow, she marched up the stairs before Mary could find proper objections. She heard a scurry of bare feet across the floor, and smiled at the agitation of blankets. "Here's your uncle, Anne." The small dark head popped up. John Thurston shook hands, his spectacles magnifying the wrinkles at the corners of his eyes. Eyes like Anne's, thought Ellen. But she pounces at things, and he never could. "I wanted to see what Ellen is so fond of," he said, releasing the child's hands.

"Me," said Anne. She snuggled under the covers. "I was afraid maybe you wouldn't come upstairs."

"Flora's married." John Thurston turned quickly toward Ellen. "A nice young chap, printer. Last month. So——" He lifted a hand, loosely, fingers curving from empty palm. "That job's done, and I'm out looking for something else. Florence sent her love to you, Ellen, if I saw you. She was grateful to you, always. I——" He ran his fingers through his gray hair. "Wish I had more time. Like to tell you about things. She got me started oi. a paper, Florence did. I'd have been a hostler all my days, only she boosted me right out of that."

"I been reading some of your pieces. I said to myself, 'John Thurston's getting back at folks now.'"

He stared, the bitter shrewdness of his lined face relaxing into a sudden laugh. "Why, maybe that's it! How'd you guess? You wait. When I come back, I'm going

to write books, Ellen. Good ones. Only I've had so far
to come . . . from nothing to start with." He turned
back to the bed where Anne watched, alert. "You're
lucky, having Ellen, aren't you? Well, so long."

As Ellen followed him toward the door, he jerked a
hand toward the hall below, grinning. "Poor Rob's all
het up, wanting me to be the prodigal, and sentimental
over hero stuff at the same time. I'm just going on a
paper job. We don't touch anywhere, Rob and I, and
when I was a kid I worshipped him. Well. You're comfortable, aren't you? Happy?" He laid an arm about
her shoulders and rubbed his cheek on hers. "It was
you I wanted to see. Now I got to go."

"There's so much I want to talk about," mourned Ellen
as they descended the stairs, his arm again through hers.

"Next time." John Thurston nodded as Rob snapped
the lid of his watch. "Time's up, eh?" His shoulders
had a twisted shrug under Mary's farewell . . . something about noble and interesting and heroic in a gulp.
Ellen watched them drive off, Rob erect and important,
John Thurston leaning out of the door to wave to her.
More than a decade, and then quarter of an hour. And
in it, he seemed less strange than Rob.

"Isn't it queer, how different brothers can be." Mary
was shooing the twins upstairs. "Although I scarcely saw
him, he stayed upstairs so long. But Rob is—well, more
finished."

Ellen was thinking: I could talk to John Thurston
about things inside of me. "Yes," she answered vaguely,
"he always was."

Rob subscribed to the New York daily for which his
brother was to write, and Ellen tried to build for herself

a picture of that remote foreign land where John Thurston
was going. She could see him, spectacled, thin, awkward,
but palm trees, guerrilla warfare, Rough Riders, all the
newspaper phrases, stayed lifeless on the paper. There
were his articles, presently, by "our correspondent, J. T.
Dacey." Mary complained that he might tell about things
without being so frank and horrid, but Rob assured her
that war was a man's affair and couldn't be nice. One
morning Ellen, searching through the paper, found no
article with his name. Fear, a rude hand, clutched at her
stomach so that she felt sick. "He's just run out of
things to talk about," said Rob. Ellen knew. Several
day later there was a brief notice. Our distinguished
correspondent, J. T. Dacey, taken suddenly ill, died on
Thursday.

Rob telephoned, telegraphed, in a blustering excitement.
Then he came home with news. The body had been
shipped to Colorado, as per instructions prior to death.

"I can't go out there! I said it was a mistake, that
the body belonged in Coldspring, in the family lot. That
damned red tape!"

"It's where Florence is buried," said Ellen. "He
wouldn't expect you to go out there."

"He never did have any consideration for the family."

Ellen couldn't argue about it. She felt acute bereave-
ment; John Thurston in his death had put an end to
possibility she had just begun to comprehend.

Through the summer people discussed newspaper headlines with relish, the remote drama adding a fillip to life.
Mary said occasionally, "Yes, my husband's only brother
gave his life there." That seemed to make the family
participators in the drama. Rob thought he ought to

look into things. John Thurston might have left a little
something, although he hadn't been, well, successful. One
summer evening he beckoned Ellen into the sitting room
and closed the door.

"Did you ever hear of a Mrs. Jackson?" he asked.
"Mrs. Flora Jackson?"

Jackson. No. But Ellen knew few of Mary's friends.

"No, not here. John Thurston left all he had to her.
Some woman he picked up. Here was his namesake,
little Thurston——" Rob's nostrils had an ugly flare. "He
had insurance, quite a bit."

"Flora Jackson!" That little girl peering through the
crack of the door. Of course. He'd said Flora had married. "It's the girl he brought up. His wife's daughter,
Flora."

"That girl!" Was there, or did Ellen only fear it,
avidity in the swift contempt of Rob's face. "Well, what
more could you expect? An outsider. When he might
have made amends by considering his own people."

"She wasn't an outsider to him, Robby." Ellen thought
an old face pushed into the contours of Rob's as she
watched, twitching at a cheek muscle. "You don't need
the money." Whose face hung there, behind Rob's?

"It's the principle of the thing. I don't like it."

Oh, she knew! Thurston, her brother, Rob's father,
with eager, sly fingers closing on every dollar of hers,
of his father's, of Grace's.

"Don't!" she said. "You sound like your father!"
Before Rob's angry amazement took words, she left him.
Her knees felt old and weary as she climbed the stairs.
But Rob never spoke of John Thurston's insurance again,
at least to her.

At the end of the summer Ellen had a letter, bulky with an enclosure.

Dear Aunt Ellen,

I always remembered the time you came to see my mother. She spoke of you often with love and so did my father. In the little bundle of his things they sent me from the camp where he died was this letter for you. He was good to me. I hope some day we can meet maybe. Yours with love even if I don't know you.   Flora.

The enclosed letter lay on Ellen's knees, the sprawling address, Miss Ellen Dacey, evoking in her eyes the long, sensitive fingers of John Thurston, fingers quiet now for months.

Dear Ellen. (Like a husky voice at her shoulder.) If, as I suspect to-night, I've caught the fever in this camp, I'm no doubt done for. I'm sorry, for I haven't done much that I meant to do before I checked off. My life's been printer's pi. I'm leaving the small bit of earthly goods I own to Flora. A woman needs a windbreak, I think. You don't, thanks to Rob. I wish I could have done it for you, instead of him. Lot's of things I'd like to talk to you about. But this damned fever's lifting the top of my head, just back of my ears . . . you know. To-morrow I'll finish this miserable letter. Good-night, with love, dear Ellen.

When is to-morrow? That old, insistent query of Anne's slipped into Ellen's mind. Beyond the tree tops, as she looked through the open windows, lay a milky-blue disk of summer sea, a small sail at the horizon like a fin, catching the sun. She stood at the window, her quiet eyes searching as the white fin disappeared. She hugged her arms suddenly to her sides; death was a hand with a chisel, chipping at you, bit by bit, until at the end of too many years, it left you . . . what?

XII

On Mary's rosewood desk accumulated a pile of neat pamphlets, bulletins of schools for girls, in Westchester, in Connecticut, in Massachusetts, even in Virginia. Ellen saw them, undisturbed, until a remark of Robert's suddenly dropped a red glare of peril over them.

"Haven't you told Ellen yet?" he was saying, as Ellen reached the door of the porch in a leisurely search for a hair ribbon Anne had lost.

"No." Mary drawled her word. "I thought when everything was settled, she . . . well, you know how she is about Anne. As if she owned her. I dread starting a discussion."

"Nonsense! If you think the child ought to go, there's nothing for her to say. She's a little sharp sometimes. I didn't like her attitude about John Thurston's death. After all, she's an old woman."

Ellen pushed against the screen door; her heart, mired in fear, scarcely moved. "I was looking for Anne's hair ribbon," she said, loudly. In the soft light through curtained windows she saw them turn wooden for a second of embarrassment.

"It's in my room," Mary said. "She can't have it for two days. I told her she needn't lose ribbons. Put on a piece of twine." Then, as Ellen strained through the warm darkness, trying to see their faces, she went on ingratiatingly. "Aunt Ellen, we were just talking over our plan for Anne. Miss Wallace advised a school where only girls went. I was quite mortified; she really doesn't want Anne back. We've selected a school that trains personalities. The principal says that many of their most charming graduates were difficult children when they came, tomboys, or tempers." Ellen saw Mary's small hand, flexed delicately at the wrist, in an inclusive gesture. "Anne does need training. The little girls all wear sailor suits in school and have music and everything. It's a beautiful place."

"You're sending Anne away from——" Ellen stopped. "From home?"

"It's a home school. They take girls even younger than Anne. We were lucky to be able to put her in this year. Some child was withdrawn only last month. It's near Boston, too."

"She's too much of a handful for you, An' Telly." Rob stretched lazily in his chair. "Winding you around her finger. I know!"

After all, I'm an old woman: that phrase lay on Ellen's tongue, so bitter, so astringent that her dried mouth could form no words.

"The sewing woman's coming in a day or so, for underclothes. The little sailor suits are ordered through the school." Mary had a tone of lightness, through which her relief breathed, relief that Ellen made no protest. She even added, "I knew you would agree that it was the best plan. To-morrow I'll tell Anne. She's so excitable. . . ."

"She's such a little girl." That thin, swiftly growing body . . . a thought that pressed against her knees and thighs and breasts, that clutched at her neck. "Such a little girl to send away from her folks."

"She'll enjoy it. All the little girls like the school. There'll be vacations, of course." Pleased finality in Mary's tone.

Ellen stood at the foot of the stairs, one hand on the mahogany ball that topped the newel post. Her cold, hard hand pressed against the dark wood; the wood was soft, warm, crumpling down like pasteboard under her hand, and the long dark shining rail of mahogany came writhing like a snake to twist about her, choking her. She stumbled forward, the edge of a step striking her knees. With the pain, the snake slid back into place, the post stood up with the proper rigidity of wood, and Ellen drew her fingers across trembling eyelids. "I better be careful," she thought. Endlessly the stairs stretched up as she started to climb. "I'm too old to feel so bad."

PART II

I

There stood her father, talking with a man, lifting his face as the train stopped, too late to see Anne's dab at the window. My darling daughter, at last you return. . . . She picked up the travelling bag, glanced about with what felt to her like cool haughtiness to see whether the few passengers lounging, heat-stupefied, in the green dusty seats, realized that she, Anne Dacey, was home from school, that her father, that distinguished gentleman in gray, awaited her. Yes, I must go at once, without waiting for the final exercises. My father's old aunt, who has always lived with us, is sinking, and wishes to see me. She has always been devoted to me.

Her father's moustache tickled her nose. "Well, Anne!" He took her bag. "Your train's late. Have a pleasant trip?"

"It's fatiguing to travel in June." Mademoiselle Bonté had said that as they waited in New York for Anne's local.

Her father beckoned to a hackman half asleep on his perch. She had expected their own carriage. "I can't get away just yet. Your mother wanted me to meet you. She's done up. You better go right out to the house."

The train creaked and pulled off as Anne sank against rusty black cushions. That picture of herself in the dap-

243

per blue and black carriage, with shining lamps. They'd
think she was just anybody! Then she remembered. "Is
. . . is An' Telly worse?"

"About the same. Remarkable constitution, the doctors say. But she's an old woman. Your mother didn't
like to send for you, right in the middle of your graduat-
ing exercises. But An' Telly worried so, asking for you.
I'll be home in an hour."

Off rolled the hack, through the wide, familiar village
street, along the winding post road, with plop, plop of
horses' feet and crack of driver's circling whip. A sharp
turn between two old stone posts into their own road,
with green dimness of afternoon light slanting through
the leaves and the crunch of gravel under steady hoof-
beats. Anne, limp in her corner, watched the fringed
tassel of the window curtain jiggle. Home-comings rolled
together into that dusty smell of felt upholstery with a
crazy tassel and a flat emptiness in her stomach. She'd
thought this time would be different; she hadn't been
home for months, with that Christmas house party; she
had finished school, she had nobly answered their summons, without a whimper, and then, in a minute, all the
drama of arrival burst into, "Well, Anne! I can't get
away." This was the last home-coming. She was finished. She had no more place in the school; that was
over a smooth wall confronting her, as impenetrable as
the wall at home . . . other people, busy with their own
affairs. Her emptiness sucked down her breath in a gasp.
There was the house, its dull red brick sprayed with
exquisite new green of ivy. My father's old aunt, who
has always lived with us. Suddenly Anne's full lower
lip quivered, and her cheeks tingled in shame. Suppose

An' Telly had heard her say that, as if she didn't care!
The child who had loved Ellen crept out from hiding,
full of scorn for the self-pitying young lady who lay so
limply against the dingy cushions. Yet . . . last summer, the summer before, wasn't I horrid to her? Anne
scrambled out of the hack, forgetting her elegance. An'
Telly was very sick, and it was Anne she wanted.

Mary met her in the hall, the ruffles of her sprigged
dimity swaying gently. "My dear child! How well you
look." Her kiss dropped coolly on Anne's mouth. "Too
bad to hurry you home, but your father thought best.
No, don't rush upstairs like that. Take off your things
and wash the train dust away. I'll tell the nurse you're
here."

Anne stood in her own room; the maple furniture, the
blue rug, the curtains tied back crisply, changed as she
looked from a quiet room into a kaleidescope, twirling
bits of Anne last year, the year before, back to the child
who stood at the doorway with her mother on that first,
infinitely remote homecoming.

"Isn't it nice, Anne? Mamma planned it for your own
room." And the child had said, "Where is An' Telly's
bed?"

"In her own room, of course. You aren't a baby any
longer."

The little thud of her conviction, her fear that An'
Telly, too, wanted to be rid of her. She had refused
to come for Anne, those first weeks of black loneliness
at school. Now she wouldn't have her in the corner of
the old room. "You mustn't bother Aunt Ellen. She is
getting old." French, music lessons, school ahead, where
that hunger for attention found more meat. "Yes, Anne's

the youngest in her class." An' Telly had still thought her a baby, pursuing her with rubbers and hair ribbons and milk. Sometimes those early years in school Anne had dreamed of the sweet shelter of An' Telly's arms, cradling her securely. Then when she came home for the summer, a little fiend stood up within her, bristling contradictions, impertinencies, rebellions. An' Telly could baby the twins; they stayed home, didn't they? Anne was finding others to love. The music teacher, Miss Dufrey. A crush, the girls called it, that dizzy thrill when her fingers straightened Anne's hand over the keys. She'd left the school . . . married, they said. Under the slanting yellow lid of the maple desk was a letter from her. Dear little Anne. Later Miss Thoms, her English teacher. Tragic eyes under her wings of gray hair; once she had kissed Anne. Two years of that devotion, with Anne hating the long summers, contrary emotions just under the skin where anyone could touch them off. The kaleidoscope tinkled with confusion of hours; Anne, slamming the door to find angry refuge against the persecuting world.

"If you wish to come in now, Miss Dacey is awake." Scattered bits of old Annes fled under the professional tone of the nurse. "You mustn't stay long. She's asked for you constantly."

"I came as soon as I could." Anne threw out a defense against the superior starched authority of the woman. She didn't dare ask: is she very sick? Is she . . .

"I'll wait here in the hall." The nurse closed the door softly after Anne. A dim room, a whiff of some drug white and dry like the counterpane, a slow whistling breath. An' Telly, waiting for her, touched into strangeness, so quietly she lay, but smiling with gentle, sunken mouth.

"Why, Anne!" A stir of her hand, too heavy for the wrist to lift. Anne kissed her. Skin papery, hot to the girl's lips, the bones hot and brittle under her hands. "You did come. That's good." Ellen's eyes were black in deep sockets, her hair made a silver swirl across the pillow.

"I'm sorry you're sick." Anne sat in a small chair close to the bed, her hands still about Ellen's. "I came right away." She wanted with a sharp longing that swelled in her throat to be comforted against the strangeness in Ellen's seeking eyes, comforted by An' Telly, holding her.

"You been growing up, Anne. It's a long time . . . a long time . . . since I saw you."

"I'm through school now. I'm going to stay home. You'll see me all the time." A swift picture . . . charming young girl devoting herself to old aunt.

"No, you won't!" The fingers under Anne's palm jerked into a hard-knuckled old hand. Not if I can help it!" The whistle of her breath inflated the words with harshness. "That's why I want to see you. Only"—her fist burrowed at her breast—"I can't talk much."

"The nurse said——"

"Oh, her!" Under Ellen's eyes was a gleam. "She's too smart," she whispered. Anne giggled, unexpectedly. The barrier of strangeness between them toppled; they were conspirators again, leagued against . . . what? "She got me scared," Ellen's hoarse whisper confided to Anne. "She and the doctor, thinking I was dying. I made them send for you. I had to tell you——" Slowly

Ellen's lids drooped over her eyes, thin lids with fine veins like tiny roots branching from the temples; in their close, sealed convexity they made a mystery of her face. Anne was no longer frightened. "I don't want to die yet." The lids folded upward again. "Mebbe I'll fool 'em. But if I should . . . I had to tell you something. About the island. I want you to get off the island, Anne. Ever since I thought about it's being an island women get stuck on, all their lives, I said, 'Anne must get off.' And I want to live to see you. It's been as good as getting off myself, thinking about you. I couldn't get off, poor Alice never could, but it's different now. You can find you something . . . if only I could talk better. . . ."

"Don't try now, An' Telly." The words danced about Anne, meaningless. Ellen's hand burned her palm. It must be fever.

"No, I'm not crazy." The black eyes insisted. "I have to explain."

"You've talked long enough this time, Miss Dacey." The crips rustle of the white uniform filled the twilight of the room. "Your niece will be here to-morrow."

"So will I, in spite of you folks!" Ellen hurled defiance at the nurse hoarsely, and her fingers pulled Anne close to her head. "I'll tell you later. You'll have to go, now. She's awful bossy."

"She's going to get better now!" Anne borrowed courage from Ellen, and tossed her words at the superior starched figure as she retreated. An' Telly wouldn't die. She said she'd be better.

"You saw Aunt Ellen?" Her mother was waiting in Anne's room. "Did she recognize you? She's been in a stupor most of the time. The doctor was afraid of pneumonia and of course at her age——"

"She feels better!" Say it, whispered a small voice; make it come true. "She talked till the nurse drove me out."

"What about?"

"Oh, nothing. Just . . . you know, how I'd grown." Islands, and Alice—who was Alice?—and getting off—— Perhaps it meant something important.

"You have grown, darling." Mary's eyes appraised her daughter. "With your hair that way, quite a young lady. We'll have to plan for next winter. It will be nice to have a daughter again. I think the boys are taller than you, a little. You must tell me all about the commencement. If Ellen hadn't been taken ill . . . but I was so nervous I couldn't risk a trip to Brookline. Is that your father?" She listened at the door. "I'll run down and see. Coming¹ Well, as soon as you are ready."

Anne could not hear her mother's feet on the thick nap of the stair carpet, but presently the light voice sounded, at a distance. She thinks I'm pretty. Quite a young lady. The boys are taller. They're always something—er. I'm to stay home now. Nice to have a daughter. No, you won't. Not if I can help it. Islands. What did An' Telly mean? Alice. There had been someone, a name, years back. Another aunt, was it? Anne looked out of the window, her head against the casement. What a horrid feeling, mixing up all your insides, school ended, forever, coming home ended. The nurse shooing you out. Like a goldfish, gaping, while someone put fresh water in the bowl. Not knowing what you'd have

to swim in next. Maybe Ellen could have told, but she
was sick. She won't die! She promised.

Anne sat on the top step of the porch, waiting for the
doctor to come out. The nurse had laid an officious finger
to her lips when Anne went to Ellen's door. Sh-h! she
had said. Anne set her feet together on the next step,
knees hunched. The June sun crept about her wrists,
her ankles, the base of her neck, softening the strained
waiting. Not just for the doctor. For everything. All
the neat harness of school suddenly gone forever. What
did you do when everything let you suddenly down, flop!
No, she didn't want to help her mother arrange flowers.
She wanted to see An' Telly.

She flung up her head. The doctor's bay horse pawed
at the gravel, arching his slender leg, plopping down his
foot. Something inside Anne arched and plopped and
scattered gravel, meaningless, persistent. Just at the
curve of the driveway—she hadn't seen it yesterday—
against the fresh green of maples beyond, a dogwood tree
spread its flat planes of white; its ordered loveliness
stopped that pawing foot of herself, stretched herself
back, level, a drift of beauty in petals, flat, quiet, under
a flat blue sky.

"Here's the young lady." Anne clattered to her feet.
"Well, you were the right tonic to prescribe. Your aunt's
better already." Anne gave him her hand. His amused
gaze, under bushy gray eyebrows, said: "Think you're
grown up, eh? Well, we remember your baby days!"

"Quite a girl you've got, Mrs. Dacey." Her mother
had followed him to the porch, with her soft flutter of
attention.

"It's too bad we had to send for Anne, since Aunt

Ellen is out of danger. It's wonderful if you can pull
an old woman like that out of death's grasp."

"Anne did it, you see." He drew on a heavy driving
glove, buttoned his linen duster. "Not me. So you're
all through school, are you? Nothing to do but catch
some unsuspecting young man for a husband, eh?"

"Not just yet, Doctor." But Mary laughed with him.
"I have to keep my little girl for a while."

"Not for long. Just look at her!" The doctor patted
Anne's shoulder. "She may even have him picked."

"I don't want any husband." Shame, like colored light,
rippled at Anne's nerve ends. They'd talked about it, at
school, the girls, but softly, at night. "I don't want——"

"Let's see your tongue! You must be pretty sick!"

Anne broke away from his hand, ran past her mother's
deprecating laughter into the house. In the hall she
stopped an instant, shame like gnats about her. What
were they saying?

"Doesn't like teasing, does she?" The doctor's laugh
was complacent. "Makes me feel pretty old, to see these
young things coming along."

Anne flung herself up the stairs before her mother came
in. They thought it was a joke. Here's another girl
ready for a husband.

The nurse frowned as Anne bumped into her.

"Miss Dacey is asking for you. She mustn't talk this
morning."

"She's better. The doctor said so."

"Yes. Her fever's almost gone. Talking irritates her
throat. You may go in, if she doesn't talk."

Ellen's hands were as heavy as yesterday against the
counterpane, but her eyes were bright, with droll wrinkles

at the corners. As Anne bent over her she whispered, "Fooled 'em, didn't I? Got a frog in my throat, that's all."

"I'll sit down right here, An' Telly, and tell you about school. If you talk, she'll chase me right out." Anne's anger burst into little rockets of chatter. An' Telly was better. To-morrow, later, oh, days and days ahead, they'd talk about islands, whatever they were. "So we had a play, and I was the prince. Very handsome." On and on. Something in An' Telly like the dogwood, calm, lifted in a plane under the sky.

II

Before Ellen was well enough to come downstairs, Anne had almost forgotten the matter of islands. The dogwood blossoms had rusted and fallen, the boys, Charles and Thurston, had come home from their fortnight in the country with the head master of their school. With them had come their tutor, a pale young man with silky black moustache, who was to see that by fall they were ready for the last year at a college preparatory school. Anne giggled at the first glimpse of their new long trousers—as if their legs had grown up earlier than the rest of them. "See, they're taller than their mother!" Mary stood between them, her hands hooked into their elbows. Thin as yet, with the air of sketch for a man, unfinished, in the planes of their young faces, in the angles of shoulders, throats, long arms. Their blue eyes inspected Anne, casualness hiding a new kind of curiosity. "One of the fellows was asking about you," said Charles. "Said he heard our sister was home. Fred Alger."

"Oh—Freddy! He's a fat boy, isn't he?" Anne saw a flicker in her mother's pleasure; she remembered about Freddy. She let her lashes droop. The tutor was staring at her, too.

"Fat? My land, no. He's going to college this fall. He plays football. He'll be around this summer. Gee, it's tough we got to grind, with all we want to do an' everything. Where's Wilson going to bunk, mother? If we hustle, we can get a swim before lunch."

"I've put Mr. Wilson in the east room, next yours. Aren't you too warm to swim?"

"Warm?" Thurston's laugh split into a high piping, as he seized a bag and started up the stairs, two steps at a time. Charles was after him, and Mr. Wilson, dropping his hat, rescuing it from Anne's feet, bowing to her and to her mother with an air of grave apology, followed the boys.

"He looks like a studious young man," said Mary. "I hope he'll be firm with them."

"He looks very firm," said Anne. She was thinking about the moustache, black and silky, and the wave of hair above his white forehead. From the living room she heard them descending, an avalanche, and the echo of the banging door hung like a taunt in her ears. She was submerged in unhappiness. "I wish I could go swimming," she cried out, as if that broke her heart. "I wish I could swim!"

"Why, Anne!" Mary seated herself at a sewing table; her small hands paused above the basket. "Swim? Why, I've lived near the water all my life, and never thought of swimming."

"Well, I've thought of it." Anne let her head droop.

Pity filled her that it was not she who had run and shouted and leaped into the water.

"I don't know." Mary lifted the square of linen and bent over it. Was she thinking, or only counting threads? Anne thrust out her lip. "Don't do that, Anne, you'll ruin your mouth. I shouldn't mind if you went into the water. But swimming . . . it might make you too muscular. Your arms are very nice now. You wouldn't like great bulging muscles, would you?"

"I don't care." Anne looked at her wrist, pushing the cuff up. "Are they nice?" That appraising scrutiny of her brothers. What did the new tutor think?

"You mustn't be vain, Anne. But a girl has to consider such things."

Anne considered them, sitting in the hammock in the shady corner of the porch. Presently the boys came back, their fair hair sleeked damply from shining foreheads, neckties crooked. "Salt in your eyebrow, kid," said Thurston, sprawling on the step. "Say, that tennis court's got to be cut. Grass's a foot high."

"Foot your granny." Charles spit on a forefinger and drew it over his gold eyebrow. "Gee, I'm starved. Where's lunch?"

"Do you play lawn tennis, Miss Dacey?" Wilson lounged against the pillar, looking over the boys toward Anne.

"Miss Dacey my—eye!" Charles pounded a fist on his brother's knee.

"A little." Anne ignored the boys.

"She plays like all girls." Charles jumped to his feet at the clang of the Chinese gong in the hall. " 'Fraid her back hair'll come down."

Anne wanted to drop into their old wrangles. "Yours won't, you skinny frog!" The words nipped at her tongue, and she swallowed them, rising with a little shake of her green linen skirts, a little arching of her eyebrows at Mr. Wilson. Amazingly Thurston spoke up: "Cut it, you cub. You like to play with girls yourself, sometimes." And the twins reverted to that first scrutiny of Anne, their sister, but a girl.

That night Anne knelt at her window sill; one great star seemed to pry apart the leaves, darting at her. He looks unhappy, she thought. As if he suffered. Well, having to teach those silly boys. His eyes had come to meet hers, often, that night. A finger stroking that black moustache. A languor crept over her restlessness, over her self-pity; anticipation, lifting her with the gentle rhythm of waves that never reached a shore to break into hard thoughts. To-morrow. And to-morrow.

The summer days ran swiftly, caught into the tempo of the twins' existence. In the mornings they were shut into the old schoolroom at the top of the house, with the tutor and books. Anne sat mornings in the new sun parlor off the sitting room, embroidering. "That school has done wonders for Anne," said her mother. Sometimes Mr. Wilson came downstairs hunting for a book. Anne's arm curved slowly, fingers poised above the disk within the hoops. At first Mr. Wilson nodded, formally, running his hand along a shelf of books. Anne saw him glance back at her. Then he came to the doorway. "Do you ravel it out at night?" he asked, "or is it a different piece to-day?"

"It takes a long time." Anne stroked the plump rose with its intricate shading of petals.

"Why don't you just pick one of these?" He broke a spray of crimson rambler behind her and dropped it on the drumhead of ivory hoop. "The things you women do to take up time!"

Anne cut her thread, lifting her eyes for an instant. "Yes?" She flaunted it, silly, useless bit of cloth, her hands curving over it, the spray of roses tumbling to the floor.

"Oh, Mr. Wilson!" Mary's voice startled the young man.

"I came down for this volume of the cyclopedia. A question. . . ."

When he had gone, Mary stood in the doorway. Anne chose a strand of pink silk.

"See, mother. Would you use this shade next?"

"Perhaps not so light." Mary tried another. Then she picked up the rambler spray. "That young man . . ." She looked at Anne. . . . "He's merely a hired tutor."

Anne's eyes were innocent. "Why, mother! He came for a book."

Later, when the boys clattered downstairs, to pedal off madly on their bicycles, to swim, Anne shrugged. Deep within her an old self tugged faintly; but it was a kite, flat on the ground, and she no longer flung it into the air, letting out string as she ran, trying to sail it higher than the world. This new self was a stranger, holding her to unfamiliar languor, fluttering at her eyelids, a thing of wiles and enticing humilities that Anne had never before felt.

Her father noticed it. He strolled into the living room before dinner one evening, where Anne sat at the piano, her dark head dreaming over the keys, the white silk

flowing away from her slim waist. "In the gloaming,
oh, my darling. . . ."

"That's a pretty song." Her father looked at her. "I
can't get used to having such a grown-up daughter."

Anne peered at him; admiration in his eyes, too. All
these years when he hadn't seen her rumbled like a threat
against the demure, half smile on her soft mouth.

"I used to think you were a little pest." Anne shared
his laughter, flatteringly. "You're much more like your
mother than I expected. Not in looks, but . . . What
was that song you were playing?"

Anne let one hand touch a chord gently. She didn't
want to move, to disturb that picture of charming young
girl. The next instant the picture vanished, with Ellen
looking in at the doorway.

"Hello, An' Telly!" Father's mood hurried to include
her, too. "You going to have dinner with the family
to-night?"

"No." Ellen's eyes were black and opaque as the onyx
brooch at the neck of her gray dress. "Bread and milk's
all I can eat this time of day. I just thought I heard you
folks."

"Pretty nice to have Anne home." Rob picked up the
folded paper, and pushed a chair near the reading lamp.
"All made over into a young lady. Surprising, isn't
it?"

"I was surprised." Ellen looked at Anne, with a little
droop of her deep, arched lids. "Yes, I was."

Anne glanced quickly down at her hands, curved so
sweetly against the creamy silk of her skirt. An' Telly
needn't look at her that way, disappointed, searching.
Why, she was nothing but an old, old, *old* maid, who

spent all day grubbing among her flowers. Anne hadn't time, with the new urgencies of life——

"They grow up like lightning." Rob settled himself with the paper. "Lord, it won't be a minute till the boys are through college and in business with me."

"Just a minute." Ellen turned, with a soft shuffle of her black, heel-less boots. "I just been outdoors," she added. "It's good growing weather, a night like this."

"Pretty smart old lady." Rob crackled the paper. "Growing weather." He laughed. "You'd know she was a farmer's daughter, wouldn't you? Old folks go back to their early days, they say."

Anne, motionless on her stool, kept for a moment that last glimpse; stooped, broad shoulders pulling at the seams of the gray dress, the old head sagging forward, lifting the smoothly pinned braid of silver. I ought to be kind to her, she's so old. She just doesn't want me to grow up. Anne flourished those thoughts against that faint, disturbing fear. What did An' Telly look for, when her dark eyes peered that way under their thin lids? For another Anne, buried?

"Good evening. May I come in?" Mr. Wilson, hurrying softly into the room, with a sleek, sidewise cant of his black head. Anne, preening her skirts with fingertips, forgot Ellen. How deferentially he stood, listening to her father. What were they talking about . . . men's talk . . . but his eyes slid off toward her, with that shiny awareness.

Then there was a birthday dance for Anne. A small, informal affair, explained her mother. Winter would be time enough for real functions. Lanterns in the trees about the house, a small orchestra, canvas spread taut

over the brussels carpets of the square drawing room and
living room behind, girls in fluffy summer dresses spilling
out of carriages, boys serious and proper in best clothes
and evening dignity. Mr. Wilson did not dance; he was
an ironic spectator, waiting—Anne knew!—for the recur-
rent moments when she swung past his corner.

They were all such kids, the boys. Friends of her
brothers, at school, whom they brought up in turn. "May
I have the next dance?" A two-step and then a waltz.
No need to say much: you just "Ohed!" and looked sidewise and laughed. A chubby little fellow with red hair
bowed in front of her. Why, yesterday she'd see him
fall off his bicycle. "My dance, isn't it?" One hand
clasped hers, moistly, the other pressed between her shoulders; his pink forehead glistened, his lips moved silently,
"One-two-three!" as he manouvered her away from the
edge of the room. Anne closed her eyes. Suppose Mr.
Wilson, with his silky moustache close to her ear. . . .
Plump! Anne's eyes flew open as she stiffened to keep
her balance. "Say!" Her partner was scarlet, and the
couple they had bumped went sliding away. Who was
that boy, bristly pompadour, prominent blue eyes? "I'm
sorry," Anne's partner panted. "I ought to'v reversed."

"Never mind. I'm tired. Let's sit down here."

"That ole Fred Alger thinks he owns the floor, always."
The boy sat beside Anne on the divan pushed under the
high pier glass. "Of course, he's a college man, and most
of us aren't yet."

Anne saw him, across the room, his head close to the
curly hair of the girl. Talking about her! Telling her—
under the glitter of light and movement which were
Anne's consciousness of the party, another feeling streaked

like a small snake, an old hatred, exciting. He was looking at her, across the moving figures, weaving toward her on the waltz rhythm. The music stopped, and Anne turned toward her companion, all soft flutters of animation. In the pier glass she could see the charming shadow of her dark head, the curve of her throat, and beyond that, moving nearer in the polished glass, the stocky, assured figure of Fred Alger. He had lost the girl in green.

"Don't you remember me?"

Her fingers moved through the string of pearls, her upward glance was discreet. Then she was dancing with him, bold swinging to the violin notes. "I wouldn't forget you." His hands held her firmly. "Didn't we use to quarrel, though?"

"Um. I hated you." Anne felt his arm draw her into its hard arc.

"Do you now?"

"I don't know."

He laughed, teeth flashing in his tanned face, pleased excitement in his tone. Anne heard it, let her head droop; she was a dream, submissive, rhythmic, in his guidance. His knee touched hers once, his fingers tightened. Past the musicians' stand, through the open doors of the sun parlor; they ran down the steps, across the grass. Colored moons of lanterns bobbed in the trees, the light from windows lay gold across the dark lawn. "Too crowded in there." Gravel of the path under Anne's thin slippers, dim fragrance breathing from the pale stock that bordered the path. Shapes came slowly out of the first blackness of the night, flowers shoulder high, moth-pale, the dark line of the hedge at the end of the garden, then below the mysterious glimmer of water, with faint light moving where the waves curled back at touch of the sand. Beside Anne, a square bulk of shadow.

"Do you still scratch?" His hand lifted hers.

"You were an awful little boy."

"You were a little wild cat!" His arm crept around her waist. "Weren't you? Why, they had to send you away to save my life."

Anne was silent. His touch was a stranger on stealthy feet, opening secret doors through which light poured.

"Do you hate me, now?" His face came close to hers, and he kissed her, until Anne pulled away with a little noise, and turning, ran through the garden, stars whirling in her blood.

She stumbled at the low step of the sun porch, and then rocked at her mother's sharp, "Anne! Where have you been?" from the doorway. "You shouldn't leave your guests this way."

A swift glance over her shoulder. No, he had stopped, back there where the colored moons swung in the branches. "I was coming back," said Anne. "I was warm. I was gone just a minute."

"No, you weren't. Was it the Alger boy? Where is he?"

"He's coming." Anne slipped past her mother, into the gay rooms. Later, as she danced past the pier glass, she saw a face, hers, with crimson, guilty lips. There was Fred Alger, with the girl in green, her curls close to his cheek. Mr. Wilson had gone. He was too old. She saw Fred staring at her. She wouldn't dance again with him.

Then it was over. She had escaped at last her mother's

inquisitive good-night, and could lie in the dark, her hands clasped lightly over her small breasts. Kissing . . . was sweet. *Anne Dacey thinks she's smart.* His mouth, hard on hers. . . . To-morrow he would come again . . . to-morrow.

But he didn't come. Anne wondered: he wouldn't wait for her to ask him. Boys didn't have to wait. . . . "Did you have a good time at your party?" Mr. Wilson asked her. How silly he looked, with his long neck and his solemn, patronizing eyes! "Oh, yes." Anne avoided the library; she didn't like to look at him. He was busy, anyway. Summer had nearly ended, and the boys had to grind hard.

One afternoon as she watched the twins dive about the tennis court, she said: "Why don't you ask some of the boys to come out, to play?" She tossed a ball toward Charles. "Fred Alger said he liked to play."

Charles scowled at her. "He's gone. He went early for football try-outs." He stood in front of her, letting the balls roll crazily on his racket. "You didn't get soft on him, did you? He thinks he's a devil with the ladies, Fred does. We saw you sneaking out."

"Don't be a silly baby." Anne's hand darted against the racket, spilling the balls.

"Well, we did!" He shrilled after her as she strolled away from the court, her hands clenched.

III

Ellen walked through the garden, a flat basket on one arm, scissors in her hand. The larkspur spikes were faded, pink edges creeping into their blue; she cut them,

holding the basket to catch the faded loveliness. Too dry
weather for second blooms, she thought. The plants'll
be stronger another year. Her feet pressed firmly against
the ground, enjoying the feel of fine, worked earth.
Beyond the larkspur was the square of zinnias; they were
nice flowers, lasting long enough for you to feel acquainted
with them. She looked at one crimson blossom; for days
she'd been watching that. She could feel it grow, expanding from the center, pushing open the smooth funnels of
its petals; like a slow fountain, a zinnia grew. At the
sound of hasty feet on the gravel path she turned from
the flower. Anne hurried past, not seeing her, flinging
herself recklessly down the steps beyond the garden
toward the beach. Ellen stared after the girl, her fingers
crumpling the silken withered petals of the larkspur in
her basket. Suddenly she followed her.

She placed her feet with caution on the boulder steps
down to the beach. The wind flapped the brim of her
old gardening hat, a southeast breeze that had merged
sky and sea at the horizon into indefinite gray, from which
the faint fog smell blew. There was Anne, farther along
the beach, motionless against the rocks as if she hoped
not to be seen. Ellen plodded across the sand, feeling
the fog in her old knees. The girl's stiff shoulders, her
hard, colorless face, shouted plainly, "Go away! Leave
me alone." Ellen moved cautiously from sand to the
rocky tip of the beach and let herself down on a stone
near Anne.

"I ought to bring a cushion for my bones," she said,
tucking her basket between two rocks. Anne's eyebrows
drew together over wary, resentful eyes. Careful, thought
Ellen, or she'll run off. "Smell the fog?" She spread

her hands, one on each knee; large hands, dull blue veins netting the knuckles, generous fingers curving. Almost like separate creatures they ached for the child Anne, whom they could have held and comforted. Something had happened to Anne. Ellen thought: now's my time. If she's hurt, there may be a hole to get in past the game she's playing, the game they've taught her, her school, her mother, all of them.

"I've been so busy with my flowers," she said, "I never could get time to finish up our talk. Here summer's most gone, and I suppose you'll be going off again."

"Where?" Anne braced one foot against a ledge. "Where would I go?"

"I thought you might have some plans or other. Are you just going to stay home working on cushions?"

"What would I do?" Anne was angry, as if some intense emotion slipped into this channel, gratified at a victim. "What are you talking about, An' Telly?"

"I 'spose, really, I'm talking about what I'd do if I was you." Ellen's face was obscured as the wind bent the loose hat brim. "That's foolish, isn't it? When you were a little girl, I got into that habit. Here's Anne, I always said to myself. She can have everything you haven't, do all the things you couldn't. But fancy work and fellows!" Ellen stopped, one hand at her mouth; her teeth always clacked if she got excited. Anne scrambled to her feet, her cheeks crimson. Ellen went on, steadily, "You used to be pretty smart, too. Smarter than your brothers, I always thought. You wouldn't catch one of them settling down in the house with fancy work, would you?"

"They're boys. They're expected to do things."

"I always expected you to. Not that I knew exactly what, but I expected you'd want something more than trying to look pretty. That's good enough for a summer. What about the rest of your life, Anne Dacey?"

"I don't care about the rest of my life." Anne's face twisted like a child's, trying not to cry. "I felt bad enough anyway, and now you talk to me this way! I can't help being a girl. I don't want to be."

One of Ellen's hands wavered up toward Anne, and then came back smartly to her knee. "You think I'm an interfering old woman. I know. Too old to guess how you feel. Nobody wants you to help being a girl. But you're going to be a woman, and I don't want you to be empty. Emptiness is terrible, Anne. Oh, you don't know what I'm talking about, do you?" Ellen stared up at the slight, belligerent figure, huddled so tensely above her, teeth worrying at the full under lip, eyes large with tears. "When I was sick, I said I wanted to tell you about islands. You remember?" Her voice pleaded, anxiously, against the girl, against an inner mockery: you're a fool, Ellen; you can't make a young girl see what you see. "Here's this house, with all of us in it." She nodded away from the sea. "Only Robby, your father, he goes away. He took me through his factory, one day, two years ago. Did you ever go there? Men, making tools for folks to use. More than that. Part of the world outside. Crops and money and the lives of lots of folks all over the world. Then he comes home, off the ocean, to a little separate island. Your mother's good; she just thinks about him, and making the island pleasant. But she never stretched off it. There's men's work and women's work, I guess. They used to go along together. They ought to now. I don't want you sticking on an island all your days. Rob's mother did, till she got fat and died. Your aunt Alice did, only she never even got a husband, and her island shrunk up till she killed herself." Ellen could see that face, down where the seaweed floated at the point of rock. "You ask your father if he'll take you through his factories. Maybe you'd see what I mean. There's more to the world than a few feelings in you. Your brothers are getting ready to get off this island. Because they'll be men. Folks think a girl can just sit around, shrivelling up, till some man's ready to marry her. Why, you can't even know how to love, that way. It'd be better if your folks was poor and you had to work." The pressure of Ellen's hands on her knees was a prayer: Give me words to show her! What's the use of me loving her so, if I can't make her see? What's the use of all the years of my life, if I can't help her?

Anne waited, a kind of sullen attention on her face.

"Here I'm trying to push you off, and it's no good if you don't want something, yourself. When you were a little girl——" Ellen could see her, intent, fiery, playing there on the sand. . . . "You had pride and you wouldn't be put upon. Maybe they broke you of it at your stylish school."

"Maybe." Anne's voice dragged. "I used to fight little boys, and now——"

"Now you want 'em to kiss you," Ellen interrupted, briskly. "That's natural. Only you need to want something else, too."

With a roar from the bank above them, down came

the two boys, golden legs flashing as they hurled themselves into the water. Behind them trotted Mr. Wilson,
his hairy legs more deliberate. Anne sat down beside
Ellen, her chin cupped in her hands, her eyes on the three
heads moving out from shore.

"I didn't learn to swim this summer," she said.

Ellen grunted as she tried to ease her stiff hips into
comfort. She'd sat too long on that rock; she was heavy
with fatigue.

"You'll have to pull me up." She'd talked herself
empty, and Anne said she hadn't learned to swim! Anne,
bracing herself for the pull, kept her hands tight about
Ellen's.

"I wanted to, first," she said, "only Mother——"

Charles had seen them, and shouted across the soft light
of the water, "Hi! Come on in, girls! Water's fine!"
His shout ended in a splash as he somersaulted, a white
porpoise.

Ellen moved her stiff legs across the sand, Anne beside
her looking at the swimmers. "There! I forgot my
basket. The tide'll get it." She watched Anne run back,
the wind moulding her slim curves of breasts and thighs.
She came, still running, withered larkspur dropping from
the tilted basket. Ellen's hands pulled at the smooth,
wiry stuff of her dress above her heart. She was that
young, wind-blown figure, running lightly, identified with
it by years of brooding; ah, no, she was an old, futile
woman. How could she touch the girl? Anne had her
own course to run.

"An' Telly!" Anne clung to her arm, as they climbed
the rough stones. "Did you hate it, being a girl? I
loath it. Being sweet and polite and delicate. Some-

thing makes me act that way, so they'll like me. Then, deep underneath, I'm ashamed. An' Telly, what can I do?" Her fingers shook Ellen's arm. "I can't bear it, feeling ashamed!"

"I don't know what you're ashamed of." Ellen's heart stopped beating for a suffocating moment. Anne had heard her! Faintly, the slow beating began again. "Nobody likes to feel ashamed. There's lots you can do, if you want to, besides waiting for a fellow. That's what I been saying, that you had to want something." Behind them came the sound of the boys thrashing through shallow water. Anne hurried her aunt along the garden path, away from the sound.

"When I was a girl," said Ellen, slowly, "I had to stay home. To work. My folks needed me. Here's your brothers, going to college, so they'll get ready for work. If it's good for them, I shouldn't think it would hurt you much. You might find out what you want, anyway." There stood Mary and the rector's wife on the porch. "Sh!" Ellen drew her arm from Anne's grasp. "Don't say anything, till you think about it."

Ellen slipped with agility through the rear doorway. She didn't want to face Mary just then, with guilt smeared all over her face. Mary'd thank her for putting ideas in the girl's head. Not that college was magic. Just another step. In her own room, Ellen sat down, forgetting to take off the drooping garden hat, her hands clasped between her knees. From her firmly shut mouth fine wrinkles radiated, as if pain ran a puckering string between her lips. Trying to send Anne away again, after years of waiting for her in an empty room. Wasn't she a fool, a doddering old fool! Her eyes ached, dry with

the need for tears. What had the child said? something
makes me act that way, so they'll like me. Underneath,
I'm ashamed. Oh, grant her weapons for her helplessness,
the richness of life for emptiness!

IV

Amazing, how simply it worked out. Anne announced
one day at luncheon that she thought she'd go to college,
too. Mary said, "Whatever for? You don't have to
teach school." Thurston and Charles looked at her, then
at each other; they began to laugh, and their laughter
encouraged each other until they rocked with shouts.
"Why, only homely girls go to college!" shrieked Charles.
"What you going for? You can get a fellow easier than
that!"

Mary added, "Not one of the daughters of my friends
is going. I scarcely know a girl who'd think of it. They
all wish to stay home with their mothers."

Mr. Wilson, stroking his moustache, said, "Our example is contagious. But think of using those eyes for
books!"

Anne argued, her enthusiasm fattening on her own
words. Her father, the next evening, said, "Ask your
mother. I thought you were going in for society.
Haven't you had enough education? I don't want one
of these blue-stockings around my house."

"Most girls would be glad to have a lovely home like
this," began Mary.

"Just to sit around waiting for something to happen."
Anne rushed headlong. . . . "And all the boys gone off
to college."

Her father laughed. "That's it, eh? No young men."
Their resistance centered Anne on the idea, until she forgot its origin, almost forgot the pit of ignominy from which Ellen had plucked her. Her mother finally said, "But you aren't ready for college. They wouldn't let you in." Then Ellen emerged from the silence in which she had watched the conflict. "She could take some studies in town. Then she'd be home, and if she wanted to go, another year, she'd be ready."

"Are you at the bottom of this, An' Telly?" Rob scrutinized her.

"What do I know about colleges?" said Ellen. "It wasn't me wanted to send Anne away from home."

Anne wondered at the ease with which Ellen's compromise worked. By the end of the winter, it was assumed that Anne would go to college. Wellesley, where she could occasionally see her brothers. "She's too young," Mary said, "for society yet. Girls these days . . ." she sighed. "When I was young, of course we married early. Now the young men wait till they are established. A girl can't expect to marry before her twenties."

V

The morning Anne and her brothers started for college, Ellen did not get up. Her rheumatism bothered her, as well as the thought of the excited breakfast table. Anne rushed upstairs, dropping a bunch of crisp marigolds beside Ellen's untouched breakfast tray.

"You aren't sick, An' Telly?"

"Just lazy. You going, now?"

"Um." Anne kissed her, firm cool lips on the puckered old mouth. "I'll write you about things. You be good till I come back. Good-by!"

Ellen sat up in bed, listening. She heard them in the hall, on the steps, heard the startling sound of that new gasoline buggy Robert had brought—why didn't they use safe horses, with all the family to carry?—heard its receding roar. For a moment she heard voices of the maids, then the closing of a door. Silence crossed her threshold, moved close to her heart as she lay down again. Silence, in which she heard only the little ticking of the clock on the table beside her bed. She reached out a hand and turned it face down. Time hurried enough without a voice. Now she wanted to wait until Anne came back again. To see. . . .

That winter and the next one drifted past. Mary complained of her empty house. "I should have kept Anne at home, now the boys are gone." Her fair skin was sagging into fine wrinkles of bewildered piteousness, and her hair, which she still arranged with great care, had dimmed into ash tones. Ellen looked at her, pityingly. "Children don't last for always," she said. And to herself she added, "It's not your house that's empty." Robert grew heavier and balder; he had bought stock in one of the new gasoline carriage companies, and he talked of trying something of the sort in farm machinery. Ellen was indignant. "Plow with one of those things? Why, a horse is part of a plow, Robby." She found her muscles tensed to the handles of a plow, saw the roll of strong flanks, the gleam of a soil-polished plowshare. "You never held a plow," she said, wagging her head. "You don't know, for all you sell them."

"Farming's different now, An' Telly. Take those

ranches . . ." He forgot her as he talked. Mary wasn't
listening, for she broke in:

"I think I'll go to the city with you next time. If
Ellen won't mind staying here. There's a new massage
I was hearing about."

Ellen didn't mind. "I'm past the need of folks around
me," she said. It was pleasant to have the house to herself. She could spend all day in the greenhouse Rob
had built in the fall, at the suggestion of Giuseppi the
gardener. Mary always fussed about her staying there.
"You'll get cold, steaming yourself up so. And you
shouldn't work so hard." With Mary gone, Ellen could
live there, in the warm, penetrating smell of rich earth
and growing things. Giuseppi didn't mind her puttering.
"You make grow the things you touch," he told her,
chewing away on a stem of a rose leaf. If she felt tired,
she could sit down, watching him build small cold frames
for the spring planting. She forgot it was winter, a season to endure, even when the snow lay in blue ridges
along the metal seams of the glass roof overhead. At
Christmas she would show Anne the greenhouse. But
Anne, at Christmas, was too busy for more than a glance.
"Lovely roses. How are you, Giuseppi?" Then she
was off, a friend in Rye, from her college, shopping in
New York with her mother, the theatre. She's happy,
thought Ellen. Out of all this, something may grow
within her.

The second summer the twins were under a cloud; conditions in math and chemistry. "Why can't you do as
well as your sister?" inquired Rob, when he had read
the Dean's letter. "Now you've got to spend the summer
grinding." Ellen saw Anne's head lift, with a sniff of

triumph in the flare of her nostrils. Charles grunted.
"Oh, girls!" he said, and Thurston broke in, eagerly,
"They take it seriously, Father, all this book stuff. It's
all they've got to do. Now a fellow's got to get out and
see something of life."

"Life! I suppose chorus girls and poker and . . . and
beer are life!" Anne crunched a piece of toast.

"Listen at her!" Charles pretended to look shocked.
"Who's been stuffing you?"

"We hear about you little Harvard boys. Life!"

"I suppose Bible classes and stoodent government meetings are life, aren't they? Anyway, our courses are stiff.
You have to bone to get 'em. No girl stuff there."

"When I was your age"—Robert rose, a heavy, important figure—"I took the job I had to do seriously. I had
to work for a chance to go back. That's how I am where
I am to-day. Now you can get down to business this
summer and clear off your slates, or I'll put you both in
the factory melting junk. You hear me? Borrow some
of your sister's brains if you can." He strode away.

Anne gave her brothers an irritatingly superior smile,
but Mary fluttered to their rescue. "I wish you wouldn't
say such things, Anne. You only bother your father.
The boys do have hard courses, I'm sure."

"That's the idea." Charles hooked a hand through his
mother's arm, and Thurston strolled on the other side.
Mary's eyes said, "My handsome big sons!" "We'll bone
this summer. Lots of fellows got plucked." The door
closed behind them, and Anne, glancing at Ellen's dry
wrinkles, laughed.

"Aren't they the limit? It's true, though, about girls
taking it seriously. You have to, don't you? If you

didn't, where would you be? Father says he'd put them to melting junk, but what would he do with me?"

"You like it, don't you?" Ellen coaxed Anne into talk. The stories, full of unfamiliar words, made a series of mosaics in Ellen's mind, in all of which one figure stood out sharp of outline, Anne, a bright, hard figure engaged in curious satisfactions. Chairman of her society, member of student government board, one of a debating team, basket ball forward, in the honors group. Ellen had no images for these phrases, but she knew the meaning of the tones in Anne's voice. She thought: it's separate, Anne's college. A little world inside the real world, where these girls play at things, as if there weren't any other world with men in it, men running it. Anne's happy, being on top; she liked to be on top. Happy, while it lasts.

VI

Anne, the first year at home after she finished college, had the same thought about her four years. They were a pleasant game, abruptly ended. She emerged slowly from that separateness. Her brothers had entered the Dacey business, Charles in the New York office, Thurston in the Bridgeport branch, learning the manufacturing side. Anne drifted, bereft of her importance.

"I'd like to close this house and take an apartment in New York," said Mary. "Then Charles could stay with us. But with the servants . . . and Ellen's so old . . . you couldn't move her now, and you can't leave her for the whole winter." Mary sighed, examining the letters the maid had left on her desk. "If your father'd only let them start here, so they could be at home this winter.

But no, Thurston must begin where his father did, and Charles must shut himself up in an office. I'm sure I don't see——" she peered near-sightedly at a card. "This sounds like an interesting display, Anne. Coats with dolman sleeves. We might——"

Anne went into the sun parlor, where pale October sunlight touched the delicate fronds of ferns.

"And, Anne!" Her mother complained gently after her. "Will you take that candy booth at the charity bazaar next week? You say you've nothing to do. I'm sure that's something."

Through the glass Anne could see the garden, with a frost-darkened patch of marigolds. Ellen was there, her thin, tall body making an arc against the walking stick her hands clutched, with Giuseppi crouched at her feet, digging up bulbs. Her head, in a funny gray bonnet, with white hair blown around her face, was like a milkweed pod. You couldn't move her into town, any more than you could break a milkweed stalk, without destruction of its last, poised moment. "She's grown very childish." Mary looked through the door for a moment. "She forgets everything and won't listen to what I say. I'll tell them you'll take that booth, then." Anne heard her small slippers on the polished floor. If she went into the garden, An' Telly would prod at her with those old black eyes. She looks at me as if she were waiting for something—I don't know what. Waiting for me to find a husband. Oh, not An' Telly! Everybody else. Dinner parties and dances, eligible young men sparring warily with angling young women. Her mother making what she thought were clever inquiries about the friend Charles had brought home last Sunday, lifting her small, ringed hands in a gesture of light despair at Anne's, "Conceited and dull!" "But, Anne, you're so terribly critical. I can't see that college has done a thing but made you restless and hard to suit. You acted as if you liked him."

Yes, I did. Anne broke a fern frond, her fingers stripping the rough leaves from the stem. I always act that way. On the half of the French doors she could see a shadow of herself: shadowy dark hair, pointed face with soft mouth, cruel restless hands. I'm sweet and soft and flattering. See, don't you want me? My red mouth, my white throat, my way of smiling as I listen? And then when they come after me, as I mean them to come . . . something shrieks and runs. I don't want them. What —what do I want?

She turned from the dim reflection. Ellen came slowly up the path, pointing her stick toward something, Giuseppi following, gesturing. The stick wavered. Anne stared at the old hand that gripped it. The gray sweater sleeve slipped away from shrunken wrist, the sunlight turned the large hand into a fist of bones and veins under mottled old skin. How did it feel to be as old as that? Did you know, then, what you wanted? The figure in the garden touched off a faint memory. Ellen had said something, years ago, crossing that garden . . . about islands, and emptiness. Anne strained back into that moment. Nothing is worse than emptiness. College was to do something, wasn't it, filling up emptiness? It just didn't hitch up, with the desultory hours now.

Suddenly the teeth of her thought set hard on the bone of her brothers. Charles, patronizing in his new importance. "Gee, you have it easy. Nothing to do, while I grind eight hours a day." Something had picked them

up, him and Thurston, and fitted them into a frame. They
hadn't done it, themselves. A pattern clicked them into
place. And I hate the pattern that is supposed to fit me.
Anne's hands were cold as she brushed the stripped fern
stem from them. Ellen's stick rapped on the stone outside the porch, and Anne moved hastily away. I have to
do it, myself. Me, Anne Dacey. If I want something
else. That's it.

VII

The next few years were to Anne a medley of attempts,
pitiful and ridiculous when she looked back, running an
emotional gamut from hope and enthusiasm through into
futile irritation. The College Settlement needed people
to help. Wasn't that what she wanted? Service? She'd
been too selfish. At her suggestion that she take a room
at the settlement, even her father grew loud voiced. "The
least you can do is to stay under our roof. What do you
think we have a daughter for?" So Anne went into town
three days a week; she found an illusion of importance in
the mere fact of having to take a train, of crowding into
a subway, of walking along the narrow, cluttered street
to number forty-five. Then: "Oh, it's Miss Dacey. Let's
see . . . you couldn't take the group in weaving, could
you? Or wood carving? Well, there are some children
in the reading room, the second door there, if you'd tell
them a story, perhaps." Anne sat on a hard chair, trying
to weave a spell for a dozen little animals, a fairy story.
An oily head close to her face, grubby hands smoothing
her furs. "Gee, ain't it soft! Like cats. Did the kink
have him a coat like yours, lady?" Or a sewing class.
Or games, for older children. Hard, shrewd, bold faces,

eyeing her with wary appraisal. Scuffles, and "Ouch!
He pinched me! Say, lady, he cheats. I seen him!"

"They don't know how to play." Anne sank exhausted
in a chair opposite Miss Winch, the resident head worker.
"They're millions of years old."

"We want to teach them." The woman's plump, grimy
hands shuffled papers on her desk. "Americanization, the
spirit of the group." Anne felt too well groomed, under
her inspection. "Of course, what we need is money.
For trained workers."

"Instead of me? You don't want people like me,
amateurs."

"Oh, Miss Dacey!" Miss Winch rubbed deprecatingly
at her small nose. "It isn't that we don't appreciate your
coming."

"Yes." Anne shrugged, fastening her coat as she
stepped into the windy twilight of the street. She'd ask
her father to send them a check. He'd be glad to buy
her off.

Later, luncheon with two girls she had known at college. "Secretarial work is what you want, Anne. That's
the only thing for women, except teaching or nursing."
Anne walked to their office building. Solid, assured, it
embraced the people who hurried in and out. Well, she'd
try that. Several months at a business college, one flight
up, on Broadway. Pothooks and Now is the time for all
good men. Brashy young girls and one elderly woman
in black. Weeks of a sedative, in spite of a snatch of
talk caught in the cloak room: "One of these rich girls
taking bread out of somebody's mouth that needs it. She's
got a nerve." It's not bread I want. Anne brushed the
moment out of mind.

Charles spent a fortnight at home in the summer, streaking about the country in a new small car his father had bought. "What's the idea, anyhow?" He peered over Anne's shoulder at the notebook she was poking out of sight. "You going out in the world as office gurul?"

"You got a job for me?"

"No, sir. I want somebody young and ignorant enough to look way up to me." Charles strutted toward the door, chin pulled into his soft collar with a pompous, "Hem! Besides . . ." he grinned around at Anne. . . . "Where'd be the kick to asking you to step out to dinner."

"Charles!" Mary brushed affectionately at his sleeve. "You don't flirt with office girls?"

"Sh! Come inside, Mother, and I'll tell you how they adore me! Say, I'm going to drive to Bridgeport and get ole Thurs to come down. Rotten shame he's tied up there, with me home. Some girl'll catch me yet, all unprotected by my twin." Anne heard his gay voice receding. Funny, that effect Charles gave, of a boy with life by the tail, swinging it in hilarious circles around his head. Just last night she'd heard her father: "Why didn't you come into the office this afternoon? I had those men, and wanted to talk over shipments with you."

"Sorry, Dad. I drove out to Rye Beach and picked up Sue Parks and her friend . . . clean forgot it." He was diving from the room as he spoke.

"Rob, this is his vacation," interposed Mary.

"Listen to him!" The roar and pop of the car, starting off with cut-out open, filled the quiet, pleasant room. "Tearing off . . . he's got no more responsibility than a two year old."

"But he works hard. He's told me——"

"Him? If he'd even pretend to be interested. I give him a start not one man in a thousand has, and what does he do? Humph. Now Thurston has settled down to business. I'll put Charles in the smelter if he doesn't watch out."

"He's so young, Rob, and people all like him." Anne had drifted away, leaving them. She had a sisterly indignation toward Charles, and she envied him.

Just before Charles went back to town, there was a dance at a new summer hotel beyond Rye. Anne, bored by the sober young man who was her escort . . . too impressed by the Daceys, he was . . . danced listlessly through part of the night. Then Charles came up, grinning. "You know Freddy, don't you, Anne?" He left her facing Fred Alger, stocky, inquisitive boldness under straight brows. They danced, a challenge in the skilful pressure of his arm.

"What years and years. . . ." Anne let the tiny bells of her femininity tinkle at him, tiny, brass-tongued bells. "You aren't married yet?"

"Nor you? Let's see . . . you went to college? Never guess it, looking at you."

Of course he wouldn't remember, kissing a child, years ago. And she had forgotten. Other kisses since then. "What are you doing?" Engineering, at M. I. T. Stiff course. Awful kick, though. Better than football. "Pretty good music. You always did dance well." His blue eyes, prodding at her. Hard long line of upper lip, oddly matured by a slash of wrinkle across the left cheek. More tinkle of bells. "What you going to engineer?" Keep him talking, while the music drifted over the floor, through windows where the night lay dark on the water.

"Dams, somewhere. South America. Or bridges, maybe."
He could talk about that, boastfully. Men's affairs. Grand
deeds. They were at the doorway as the music stopped.
"Me married? I'm surprised at you, though." His fingers moved, like a question, along the cool satin of her
arm from elbow to wrist. "He travels swiftest who travels
light, you know. I've a long way, oh a long way to go."
They walked across the veranda, down toward the stretch
of sand. Tell me about it. All Anne's bells tinkling, isn't
it wonderful, what you will do. Two of Anne walked
there, silver slippers on fine white sand; one swaying
gently, listening, mist on her hair, hunger on her lips;
the other hard, flame bright, crying, he's blind and stupid,
he doesn't know I'm here, me, as much as he is here; he
doesn't know, this soft, silly thing is all he can see, ever.
"You didn't scratch, once." Ah, he was excited; all her
bells ringing in his ears, in his blood. She let him kiss
her, with the little sound of dark water near her feet.
"Once more, Anne." Easing her hunger, whetting her
scorn. "Let's dance, here!" Faint music twisted with
the soft water noises And later, "I've just one day
before I have to go to Boston. Can I see you, to-morrow?"

"I'm going to town to-morrow. So sorry." Anne
saw the line at the corner of his mouth deepen.

"What for?"

Anne waved a languid summons toward the solemn
young man who had brought her.

"I'm going to look for a job," she said. "Don't laugh!
I mean it. Some time, years after, we may meet again."

Charles waited, Sue Parks tucked beside him, to drive
them home. Anne felt the night air divide along her

flushed cheeks. Oh, fool, she thought. Why not have
let him come? You've tangled him. You might do
more. No. She shut her eyes, to feel the wind cool on
her lids. If I could bend him down, as he bends me; if
he had to come with tinkling bells, instead of all a-swag-
ger, as a man . . . Oh, what do I want?

A note from him.

Dear Anne,
   More ways than one of scratching, aren't there? You've
got me going. Wait till I see you again, which will be the
next time I'm in your town.
                                                    Yours,
                                                       Fred.

Anne tried that fall to find some use for her pothooks
and typing. Nobody wanted a "part-time stenographer,"
as the employment agent classified her. She tutored for
a few weeks, an adenoidal child who was behind his
class. Then she typed a few hours a week for an elderly
man. His genealogy. Anne worked copying his fussy,
interlined pages into neat sheets. It's not getting me anywhere, she thought. I'm still just an amateur, fiddling
along. If I were a genius at something. . . .

By Christmas the last page of the genealogy was typed,
and Anne was at home. Fred telephoned. He'd busted
away from his job for a few days, just to see her. They
rode together across fields brown through the thin snow,
blackened knobs of sumach left from October flame in
the fence corners. "You ride well." Fred urged his
horse close, reaching to grasp her rein. Anne brought
her crop down on her horse's flank. She was escaping
him, the swift, hard motion of the horse quickening her
heart. He's thinking about kissing me. A glimpse of

his wind-reddened face, sulky, threatening, excited her. She raced him back to the stables where she slid from the horse before he or the groom could touch her hand. He caught her as she walked toward the house, his fingers burrowing under the cuff of her gauntlet. The earth cantered faintly. "Stay to luncheon?" Anne eluded him at the door, just as Mary came into the hall. She saw her mother prick her nose, as if that lunge of Fred cluttered the air. Through luncheon her mother maintained an air of pleased speculation. She hadn't seen Fred for years, although she saw his mother often and had heard how well he was doing. Fred furnished details about that, flirting with her until she preened and fluttered. Ellen, sitting opposite Fred, pretended to be deaf, cupping her gnarled hand behind her ear with frequent, "Eh! What's that?" Fred explained again. He'd finish the Boston job in the summer. He had an offer from a construction firm in New York he might accept. He watched Anne as he talked. Settle down somewhere . . . good offer.

"What about dams in South America?" Anne jeered.

"More money right here. I begin to feel as if I'd played around long enough." White teeth flashing in a bold grin. He meant something.

After luncheon, an hour in the living room. Anne lounged, drowsy, in the corner of the davenport drawn near the fire of logs. Mary talked brightly, and then, with significant eyebrows, withdrew. Fred looked down at Anne, his face flushed under his prominent blue eyes. Then he had her in his arms, Anne's eyelids shut under his hard mouth. Sweet . . . just lying there, a kind of giving up, drugging everything but the turmoil of senses.

Anne stirred, lifting her head. Footsteps above her, old feet dragging. She pushed away, lifting her hand to brush her hair from her face. "What a mess?" She rose, smoothing her crumpled riding shirt. "Look what you've done to me!"

"I'd like to do more than that." Fred was at her side, his breath on her cheek, but Anne retreated.

"That's enough!" she insisted. "No. Time you went home."

"Anne, listen, Anne! If I come back, in the summer. . . . Can't we fix it up? I'm crazy about you. I mean it, about settling down. You . . . you're just the wife I want."

Anne turned the door knob. "I don't know." She couldn't think. The languor of her body held her darkly quiescent. "I don't know."

"Well, I'll make you know!" He let her go, stood looking up the stairs after her.

Anne lay awake that night. Just the kind of wife he wanted, was she? And she . . . did she want him? Sharply, out of the twist of feeling, came a decision.

She announced that she was taking a real job, every day. If the family wouldn't let her live in town, as Charles did, she'd go back and forth every day. Plenty of trains. Mary cried a little. "I thought you'd get over it. So much you could do here . . . the church . . . clubs . . . and Fred Alger is coming back." Anne said: "I'll live here, but I've got to try this."

She tried it. Long days, from the early train, crowded and stuffy, through hours in a dark rear office, typing form letters for the small publishing house: sets of the classics, sold by mail order on the installment plan; to the rush for the evening train, crowded and stuffy again. Anne counted the bills in her envelope at the end of the first week. If I had to live on this, she thought, all the work might seem real.

She stuck it out. Her father said, "I don't see what you're getting out of this. You make yourself so tired you're no good to us or anybody else." Anne thought: if I stick, I may get something.

Then, abruptly, Charles produced a crisis. Something about a woman. Anne picked up stray crumbs. Her mother knew only that Rob had extricated the poor boy from some adventures and now insisted on sending him off to Europe. "He can go along with Pendleton." Rob looked older, deflated, under his righteous anger. "Pendleton's booked to sail next Saturday, on this foreign market business. May make a man of Charles. Give him a chance, break him off from this crowd he's running with." He roared down Mary's protests that Europe was so far. "Far? I'd send him to China if I could. Africa! A son of mine! Thank God it didn't get in the papers." A subdued Charles appeared to bid his mother good-by. Mary, by the day he was to sail, was in bed.

"I think, Miss Dacey"—the doctor had been talking with her father—"you ought to realize your mother's condition. At her age she shouldn't have worries . . . critical period. . . . Why not stay home for a while? You look fagged. Relieve her mind about you, anyway."

So Anne dropped her work. You're glad to have an excuse, you fake, she accused herself. Save your face. Pleasant to stretch in leisurely days of reading, riding, nothing. Why not just wait for Fred to come again? A proper match. . . . Unbidden pulses leaped, drawing her under the net of phantasy, so that she seemed again to lie in his arms; then, violently, she would beat away the net, as if such dreams leagued themselves with him to beat her down, to destroy some part of her more native than her soft flesh.

Her mother recovered, plaintively, waiting for the first letters from Charles, assuming Anne's presence as the proper thing. "Have you written to Fred?" she asked one evening. "His mother called to-day." Anne's silence did not deter her. "She's very pleased. I judge there've been lots of girls just throwing themselves at his head. He is attractive."

"I should think myself lucky to land him. Is that it?"

"A suitable match." Mary was offended at Anne's tone. "Your father would like it. Not that we'd try to force you, but we have done a great deal for you, and of course we'd like to see you married to some good man."

"Suppose I hate him——" Anne s tension broke into recklessness. "For his conceit, for the way all his thoughts belittle me . . . because I'm a woman, and he's so far above me——"

"Sometimes you say dreadful things, Anne! I'm sure if a man wants to marry you, he is doing you an honor." Tears brimmed in Mary's eyes. "I don't know what to make of you, and all this difficulty about Charles, too." Her tongue caught a tear at the corner of her quivering mouth. "I'm your mother and I know more about such things than you do. Oh, I know, you've been trying to be one of these modern women, pretending they're as smart as men. You'll be sorry, if you turn out another Dacey old maid. What's more, the longer you wait, the harder it'll be. You never have been a comfort, the way a daughter should."

"I'm sorry, Mother." Anne moved uneasily away, staring with surprise at her mother, a small, tearful, accusing figure. It's years and years of me she's really complaining about. Anne had a clear moment of pity, feeling her mother's bitterness. But she had no words, except a repeated "I'm sorry," as she went away.

In the days that followed, Anne went often to sit in Ellen's room. The old woman had developed an unusual garrulity, a need to pour out stories of her early days: of her mother and the old farm cut from the wilderness, of men going off to hunt for gold, of the Civil War, of Rob as a little boy, of a forgotten uncle. Anne listened tolerantly at first, and then with a growing compulsion to listen, as if in those stories lay hidden significance for her. There was an abruptness, a lack of sequence in them; they pushed into words like chips whirled to the surface of a secret, flowing river. "You look like Martha." Ellen had been nodding in her chair at the window when Anne entered her room. "Like Martha, my mother. I dreamed I was a little girl and saw her. But you're uneasy and afraid of something. Martha wasn't."

Anne thought about Martha. Ellen's stories made her a figure with grandeur. Well, life was like an epic in those days; easy to be heroic. Simpler than to-day.

"Yes, it's the eyes that's like Martha's. The mouth isn't."

Anne laid her fingers involuntarily across her mouth. "I'd like to start out into the wilderness." Her words pushed against her fingers. "What do you think I'm scared of?"

"You think that would be easy, don't you?" Ellen's dry laugh crackled. "You're scared your pride will be hurt. I know. There's still wildernesses, if it isn't woods, I guess. You going to marry that Alger fellow?"

"Would you?"

"Not if I was after wildernesses. He's smart enough. He's like your father. He'll get ahead." Ellen nodded wisely. "He'd make a real pleasant island for you to settle down on. Where's my spectacles?" She fumbled in the folds of her gray dress. "You find 'em for me, Anne." The wrinkles down her cheeks deepened, like parchment with secret symbols of derision and disbelief.

"I'm going to work again, to-morrow." Anne found the glasses in a work basket. " They need a secretary at women's suffrage headquarters. Doesn't that sound grand?" She offered the news placatingly.

"What's that?" Ellen got her glasses in place, and glanced up, her black eyes magnified.

"Get you a vote, so you'll be good as any man."

"I've been that, inside me, quite a while."

VIII

The family did not like her new job. "You'll make yourself conspicuous, Anne. Only fanatics make such a fuss."

I wish I could be a fanatic, thought Anne. That's what An' Telly would like. I'm useful, anyway. They need a secretary. Letters about speeches, funds, lobbying. She liked the excitement of the office, with its outer air of devotion to a great cause, its inner multiplicity of personal moods. She liked the differing women, so articulate and sure about the world and what it needed . . . the emancipation of women from the slavery of the ages. Anne wound herself in phrases: the trouble with women is . . . oh, any number of things: they're too submissive, too isolated, too personal. The trouble with men is . . . all sorts of opposites. She thought: I will care about this intensely. She wrote letters, she interviewed people. She, Anne Dacey, would submerge herself in the cause of women. But sometimes, at night, or when she walked across the fields and into the woods, as spring came on, a part of her thrust up a stubborn head through the swaddling phrases, yelling at her, "You don't really care. You're bluffing!" Oh, she was tired. She wanted to be swallowed up, whole, and here she was, thoughts sticking out in every direction: a willing mouse, with nose and tail and small limp feet hanging out of the cat's mouth. Spring fever, perhaps. If there was such a thing. Ellen's story about her mother, the Martha with eyes like Anne's, lining up her children for a spring dose. The trouble with women . . . a phrase from her swaddlings . . . is that they don't care enough about ideas. Well, who did?

The woman in charge of publicity was taken ill. Would Anne try her hand at that? They had to keep in print, some way. Anne tried, vague as to what she might do. The little office girl who kept the clipping book said there just weren't any stories to clip any more. "Call up Tom Vining, at the Gazette office, Miss Dacey. He's always slid our stuff in. Ask him what's up." Anne called him, asked her question. His voice answering sounded so loud that she glanced about the crowded office, her cheeks scarlet. "Trouble is the stuff's no good. Who's doing it?"

"I am." Anne snapped back. "What's wrong with it?"

"Everything. Why don't you let Josephine go on with it? She had some idea."

"She's sick. I've got to do it." Anne grew humble, under that loud serene voice. "You couldn't tell me. . . ."

"I'll drop in some time. You got to think about the folks you're writing for. Get some human flavor."

Anne stared at the telephone. She could see the owner of that voice. Checked suit and yellow shoes. Bullying her. . . . A few days later when she reached the office she found a man waiting for her. "I'm Vining, Miss Dacey." Her brows puckered faintly at him; awkward, slouching a little in wrinkled clothes, a curious face . . . something accidental in the juxtaposition of the features, clumsy modelling of the broad forehead and heavy chin, the thrust of nose between sandy brows. "If I can help you——" He needed the protection of the telephone, Anne saw, to bully her. He fumbled with his thoughts, blurting out phrases at her, while she looked down her fine nose at him, her lashes delicately satiric. "You, that is, have I made it clear? I can't make them . . . the paper . . . use stuff unless they like it, you know." He stared at her, the fingers of one hand opening and closing in an indecisive gesture, and suddenly, without another word, went away, his head held forward from his loose shoulders. Anne heard him in the entry, bursting into a laugh as loud, as assured as his telephone voice. One of the field workers came in. Had he . . . oh, had he dared make a joke of Anne to her? The boor! She'd show him. Suddenly, in a breath, Anne dug herself into a job. Cold, was she, and too remote? Didn't know what ordinary folks were interested in? That street meeting in Harlem, with the

colored man hauling away his fat wife, bundle of laundry
in her arms. Was that it, a story? Funny? That law
about guardianship of children, and the barber. . . . Anne
sharpened pencils and scrawled pages of yellow paper. A
fortnight later Vining's voice assailed her ear again. "Miss
Dacey? I can rewrite some of that stuff you sent yesterday, if you want me to. No, it wouldn't do as you
wrote it. It's better, but you can't write like Pater for
a New York daily."

"I'd like to talk to you again, some day." Anne slid
down the path of an impulse into swift words. "I want
to get this right. You were so helpful. I've just got to
learn how to do it."

"I'm awfully busy now." His voice retreated, alarmed.

"Oh, any day. Drop in when you have time."

Now, why do I want to see him? Anne pushed the
telephone back on the desk. Under the rim of thought
burrowed something, more vague than feeling, a mole
waving soft blind snout, the delicate pressure of herself
against the awkward, silent, withdrawing self of that
man. He doesn't want to come. Doesn't think me worth
a second look. She asked about him. "Vining? Oh, sort
of a bore. Good head . . . ever seen his articles? He's
so shy it's painful."

Josephine Waite came back, her hatchet face thinner
above the severe tailored suit. Anne said, "Do you mind
if I try a story once in a while? It's interesting, and I'd
like to get the knack."

"Try all you like." The woman glanced over recent
clippings. "Some of this is good. We need more. This
one, now——"

"Mr. Vining rewrote that one."

"Tom?" Josephine laughed. "You must have turned those lambent orbs of yours on him." She laughed again at Anne's protest, "I saw him about two seconds." A few days later she said, "Tom Vining was asking about you. He had some notion about your being a poor girl trying to do news stuff, till I told him who you were. He seemed"— Josephine grinned,—"real disappointed to hear you are a daughter of the idle rich."

When she had bustled away Anne seized the telephone, in haste before sober restraining thought could catch her muscles. Since Mr. Vining was so busy, how about Saturday or Sunday? The country was heavenly now. Why couldn't he come out? She'd meet his train. For a moment she thought he had dropped the receiver, dodging the lasso of shining wire she hurled at him, and then, "Why, thanks. I might."

Sunday was rainy. Anne sent the car to meet Vining's train and waited restlessly in the living room. Too warm for a fire. Silver rain beyond the windows, and roses spreading above their shadowed reflections in polished mahogany of tables. What had she ever asked him to come for? "Who is this young man?" her mother had been curious. "I know you said he worked on a paper, but who is he? Where did you meet him?" What is he coming for, her eyes had insisted. "I'm sure I don't know," Anne said. "Yes, he'll stay for tea, I suppose."

As he hesitated at the door, she wondered why he had come, so evident was his own reluctance at being there. She sat across from him, chattering, hurling at him gay tinsel balls of nothingness which burst because he wouldn't catch them. I'm just tinkling at him, and he thinks I'm a fool, and I can't stop. He sat somewhere behind that curious, roughly modelled face, jeering at her, or just not listening. Tinkle at him, dazzle him! On she ran, and he shifted in his chair, ramming one hand into a pocket, frowning, saying, "Oh, yes. Yes." If she stopped tinkling, he might ask, "What did you want of me?" You know what you wanted, cried a small voice, you wanted him to look until he saw you, small wrists so white along the dull blue velvet of the chair, curving throat, and wave of dark hair, and more. He won't look.

No, he couldn't stay for tea. Even if he had come so far. No. He was determined to go. "Such a pity it's rainy. The woods are lovely. We could have ridden. You ride, of course?"

Just bicycles. He edged with obstinacy toward the door. Anne grew silent, standing with hands linked loosely. He looked at her, past her at the room . . . rugs, hangings, charming pieces of old furniture. "What"—he hesitated as his eyes came gravely back to her—"what do you come in to that office for?"

For an instant a wave lifted in Anne's heart, but it broke into froth the next instant. "Oh, it's dull, doing nothing at all."

He nodded, as if he said, "I thought so." No, he wouldn't have the car. He preferred to walk.

"Well, the young man seemed in a rush!" Mary was on the stairway. "I was just coming in to meet him." Her eyebrows hinted at amusement.

IX

Summer settled into a persistence of heat, so that Anne wondered a little that she continued to go in to the office.

Perhaps she went from stubbornness, against the repeated protests at home. Or perhaps. . . . Tom Vining came occasionally to the office, on casual pretexts. He would look across at Anne as he talked with Josephine, hidden speculation in his crooked, secretive mouth. Each time he came he seemed to nod to himself at finding her still there.

There were letters from Charles, with amusing details of food he had met and the way foreigners did things. Rob lost his deflated look. "Pendleton says the boy's trying to take hold," he announced. "Getting interested in the idea of spreading Dacey implements over the world. I told you it was a good scheme, sending him." Thurston came home for a week, bringing with him the girl he was to marry. Anne watched them with curious uncertainty. Dorothy was soft and polished, with effective lashes and a small red mouth. She flirted with Rob, she was confidential with Mary until she wore through the first maternal suspicion. Toward Anne she showed an edge of wariness. Her manner whispered, slyly, "Oh, you're too clever for little me. But what of it? See the perfectly good man I've caught."

Anne watched her brother's pride, his swaggering adoration. "I wish ole Charles was here. He'd be crazy about Dot. All the men are." That was at breakfast, with Dorothy not yet down, and Anne dressed for her trip to the city. "Frankly, Anne——" Thurston shook his head. "All this stuff you're messing around with isn't doing you a bit of good. Men hate it in a woman. When Fred comes home, he'll make you chuck it."

"Yes?" Anne rose, pulling on her gloves. Retorts bristled like rising quills, but before she spoke Thurston's face altered from the faint hostility in nostrils and mouth. Excitement leaped in his eyes. With a charmed, poised moment at the doorway, Dorothy entered.

When Fred comes back. Soon, now. He'll make you chuck it. What was it Ellen had said? He'll make a pleasant island for you . . . and see that you stay on it. Well—Anne sat away from the sticky wicker of the train seat. Fred had written," Mother says she'll go to a hotel and we can have the Alger place. That'll do for a year or so, and then I'll buy you a house in town." He was as sure as that!

In the afternoon Anne sat in the deserted office, the electric fan droning overhead, stirring the dead warm air against her neck. The heat pressed around her, making of her a small, irritable creature, with nerves curled. I might as well go home, she thought. She felt in her muscles that moving down the stairs and through the street, the heat dividing reluctantly to let her pass. Behind her a door swung open and feet shuffled to an abrupt pause. Anne pushed herself around. Tom Vining, his bumpy forehead moist, relinquished slowly his impulse to turn and go. "Hello. You here? Alone?"

"I can't move." Anne sagged in her chair, her hands limp.

Vining pulled a chair to the corner of her table.

"I should think——" his eyes, sunken under slanting lids, regarded her, while Anne stared at his necktie, badly tied, falling out from his coat with frayed end. "I should think it wouldn't be amusing enough, days like this, to come in."

"Amusing?" Anne's fingers curled into her palms.

"That's what you said."

"Does it amuse you, seeing me here?" Her crinkled nerves snapped; he was ridiculous, uncouth, wrinkled, heat-worn, peering at her.

"No. But I don't get it figured out. You don't care about all this—this suffrage business. You aren't married to it, the way Jo Waite is, and others. You live out there in that grand house, with all the money in the world. You're just playing, aren't you?"

"What difference does it make to you?" Anne poked herself upright, her lethargy squeezed out of being by tight anger.

"I don't know." He rubbed one hand over his head, dragging up ends of lank hair. "I just had to ask you. That's what I came for. To see if you were here. To ask you what you are after, anyway."

"Why?"

"Because you bother me, that's why." Vining thrust his chin forward, under grim lips. His body rose in the chair, as if his muscles stiffened for a plunge. "I want to get you out of my head. What have we got in common, you and I? Look at me!" He dug his fists between his knees, rocking forward. "All my life I've worked. To be something. I mean to write. Things in me. . . . I don't want to make money. I don't want a woman like you . . . spoiled and idle and soft. I know what your kind does to a man. I don't want you! I want someone who'll go with me, a hard way, working, helping. . . . That's what I want. Now laugh at me, the way you did that Sunday, at your house." He got to his feet, a glistening pallor on his face. "It must be this damned weather." He pawed at his cheek. "I didn't mean to talk this way."

"Is it just that I'm . . . that my father's rich, that you

call me names?" Anne's palms clung together, cold and damp. Vining stood above her, aghast at his plunge. Anne looked at him down a long telescope of rage so that he retreated, a diminished figure, grotesquely dismayed. "I didn't laugh at you, then. I'd like to, now." Oh, to keep her rage whirling, blurring the thing that crouched, humble and eager and unseen behind it.

"Yes, it is funny. Me, a hack writer, lonely, clumsy . . . oh, I know what I'm like! . . . and you. Laugh some more. Then your eyelids won't beat at my brain all night. I won't love you, do you hear? I won't be part of your amusement." He backed away from her, his face crimson. "Now I've said all this, I'll have to keep away. Till you get tired of this, too."

Anne sat motionless when he had gone. Within her the wheel of anger stopped, and under it climbed that hidden thing, eager, humble. She lifted her arms to the wooden chair arms, letting her hands hang limp, the breath from the droning fan touching her wrists. Bit by bit she called him back, building him before her: slouch of shoulders, stubborn heavy head, wrinkles, rough hair, hard tormented mouth. Why . . . he wanted to hate her. He accused her for being what all her life she had hated men for wanting in her. And she had let him go, thinking that she wanted to laugh. A hard way, he said. Harder than he knew. She could see him, blundering, uncompromising. He needs an angel, not a woman. Someone to put up with him and work for him and not mind his . . . his boorishness, and love him. Anne stood up, shrugging, shaking into place her thin silk. He doesn't want me. He said so. She waited, her fingers at her lips. And I?

When she came to the foot of the stairs, her eyelids flickered. There stood the car, her father's chauffeur jumping out to open the door. "Your father told me to wait, Miss Dacey. The train's pretty bad, a day like this." Anne, settling herself, thought: Tom Vining saw him. That was partly what had set him off. "I don't want to have to make money." She wouldn't think. Just lie back, for miles of no effort. Home, with the faint odor of the sea in shaded, wide rooms. Fred Alger had telephoned. Amusing that he should come to-night. Anne moved langorously through the business of dressing, through the dinner, with Dorothy sparkling at Thurston, at her father. Spoiled, idle . . . and these were pleasant things, iced bouillon, crisp salad. "I'm afraid of some trouble in Europe." Her father frowned. "This archduke they've shot over there." Thurston poohed at his idea. "Do send for Charles, then," cried Mary.

Then Anne, cool, relaxed, in a low chair on the screened porch, waited for Fred. Through the open French doors came the metallic rhythm of the phonograph, and across the lawn moved at intervals the grotesque shadows of Thurston and Dorothy, dancing past the light. "No, I won't dance any more." Dorothy crossed the porch, not seeing Anne. "Much nicer out doors in the dark." Thurston followed her, his arm a black slash across her light gown as they disappeared down the dark road. The phonograph squeaked horribly and died. Through the wood rushed a funnel of light, a blare of harsh sound through the still summer night, making trees and roses and house theatrical, smiting Anne low in her chair. A car rushed behind the light, grinding to a stop. The darkness was a wave of silence again. "Hello, Anne!" He'd

seen her, of course. He crashed down upon her like the
light. Anne twisted away and his kiss bumped her ear.
"Too hot. Go sit down over there."

"Well, you're cool enough." Fred glowered; she got
the angry duck of his head in the dim light as he dropped
into a chair. "After months. You never even wrote to
me. I don't want to sit way off here!"

"I do. I want to talk."

"What's the good of talk?" He hitched his chair along
the floor nearer her. "What's the big idea, freezing me
out?" Into her silence he flung a sudden, "Someone been
stuffing you with yarns about me?"

"Are there yarns?"

"Not since Christmas, I swear. Before that . . . well,
no fellow's a monk Anne. But listen——"

"I don't want to hear them. I knew, anyway."

He had her hand, his fingers slipping from wrist to
elbow, to rest in the hollow there. "Feel your heart
jump?"

"No. That's yours." She pushed his hand away, sitting forward, her arms about her knees. "Fred, we're
through." She could see him crouching upon her. "You
won't mind, after a minute. You'll get another girl.
You're handsome and rich and——"

"You mean you've got another man?"

"No. Not yet."

"But at Christmas——" his hand pried at hers, locked
about her knees. "You're crazy. Come here."

"No. When you kiss me, something dies in me. I want
to stay alive."

"This is some damned nonsense you've picked up in
town." Fred was on his feet, roaring at her. "Mother

warned me. I said I'd stop it, once we were married.
Why, everybody expects me to marry you! It's . . . it's
all settled. What more do you want? I'm giving you
anything a woman could want. I'm crazy about you.
Why, I dream about you." His voice dropped into pathos.
"I even brought a ring." He clutched at a vest pocket.
"You've just been playing with me, is that it?"

"I tried to play your way." Anne felt her thoughts
climb slowly a long spiral, up, up. "I thought love had
to be a kind of death, shutting out all of me you never
cared to see. But now——"

"Who's the other man? I don't know what you're
talking about."

"That's enough, isn't it?" Anne had to stand up, away
from the threatening curve of his body. "I'd be sorrier
if I'd hurt you. Your pride hurts a little . . . that's all.
Good-by."

"You needn't think you can whistle me back!" His
anger swept after her. "There are other women!"

Anne stopped at the door. "Yes. Plenty." She sighed
into a laugh as he pounded down the steps, ground at
his motor, and roared away.

Ellen's door stood just a crack ajar, and within sounded
the bang of a drawer shoved into place. Anne pushed at
the door, bent to pick up the slipper with which it was
wedged.

"I can't lay my hand on it." Ellen padded busily across
to the table beside her bed, the braid of white hair slapping at her bent shoulders, her gray bathrobe tucked
under her arms, as if she had found its folds a nuisance.
She jerked open the small table drawer.

"What you looking for?" Anne closed the door.

"That bankbook Matthew sent me." She sat down on the bed, running trembling fingers along the neat triangle of turned down sheet. "Do you think Thurston took it?" She thrust her fingers under the pillow, burrowing along. Then she glanced up at Anne, her eyes dim under crinkled, heavy lids.

"Thurston wouldn't take anything." Anne touched the bent shoulder gently. "An' Telly—"

"Another Thurston." Ellen's hand clawed up toward Anne's, and suddenly the puckered mouth smoothed into a smile. "My land, it's Anne. Sit down. I"—her eyes cleared into focus again—"I knew better all the time, looking for that." Her laugh scattered a half century like crumbs. "It's been so warm, I couldn't get to sleep."

"You let me tuck you in." Anne pulled the bathrobe off, held back the sheet while the old body twisted into place, head cocked forward on the pillow, chin jutting over the frill of embroidery. "An' Telly——" Was she listening, or had she wandered down some other path of years? "I wanted to tell you something."

"About that fellow!" Ellen pried up her head. "I heard him honking up. Mary told me."

"Did you hear him honking away?" Anne saw, faintly, the old gleam of conspiracy; she and An' Telly. "He was angry. They'll all be angry, won't they?"

"Sent him off, did you?" The withered cords of Ellen's neck relaxed and her head dented the pillow. "High time. Ditch water, shallow and muddy. That's him." The hooded eyelids shut down. "Never did see what you were up to."

"He made love to me. I thought that was all I could

get, excitement—I thought, men are like that." Anne
bent toward the old woman. "An' Telly, are you listening?" Hurry, tell her, or she'll never know! Like telling God, so thin the wall seemed that held the present moment away from all the past and all the future in whatever
consciousness lay behind that wrinkled parchment mask.
"An' Telly, I told Fred I wouldn't have him. Because
another man called me names. Silly and soft and useless.
All the things I made myself for Fred. He says he won't
have me. He thinks I'm not enough for him. And all
my life I've had this hate in me, for men, for wanting
less. Where's my pride, An' Telly? He's homely, and
poor, and wonderful, this man. He——" Anne laughed,
lifting her arms in a long ripple from throat and shoulder
to wrists. "He says he won't love a woman like me. But
I'm not. Am I, An' Telly? I'm going to make him have
me."

"Well, I guess you can." Ellen blinked at Anne's face,
close above hers. "You go ahead." She closed her eyes
again and slept. Anne watched her, thinking how strange
sleep was, this old sleep, carrying Ellen out of reach. She
might have waited, to listen. Anne turned off the light
and moved toward the door. You've come together, in
one piece. Her hands, extended, seemed to sing as they
touched the smooth wood of the door. Ellen had known,
before she slept. It was true, all her body swinging to
the rhythm of her heart. At her window she pushed
aside the curtains, looking into the soft black night, with
its faint undertone of quiet black water on the shore. Into
one piece, she thought, and then, *peace*. Peace wasn't a
quiet, still place, white and separate, as she had always
dreamed. Motion, strong, marching, a flowing rhythmic

movement. Not silence, but music. I can't get it with my mind. It's me, all of me, living.

X

She did not go into town the next week. Under the flurry of angry protests about Fred . . . his mother had telephoned the next morning . . . some part of her mood persisted. Mary buzzed at her constantly, but to Anne her buzzing was that of a bee outside a window, until her mother cried, "I can't touch you! You act as if you didn't even hear me, as if you were walking in your sleep. I wash my hands of you. I've done my best."

Then Mary forgot Anne, completely. Newspaper headlines about an archduke slain a month earlier, Germans marching into Belgium. "You sent that poor boy away from home!" She flew at Rob. "Now there's a war! Get him back. My son, my son Charles!" Rob paced the floor, working his mouth under his gray moustache. "Can't sell plows now. Have to make guns. Business is crazy wild. War, why, incredible! War, to-day?"

"Maybe Charles is in Belgium." Mary beat her hands together.

"I've cabled them. Don't work yourself up so. He's an American, safe enough."

An answering cable from Pendleton, in England. They would sail as soon as they could get passage. Ellen made articulate the fear under their waiting. "Charles won't come back. Not with a war going on. I remember your father, Robby. Why, he couldn't wait to ride away!"

Nor did Charles come. Pendleton, arriving on one of the jammed, hysterical boats, brought a brief letter from

him. A friend of his, a Frenchman, could get him into
ambulance service. Thurston, home for the week-end,
said, "The lucky dog!" Mary clung to him, while Rob
growled, "When you're through talking to your mother,
come into the study. We've got a problem in that stuff
we were planning to ship."

Anne wondered at her mother. After the letter from
Charles, she steadied herself into a kind of excited dream,
in which she dropped words about a mother's feeling,
planned boxes for Charles, wrote him long letters, and
read, the spectacles she had hitherto refused to wear sliding down her small nose, the countless papers with which
the house was littered. She seemed scarcely to mind
Charles's being there. No, not that exactly. She'd
needed a cause, perhaps, and this was it. She has let herself down in the war, through Charles.

Anne read the *Gazette* each day, thinking; Tom Vining
wrote this, or this. She found an article in a weekly,
with his name, and read that, her mind trying to search
him out in the pattern of words he made. Hard, simple
phrases. She heard his voice under them and was humble,
thinking, that's his life, shaping ideas, words, piling them
into form, lances to hurl into the minds of people; himself extended, strong, articulate. He's afraid I'd stop
that. Afraid I'd cling about his neck. She laid her hand
over the column, fingers tight to hide the small black letters. Away from that part of his life, wasn't he baf-
fled, inarticulate? He's in pieces. Anne curled her hand
against her cheek. Thinks I'd scatter him further. Why
don't I go to him? He won't come. Behind her eyelids
she could see him climbing the dusty stairs to the suffrage

office. They'd say, "Miss Dacey isn't coming in. No, she didn't say why." Huh, he thought so! That jerk of his head.

Dear Tom. Her fancy moved in letters to him. Dear Tom. And stopped there, words bending, crumbling under the longing of her whole self toward him. In fancy she moved to the telephone. A number, a moment of waiting, and his voice beating at her ear. To-morrow, perhaps. She wondered at her inertia. It wasn't fear, nor doubt, nor modesty that held her. More as if she needed a little time for this new self to learn to walk before she turned it loose. To-morrow or the next day I shall want more. To-day. . . . Her mother hurried into the room, her arm full of spikes of gladioli, scarlet and white sheathed blossoms. To-day I want more peace than I shall have, later, when they know. Her mother bristled over her flowers, and Anne felt them launched at her, incredulous reproaches.

That evening a comment of her father, as he looked through the evening papers, crashed into her mood of waiting. "I see they're sending some of these newspaper fellows across. First hand stories. That'll be good."

Oh, fool, fool! The days she had wasted, and it might be Tom who went, who had even now gone! She crouched in her chair, impulses tearing her into separate fibres. Telephone. But where? It was late. She didn't even know where he lived. He might be at the office. Rush into town . . . where, again? Who would know? Josephine Waite? She felt her father's mildly startled gaze follow her as she plunged from the room. She couldn't talk from the house telephone, with them sitting there. At the village. As she reached her own door, had her hand out for a purse, she heard from Ellen's room a thud, a splintering of glass.

The room was dark, but in the shaft of light from the hall Anne saw a huddled body, the night table over-turned, bits of glass winking brilliantly. Anne could not lift her, couldn't pull her straight from that awful crumple of limbs. Her call brought her father, one of the maids.

Through the pity and confusion of the next hours prickled that fear. If Tom had gone! The doctor shook down his cuffs, pulled his coat sleeves smooth. Not a bone broken, as he had feared. At her age. Just shock, from the fall. She'd stumbled, or fainted. Her heart was almost worn out. Good many years it had served her. Anne trembled with sharp pity. An' Telly's heart . . . its valiance, its love, beating into her own life. He'd send a nurse as soon as he could. By morning. She might never regain consciousness. He couldn't say. He'd given a hypodermic.

"I'll sit here." Anne looked at the long, still ripple of the sheet, looked at the papery mask of face. Little enough to do. If she lost Tom—oh, she couldn't, not in the few hours before day came.

"I'll stay with you, Anne." Mary screwed a fresh globe into the night light, set the little clock in place. "It's still going," she whispered, "although the face is broken."

"No. You must go to bed." Anne drove her gently away.

Hours, then. When morning comes, I will have to go. Anne leaned forward, her own breath hushed. Too faint to seem like anything in life she caught the slow, remote sigh of Ellen's breathing. I ought to think about you, not of myself and Tom. Of you . . . all those stories of Ellen's life, dead people back of Anne, women. Why, it's as if you'd been getting ready, isn't it? Winding up all the threads. Anne drew back in her chair. Some day I shall lie, dying. The thought shut over her like a black wing, beneath which she crawled, infinitesimal, incredibly humble. Oh, Tom! She couldn't find him quickly enough; between her and death Tom made a wall. He was light in which the black wing vanished, a shadow not there.

She slept, dreaming she was a child who ran after Ellen. She woke to find the night light a prick of saffron in the clear pallor of dawn, and Ellen's eyes open, dark.

"An' Telly!"

"Huh?" Ellen's hand, the fingers cupped, moved with a jerk along the edge of the sheet. "Six beans to a hill. One for cutworms, one . . . Eh? You been asleep. I saw you." She clucked in her throat. "I thought . . . you ought to show me your young man." Her eyelids closed, her cupped fingers relaxing.

Anne's heart beat quickly, not in its proper place, but all through her blood, in her wrists, behind her ears, where her shoulder touched the chair. Bring Tom! She would. That in a single stroke, would end it, this dallying, would start . . . oh, all of life! She stared at the little clock. Its pasteboard dial was crumpled on the line of eight. She'd take that for a sign. At eight, then.

The nurse came shortly after seven, and Anne tiptoed away. Her eyelids ached. Coffee, and then she sat at the desk, the hard circle of the instrument the only solid thing in the world. Delay, with time strung into wires that clicked and whirred, and then—"Hello! hello?" Anne swayed forward, to hear above her singing blood that voice. "Hello. Yes, Anne Dacey." He wouldn't understand who it was. Then he repeated her name, and said nothing else. "You haven't hung up? You're there? Tom, come out here. This morning. Do you hear me? You see——" She lifted her eyes, to find in the doorway her mother, blue silk and ribbons floating about her amazed strut. Anne shut her eyes. "You see, there's someone dying. An' Telly. She loves me, and I told her about you. I told her I was going to marry you. She wants to see you." Was it his shouted "What?" or only the silent *what* of every line of her mother's rush upon her. "Will you come? At once?"

"Who are you talking to?" Anne's fingers lingered on the telephone, trying to keep the vibrations of the few words. "Anne! I get up, after a sleepless night, and find you. . . ."

"It's Tom Vining, Mother. You . . . oh, you didn't see him, did you, that Sunday? He's coming out. An' Telly asked to see him."

"Anne!" The folds of soft skin under her mother's chin quivered. "You aren't engaged . . . to that nobody? I've waited, patient, till you came to your senses about Fred . . . and you've been deceiving me. Telling your aunt instead. Oh, all your life she's put you up to things, against me! I won't have it. That's all. If she is on her death bed!"

"I'm not engaged." Anne's smile twitched. "I want to marry him, if he'll have me. That's all." She glanced at the telephone; it looked the same, in spite of those amazing words of hers! "I can't talk . . . not now."

She fled, hearing her mother's flood of incoherent protest break as the maid came in from the dining room. The nurse sat outside Ellen's door, her nose sharp at the crack. "She insisted on being alone," she whispered up at Anne. "She's just lying there. I keep an eye on her. You have to humor them. She just insisted." Anne nodded, and shut herself into her own room. She must hurry to bathe and dress . . . that queer tremble of her knees, that clutch of fingers inside her body! Tom was coming, her lover was coming; death was coming.

XI

Anne peered through the crack of the door, above the frill of the nurse's cap. Ellen lay, masked in sleep. She stopped in the lower hall. From some room came voices, in a steady rhythm of injury, her mother talking to her father. She walked across the lawn, a little way into the wood. The morning sun dropped light through boughs, bars to hold her, bending for her as she passed. She stood near a tree, her fingers pressed against the bark, tingling. He would come, soon. She heard the rattle of a station taxi, saw his face. She thought the tree swung under her fingers. The taxi backed and churned and lurched away.

"I think"—his face was white, the sandy eyebrows meeting over his eyes—"I couldn't be sure I heard you. You said——"

She was steady, rooted like a tree. "I said An' Telly wanted to see you. She loves me. I told her I was going to marry you, if you would have me."

He stood close to her, his arms hugged to his sides,

the sunlight striking across his doubting mouth, his hungry eyes. "But I told you——"

"I don't mind anything. How hard it is, how poor you are, anything. If you want me." Then as his fists lifted, opened, Anne caught one of them. "Not now. There's all our lives. Hurry." She went toward the house.

"When will you marry me?" He drew her back as she touched the door.

"To-day. To-morrow. Any time!" Anne's hand clung in his. She led him up the stairs. "Stay here, I'll call you, if she's awake." She ignored the protest of the nurse, and pushed Ellen's door wide, moving across to bend over the bed, whispering, "An' Telly!"

XII

Ellen woke, coming slowly to the margin of the blackness in which she rested. Was that her heart, beating somewhere outside her in a hurried, clicking whirr? No. That silly clock. She'd forgotten to turn it face down. No, she'd turned it, and stumbled, fallen. She couldn't remember, exactly. But her heart didn't go at that rate. She shifted her head up the pillow. I'm still here, she thought, with drowsy surprise. She'd heard them whispering: she'll slip away in her sleep. Nothing to do, her body's just worn out, and her heart. They'd wanted that strange woman in apron and doodab on her head to plant herself there by the bed. "I won't have you in my room!" She'd made them understand that, finally. "There's things I got to do." She'd got rid of her. She couldn't trouble to explain, but people bothered her, throwing a shadow over the faint light that still shone. Only

alone could she finish what she had to do. Even alone a
shadow fell across her thoughts, like sleep, and she had
to wait for it to drift away. I'm almost through, she
thought. Almost to the bottom of my mind.

When was it her thoughts had begun that crazy clacking
and whirring, so that she'd talked and talked, trying to
be rid of the jumble? The days of her life, hundreds of
them, melting together into the small moment of now, so
that time was no longer a succession of hours, of years,
but was contained within her in bewildering instancy,
fused into now. She'd talked, letting her thoughts run
into words, while she hunted under the jumble, hunted
for some secret, something clear and orderly. Set my
house in order. She felt sleep, a gentle finger, brushing
her mind empty. Not yet! She had to finish, first. "Old
people like to talk about their past." Robby kept saying
that. He didn't know. The past came up around you
when you were old. It was you. All her life alive in
her, wanting something of her. All the people of her life
crowding close, closer than hands or feet. Before she
finished, she had to let them go, free of her love, or jealousy, or hate. Martha, all the Thurstons, Matthew, Sarah,
John Thurston, Alice, young Robby. Not ghosts, not
dead people, but a feeling each made in her, before they
slid away, releasing her. When they're all gone, at the
bottom, I'll find it . . . me. Sleep crept over her, black
and velvet nothingness.

A breath on her cheek, like a moth's wing. Slowly she
lifted her eyelids. Anne bending near her, dark eyes
heavy with . . . was it pity? . . . or love?

"Eh, Anne?" A child, running to her. Steady, now,
the shadow moving from the faint spark. "My mother

had sunflowers along the garden." Disks of gold nodding above her head. Why, at the bottom, nothing but tranquil emptiness. It had been herself that slipped away, not other people.

"An' Telly! Wait! He's coming."

Ellen heard her, remotely. But she had at last to let go of Anne.

AFTERWORD

I

The "Woman Question" was still a topic of heated debate in the United States in the 1920s following women's protracted struggle to secure the right to vote. When *Islanders* was published by Macmillan in 1927,[1] the story of Ellen Dacey's life was received as a significant and moving contribution to the discussion. Ellen was seen as a prototypical unmarried woman whose experiences from the late 1840s to the beginning of World War I reflected the isolation and powerlessness of women as they were increasingly relegated to spheres of activity separate from men's. Ellen's life became symbolic of the widespread, multifaceted effects of economic and technological change on the lives of women in the United States.

Critical reaction to the book, which included approval of Hull's feminism, serves as a commentary on the political/literary preoccupations of the 1920s. The reviewer for the *Boston Transcript* concurred with Ellen's perception that nineteenth-century American women had become "islanded" in homes owned by their male relatives, cut off from the mainland of activity, decision, and reward. The Boston reviewer described *Islanders* as the story of "women ... marooned on an island of feminine restriction entirely surrounded by masculine privilege."[2] The *Woman Citizen*'s reviewer noted that "Some people will call *Islanders* a feminist novel of perennial importance and interest."[3]

It was Ellen Dacey's character that secured readers' loyalty to the book and drew praise even from reviewers who found Hull's feminism unpalatable. In fact, critics could not find enough good things to say about Ellen. In periodicals such as the *Saturday Review of Literature* and the *New York Times,* she was described as a woman of "rich beauty, sturdy honesty, lovely vigor"; as someone "fine, vital, beautifully courageous"; as "a woman of rare courage and inquiring mind"; as "a brave spirit, a clear-thinking, self-reliant woman."[4] The reviewer for *Outlook* observed,

> Always the central figure, and holding the whole together, is Ellen Dacey ... able, shrewd, courageous, maternal, tolerant, wise.... If only there were a synonym for "inspirational" which did not suggest sermons or consciously uplifting literature—but never mind. Ellen needs no fine adjectives. She is as solid and unsaintly and prosaic and genuine as some of those good small-town women many of us have been fortunate enough to know.[5]

Ironically, Lawrence Cornelius of the *Saturday Review of Literature* argued that Ellen Dacey's strength and her endurance in the face of decades of male abuse save *Islanders* from being a truly feminist book. Cornelius finds *Islanders* superior to Hull's first three novels because it is not marred for him by an "aggrieved knitting of the author's brows at the horrid spectacle of woman's domination by man." This novel, he argues, is not propaganda because its "central truth, woman's dependence on man, is implicit in the living out of people's lives, and [Hull's] feminist indignation is not the real occasion for the novel." In fact, he is so enthusiastic about both *Islanders* and Ellen that he places her with "that undaunted company which includes Willa Cather's Antonia and Alexandra, Zona Gale's Lulu Bett and Ellen Bascomb."[6]

Despite his professed admiration for Ellen's strength, however, Cornelius ultimately finds her appealing not as a representative of the endurance of generations of women but as an individual woman who is "brave and lonely." Ellen's character and what he sees as her life of "vivid pitifulness" are much more attractive to him than the circumstances of the heroines of Hull's first three novels: *Quest, The Surry Family,* and *Labyrinth.*[7] In those novels, defiant young Jean and Marjy pledge themselves to lives different from their mothers', and Catherine Hammond reluctantly gives up her hard-won job to follow her husband to his new position in the Midwest, swearing that she is not yet beaten. *Islanders,* in fact, offers a far more sweeping condemnation of patriarchy than any of those first three novels, but Ellen's character is so strong and so appealing that it distracts Cornelius from Hull's feminist analysis.

Meanwhile, in *The Nation,* Johan Smertenko appreciated Hull's political insight and welcomed the fact that, in her first four novels, she takes "the contemporary woman question as her underlying theme." *Islanders,* he says, continues the discussion begun in *Labyrinth* ("one of the most intelligent studies" of the problems faced by modern women) by going "back to the more fundamental question of the status of woman in the mind of man as well as in his social organism." He credits Hull with seeing that the "chivalrous view of women" (which considers them frail beings in need of protection) "is the illusion of a secure and affluent society." In difficult times, women bear most of the burden— in addition to suffering from a double standard. Unlike Cornelius, Smertenko would have been pleased with even more political content, and he regrets what he sees as an "overemphasis on the emotions of its characters."[8]

II

Helen Rose Hull was born in Albion, Michigan, on March 28, 1888, the oldest of four children. Her father, Warren C. Hull, was for a while the superintendent of schools in East Lansing, but eventually he went into real estate and then into lifelong unemployment following World War I. From then until his death at ninety-six in 1956, he was supported by Hull and her brother Frederick. Hull's paternal grandfather, Levi T. Hull, was a printer and newspaper publisher who encouraged her childhood literary ambitions by printing her first stories. Hull's mother, Minnie L. McGill Hull, was a schoolteacher before she married, but left paid employment for a life that remained centered on her family until her death in 1933.

Hull commuted from home to attend Michigan Agricultural College (now Michigan State University) and then held several teaching jobs, mostly in rural communities. After completing a Ph.B. and some graduate work at the University of Chicago, she was hired to teach English composition at Wellesley College in 1912, whereupon she left the Midwest permanently. In a 1914 letter to her mother in which she announced that she wanted to leave teaching, Hull insisted that she was a teacher not because she was drawn to the profession itself but because teaching was the only way she could support what she had long seen as her true vocation: writing.[9] Hull in fact remained a teacher for the rest of her life, but she was able to reach a happy professional compromise by teaching creative writing and having her summers free for her own fiction.

Although she found Wellesley unsatisfactory professionally, it was during her time there that Hull became committed to feminism. First attracted to political analysis through a socialist instructor at Michigan Agricultural College when she was a student, Hull published several of her earliest stories in the leftist Greenwich Village magazine *The Masses,* beginning in 1914. While these pieces address class issues, they also demonstrate Hull's concern with feminism, focusing on such topics as spousal abuse, "illegitimate" birth, rape, and women's economic disadvantages. Also in 1914, about the same time that Hull published a one-act play in the suffrage magazine *The Woman's Journal,* Carrie Chapman Catt offered her a position as publicist for the New York State Suffrage Association. Under considerable pressure from her mother to avoid such "fanatics," Hull regretfully turned down the offer. Determined nonetheless to leave what she saw as the artificial environment of Wellesley (a perception that works its way into descriptions of Anne's experience in *Islanders*), Hull accepted a slot at Barnard in 1915; in 1916 she became a member of the English Department at Columbia University, where she remained for over forty years.

Although her mother may have thought she rescued Hull from the clutches of feminism, Hull became part of an active group of feminists as soon as she moved to New York City in 1915, particularly when she joined the Heterodoxy Club. During these first years in New York, she published short fiction concerned primarily with the problems, experiences, and insights of women. For example, a series of six stories appearing in both mainstream and little magazines between 1917 and 1921 focus on a character (or characters) called Cynthia; taken together, these stories offer a feminist model for growth.[10]

While she was at Wellesley, Helen Hull not only became committed to feminism; she also met the woman with whom she would spend the next fifty years: Mabel Louise Robinson. In 1914 she and Robinson began their lifelong pattern of summering in North Brooklin, Maine, where they first rented and eventually bought Bayberry Farm. It was there that they did their writing, each in a small building separate from the main house. In the late 1910s they shared the house with a friend from Greenwich Village, a teacher and writer named Eleanor Wheeler. In 1920 Hull and Robinson bought the farmhouse, and Wheeler bought the house across the road. Wheeler's New York housemate Mabel Jettinghoff joined them during the few summer weeks she had free from her publishing job. Several other women from artistic or literary circles in New York also purchased or rented houses in North Brooklin, and they formed a small and unpretentious but lively summer community whose principal interests were writing, gardening, dog-walking, sailing, and sleeping outdoors in Gloucester hammocks. The permanent residents viewed them with considerable suspicion, particularly in the late 1910s and early twenties, but times were not easy in Maine, and the cash these modern city women brought into the local economy was welcome even if their new ideas about appropriate roles for women were not. As one woman who was a young girl at the time puts it, "They used to go flying down the roads on their bicycles in their khaki knickers and middy blouses, their hair flying out behind them. They were very strong-minded."[11]

By the time Hull moved to New York City in 1915 to take up her job at Barnard, Robinson had already moved there to work for the Carnegie Foundation. Robinson, too, was hired by Columbia, where she completed a Ph.D. in Education with a dissertation on the curricula of women's colleges. Both Hull and Robinson remained at Columbia for the rest of their professional lives and were central to the university's creative writing program for adult students.

Helen Hull's publishing career spanned nearly fifty years, beginning in 1914 with the appearance of a play in *The Woman's Journal* and a short story, "Mothers Still," in *The Masses*.[12] Her last novel, *Close Her Pale Blue Eyes*, was issued by Dodd, Mead in 1963. In the intervening years, she published sixteen other novels, some sixty short stories, four books about writing, and a short biography of Madam Chiang Kai-shek.

Hull wrote about a range of subjects that we find compelling today, and she did so with seriousness and literary maturity. Some of the subjects Hull addresses in her fiction are the nuances of family interaction, the psychological and practical ramifications of women's economic disabilities, gender differences, the advantages and disadvantages of various models for relationships (especially in marriage), child/parent conflict, and racial and class tensions. These subjects are concerns her characters face in their daily lives and for which they find no simple solutions. As one reviewer said of *Islanders*, "For all its protest, its people are human and act accordingly."[13]

Even though Helen Hull's work is largely unknown today, she was highly regarded during most of her years as a publishing writer. In fact, Hull's fiction was admired from the very beginning of her career. For example, of her five stories that appeared in *The Masses* between 1914 and 1917, two of them were lead articles for the magazine. From 1917 to 1921, twelve of her stories also appeared in *Touchstone*, a little magazine published by Mary Fanton Roberts. Roberts repeatedly featured Hull's work as the lead article, beginning with "Blight" in the first issue of the magazine in May 1917. During her career, Hull published short stories in at least twelve different American magazines, including *Collier's, Saturday Evening Post, Harper's, Cosmopolitan,* and *Ladies Home Journal*.

Hull's novels were consistently reviewed favorably until about 1950. Following the enthusiastic reception in 1922 of *Quest,* her work received increasingly laudatory notices, especially in the *New York Times,* the *New York Herald Tribune,* the *Saturday Review of Literature,* and the *Boston Transcript.* By the time *Islanders* appeared, Hull was well established as

a serious and talented novelist, and *Islanders* sealed that
reputation. When *Heat Lightning* was selected by the Book
of the Month Club in 1932, she began to reach an even
larger audience. In 1940 the *New York Times* ranked her
novella, *With the One Coin for Fee*, with *The Red Badge of
Courage* and *Ethan Frome* and predicted for it a long life as
a frequently anthologized classic.

During the 1950s, however, the critical climate had
shifted so that Hull's novels were reviewed—and dismissed—as "women's books." In the early 1960s, she published two mysteries. The first, *A Tapping on the Wall* (1960),
won a Dodd, Mead prize for the best mystery written that
year by a faculty member. The writing of this book, which
she took on almost as a joke, provided only slight distrac-
tion from the terminal illness of Mabel Louise Robinson,
who died in 1962; the book's success offered only small
consolation for the waning popularity of what she regarded
as her more serious work. Hull herself died in 1971, greatly
disappointed that her work had disappeared almost entirely from both literary and popular view.

III

Hull began writing *Islanders* in the Alps in 1926. As she
remarked to the publicist for Macmillan, "Fortunately, my
partner is a writer, too, and so all things worked together," a
point she repeated to a reporter from the *Lansing Capital
News*. "I was with another woman who was writing. Conditions were ideal," she said.[14] Her belief in the importance
of the support of other women echoes Edith Somerville (of
the female writing team Somerville and Ross), who said in
her *Irish Memories* (1917), "The outstanding fact ... among
women who live by their brains, is friendship. A profound

friendship that extends through every phase and aspect of life, intellectual, social, pecuniary."[15]

This sense of community, of shared intent and support, is clearly lacking in Ellen Dacey's life. In fact, her central perception is the isolation of women in late nineteenth- and early twentieth-century American middle-class homes. Ellen's realization that women live on metaphorical islands comes to her very slowly over the years, entirely without the aid of an organized feminist movement. The only woman with whom Ellen has a truly cooperative relationship is her mother. After her mother's death, Ellen recognizes that Martha reserved her loyalty—and her real love—for her sons and her husband, but "she had lived with Ellen, and it was to Ellen she had given her farewell" (50). Ellen and Martha were collaborators in survival, and Martha's legacy to her daughter is the ability to endure.

While the endurance Ellen sustains over the years is admirable, *Islanders* is not simply the study of a determined personality. Penniless and dependent in her old age, Ellen says explicitly, "This has happened because I am a woman" (167). Through Ellen's life we see U.S. culture over a span of some sixty-five years, and through her experiences Hull traces the damaging effects—especially on women—of major social institutions including marriage and the family, the economy, organized religion, the military, and the myth of the American dream.

When asked once why she wrote about family life, Hull replied that she saw the family as a microcosm of the world.[16] In her fiction she presents domestic or "private" life not as a retreat from the larger world but as a reflection of it; her fiction explores social, sexual, political, and economic issues that operate within the family and extend well beyond it. In her view, the individual family and larger social structures are interdependent systems, each affecting the other in direct and indirect ways.

Hull's earlier novels *Quest* and *The Surry Family* focus on the development of adolescent girls as they outgrow their families; the novels serve as indictments of the white, middle-class, American family as it functioned at the beginning of the twentieth century. Hull presents the family in both books not as a haven or a retreat but as an unhealthy, unsafe place for the people living in it, especially children whose interests are supposedly being protected by parents who refuse to divorce. All of Hull's novels demonstrate that women's economic dependence on men and the restriction of their activities to family life make the women themselves unhappy and also work to the detriment of other family members. In these two early books she sees women, men, and children as victims of a social arrangement that works to everyone's disadvantage.

In *Labyrinth* and *Islanders,* both men and women suffer from the ill effects of patriarchal family structure, but in these two books, Hull makes it clear that the men also profit immensely from the system and are quite content—in most cases even eager—to perpetuate it. *Labyrinth* focuses on the contemporary debate on marriage versus careers for women that was also being conducted in such novels as A. S. M. Hutchinson's frenzied *This Freedom.*[17] What Hull documents in *Labyrinth* is the persistence of such social institutions as marriage, whose very familiarity and seeming inevitability help mask their destructiveness.

In *Islanders* the kinds of loyalties assumed to inhere in the family tend to work to the advantage of the male relatives but not the females. Martha and Ellen are rewarded for their devotion with abandonment, years of heavy labor, loneliness, theft, insult, and betrayal. No matter which family unit is "protecting" Ellen as an unattached female—her parents Martha and Thurston, her brother Thurston and his wife Grace, or her nephew Robby and his wife Mary—Ellen is exploited for her labor at the same time she is relegated to a status inferior to the other women in the household. In fact the status of the other females (the ones who are attached to the controlling male) is defined by the extent to which they can unload their household labor onto Ellen. Their idleness is an index of the success of their husbands, the standard by which the community measures them as well, and neither Grace, Alice, nor Mary hesitates to use Ellen. As the family unit's socioeconomic position improves, the family also insists on Ellen's conformity to gender expectations for middle-class women, Thurston claiming that she makes them all look bad by working like a man (farming) and wearing men's boots in public. They still want her to labor; now she is supposed to do so invisibly in their houses.

Islanders explodes the myth of female dependence. The more her family insists that she is a dependent, the more labor they expect Ellen to give them in return for her "keep," until it becomes perfectly obvious that the various households are in fact dependent upon her and would founder without her work and household management skills. Ellen is transformed from an independent farmer into that nineteenth-century plague, the spinster. The spinster's unmarried state was the excuse for her being an object of scorn at the same time that her labor was crucial to the operation of most middle-class households. In another fictional treatment of the lot of the spinster published about the same time as *Islanders,* Sylvia Townsend Warner portrays a heroine, Lolly Willowes, who would prefer literally to sell her soul to the devil than to continue in her status as a female "dependent" in her brother's house.[18]

By the time Hull was writing *Islanders,* the spinster was considered—at least in the popular press—a nearly extinct species, a change caused largely by the new economic status of single women in the 1920s. While Ellen is caught in a generation of women for whom "careers" were simply not a possibility, single women in the twenties were able to take advantage of the combined effects of the women's movement and the shortage of male labor during World War I, which brought women into the labor market in significant numbers. By 1930, the phrase "family parasites" appears in the *Saturday Evening Post* not to refer to unmarried women, as it had earlier in the century; rather, Elizabeth Jordan uses the term to refer to the families who continue to exploit unmarried relations, now no longer laboring invisibly in the home. Instead, the new "old maid" brings in cash from a career, cash that is siphoned off by greedy, insensitive, or irresponsible family members (female and male) who rationalize their behavior and manipulate their female relations by insisting that the spinster has nothing else to spend her money on anyway.[19]

At the same time that Ellen is cast in the role of household drudge, mostly by her female relations, she is also assumed by her male relatives to be wholly ignorant about "important"—that is, business—matters, and she must stand by as her father and her brother sell off the land she has farmed for eighteen years for a foolish investment scheme. Later, her brother Thurston also loses the money he has stolen from Ellen while she is unconscious. In fact, the men are the ones who waste, who squander, while giving themselves credit for being the managers of the world; the women actually keep things going. It is Martha who recognizes that there is "gold" in their land, and Ellen who stays to work it. In fact, it is Martha and Ellen who make the only sensible plans for the family, always in the face of great male opposition and blustering. Martha succeeds in keeping her son Thurston home by appealing to his thirst for fame, power, and riches, while Ellen must resort, essentially, to blackmail to make him choose correctly for Rob's

future. All the while, of course, Thurston insists that
"women had no sense. Selfish, scheming creatures. A man's
life had to reach out, shaping the affairs of the world. No
woman knew anything about a man's concerns" (83).

In *Islanders* Hull traces the shift from an agrarian to a
cash economy and documents the tremendous economic
disadvantages women suffered as they were pushed to islands of economic activity separate from men's. Although
men and women both continued to labor, only men received direct compensation for their efforts. When Ellen
learns of her legacy from Matthew (she is nearly fifty at the
time), she immediately grasps the significance of the inher-
itance: "Now I can do what I want, myself," she thinks. "I
am delivered out of bondage" (74). She thinks of her money
in terms of freedom, safety, invulnerability; when Thurston
steals her bankbook, he literally removes something from
her heart.

While her mother finds consolation for the hardness of
her life in religion, Ellen learns that organized religion is
every bit as much a bastion of male privilege as the patriarchal family or the economic system. She discovers that
men abuse their privileges as "instruments" of God, that
much of what passes for spirituality is really sexuality, and
that religion offers neither consolation nor meaning for
her life.

The male clerics in *Islanders* are not only arrogant but
also predatory, and Ellen is conscious of them as a source
of danger rather than solace or salvation. The men of God
always appear dark and threatening to Ellen, who is made
uneasy by the undercurrent of violence she immediately
detects in them. In the scene in which Brother Laing pre-
tends to try to "save" Ellen, he takes advantage of her sex-
ually under the guise of spiritual contact; the minute Ellen
resists, he turns the tables and accuses her of leading him
astray. In this, of course, he echoes the Judeo-Christian tra-

dition that insists that Adam's sin was Eve's fault because she tempted him. Martha acts as Laing's apologist, claiming that Ellen is "young and stubborn" and that the real problem here is not Laing's behavior but rather Ellen's failure to be understanding and compassionate. Laing, Martha insists, is an instrument of God, but also "only a man" (31). In this exchange, we can hear generations of excuses for men who claim not to be able to control their sexual impulses in the presence of a "temptress" (at the same time they maintain that their rationality makes them superior to women). Even in the relatively genteel setting of Rob and Mary's church, the rector salivates at the thought of what he assumes to be Alice's fortune, and Hull makes it clear that he is at least indirectly responsible for her death.

Ellen also recognizes the sexual nature of much of what passes for religious experience, beginning with Martha's intense anticipation of the revival meeting. At the meeting itself, Ellen remains unmoved while the people around her—especially the women—sigh, gasp, groan, sway rhythmically, and swoon, all in the name of the Lord. Ellen, however, feels "no inrush of God." Perplexed by the response of the others at the meeting, Ellen wonders "How did it feel? That strange glow on her mother's face, the pleased, dazed look Sarah lifted?" (26). What comes to her immediately is a vision—a very physical sort of presence—of Matthew, who becomes the symbol of sexual longings she does not put a name to. Later, she identifies her mother's relationship with God as basically sexual in nature, but backs off from her perception of her mother's "intimacy of religion." Such a thought, she concludes, is "the dangerous edge of . . . irreverence" (55). Although Ellen lacks sophisticated analytical language, she quickly enough sees the patriarchal nature of organized religion: God, she realizes, is a man.

When Ellen flees to her room after the encounter with Brother Laing, she weeps for what she assumes must be her "wickedness," but also for "bewilderment at the ways of God, for pain at the treachery of her soft, yielding body, in which those dark caresses had stirred blind hunger." She falls asleep, dreams of a black-bearded God pursuing her over the edge of a cliff, and wakes in "an agony of fear." Ellen's encounter with what was supposed to be the consolation of religion leaves her feeling guilty. "Afraid and small, in an empty cold world," she is confused and ashamed by her feelings, convinced that she has been betrayed by her body, and utterly alone (29–30).

Ellen also rejects religion as a potential source of meaning. Following her illness, she enters a period of depression that gives way gradually to what she calls a "quickening search. . . . Was it God she wanted? She could see her mother, the Bible on her knees. No. She might be wicked, but God wasn't her answer. Something deep in her own heart" (89). The preacher's wisdom, she concludes, is as inadequate as an old bit of canvas tied at each corner over a bulging pile of hay. Religion, then, fails all its tests for Ellen: socially (its leaders are predatory and unprincipled), spiritually (its nature is more sexual than spiritual, and it offers no real consolation to people in need), and philosophically (it does not provide the core of meaning that its adherents claim for it).

In addition to attacking religion, *Islanders* examines some of the ways in which men seek what they think will be simple solutions or easy success. The quick fix, of course, proves ever illusory, whether in military campaigns, gold mining, or "sure-fire" investments. Hull presents the all-American rags-to-riches philosophy not as an ideal but as a form of male adolescence, the indulgence of which exacts its major price from women and children. In *Islanders* the Golden West appears not as a frontier of great opportunity but as a male myth with the power of other patriarchal institutions to distort the lives of those it touches, especially the women who must constantly mend the social fabric rent by their starry-eyed and selfish men. In *Islanders* it is the men, not the women, who are incurable romantics, and the consequences of their escapades cannot be lightly dismissed.

Ellen watches most of the men in *Islanders* constantly riding away—or longing to do so—whether in search of instant success, instant glory, or (as she sees much later in her life) perhaps in search of meaning or significance. She is convinced, however, that none of them will find it riding *away*, whether into the sunset or into Wall Street. The only man in the novel who seems to hold some promise is John Thurston, whose relative lack of male privilege has made him sensitive personally to the plight of Florence and politically to the plight of workers. His brother Rob, however, is incapable of understanding either their sister Alice or his employees, insulated as he is in his strong and successful maleness.

Literally riding away is not a choice for the women in the novel, but Ellen recognizes that the other women in her family develop their own forms of escape, once they no longer need to struggle to survive. Mary retreats into her social role; Alice, into delusion; Grace, into obesity and paralysis. Ellen, on the other hand, turns not away but toward: toward the natural world (whether her oak tree, the sky, or the sea) and toward other people, for nurturance, inspiration, and meaning. Ellen is the one true adult in this book. Hers is the maturity born, yes, of suffering, but also of patience, of love, of honesty, of a refusal to be drawn into those patterns of behavior assumed to be so necessary and so patriotic: competition, military glory, individualism, escape. What she wishes for women, and specifically for her grandniece Anne, is a way off of their islands of restriction, a way into a mainstream of activity that will enable them to live not like men but like women who can grow into the full use of their powers.

Throughout her life, Ellen maintains a firm sense of her own worth despite her role as a "dependent." When Anne explains to her that the suffrage movement means "Get you a vote, so you'll be good as any man," Ellen seems surprised that anyone would look to external sources for her sense of her own value. "I've been that, inside me, quite a while," she says (288). She yearns for change (what we might call institutional or systemic change) not to feel worthy but to have a fair chance in a world that is difficult enough without the extra burdens imposed on women by men, both individually and collectively. Her strong sense of self coupled with her determination to endure save Ellen over the years, and it is her spiritedness that she tries to instill in Anne. Ellen waits to die until she is certain that Anne has learned to think not so much as Ellen herself would, but to think for herself.

IV

In much of her early fiction—especially the Cynthia stories, *Quest,* and *The Surry Family*—Hull presents adolescent female characters who begin to think independently and who pledge themselves to a more or less defined quest: to seek love, work, and self. In this, they see themselves setting a course different from their mothers'. When Hull considers the future of her heroines, she never stops at their need for both love and work—the standard 1920s argument about women and careers. These characters also perceive the need for a self, not in the sense of personal fulfillment, but in terms of a kind of basic integrity of self, a core that is so firmly in place that years of battering (such as Ellen experiences) cannot violate or destroy it. These young characters must work to create or identify this essential self and then develop enough confidence to insure that no one (especially not a lover) can erode it. For example, Marjy in *The Surry Family*, who is quite determined to have meaningful work, ends up agreeing to marry, which she acknowledges will impede her career; she does so, however, only when she has her *self* firmly established. Then she chooses a husband who will not seriously threaten or violate that inner integrity, unlike the young man she instinctively rejected earlier because he is basically predatory and invasive.

In *Islanders,* Anne is one of a series of Hull's late adolescent characters who try to determine the appropriate roles of passion and work in their lives. Unlike most of Hull's other adolescent characters, Anne's privileged life works against her development into a fully mature human being. But like all of Hull's female characters—both adolescent and adult—Anne cannot fully resolve this question about the place of love and work in her life. It is not that she is inept but that her dilemma reflects a wide-ranging set of social and economic problems that cannot be solved by individual women simply making "correct" choices.

By the beginning of World War I, as *Islanders* draws to its close, the status of women has changed from what Ellen knew as a young woman, but Hull suggests that it may not have changed all that much. Anne's fate is important insofar as it serves as a coda to Ellen's life, updating the prospects for middle-class women. Even though Anne can go to college and consider a career, she herself perceives that external forces still determine gender-appropriate behavior, and that the dice are loaded against women who want anything other than the most traditional life. She realizes that her brothers' success (for which, of course, they claim full credit) is not entirely their own doing: "Something had picked them up, him and Thurston, and fitted them into a frame. They hadn't done it, themselves. A pattern clicked them into place" (276–77). While an entire patriarchal structure ensures that Charles and Thurston will prosper, Anne realizes that the same structure guarantees her frustration and demands of her tremendous personal effort if she wants to live in a way that will not make her a replica of her proper but vapid mother, her pathetic and deluded aunt Alice, her bloated and paralyzed grandmother, or her spirited but restricted great aunt Ellen.

Critic Johan Smertenko in *The Nation* misses the point when he complains about the "hack trick" of Anne's marriage as an easy way to achieve a happy ending in *Islanders*.[20] While Anne's decision to marry offers a conventional "resolution" of the plot (or of part of it, anyway), Hull suggests that it is not necessarily a happy ending. Anne's young man will probably go to the front, and the fact that he wields a pen rather than a sword really doesn't make that much difference. What will attract him, like the other men in the book, is the chance to run off to a glorified frontier populated by a company of gallant males. The one mark of some progress is that Tom expects Anne to be "useful," to work along beside him, like the generations of frontier women who came before Ellen. That he expects Anne to help him in *his* work—that his concerns will be the focal point of their union—is, Hull suggests, a typically male attitude, born of centuries of being at the center of their universe. Even Anne recognizes that Tom's particular brand of male arrogance requires for a marriage partner an angel rather than a woman. That he would probably expect her to take her place at his side *after* he returns from his important male business in the European theater of war places him and his generation of men developmentally right back in 1849. Tom Vining, then, is a step in the right direction, but marriage to him (which Anne sees as her best option) is no ideal solution.

Ellen can finally let go of Anne not because her marriage is safely arranged, but because she has developed enough spirit to look after herself. By the end of the book, Anne has absorbed enough of Ellen's spirit that she can take over her metaphor as well: When Tom arrives, Anne is "steady, rooted like a tree" (309). Her spirit is identified with a vital, natural world and not with artificial or dangerous social constructs. Anne reaches what she describes as peace, that inner integrity so important to Hull's heroines. This kind of peace, however, is not at all the passivity traditionally associated with femaleness. It is, rather, "motion, strong, marching. . . . It's me," she says, "all of me, living" (302–3). Although Anne lacks the level of insight that it has taken Ellen years to command, she has begun at least to get the basic idea. She recognizes that this new-found peace, this feeling of wholeness, stands in sharp relief to her sense that part of her died every time Fred kissed her. What Anne finally achieves (at least in theory) is the best fusion of love, work, and self that she can manage—the feminist model for maturity that typifies Hull's fiction beginning in the mid-1910s.

Anne's maturity is reflected in her growing interest in the world beyond the domestic island, her rejection of Fred's proposal and the passive life it represents, and her willingness to take on the displeasure of her family in order to marry outside her class and all its expectations for her. Under the circumstances—that is, coming from a privileged family in a patriarchal culture—Anne is doing about as well as could be expected of her. She is not Ellen reincarnate, for part of Hull's point is that the vigor of middle-class women has been sapped by decades of their being islanded.

A late twentieth-century desire for Anne to be somehow more resolute herself or to reach a more "feminist" resolution of her situation demands of her that she step outside the world she inhabits. What Hull says again and again in her fiction is that there are no simple solutions. And repeatedly she concludes pieces of fiction with marriages that only superficially resolve conflicts. In such cases, the weight of the narrative indicates that the marriage is not necessarily a happy ending and/or that the real resolution has taken place *inside* the heroine, who intends to resist the kinds of personal destruction typical of "selfless" wives and mothers.

Because of the historical moment and the socioeconomic class into which she is born, Anne has a relative luxury of choice not available to Ellen. One of the reasons we are so drawn to Ellen, however, is that she is, in a sense, not limited by these limitations. Of all the characters in the novel, she has the best understanding of external restriction and is at the same time the most compassionate toward others, the most generous, and the most insistent on people's responsibility for their own lives. For example, although Ellen fully recognizes the disastrous effects of certain social and economic institutions on Alice's life, she nonetheless observes, "It seemed dangerous to blame the country for the girl's pinched face. . . . If you got to blaming hard times and distant places for what happened to people, where would you be? If you weren't responsible for your affairs, what was there to keep you going?" (102).

Ellen reaches this conclusion not out of self-righteousness but rather out of a recognition that one can and must maintain a certain integrity of self regardless of the battering of a whole range of external forces. It is this mature and eager acceptance of responsibility for herself that sets Ellen apart from those about her and also places her firmly at the heart of *Islanders*. When Ellen hopes for a better life for Anne, she notes wryly, "You'd think I was one of these bloomer women, and here all my life one man or another has decided what would become of me." But "the strong fibre of her heart tightened in protest" at this thought, and she insists that Matthew, her father, her brother, and Rob "had decided things that happened about her" but not what became of *her,* that is, of Ellen herself (208).

Like the good and prudent farm woman she is, Ellen has unostentatiously tended the growth of her own self—of her secular soul, if you will—in accordance with the seasons of her life. Consequently, she is able to survive the devastation inflicted by a whole range of institutions and individuals that the novel relentlessly documents. The result for Ellen is not a retreat into passive femininity but rather endurance and an active kind of peace that Anne only begins to understand: not a "quiet, still place, white and separate ... [but] motion, strong, marching, a flowing rhythmic movement. Not silence, but music" (302–3). It is Ellen's inner harmony that plays through *Islanders,* not lyrical perhaps, and not dramatic, but quiet, steady, attuned to the natural world, persistent, and clear in spite of the clamor around her.

Patricia McClelland Miller
Ashford, Connecticut

NOTES

1. Helen Hull, *Islanders* (New York: Macmillan, 1927). All subsequent references will be cited parenthetically in the text.

2. F.B., "Islanders on the Mainland," *Boston Transcript,* 20 April 1927, p. 4.

3. *Woman Citizen,* June 1927, p. 38. This article also contains a review of Virginia Woolf's *To the Lighthouse,* which is described somewhat less favorably than *Islanders.*

4. Lawrence Cornelius, "Woman's Place," *Saturday Review of Literature*, 23 April 1927, p. 753; *Woman Citizen*, June 1927, p. 38; *New York Times*, 26 June 1927, Book Rev. sec., p. 5; *New York Times*, 1 May 1927, Book Rev. sec., p. 9.

5. *Outlook*, 22 June 1927, pp. 257–58.

6. *Saturday Review of Literature*, 23 April 1927, p. 753.

7. *Quest* (New York: Macmillan, 1922); *The Surry Family* (New York: Macmillan, 1925); *Labyrinth* (New York: Macmillan, 1923).

8. "The Woman Question," *The Nation*, 27 July 1927, pp. 89–90.

9. HRH to Mrs. Warren C. Hull, 6 May 1914, Frederick C. Hull Collection, Pittsburgh.

10. These stories have been reprinted in Helen Hull, *Last September*, ed. Patricia M. Miller (Tallahassee, Fla.: Naiad, 1988).

11. Gertrude Voight, interview with author, 25 June 1985.

12. "The Hallway," *The Woman's Journal*, 23 May 1914; "Mothers Still," *The Masses*, October 1914, pp. 14–15.

13. *New York Times*, 1 May 1927, p. 9.

14. HRH to Rosa Hutchinson, n.d. Macmillan Archive, New York Public Library; *Lansing Capital News*, 30 December 1926, p. 1.

15. Quoted by Gifford Lewis in *Somerville and Ross: The World of the Irish R.M.* (New York: Viking, 1985), p. 195.

16. "Why I Write about American Family Life," transcript for radio broadcast, Helen Hull Papers, Rare Book and Manuscript Library, Columbia University, New York.

17. A.S.M. Hutchinson, *This Freedom* (Boston: Little, Brown, 1922).

18. Sylvia Townsend Warner, *Lolly Willowes* (New York: Viking, 1926).

19. Elizabeth Jordan, "Family Parasites," *Saturday Evening Post*, 5 April 1930, pp. 39, 165–66.

20. *The Nation*, 27 July 1927, p. 90.

ACKNOWLEDGMENTS

In the preparation of this volume, I gratefully acknowledge the assistance of Frederick C. and Eileen Hull, the Rare Book and Manuscript Library of Columbia University, the Special Collections and Interlibrary Loan Departments of the University of Connecticut Library, Gertrude Voight, Helen and Jose Yglesias, Jean Henley and Barbara Jones, Judith A. Schwarz, Barbara D. Wright, Barbara Sicherman, Joan Joffe Hall, William D. Curtin, Joanne O'Hare and Florence Howe of The Feminist Press at The City University of New York, and my parents, Jane and David Miller. Special thanks to David Garnes and Jan Merrill-Oldham of the University of Connecticut Library for providing the copy of *Islanders* here reproduced.

337

For a free catalog, write to The Feminist Press at The City University of New York, 311 East 94 Street, New York, NY 10128. Send individual book orders to The Talman Company, Inc., 150 Fifth Avenue, New York, NY 10011. Please include $1.75 for postage and handling for one book, $.75 for each additional.